NO HOLES BARRED

Kimberly Zant
Shizuko Lee
Angelia Whiting
Shelley Munro

Erotic Futuristic Romance

New Concepts

Georgia

Be sure to check out our website for the very best in fiction at fantastic prices!

When you visit our webpage, you can:
* Read excerpts of currently available books
* View cover art of upcoming books and current releases
* Find out more about the talented artists who capture the magic of the writer's imagination on the covers
* Order books from our backlist
* Find out the latest NCP and author news--including any upcoming book signings by your favorite NCP author
* Read author bios and reviews of our books
* Get NCP submission guidelines
* And so much more!

We offer a 20% discount on all new Trade Paperback releases ordered from our website!

Be sure to visit our webpage to find the best deals in e-books and paperbacks! To find out about our new releases as soon as they are available, please be sure to sign up for our newsletter (http://www.newconceptspublishing.com/newsletter.htm) or join our reader group (http://groups.yahoo.com/group/new_concepts_pub/join)!

The newsletter is available by double opt in only and our customer information is *never* shared!

Visit our webpage at:
www.newconceptspublishing.com

No Holes Barred is an original publication of NCP. This work has never before appeared in book form. This work is a novel. Any similarity to actual persons or events is purely coincidental.

New Concepts Publishing, Inc.
5202 Humphreys Rd.
Lake Park, GA 31636

ISBN 1-58608-789-4
© Kimberly Zant, Shizuko Lee, Angelia Whiting, Shelley Munro
Cover art © copyright 2006 Dan Skinner & Eliza Black

NCP books are available at special quantity discounts for bulk purchases for sales promotions, premiums, fund raising, or educational use. For details, write, email, or phone New Concepts Publishing, Inc., 5202 Humphreys Rd., Lake Park, GA 31636; Ph. 229-257-0367, Fax 229-219-1097; orders@newconceptspublishing.com.

First NCP Trade Paperback Printing: April 2006

TABLE OF CONTENTS

Missing   Page 5

Mating Dance   Page 57

The Awakening   Page 86

Stranded   Page 154

MISSING

Kimberly Zant

Chapter One

As I sat in my car, staring at the unprepossessing building that housed the exclusive adult club, No Holes Barred, I was more aware of my body than I had ever been in my life. I'd spent the past two hours trying to convince myself that the humming within me was pure adrenaline flow from the danger inherent in the job I'd taken upon myself. The edge of excitement I'd put down to the thrill of the chase.

The plain truth was, although there was a dollop of each within me, I knew it was more than that. I was sexually aroused as well, so much so that I could hardly keep my mind off of my tits or cunt and concentrate on the task at hand.

If anyone had ever asked me if I was 'in' to bondage or S&M I'd have told them they had to be out of their mind, but I'd discovered that tonight, when I would be going into a place such as I'd never known, impersonating a woman I'd never met, my mind simply wouldn't allow me to lie to myself.

I might have been a little unnerved about facing the unknown, but I was far more excited by the prospect of my experience than I was afraid or reluctant.

Solving mysteries wasn't just my bread and butter. I loved it. I was fascinated with unraveling puzzles. I relished the adrenaline pumping excitement, and even fear, so often associated with my job.

Obviously, whether I actually wanted to admit it or not, I was a glutton for punishment--prone to self-inflicted S&M, or at least indifferent to the possibility of having to experience it. Otherwise, I'd have chosen a less dangerous job.

By day, I was a cop. I moonlighted for a private investigations firm, though, because I'd been stuck behind a desk in my chosen career and it didn't seem likely I'd be seeing daylight any time soon.

Besides that, the pay sucked and I figured if it took two paychecks to make ends meet, this was the best way to do it.

With all due modesty, I knew I was good--maybe not Sherlock Holmes, but still damned good.

It irked me that I'd been chosen for this assignment solely on my appearance.

Our client's daughter, who'd become a member of the club only a few short weeks earlier, had visited the club the weekend before and hadn't been seen since. The client had gone the usual route but was too frantic to find her daughter to simply wait for the police to do their job. Preliminary investigations had turned up nothing except that Julia Hutchins appeared to have vanished from the time she'd gone into the club. She'd been seen entering, but no one had seen her come out and she hadn't been spotted since.

My boss had decided I was a dead ringer for the missing woman and the quickest way to discover if any of the club members had had anything to do with her disappearance was to pose as the missing woman. I was willing enough, but I couldn't see it myself. I was the same general height, weight and build. Otherwise, I didn't look much like the woman at all. I didn't sound like her either, for that matter.

I didn't argue, though. I would be wearing her clothes. It was dark inside the club. Like the boss, I figured I was close enough to smoke the bad guy out if he was inside. Mostly, I was here to find out if anyone would react violently to the missing woman's sudden reappearance, but in the back of everyone's mind, we were all hoping that the charade would break the case wide open, not just give us a lead to pursue.

It could be dangerous, and that was one of the reasons I'd agreed to do it. It wasn't that I had a death wish or anything. I knew, though, that the boss would just find someone else and I figured I was probably more qualified to handle a dangerous situation than most anyone he could come up with.

If I could just get my mind off of sex, sex, sex.

I hadn't been laid in a year, though, and even that had been pretty much a washout as far as I was concerned.

My imagination was running riot, visions of sweating, writhing bodies flickering through my mind's eye, the pungent, musky smell of sex in my nostrils and it was making me hot and wet and jittery in a way that had nothing to do with anxiety about the gig.

I shifted uncomfortably. My radio squawked abruptly, causing me to jump as if I'd been caught playing with myself.

"Candice?"

"Yeah?"

"Ready?"

No. "Sure."

He must have heard something in my voice. "We've got somebody inside to keep an eye on you and Junior and I are watching the exits. You'll be fine."

That 'somebody' was the new guy, Jerico. I wasn't certain how I felt about him 'watching' over me. In the first place, he was an unknown quantity. His background sounded impressive, but I had to wonder what he was doing working for the agency if he was even half as good as I'd been told.

And then there was the fact that he was so hot, just looking at him was enough to make me warm, breathless, and wet. I was inclined to think he was pretty much every woman's wet dream, tall, dark, well built, stunningly handsome and not even a dick wad jerk as far as I'd been able to discover. I didn't know if I liked the idea of him watching me perform--or if I didn't like it--but I was certainly not indifferent to the possibility. I hoped that wasn't going to get in my way at a really bad moment.

Shaking those thoughts off with an effort, I dragged in a deep, sustaining breath and let it out slowly. My heart was still pattering along about 100 miles an hour but I didn't feel quite as lightheaded. Resisting the urge to check my appearance again, I grabbed my purse and climbed out of my car. A flash of light caught my attention as I looked at the building across the street. I looked up, curious, just in time to see another thin, bluish streak cut across the night sky, almost like a comet except for the fact that it was headed out, not inbound.

I frowned but finally decided maybe it was some sort of laser thingy to attract attention. It seemed a little high toned for a place that was really very ordinary in appearance, but who was I to judge?

Without a backward glance, I left the car and crossed the street. I didn't' lock it. I'd never seen the point. No body was going to steal that old rattle trap and if they stole the garbage out of it--well, so much the better. It would save me having to clean.

My knees felt like silly putty as I tried to stroll casually across the street toward the club. I hoped I looked more confident than I felt. I hoped I looked sexy as hell, but the moment I got out of the car my confidence slipped a couple of notches.

I wasn't used to the get up I was wearing. The fucking corset was one of the reasons I couldn't even drag in a decent breath of air, and then there was the skirt, which barely covered my ass--actually I wasn't convinced it did cover my ass. It felt airish back there, but that might have been the thong residing between my ass cheeks and leaving my buttocks bare--which I also wasn't used to.

The top I was wearing was almost worse. It was black like the leather skirt, but virtually transparent and I wasn't wearing a bra--just the corset which pushed my boobs up as if offering them for a taste.

It wasn't the sort of clothing any woman could actually be comfortable in, but then it should have made me feel sexy as hell and boosted my self-confidence, instead of filling me with the anxiety that someone would think I looked ridiculous.

I didn't mind the idea that anyone would think I looked slutty. Ridiculous was hard to swallow.

A tiny panel on the solid metal door slid back almost before I'd rapped on the door. Video surveillance, I realized, flicking a quick look around to see if I could locate the camera. "Member," I muttered to the two eyes peering at me and held up my hand, palm up, so that he could see the symbol I'd drawn--the one Julia's best friend had said she'd seen on the missing girl's palm.

The panel slid shut again. I'd just begun to wonder if my ruse would even get me in the door when I heard a distinct click and the door opened. Relief and tension and reluctance smacked me all at the same time. It took an effort to stroll casually inside--I hoped it looked casual.

This was where it got tricky. I hadn't a clue of what the place was like inside. The missing woman hadn't kept notes--which would have been damned helpful--or, if she had, somebody had gone through her place and removed them. We'd gotten what information we had about the club from a close friend of the missing woman but she'd never been inside it herself.

I found myself in a wide corridor. The lighting wasn't quite like I'd expected, not quite like anything I'd ever seen before actually. It was dim, which I *had* expected, but ambient light surrounded me, leaving nothing in actual shadow. Without glancing back to see if the man who'd let me in was actually standing behind me, or if he'd used an electronic door release--which I suspected--I followed the corridor as casually as I could. The floor and walls were thumping. My heart caught the rhythm and matched it before I even realized there was a bass beat filtering through every solid object.

Reaching a door at the opposite end of the corridor, I pulled it open. The moment the door was cracked the music washed over me like a tidal wave. Blinking in surprise, I closed the door again. The music vanished and only the beat remained. "Way cool," I muttered, impressed enough with the acoustics that it penetrated my self-absorption with my mission--and my excited cunt.

Opening the door wide enough to enter, I stepped inside. The scene that met my curious gaze was almost anticlimactic. The room was huge. The dance floor took up most of it, but a narrow strip of tables and chairs ran all the way around the pit. In the pit, couples gyrated to the beat of the music. The same strangely ambient light lit this room, but a ball of colored lights rotated just above the dance floor, sending jewel toned colors across the bumping, grinding, wildly gyrating dancers that were pretty much like those I was familiar with seeing in social clubs like this.

I studied the room for several moments, feeling oddly deflated by the fact that it looked very much like every other club I'd ever been in to. The only difference that I could see was that pretty much everyone was dressed as I was, in skin tight black leather that left almost as much flesh exposed as was covered.

After surveying the room for several moments, I noticed that two sets of circular, wrought iron stairs led upwards. At the top of those stairs was a balcony mezzanine that circled the dance floor.

My heart skipped several beats. This was where the real action could be found. Upstairs, the people were 'dancing' to a different beat altogether. Slowly winding my way through the crowd, I headed for the nearest stairs. No one seemed to pay the least bit of attention to me, which was not only strange but extremely disappointing. We had all expected varying reactions from the people the missing woman regularly hung around with. We hadn't expected *no* reaction.

I tried not to think about the fact that I'd thought I was dressed to kill and *I* was being ignored.

On the other hand, I had to admit it was hard to stand out when one was dressed so similarly to everyone else.

So much for the 'disguise'. I could've probably picked up an outfit anywhere and nobody would have known the difference.

A bouncer built like a wrestler met me at the top of the stairs. My heart leapt into overdrive, but after surveying me from head to foot, he merely nodded and stepped back. Relieved but curious about the security, I moved past him.

Why have security if they weren't actually going to check IDs?

Shelving the puzzle for the moment, I glanced around the mezzanine. There were four fantasy worlds to explore, I saw. At the far end, directly across from me, I saw the one I was looking for. The informant had said 'gallery of dates and mates, or something like that'. The sign actually read 'galactic dates and mates', but I figured that was as close as I was going to come. Besides, if I guessed wrong, I could always check out the other areas next time.

"Galactic dates and mates," I murmured quietly, wondering if my backup could actually hear me. A burst of static was my only answer. I didn't dare try to adjust the transmitter or receiver while I was in plain view, however, and pushed the prick of uneasiness the static produced to the back of my mind. When I found a lady's room, I'd check the damn thing. Otherwise, I was in no immediate danger unless I gave myself away.

I headed for the sign. The door wasn't locked. Pulling it open, I stepped inside. A long corridor much like the one at the entrance greeted me. The similarity ended there. Peepers, mostly men, were lined up along each wall, staring at something I couldn't see. Curious, I moved to the first window and stopped. There was a man and a woman inside. The woman, who didn't appear to be wearing anything but manacles and a corset around her middle, was bound by her wrists to a chain that disappeared into the darkness above her. She was blindfolded. A circle of light surrounded her. Next to her, a man wearing a mask that covered his head, and absolutely nothing else, was toying with something that looked like a whip.

The dialogue sounded like something from a bad porn, but I hardly noticed. My attention was riveted to the whip. I gasped when he abruptly struck the woman with it, expecting to hear screams of pain and terror. Instead, she merely moaned.

I saw then that the 'whip' hadn't left a mark on her. Whatever it was made of, it was obviously too soft to cause actual pain.

Domination. Losing interest in the couple--I really wasn't 'in' to watching and I was working besides--I peered at the room around them, trying to figure out why this area was designated as 'galactic dates and mates'. I saw then that the shadowy walls that surrounded the couple depicted deep space. Murals? I supposed that was what it was, but it had been treated with some sort of phosphorescence, because the stars glowed faintly.

Mentally shrugging, I moved on to the next window. This one gave me a bit of a jolt. The creature inside was roughly the size and shape of a human, but it sure as hell didn't look human.

Kick ass make up job!

There were several men plastered to the window and I wasn't tall enough to see over their shoulders. I moved a little closer anyway, trying to peer between their shoulders. The woman was spread eagle, but she looked like she was floating in the air.

Cool! I couldn't see a sign of the filaments I knew must be supporting her.

As I watched, a long, tongue like thing slid out of the 'alien' creature's mouth and went straight for her pussy-- like a prehensile elephant trunk. Despite the fact that I'd assured myself that I wasn't in to watching, I couldn't pull my gaze away. My own cunt clenched as I watched that long tongue slide inside of her. My nipples hardened. My breath grew short.

It was amazing. I'd never seen anything like it and yet it looked so real!

From the whimpers the woman was making it must have felt real too.

I jumped guiltily when someone touched my shoulder, glancing around quickly as if I'd been caught doing something I shouldn't.

I didn't know whether to be relieved or pissed off when I saw it was Jerico--my inside man. Frowning at him, I jerked my head slightly, trying to shoo him away. He wasn't supposed to approach me, the numbskull. He was just supposed to watch for someone else to approach me.

He shook his head slightly. Wrapping his fingers around my upper arm, he pulled. Rather than attract attention, I went with him, wondering what the hell was going on. It looked like either our cover was blown, or something had gone sour.

Containing my curiosity with an effort, I allowed him to lead me to the end of the hallway and into a room to one side of the corridor. He placed a finger on my lips before I could say anything and shook his head slightly.

Nodding to let him know I'd understood the warning, I followed him meekly as he led me to the center of the room.

"Undress."

I stared at Jerico blankly at the command. He couldn't be serious. It occurred to me after a moment, though, that the place had security everywhere, which probably meant cameras.

We were being watched.

I still didn't like it. I'd known when I took the job that I might have to do something I might not especially like. I hadn't expected to be doing it with my partner. Not that I would've minded *that* under other circumstances, because I hadn't been able to actually look in Jerico's direction since I'd first met him without fantasizing about being in bed with him. But I didn't want it to be a 'job', something to throw off suspicion. This sucked a hairy one.

Mentally shrugging, I reminded myself that I had to play along if I didn't want to risk blowing my cover.

I was almost sorry I hadn't taken strip lessons. Here I was being offered the opportunity of a lifetime and I felt awkward as hell stripping while he watched. When I'd discarded everything but the thong and corset I was wearing, he touched my hand, a signal to stop. Wondering wryly if that meant he'd seen all he wanted to see, I did as I was commanded and tried to act casual while he walked around me, examining me, skating a curious hand over me here and there and sending shivers of delight all the way through me that I tried really hard to hide.

Maybe this was another security measure? He was looking for bugs? I was wearing a modified cell phone-- which he knew. Everyone carried the things these days and it was a lot less conspicuous than trying to hide a wire, particularly considering what I'd had to wear this time.

Despite my pose of unconcern, I glared at him pointedly when he was facing me again. He ignored it. Reaching for my earpiece, he removed it, wound the cord and then removed the tiny 'phone' at my waist.

It took all I could do to maintain my cover then. I couldn't carry a weapon. The 'cellphone' was my only backup-- besides Jerico.

Calming myself with an effort, I reminded myself that we were undoubtedly being watched. Jerico would explain the situation later. All I had to do was to play along, keep cool, maintain my cover and everything would work out just fine.

My heart slammed into my ribs at that thought and tried to beat its way up my throat. I swallowed with difficulty, trying to dislodge it and force it back into its proper place when he calmly reached for my thong and pulled it down my legs. I was so unsteady by the time he reached my ankles it took a moment to lock one knee and lift my other leg. When he'd tossed the thong aside, he curled the fingers of each hand around my ankles and slowly slid his hands upward. I stared down at him as he rose, trying to ignore the way his hands felt as they glided up my legs, trying not to think about the way my belly was shimmying and the warm wetness that gathered in my nether regions.

My belly went weightless as he passed my knees and continued upward until his thumbs brushed my nether lips. They lingered there for two painful heartbeats and then he slipped his hands over my pelvic bones and around behind me to cup my buttocks, his fingers curled teasingly along the edges of my cleft--touching just enough sensitive flesh to make it impossible for me to get my mind around anything else.

"You please me," he murmured, his face mere inches from mine so that the warmth of his breath wafted across my face, sending a dizzying rush of pleasure through me. "What can I do to please you?"

I felt my jaw go slack with surprise. My mind had gone mushy, however, and disjointed, like a motherboard that had overloaded, and only sporadic bursts of random data registered. Nothing I could actually grab onto.

Lifting a hand, he traced his thumb lightly back and forth across my lower lip, studying me speculatively. "We will discover it together," he murmured finally. Lifting his hand, he cupped it over my eyes and brushed downward. Blackness followed.

I was totally disoriented when I became aware of my surroundings again. There was no drifting upward, no cobwebs of drugs or sleep. It was more like a switch coming on.

The confusing part was that I couldn't see a damned thing and I had the most peculiar sense of weightlessness. That scared me worse than the blindfold, which I'd almost instantly identified. Before total panic could set in with the fear that I'd somehow lost all feeling from the neck down, I felt something touch my foot.

I frowned, trying to identify the inquisitive touch--not a finger, certainly. It was neither warm nor blunt like a digit. It wasn't hard either. On the other hand, it didn't feel as softly yielding as cloth.

As it wandered almost idly along the sole of my left foot, I came to think it must be something like a feather. The light touch tickled the sensitive flesh on the soles of my feet, not in a way that made me feel even a vague urge to giggle, but in the sense that it produced little electric bursts of sensation I wasn't altogether certain I liked.

"You've only to say 'stop' and I will stop," he whispered, close to my ear.

I recognized his voice--Jerico.

What the hell did he think he was doing? I mean, there was playing along and then there was going way over the top.

I cleared my throat with an effort as I felt the stroke of the feather begin again after a significant pause. This time, it traced a pattern across my lower belly that sucked the breath right out of my lungs.

I was still trying to catch my breath when I made a new discovery.

Despite the fact that I couldn't actually feel anything that could be preventing me from moving, I couldn't move. I would have thought it was paralysis except that I was having no trouble at all feeling that damned feather--or whatever it was, because it was driving me crazy, sending little jolts of electricity through me every time he discovered a new batch of exposed nerve endings.

Just as I was about to scream at him to stop, I felt his hands pushing my thighs wide. Cool air wafted against my warm genitals. Blood rushed into the flesh there, making it more sensitive. Blood gushed into my nipples, too, making them stand erect.

The feather--I decided it had to be a feather--teased me, tracing narrowing circles around the place that was throbbing for attention by now. I became so focused on the movement all other thought fled as I held my breath, waiting--in vain. Instead, he teased me with the damned feather until I was tense from head to toe, dying for him to touch me in just the right spot, and then he began to trace my sensitive inner thighs.

He'd get back to the spot, I assured myself. He wouldn't just tease me like that and go away.

He moved back to my belly. I let out a whimper of protest before I even realized it was there, then bit my lip.

Ignoring my objection, he continued up by belly, down my arms, over my back and buttocks and along my neck, finding every supersensitive spot on my entire body, places I hadn't even known about myself.

He stopped when I was a mindless massive of tingling, sparking nerves.

I waited, hopeful. I hadn't said stop. As crazy as it was making me I didn't want him to. When nothing happened for so long that I began to feel the jolting nerves begin to settle, I turned my head, trying to see if I could see him beneath the edge of the blindfold. I couldn't. I licked my dry lips. "Why the blindfold?"

"So you can focus on what you feel."

I wasn't sure I needed more focus. I'd begun to feel like I might come just from being stroked, a genuinely unique situation for me. All I really wanted him to do was finish me off. It was all I could think about for a time--that and the fact that I could feel the opportunity slowly slipping away from me.

As it did, I tried to put my legs together. That was when I made a brand new discovery. I couldn't. Before I could get either alarmed or indignant about the situation I felt something readily identifiable--his tongue. It was in the wrong damned place though. My pussy instantly began to clamor for attention. Instead, he started at my feet again.

I was definitely not a foot person. My feet were too sensitive. My belly clenched. I think everything on and inside of me clenched all at the same time, almost painfully. Dizziness washed over me while I tried to cope with the intensity of the sensations as he slowly and very deliberately explored every tender inch of skin with his tongue and the edge of his teeth. I would've been clawing at something if I'd been able to reach anything besides air. Finally, I merely squeezed my eyes tightly shut and balled my hands into tight fists.

It didn't occur to me *once* to yell stop.

I think that was because, in the back of my mind, I just *knew* he would go for the gold next. Men were typically not creatures of finesse. They knew what a woman really wanted and they planted their face right in the middle of it right off, just to get 'hers' out of the way so they could concentrate on their own goody.

Within five seconds I began to have a nagging suspicion that this guy had missed Man101. He started with the left foot, gnawed his way all the way up that leg, skipped the best part and moved down the other. I was in a fever by the time he began to torture my right foot.

I gritted my teeth. I could take this. I was going to take it, because I needed his tongue on my clit and I wasn't going to give him the opportunity to stop until he'd given me what I wanted. Relief flooded me when he finally ceased to suck my toes and gnaw along the sensitive sole of my foot. I'd been so tense, I could feel tiny beads of moisture popping from every pore. My pussy was almost embarrassingly wet. I tried not to think about whether or not it was noticeable, then decided I hoped it was and that it would entice him.

Because he'd stopped again, damn him!

The next touch I felt was on my buttocks. I clenched them, trying to evade that touch but there was no escaping it. By the time he began to weave his way up my back I was nearly mindless but also confused. How could he reach me everywhere? Was I hanging? And if so, why didn't I feel the strain?

I forgot all about that when I felt his tongue tracing a teasing pattern around my breasts. My nipples were so sensitive I'd come before just from having my breasts fondled and I was so ripe by now I knew I could if he was even half as good at sucking as he was at licking. I held my breath so long, waiting, till I was on the verge of passing out, or erupting into the behavior of a woman possessed by a demon, speaking in tongues and screaming 'Fuck me! Fuck me!'

The deceitful, low down snake skipped my nipples just as he had my clit and pulled away again.

I fumed, too pissed off to even find words to express my outrage.

The ice on my heated skin sent a painful jolt through me. I gasped, wavering toward unconsciousness as he slowly drew the chilling fragment over every intensely heated part of my body, making it clench in a whole new way. By the time he'd stopped, I couldn't even catch my breath, let alone scream.

I wasn't altogether certain when he stopped. I was too busy trying to drag a decent breath into my laboring lungs, struggling against the darkness that kept threatening to overwhelm me. The heat of his mouth on the chilled skin of my inner thigh was like fire. I jerked, thinking at first that it was. "No," I managed to gasp out, forgetting the safe word altogether and wracking my brain frantically for it when he not only didn't stop, but nibbled a teasing path upward toward my pussy.

I'd just managed to wrap my mind around the word I needed when his mouth closed over my clit. Mindless pleasure went through me, instantly banishing all rational thought. I bit my lip but groaned anyway as his tongue danced along my clit. Yes! I thought, feeling my body respond instantly, shooting skyward at dizzying velocity. I felt myself hanging on the very verge of explosive release when he ceased to suck and fondle my clit and began to explore my cleft, pressing his tongue into the opening of my passage.

I felt like screaming with disappointment. No! Not there, *up*, higher!

Finally, he moved to my clit again, but I'd fallen. Fighting the frustration that was destroying my focus, I concentrated on the wonderful feel of his tongue and mouth. My body responded again, the tension coiling inside of me, lifting me toward what I needed.

When he stopped just shy of taking me there I was too stunned for several moments to actually grasp that he'd stopped. Slowly it filtered through the magma my mind had been that he had, once again, left me hanging.

Anger surged through me, but I was way beyond self defense by this time. All I could think about was gnawing free of whatever device held me and raping him if I had to. That thought cooled my anger. I was going to die if he left me like this. I had to have relief.

He couldn't intend to tease me and leave me hanging. I knew he couldn't be that cruel.

But he had no intention of allowing me to breeze through either. I was going to have to enjoy as much as I could stand before he gave me what I needed.

He proved that theory true when he touched the ice to me.

That time I did faint, but I wasn't out nearly long enough.

I wished to hell he'd taken off the damned corset so I could drag a decent breath of air into my lungs.

I wished it harder when he began to tease me again, this time starting with my breasts. I tried to focus my mind elsewhere. The sensations were maddeningly wonderful, but I couldn't be satisfied with a 'dry' release by now. I had to have cock--or tongue--finger would do if he had his mouth on my clit. I wasn't that choosy. But the kind of lightweight climax I usually got from having my nipples fondled just wasn't going to satisfy me.

I almost came anyway. It was almost as if he knew exactly how far to push, exactly where my breaking point was.

I don't know when I began to moan incessantly, like someone dying from fever, but my mouth and throat grew so dry from gasping that I could hardly gather moisture to swallow.

The moisture was all down at the other end.

"No more," I managed to moan at some point, long past the point of being able to remember anything as simple as 'stop'.

Apparently it was the key words for something, however. He lifted his head from my pussy. I felt as if he was studying me, but I'd just decided he was only waiting, as he had before, to start again.

I was wrong. He dipped his head again. His heated mouth covered my clit and he sucked and nibbled it until my body almost seemed to explode with keen rapture. I screamed as it hit me. Before the aftershocks had even begun to dissipate, he lifted his head again, pulling me toward him. I felt the head of his cock as he probed me. It felt huge, but my body was clenched so hard in spasms of ecstasy, he would've had a hell of time shoving his index finger into me.

He struggled, gripping my hips tightly and driving forward. I gasped, tried to relax my spasming muscles to allow him to claim me. The scrape of his cock along my passage only set off more convulsions, though, and he was damp with perspiration by the time he drove deeply inside of me. I was damp with everything, but all I could think of was wrapping myself so tightly around him I became a part of him. I couldn't. My arms and legs were still bound. I could only allow him to move as he pleased.

It pleased him to pound into me like a piston engine. It pleased me too. I'd hardly touched down when my body responded to his fierce possession by coiling for another release. My second followed so closely upon the heels of his that it was almost like I'd experienced both my culmination and his and it was so divine it pitched me beyond the known world.

Chapter Two

I stared at the furnishings of my apartment bedroom for a good five minutes before it sank in that I wasn't dreaming. Frowning, trying to shrug off the mind dulling remnants of sleep, I pushed myself up and looked around me. Morning light streamed in around the room darkening shades at my windows.

I looked at the clock. Ten. My mind struggled with that number for several moments before it clicked together with the light. A.M. There was too much light for P.M.

Good thing I was a detective, I thought wryly. Now, what day?

"Shit!" I exclaimed as it sank in on me that it was a work day. "Two fucking hours late. Jeff is going to kill me. Then he's going to fire me."

My feet hit the floor before anything else could sink in-- like the twinges from muscles recently used that hadn't been in a while. My inner thighs felt like someone had grabbed each of my ankles and yelled 'make a wish'. I plopped back down on the edge of the bed, massaging my aching groin area. It responded by hurting worse.

This was as real as it got.

So if I hadn't had the mother of all wet dreams, how the hell did I get home?

I struggled with that for a few minutes but to save my life I couldn't remember anything after the fade out of the dream –which couldn't have been a dream at all unless I'd been up doing splits in my sleep.

Date drug? That didn't seem quite right, not unless this was a brand new high. I wasn't having any trouble remembering what had happened before I woke up and I didn't feel like I had a drug hangover, just the typical 'up half the night and half as much sleep as I needed' sort of grogginess.

Shaking my uneasiness, I pushed off the bed and scrambled to get ready for work. As tempting as it was to just make up a believable lie and call in sick, I couldn't afford to, especially when my job might be hanging in the balance. On my salary, I could barely get by with two jobs and I had no desire to experience what the life of a bag lady was like.

"Hey, who's that woman?" Marvin quipped when I dashed in the door at work.

I sent him a drop dead look. "You're so funny, Marv."

"Jeffie's pissed."

"When is he not?" I muttered, hunching over and heading for my desk.

My ass hadn't even touched down with his door swung open. "MY office. NOW!"

Fuck! I slunk into his office, trying to look contrite.

"Shut the door."

"If you're going to yell, I might as well leave it open," I muttered.

He was glaring at me when I turned around. "You got any idea what fucking time it is, Cavanaugh?"

I decided I'd better be meek. He didn't look like he was in the mood for wisecracks. "Uh … actually my clock broke last night," I hedged. It wasn't exactly a lie, I reasoned. The fucking alarm hadn't gone off even if the clock did seem to be still working. Of course that might have been because I didn't set it since I didn't remember getting home, or getting into bed. Fortunately for me, I hadn't had the chance to have hysterics over the lost time yet.

"*That* is your excuse for coming in three hours late?"

I shrugged. "I did a gig last night, worked late. My alarm didn't go off."

"Well, you better really like that other job, Cavanaugh, because if you come in late again…."

"I'll pick up a new clock at lunch."

"You expect to take lunch when you just got here?" he demanded as if I'd asked him to let me fuck him in the ass.

"How else am I supposed to get a clock?" I demanded irritably.

He looked a little taken aback when I growled back at him, but to my surprise and amazement, he let it go. "Get to work. You need to process those reports before you take lunch."

There was a stack nearly two feet high teetering on top of what was supposed to be my 'in' box. Gritting my teeth, I set to work. It was hard to focus. My mind, which could never leave a problem alone, kept going back to the personal one of 'how the hell did I get from the club to my house?'. When it wasn't toying with that unnerving question, it was reliving the moment. I had to tamp that tendency. Everything on my body throbbed every time some fragment of memory from the night before popped into my head and I was afraid somebody was going to notice if I kept squirming in my seat.

I skipped lunch. No way was I going to get through all of the damned reports if I took off for an hour. Mid-way through the afternoon, I noticed Jeff hanging over my desk like a buzzard waiting for its victim to stop squirming. I looked up at him blankly. "My office."

I frowned. What the hell had I done now?

Sighing, I got to my feet and headed into the captain's office. "As of tomorrow, I'm reassigning you to a patrol unit."

I blinked several times and finally decided I hadn't heard him right. "Patrol?" I echoed, as if I'd never heard the word before. "Did somebody di--quit?" I added, abruptly feeling like a bird of carrion myself. Something besides just paperwork? A raise?

"Peterson transferred out. We've got a new rooky. You'll be partnering with him."

I stared at him. Two rookies together? I might have been on the job a year and a half, but I hadn't driven anything but a desk. They must be seriously short on patrol units. "When?" I asked, hardly able to control my excitement.

"Tomorrow. Be on time, Cavenaugh."

"Yes, sir."

My concentration was totally shot after that. I realized I hadn't asked him what shift I was going to be working. I'd have to find out if it was going to create problems with the agency. I didn't think it would, but one never knew.

I glanced at the clock and saw it was nearing the end of my shift. If I didn't kick it into high gear, I was going to be stuck finishing the reports and I needed to check in with Bill to find out what had happened the night before.

Now that I thought about it, I'd been so wrapped up in all the fun I was having the night before it hadn't occurred to me to wonder why my backup had never arrived. True, I'd been with Jerico, but he hadn't checked in and my link had gone dead. Why hadn't they burst in to see what was going on?

I dismissed it, realizing Jerico must have checked in at some point, otherwise they would have.

Chapter Three

"Where the hell have you been?" Bill roared, leaping up from his desk and looking like he was about to have a heart attack.

My gaze went immediately to the clock on the wall behind him. "Jeeze! I'm only ten minutes late. Cut me some slack. I was late getting in to the precinct today and had paperwork backed up to my eyeballs."

Bill dropped into his seat like his legs had just given out. I couldn't help but notice that he was staring at me like he'd never seen me before. His complexion looked a little nasty, too, all gray and shit. "You all right?"

"No, I'm not fucking all right! What happened last night?"

"Something happened?" I asked uneasily. I wasn't about to divulge a damned thing until I knew how much he knew about what had happened the night before.

He looked at me with that same expression, as if we were speaking two different languages and he couldn't quite figure out what I was saying. "Sit down. Tell me what happened."

I sat, resisting the urge to demand that he start, so that I'd know how much I *had* to tell him and what I could keep to myself. I didn't think he'd be interested in learning that I had experienced the best sex I'd ever had in my life and felt like someone who'd just spoken to god--or a god. I didn't know what I was going to say when I saw Jerico again, but I got hot every time I thought about him. "Uh. Well, I went into the club without a hitch. When I got to the main room, I noticed stairs leading up and followed them. I saw the sign the informant told us about right off--galactic dates and mates." I shrugged. "That's about all there was to it, actually. No body even looked at me twice, so either the get up didn't fool anybody, or whoever it was that disappeared the client's daughter wasn't there last night."

Bill frowned. "That was it?"

I shifted uncomfortably. "Pretty much," I lied. "Actually, I don't remember getting home last night, which is the weirdest thing about the whole gig. One minute I was there, the next I woke up at home in my own bed and I was late for work."

"Drugs you think?"

"I thought of that, but I didn't drink anything and I sure as hell didn't pop anything voluntarily."

He frowned. "I feel like I had a bad 'trip'. I don't think I've ever worked on a weirder case. You know, we searched every inch of that place and there wasn't a sign of you--or anybody else for that matter."

I stared at him blankly. "When?"

"Last night! Your wire went dead. We didn't want to blow your cover, but I don't like taking chances either. As soon as it went dead, we went in. The place was deserted."

I felt like I was tripping on acid. "Wait a minute. You went in? To the club?"

"That's what I'm telling you. We went in not thirty minutes behind you and there was nothing and I mean nothing. The place looked like it had been deserted twenty years."

"That's not possible--unless you went into the wrong place. There must have been a hundred people on the dance floor alone, plus the DJ and the bar--the place was packed. No way it emptied between the time I got there and the time you did. Besides, there would've been all sorts of things lying around that had been left behind even if they did haul ass out the back."

"We went in the back."

I frowned. "Well, maybe that was the problem. Maybe you got the wrong door?"

He gave me a look. "I've been doing this for twenty years. I don't make that kind of mistake. I was right outside when you went in, for chrissake! How could I possibly have gotten the wrong building?"

I frowned, trying to shake the feeling that I'd walked into the twilight zone. "Did you lose time?"

"No, I didn't. We searched the building from top to bottom, and then the buildings adjacent to it. I finally called the cops. You know how I feel about that--not that it helped at all. They think I'm crazy."

I rubbed my temples. "This is the most bizarre thing I've ever encountered. Looking at it from a stranger's point of view, I'd have to say that one of us was crazy. I don't doubt what you're saying, but I'm telling you it wasn't like that when I went in."

"But you don't remember leaving?"

"I blacked out," I responded reluctantly, unwilling to tell him why or how I'd blacked out.

"Somebody clock you?" he asked, frowning.

I shook my head. "No. I'd be in the hospital now if anybody had hit me that hard. I'll take a blood test, if you like, but I'm telling you they're not going to find drugs in my system."

We sat pondering the situation for a while, but I wasn't any closer to figuring out what had happened and I could tell he wasn't either. "What do you want to do now?"

He frowned. "Mrs. Hutchins paid me half up front," he muttered slowly.

I knew how much he hated to part with money. I shrugged. "So, we go again."

To my surprise, he shook his head. "I'm not sure that's a good idea."

The moment he said that I knew I was going--undercover or otherwise. I had to. Nothing like the night before had ever happened to me in my life and I wanted to know if it was real, or some kind of mental trip. "You're going to give her the deposit back?" I asked pointedly.

He looked unhappy. "I've already spent half of it on the equipment. Speaking of which--what happened to your wire?"

Why didn't I know that was coming? "Jerico didn't bring it back?"

He looked at me blankly, frowning in puzzlement. "Who's Jerico?"

If he'd punched me in the jaw I couldn't have been more stunned. "The new guy? Jerico? My inside contact?" I prompted.

He still looked blank. "I don't know anybody named Jerico, Candy. We don't have a new guy."

Ignoring the shortening of my name to Candy, which, in a general way, irritated the shit out of me, I concentrated on the important thing. It took me all of thirty minutes to convince Bill we had to try again. If we didn't he was going to have to return the biggest part of the deposit and he didn't want to do that in the worst kind of way.

After we'd set up a time and place to meet, I returned to my apartment to get ready.

I hadn't had to pretend confusion after Bill's last revelation and I hadn't tried to explain. He didn't ask. I think he was already suffering overload on the weirdness of the case himself and wasn't sure he wanted to know.

When I had a little time to myself to think about it, however, I sat down and tried to piece the puzzle together. Deep concentration produced information I hadn't really considered before.

I hadn't once met Jerico *at* the office or when I was with anyone else *from* the office.

That explained how it was that I knew him and the boss didn't. It didn't explain why he'd deceived me.

What could he possibly have to gain?

One possibility, and only one, presented itself and it made cold shivers climb up and down my spine.

He was the perp we were looking for, the one that had made our client's daughter disappear.

I examined that theory from every angle, ignoring my reluctance to accept it as even a remote possibility, but it seemed to fit and it was the only thing that seemed to fit. There was a huge flaw in it, though. He hadn't actually done anything but fuck me six ways from Sunday and give me the best ride I'd ever had. I could see trying to distract me from my investigation, but that seemed a little excessive, particularly when I had felt no threat at all at any time--beyond the possibility that he was going to tease me and not give me my cookie.

I was paranoid, I decided, feeling relieved. There had to be some other explanation. Maybe the boss had had a seizure or something and it had screwed up his head? It was certainly a very selective memory loss, but then there was what he'd said about the club, too. One of us obviously wasn't playing with a full deck at the moment, and of the two, I was more inclined to lay it at *his* door. After all, I hadn't *not* seen a hundred plus people on a dance floor. I didn't remember getting home, but there was probably a lot more reasonable explanation for that than him bursting into a packed club and seeing no one.

And him not remembering a new employee.

And, just because I couldn't remember a particular incident when I'd been around Jerico and also around Bill or Junior didn't mean there hadn't been any such occasion. In all honesty, from the first time I'd set eyes on Jerico, I was a goner. I couldn't get my mind on anything else when he was around me. I could hardly concentrate on anything Jerico said to me for that matter because I absolutely loved the sound of his voice and I had the tendency to simply go into a deep trance when he spoke.

Maybe I should talk to Junior about it and see if he'd noticed any other strange behavior by his dad?

I meant to talk to Jerico, too. Sadly, I'd have to before I could allow any more games, because I wasn't taking any chances that he actually *was* involved in that woman's disappearance.

I moved my car into almost the same position as I'd occupied the night before, killed the engine and waited. Ten minutes later, I saw Junior's car come up the street and turn into the alley. I waited until he'd had time to park and cut the engine. "Junior?"

"Yeah, come back."

"This wire sounds better than the one I had last night."

"Good, because if we lose contact again, Dad's going to freak."

I stared at the building. "Maybe they've got some kind of equipment inside that's blocking the signal?"

"I didn't see anything when we searched the place last night."

That comment unsettled me. I wanted to pursue it but decided to wait until 'Dad' wasn't also tuned in. He hadn't said anything, but he'd been parked on the other side of the building when I arrived. I knew he was listening.

My body was already humming when I got out of the car. I hadn't even tried to lie to myself this time, but I had tried my best to tamp its enthusiasm. "No cock for you tonight," I muttered. "Bad pussy, down girl!"

My attempt at humor lightened my mood slightly, but only slightly. Pussy wasn't listening and neither was the rest of me. The closer I got to that door, the higher the hum. I paused when I reached the curb and glanced toward Bill, but I didn't want to attempt a signal that might be seen and it was too dark for him to see my expression. Straightening my spine, I marched up to the door in my stiletto heeled, thigh high black leather boots.

My fucking pistol dislodged itself from the thigh area and began slipping downward. By the time I rapped on the panel, I could feel the frigging thing wedged between my ankle and the zipper of the boot.

Shit!

So much for Plan A.

Too bad I hadn't thought of a Plan B.

As soon as I was inside, I began to circle the dance floor. I finally located the lady's room at the rear of the building. The window I'd hoped to find wasn't there. The room was huge, but like a closet, containing nothing but a row of stalls and a row of lavatories.

Irritated, I went into the last stall and struggled with the boots. I was sweating by the time I managed to wrestle the pistol out. My ankle was bruised, too. I stared at the small .22, trying to figure out a better place to hide it, but the reason I'd put it in the fucking boot to start with was because there was barely room in my clothes for me, much less a gun, however small.

I had two options as far as I could see--try the boot again, or discard it.

I didn't really feel like I needed it, but I didn't trust my instincts either. Sighing with irritation, I slipped the pistol into the inside of the boot. It was hidden better there anyway since the skirt I was wearing didn't even reach the top of the boots and hadn't covered the bulge.

I used the facilities and freshened up as long as I was there anyway. About halfway through the process it occurred to me that I was being extremely conscientious about clean up for somebody that wasn't going to get laid anyway.

Irritated with myself, I shoved the tiny bottle of perfume back into the equally tiny purse I was carrying without using it, left the restroom, and headed for the stairs. My heart was thumping in time to the music as I crossed the mezzanine to the door that had opened me up to a whole world of pleasure I'd never even guessed had existed.

I'd left virginity behind me years ago and without any regrets. Since then I figured I'd been a typical red blooded woman--had a few relationships, some extremely short and others shorter even than that. I'd had good sex, bad sex and god awful sex. Up until the night before I'd considered the good sex great, but now I knew that it hadn't even come close.

I was never, ever going to be the same again. I was going to be crushed if I discovered Jerico was my bad guy.

Thrusting that thought aside, I pulled the door to 'galactic dates and mates' open and went inside. Jerico was standing at the opposite end of the hall, as if he'd been waiting for me. Despite the distance, I could see his expression change as he saw me. I saw relief, desire, welcome. I didn't see deception, evil intent.

Maybe I didn't want to see that?

Ignoring the debate in my head I walked toward him. He met me. His gaze flickered over my face in a way that made me feel more than desired. It made me feel like I was special, wanted, needed.

I decided I was imagining it.

"I didn't think you'd come back," he murmured as he leaned close and nuzzled his face against mine.

My heart executed an odd little flutter at the comment, the intimacy and affection inherent in his actions and his scent, a mixture of cologne and man that instantly resurrected memories of the night before. The words might have been interpreted several ways. The nuances only one that I could see, and I was still skeptical. I'd found the experience shattering, soul altering, but I was a realist. For men who looked like Jerico and frequented places like this each new conquest was as thrilling to them as the last and they were always on the prowl. "Why?"

He shook his head. "Not here." Stepping away from me, he caught my wrist and led me to the room we'd shared the night before. The moment had arrived to execute Plan A and I wasn't entirely sure I was up to it. My blood was pounding against my ears with more than desire when he closed the door behind me and pushed me back against the hard panel, pressing his body tightly against me.

The move took me completely by surprise.

He'd kissed every square inch of my body the night before--except for my lips. I wasn't at all prepared for the impact his kiss would have on me. The moment his lips brushed against mine, covered them hungrily, my mind, my entire body turned to pure putty and I forgot all about Plan A. His taste was like a drug entering my system. The heat of his mouth, the faintly rough texture of his tongue as it caressed mine, quickly stoked a hunger in me to match his. I stroked his body mindlessly as he stroked mine, exploring every part of him I could reach as I had not been allowed to the night before when I had been bound, learning the feel of his body with my palms and fingertips.

It wasn't until he finally broke the kiss that some small fragment of sanity reared its unwelcome head.

Plan A popped into my mind as he wove a heated trail of kisses down my throat. I groped blindly for the pistol I'd stuffed into the top of my boot. The moment I shoved my hand into the damned boot, however, the pistol began its downward slide again.

He caught my hand, turned it, cupped it over his erection. His cock was hard as rock, hot, huge. My mind immediately leapt to the feel of that hard length thrusting along my passage.

Fuck it! I decided instantly. Plan A could wait.

He, apparently, was in no mood to. The moment he released my hand, he gripped my hips, sliding them upward and pushing my skirt with it. Planting one hand on my ass, he slipped the other between my thighs, rubbing me lightly. Moisture immediately gathered there. Heat traveled upward from the point of touch, frying my brain and electrifying every point in between.

Groping blindly, I managed to unfasten his pants and unzip them. The headiness of success went through me as my hand closed around the heated length of his cock. I stroked him from tip to root, dug a little deeper and stroked his balls. He grunted, released me long enough to push my hand away and disentangle his cock from his pants. Impatient, I grabbed it the moment he did so and pushed it between my thighs, clenching them tightly around it.

I could hear him grinding his teeth, heard his breath hiss between them, and hoped it was from exquisite pleasure, not pain. His erection butted against my cleft, followed it, but there was just enough fabric to the thong I was wearing to frustrate me. Before I could push it out of the way, he did. The head of his cock delved my cleft, rubbed along it, gathering the moisture my body yielded for him.

His cock head nudged the opening to my body, burrowed inward and met resistance. I shifted, going up on my toes to give him better access. He pushed deeper, but the awkwardness of our position made it impossible for him to delve as deeply as I wanted, needed. Dizzy with desperation by now, I tried anyway.

He caught my buttocks in the palms of his hands and lifted me upward. I teetered, off balance, then wrapped my arms tightly around him as he hoisted me higher, finally sheathing his cock so deeply inside of me I thought I might pass out from the pleasure of it.

I clung as he pressed me more tightly against the door to gain purchase, but his attempts to set a rhythm were thwarted by gravity and emphasized by the squeak of my bare ass sliding down the metal door.

Panting for breath, he glanced behind him, then struck the wall with the palm of his hand. I was still trying to figure out why he had when he backed up several steps and half sat half fell backwards. A gasp of surprise huffed from my lungs about the same moment we touched down on a bed.

I hadn't noticed it when we came in or seen it the night before but discovered I had little interest in its appearance beyond relief. I spread my thighs wider and pressed downward, bringing him deeply inside of me, groaning at the currents of pleasure that movement created. He caught a fistful of my hair, dragging my head back so that I had to arch backwards to ease the pressure. The movement lifted my breasts in offering and he covered one taut nipple, sucking. I almost came that very moment. With an effort, I fended culmination off, slowly sheathing his cock, lifting up to allow it to stroke downward and then pressing down on him again, reveling in the growing flow of ecstasy created by the friction of his cock rubbing along my passage.

I lost it when he moved to my other breast. Almost the moment the heat of his mouth closed over my engorged nipple and he began to suck and tease it with his tongue, the eruption I'd been trying to stave off broke free. I cried out as convulsions of rapture shuddered through me, shaking, unable to continue the rhythm I'd set. He grasped my hips, thrusting upward hard and fast and deep until he joined me.

Gasping for breath, he released me and fell back against the mattress. Weakly, I fell forward, catching myself with my palms splayed on either side of him. The haze of bliss dissipated slowly as my heart and lungs regained a more normal rhythm. As tempted as I was to simply flatten myself against him and drift away, reason had begun to tickle at my self-conscious as delight faded into nothingness.

Still panting, I unzipped my boot and dug for the gun.

Withdrawing it at long last, I sat back on his pelvis and pointed the business end at his head. "Who are you?" I managed in a gasping breath.

He cracked an eye at me, stiffening slightly when he saw the gun.

I had to hand it to him. A lesser man would have withered forthwith. Disconcertingly, his cock, still inside of me, began to grow hard again.

My eyes widened, but there wasn't a hell of a lot I could do about the situation now. I had him by the cock. He had me by the pussy. Jeez!

"Jerico."

Ignoring the tightness, the less than threatening position I was in, the faint muskiness of sex and the perspiration of our recent activities, I gave him as hard a look as I could manage.

"Try again."

Amusement curled the corners of his lips. Very slowly, he lifted his arms and locked his hands behind his head. "Jereeko Taune."

I frowned. "What kind of name is that?"

"Ren Jtanie."

"Ren-what? Where the hell is that? Never mind. What happened to the girl that was here before? The one that went missing?"

He studied me for several moments, trying to decide, I knew, whether to lie or tell the truth. Without blinking, he spoke again. "She left."

There was nothing in his body language to indicate that it was a lie, and yet we knew she hadn't left--we thought we knew that much, anyway. "So you knew about the woman who disappeared?"

He shrugged. "I run the club. I know everything that happens here."

I gaped at him in absolute shock and disbelief. "You run … you mean you own this club?"

"I'm one of the owners. My job is to set up the new clubs and see to it they're running properly."

This was more information than I'd expected to get out of him. Why hadn't any of this turned up in the background check Junior had run? He'd checked every available source and had come up with zilch--no owner names, and certainly not the fact that it was a chain. I wasn't certain that that had any bearing on my case, but it could have.

Maybe this was some kind of front for white slavery. Maybe they were catching women and sending them off to god-only-knew where.

"Exactly what is the purpose of these clubs?" I demanded.

His dark brows rose. "Dates and mates."

Irritation flickered through me, but after a moment a new possibility presented itself, one we'd dismissed. "She met somebody here."

"Yes."

"And left with him?"

"Yes."

I lowered the pistol, studying him. "Why didn't you tell anyone that when the cops were investigating her disappearance?"

Instead of answering, he caught my wrists. I was so stunned by the lightning quick move, I merely stared at him in stunned surprise. Lifting my arms up, he rolled, tipped me off, and then sprawled half on top of me. Still holding my wrists above my head, he leaned toward me and nuzzled my neck, placing light kisses along the side of it from shoulder to ear.

My flesh prickled in reaction.

"Why did you take the job at the agency?" I asked, determined to get the answers from him if he had to torture them out of me with pleasure.

"To assess the situation."

I frowned, struggling against the warmth seeping into me. "But--you posed as my inside contact," I reminded him, trying to sound indignant.

"Mmm. I couldn't resist."

I digested that while he investigated the swirls of my ear with his tongue, wreaking havoc with my concentration. "I don't--understand," I said, gasping the last word out.

"It was the opportunity I needed."

"For what?"

"Dates--and mates," he murmured, as if that explained everything. "You weren't looking. If not for the case, you would not have come. So I ... waited."

That penetrated my absorption in what he was doing. "For a date?"

"I should tell you the rules of the club--twice are dates, thrice a mate."

It sounded nonsensical, but then he'd stopped teasing my ear and was making his way to my breasts. I lost my grip on the pistol when he covered one puckered nipple with his mouth. I lost interest in the conversation altogether when he pushed his knee between my thighs and moved over me.

I needed no further encouragement and opened myself to him. My body burgeoned as I felt his cock glide slowly inside of me, stroking the wonderfully sensitive walls of my passage and setting off currents of enjoyment. Releasing his grip on my wrists, he slid his arms under my shoulders, dipping his head to nipple teasingly at my lips and finally covering them, thrusting his tongue into my mouth and stroking that cavity with the same rhythm he had set in thrusting his cock into me. The double penetration set my heart to racing, heated my blood.

Without a whimper of protest I allowed myself to be submerged in the thrill of his possession, caressing him as he caressed me, arching to meet his every thrust. As slowly as he began, the assault was powerful, building passion swiftly, building it higher than before.

My body reached pinnacle, convulsed briefly in release and, without missing a step, coiled tighter, climbed higher. We became slick with the heat of our desire and labors. Almost as one the first quakes of release caught each of us. Jerico began to move faster, as if racing to catch the crest of a wave. His need pushed mine to the brink and finally over it. My body clenched around his swollen member, milking him. I cried out as the waves of ecstasy washed over me, through me, turning me molten inside. He groaned, his body convulsing in time to mine.

I groaned as the molten tension began to mellow, slide away from me, taking every ounce of strength with it.

"Come back to me," he whispered hoarsely as I drifted past consciousness into sated, peaceful nothingness. "Promise."

Chapter Four

I cracked an eye and peered at the room around me before I was even fully conscious. It looked familiar--real fucking familiar. Groaning, I pushed myself up on my arms, blinked my eyes a couple of times to try to focus and tried again. It was my bedroom alright.

I collapsed on the bed again. "What the fuck?" I muttered wondering briefly how I could get from the club to my apartment without remembering a damned thing about the trip.

Closing my eyes, I struggled to focus my thoughts into something coherent. Last memory--absolute ecstasy. Nope. Jerico had said something. I had to think for a while before that came back. By the time I'd remembered it I was wide awake.

Rolling over, I checked the clock. Dismayed when I discovered what time it was, I rolled to the edge of the bed, tangling in the covers on the way and landing on the floor when I misjudged the edge. "Ow," I managed to get out after a mental examination to see if I'd hurt anything besides my pride.

Fighting free of the sheets, I tossed them in the general direction of the bed and headed for the shower.

I'd overslept again. I still had time to get to work before my shift started, but just barely, not enough time for a lot of primping and certainly not enough time to eat. I grabbed a coke out of the fridge and a couple of energy bars. Traffic was a bitch. I discovered I couldn't eat and dodge cars at the same time, much less comb my hair. I used the traffic lights for grooming and snatching bites of one of the bars. By the time I arrived at the precinct I'd managed to comb my hair and bundle it into a reasonably neat ball on the back of my head and I'd eaten--and I had the indigestion to prove it.

Wiping my mouth on the sleeve of my uniform as I parked, I checked the buttons, zippers, etc., climbed out of my car and walked briskly inside to meet my new partner. I discovered, not very happily, that my new partner was outside in the patrol car, waiting for me.

Gritting my teeth, I turned around and left the building again, this time by way of the garage. The car I'd been assigned was on the second level. I found it at the end. My partner had already parked his ass in the driver's seat.

I'd had a hell of a morning already and damned little sleep for days. Appropriation of my seat was enough to set spark to tender. I stomped around the car to the driver's side and tapped on the window. The man at the wheel, rolled the window down and peered up at me.

My mind went perfectly blank.

I blinked, slowly, wondering if my mind had snapped. After all, I'd gone out to a club my boss said didn't exist-- twice--had the best sex I'd ever had in my life--with a man my boss said didn't exist--and ended up in my own bed the next morning with no memory of how I'd gotten there. And now, my new partner was looking up at me with Jerico's face.

"You're the rooky?"

He smiled, a slow, sweet smile that looked exactly the way Jerico smiled--except different. I couldn't put my finger on the 'different'. The difference was in his eyes. There was absolutely no recognition in them, as if he was looking at a complete stranger, and the smile was polite, not intimate. For that matter, I couldn't detect so much as a touch of devilment, or the self-confidence Jerico exuded like strong cologne. He looked almost--shy.

"I guess I should be on the other side. I wasn't sure you were going to make it today, though."

I blinked again. His voice wasn't quite the same either. Dumbfounded, I merely stumbled back as he pushed the door open and stared at him as he climbed out of the car and moved around to the other side. I finally managed to will my legs to propel me forward when he'd slid into the passenger seat, and sort of fell into the driver's seat, partly because my knees had lost their starch and partly because he had the seat pushed way back to accommodate his long legs.

"Are you all right?"

I turned to look at him, still too numb with surprise to bring order to the chaos inside of me. He looked like Jerico, but he didn't sound like Jerico and he didn't act like Jerico. Where did that leave me?

Jerico was either a damned good actor--or he had an identical twin. What were the odds, I wondered, of Jerico's identical twin just happening to show up at my precinct for job? For that matter, how had he managed the paperwork to get it?

"Jerico?" I managed to say, though my voice sounded weak and distant.

Something flickered in his eyes--I wasn't sure what--and then I saw both devilment and laughter in his eyes.

"Jared."

That threw me. I'd just convinced myself that it *was* Jerico. I held up a hand before he could say more. "Don't you dare tell me you don't know Jerico, because I'm not going to believe that for one minute."

He twisted, settling his back against the door and giving me a thorough once over. "He's my brother."

I studied him suspiciously. Now I didn't know what to believe. Was it Jerico pretending to be a twin? Or was this really Jerico's twin? And if he was, why hadn't Jerico mentioned it?

All right, there hadn't been a lot of time for discussing a family tree, I admitted, but it was a hell of a thing to leave out. And now that paranoia had set in, I wondered who I'd been with. Jerico? Or Jared? I could've been with either or both and I wasn't sure I would've known the difference.

He hadn't seemed to know me, but could I trust that?

After a moment, I scooted the seat forward and started the car. I had questions but I wasn't about to ask them in the precinct garage. I didn't have any particular destination in mind, but when I discovered I'd turned down the street where I lived I figured it was as good a place as any. Pulling into my space, I put the car in park and switched off the engine.

Jared glanced at me curiously but said nothing.

"What's going on?"

He turned to study me, lifting his brows questioningly.

When he said nothing my temper sparked again. "Are you aware that it is against the law to impersonate a police officer?"

"Earth law?" he asked with interest.

"What?"

"Earth law?"

"United States Law--I don't know. Everywhere I guess," I said testily. "Don't avoid the question."

"No."

"No, what?" I asked suspiciously.

"I didn't know."

I gaped at him, feeling that twilight zone thing settling over me again. "How could you *not* know?" I demanded.

He frowned. "Why did you ask if you were so certain I did?"

I gripped the steering wheel, resisting the urge to wrap my fingers around his throat and choke the life out of him. Questioning him was about as useful as questioning Jerico. That much was certain. "I should just turn you in. I don't know why I didn't arrest you right off and march you inside."

He seemed to think that over for several moments. "I don't think you can do that."

"I happen to be a trained police officer, I'll have you know. I can take you down if I have to," I snapped.

He looked both interested and amused, but not the least bit intimidated. "But you don't have to. I'm a police officer."

"My ass!"

His gaze immediately dropped to my lap. Abruptly, I had the strangest feeling that English was not his native tongue. I don't know why, except that he seemed to take the slang literally, because he didn't have any accent at all that I could detect. "Do you have trouble understanding English?"

He hesitated a fraction of a second, just the sort of delay one makes when they're interpreting. "No."

"But it isn't the language you usually use, is it?"

He thought that over a bit longer. "Why do you ask?"

I sucked my bottom lip in and gnawed on it thoughtfully, trying to tamp my impatience. Clearly I wasn't getting anywhere. It seemed unlikely that trying to arrest him was going to get me any further. He wouldn't be sitting here now, in a uniform, in a patrol car, if he hadn't had everything he needed to establish his identity and get the job. If I cuffed him and marched him into the station swearing he was impersonating a police officer, the likelihood was that I'd be sitting in the shrink's office before the day was out.

"Why are you here?" I asked finally.

"To work."

I had the feeling his 'work' wasn't what those two little words seemed to imply, but I realized that there wasn't anything I could do without evidence of some kind. Sighing, I started the car, dug a city map out of the glove box and headed toward my patrol route. The entire shift went pretty much like the first part had. He was quiet unless I asked him something directly. When I did, he usually answered the question with another question and managed to avoid divulging any information at all, remaining exquisitely polite throughout.

It was just as well I had Jared to entertain me, because absolutely nothing happened on our shift. By the time we returned to the garage I was convinced that the captain had taken great pains to place the two rookies in the only area of the city that had no crime at all.

Brushing the dust off, I hit for home to change and head to my other job. Bill was holed up in his office with a client when I arrived. Balked of that prey, I went down the hallway and tapped at Junior's door, opening it and poking my head in when he called, "Yeah?"

"Do you have a few minutes?"

He blinked a couple of times and finally nodded. "Whatcha need?"

I frowned, wondering where to start. Finally, I decided just to take the bull by the horns since Junior kept glancing at his computer screen and I knew I was going to lose him if I didn't make a move. "Do you remember a guy named Jerico that was here last week?"

He stared at me blankly. "Jerico? A client?"

"You don't remember?" I asked glumly.

He shook his head. "It doesn't ring any bells. Why don't you ask Dad?"

I wasn't crazy. I knew I wasn't. But how could I be the only one that remembered Jerico working at the agency?

"Just one more thing--the other night--the first night I went into the club, No Holes Barred, and my wire went dead. Did you and Bill find anything?"

He frowned. "Your wire went dead? I don't remember having any problems on our end. Where is it? I'll check it out."

"Uh--I don't have it with me. I'll bring it by tomorrow."

He nodded, then glanced at me. "Oh. You need to talk to Dad about that, I guess."

Frowning, I left his office and went back to the reception area. I'd just settled in the seat at the receptionist's desk when the door to Bill's office opened. A woman preceded him out. I stared at her. It was Mrs. Hutchins, the client with the missing daughter.

She was smiling.

Bill was smiling too, though he didn't look terribly happy.

I waited until she'd closed the outer office door behind her to barge into Bill's office. "Something happen with the case?"

He looked at me glumly. "Her daughter contacted her. Told her she'd met some man and took off with him. Looks like the gig's over. At least Mrs. Hutchins didn't demand her deposit back," he added.

I sank into the nearest chair. It was a good thing one was handy. Otherwise, I'd have sprawled in the floor. "The woman that was missing?"

"I just said that, didn't I? Look on the bright side. You could probably use the rest. I'll give you a call in a few days if anything comes up."

Just like that? I was dismissed?

That wasn't the real reason I was so stunned, though. I'd been working for Bill for a while. When he had something for me, I worked, and when he didn't I only had one paycheck to live on.

It sucked, but such was life.

Gathering up my purse, I headed back to my apartment, too numb to think. Nothing really registered in my mind, though, except that the job was done and now there was no reason to go back to the club.

It had been a while since I'd been home for an entire evening. I wasn't sure what to do with myself. After pacing a while, I settled on the couch in my tiny living room, turned on the TV and then just stared at it wondering if anything I thought I'd experienced over the past week had actually happened or if I'd had some sort of weird mental episode.

I'd been too stunned by what Junior had told me, and the discovery that the case was abruptly over to ask Bill any of the questions I'd had in my head, but now it seemed doubtful that would have made any difference.

Neither Bill nor Junior remembered anything--not Jerico and not the search of the club. Hell, by tomorrow, they might not even remember the club.

I was tempted to drive down for a look, just to see if I'd lost my mind, but I resisted the urge.

I discovered the following day when I reported for work that I hadn't quite escaped the twilight zone. The man sitting in my patrol car when I climbed in wasn't Jared. It wasn't Jerico either. Marvin Cohen winked at me. "Ready to rumble, rookie?"

I didn't even ask. I knew if I did I'd discover Marvin didn't know anything about any rookie named Jared. No body else in the precinct would know either, including the captain, who'd assigned him to partner with me only two days before.

It was a busy day, just the distraction I needed from personal problems. By the end of our shift, we'd handled two domestic disturbances, answered a call on a shoplifter caught at a local boutique, and sifted through three dumpsters looking for a weapon discarded by a murder suspect. We caught a couple screwing in the forth dumpster. Jeez!

My ass was just about dragging the pavement by the time I crawled in at my door and collapsed on my couch. Despite the shower I'd had after dumpster diving, however, I was certain the stench was still clinging to me and finally managed to get up the energy to drag to the bathroom where I soaked until I was shriveled from the neck to the tips of my toes.

I sat down in my kitchen with a scratch pad and a tuna fish sandwich later and scribbled down all of the questions running through my head. Underneath those, I wrote down the very little I'd discovered from 'questioning' Jerico. I puzzled over what little I knew until I had a blinding headache and finally gave it up for the night.

A week passed in pretty much the same way. In a sense, I fell back into a familiar routine, and that helped, but the questions just refused to go away. One thing I finally settled in my mind was that everything I thought I knew was real. It sounded crazy, even to me, that I could take that attitude when I was the only person who remembered anything. Still, I wasn't off my rocker. I damn sure hadn't dreamed everything that had happened to me at the club.

In the first place, I distinctly remembered the 'day after' and the discomfort I'd felt wasn't from a dream. It was from having sex when I wasn't used to having sex because I hadn't in forty fucking forevers--and never like that.

In the second, I was more miserable than I'd ever been in my entire life, suffering withdrawal from a man, and no dream, no matter how real it might have seemed, would have that effect on me--unless I was a basket case.

So, if I accepted that that was real, how had Jerico managed to make everybody else forget his very existence? And what had Jared--if it had been Jared and not Jerico--been doing posing as a cop?

Clean up.

Mrs. Hutchins had reported her daughter missing. There'd been an investigation underway that had connected her disappearance to the club. Of course, it would have been closed when Mrs. Hutchins reported that her daughter had spoken to her and she was no longer considered missing, but maybe they hadn't known that? Or maybe they hadn't wanted to take a chance that any information about the club would linger in the police's hands?

It seemed a little farfetched, even to me, but then what else could it be?

Almost another week went by before I got the chance to check my theory. Sure enough, the files were clean, gone, vanished. There wasn't a single trace that a report of a missing person had ever been filed at all, no mention of the club, none of the background checks--and the guy that had supposedly been handling the case didn't remember anything about it.

The more I thought about it, the more certain I was that I needed to go back to the club for answers.

All right, so it also happened that I missed Jerico with a desperation that only got worse with every day that passed.

I wanted to see him, just one more time. I could use the 'mystery' as an excuse.

I parked my car in the same spot I'd used the only two times I'd ever been to the club. I'd passed it on a regular basis in the past couple of weeks, debating with myself each time and never stopping.

I wondered if Jerico knew I'd been driving past the club like a stalker.

I hoped not.

But then, maybe there was no Jerico?

My knees were weak and I was shaking with nerves by the time I finally gritted my teeth and got out of the car. I almost lost my nerve three times between the car and the door of the club and when I finally reached the door I simply stared at it for a while, trying to decide whether to go in or not.

I knocked before I completely lost my nerve.

The panel slid back at once, which was a tremendous relief all by itself since I'd begun to doubt that the club even existed.

I glanced at the door man when I went in. To my surprise, he looked pleased to see me. His smile broadened at the expression on my face and he gestured toward the end of the hall, as if encouraging me.

I don't know why, but that one thing seemed to remove all the doubts that had been plaguing me forever, not just about what I'd remembered, but about Jerico. Because one of the reasons I'd been so reluctant to go back to the club was that I was afraid it *had* been real, but Jerico might not be particularly pleased to see me again and I didn't think I could handle that.

As before, the main room was crowded when I opened the door at the end of the hall and went in. The music was rocking, the dancers gyrating. My heart picked up the beat of the music as I made my way around to the stairs and slowly climbed them. The bouncer at the top of the stairs nodded, and, as the doorman had, held his hand out as if encouraging me, or perhaps pointing me in the right direction?

I was a little puzzled, but dismissed it as my gaze settled on the sign--galactic dates and mates. My heart fluttered uncomfortably and I grew short of breath as I moved toward it.

Dates and mates--what was it that Jerico had said about the club rule? Twice was nice, but--no, that wasn't it. Twice are dates, thrice are mates?

I frowned as I reached for the door. Dates and mates. Pausing, I turned to look down at the dance floor below. No holes barred. I'd never really considered the name before. It was just a club, I'd figured, and like most clubs where people socialized, there was a whole lot of screwing going on, with some people searching desperately for a mate, and others just looking for a lay.

Something tantalized me about that, but I couldn't quite grasp it. Finally, I simply shook it off and opened the door.

The corridor was crowded tonight. I threaded my way through, my heart trying to beat me to death, my mind pure chaos. I'd begun to think I was going to be disappointed and Jerico wouldn't be there, waiting for me, like he had been before.

It was stupid to think he would be, I knew. In the first place, it had been more than two weeks since I'd come. In the second--well, I tried to be a realist. It was very doubtful that he'd ever been waiting for me. He'd probably just been looking for a likely candidate for the night.

I froze when I saw him, too petrified for several moments even to move. He was leaning against the wall at the end of the corridor, his arms folded over his chest. He looked pensive. I was just wondering if I should retreat again and forget the whole thing when he looked up and saw me.

He came away from the wall at once and started toward me. I couldn't tell anything about his expression though, whether he was glad to see me--if he meant to show me the door.

I wasn't really a member after all. I'd used the missing woman's code to get in.

I was still debating with myself when he stopped in front of me. His cologne drifted over me, bringing back memories that made me quake inside.

I saw his throat work as he swallowed. "I thought you wouldn't come."

Something warm blossomed inside me that was more than just desire. "I wasn't sure if I should."

He lifted a hand and brushed his fingers lightly over my cheek. "And now?"

I had the sense, suddenly, that there were undercurrents surrounding me that I didn't understand. He seemed so serious--and nervous. I searched my mind, trying to capture the elusive idea that never quite coalesced and finally said the first thing that popped into my head--the truth. "I missed you."

He smiled faintly. "Not half as much as I missed you, I think, or you would have come sooner."

Without waiting for a reply, he caught my hand and led me to the end of the corridor. A thrill of excitement went through me. The moment he dragged me inside, he gathered me close, kissing me hungrily. Full blown desire rushed through me and I kissed him back with a need that matched his, reacquainting myself with the feel of his body.

To my surprise and disappointment, he broke the kiss just about the time I was getting really wound up, catching me by the shoulders and setting me slightly away from him. "You're certain?"

I blinked at him in confusion. "About this? Yes."

He examined my face. "You don't understand, do you?"

"I don't understand a lot," I responded a little tartly, vaguely disappointed that he seemed to want to talk when I had other things on my mind. Of course, I'd told myself it was answers I was after but deep down I knew I didn't particularly care what the answer to this puzzle was. I just wanted Jerico.

He frowned, releasing me. "This is Galactic Dates and Mates."

"I know that."

"It's a matching service."

I blinked. Slowly, the words began to actually make sense. "Is *that* what you meant? Twice are dates, thrice are mates?--Wait a minute! Mates? As in--paired? Married? Till death do us part, and all that stuff?"

He looked angry. "That is what this is for, what it's all about. The social club is fine for flings, but the services *here* are for those looking for their soul mate. The concept was mine, but of course we've improved and extended the service. There *is* someone for everyone, but not everyone can find that someone--sometimes because they haven't the opportunity to look for them." He shrugged. "Although naturally everyone has their own concept of pairing, their own customs or rituals--when two have been together twice and feel the draw of passion, they know what they want. I know what I want."

I simply stared at him while that sank in, grappling with the idea that he actually wanted me--permanently. I'd never had a real proposal before. Actually, I wasn't completely certain this qualified as a proposal, but it certainly felt like one. "Me?" I asked a little weakly.

"I asked you to come back to me."

"But--I wasn't even sure I remembered that. I didn't remember anything afterward, not even getting back to my place."

"Then--you didn't come to consummate the mating?" he asked a little stiffly.

I supposed it wouldn't sound terribly romantic if I confessed that I'd come in hopes of getting my brains fucked out, but now that he'd put the idea in my mind that I could have this, have him, on a permanent basis I discovered I had been thinking along much the same lines all the time. Of all the things to base a significant relationship on, mutual desire seemed to make the most sense--to me, at least.

I moved closer to him. "Actually, I think I did. I just didn't realize that was why it was such torture to stay away."

He simply stared at me for several moments, as if he was examining what I'd meant. Finally, both relief and desire lit his eyes and he pulled me close and covered my mouth with the dizzying heat of his own. The desire that had been simmering just below the surface caught, enflaming both of us as our bodies merged at that one point. His taste and scent engulfed me, driving all thought from my mind. Purest animal instinct took over. My senses focused inward, channeling the pleasure of his touch and his nearness until it began to pool inside of me, building, expanding, feeding off of itself and, at the same time, feeding his need.

When he pulled away at last, it was only to strip me of the clothing that thwarted the need to touch skin to skin, to feel the texture and heat of each other. He caressed my flesh as he uncovered it and I shivered as every nerve ending came alive at his touch, quivering, sending minute jolts of sensation through every pleasure center.

I was so dizzy with desire I was hardly aware of the words he whispered against my skin.

"We are grateful that the force that creates all things in this universe saw fit to bring you into our path. We desire you above all others, with all that we are. We will cherish you as our soul mate, accepting and understanding that the differences between us are not insurmountable but the spice that seasons a relationship."

He stepped away from me then and began to remove his own clothing with the fumbling haste of need. I stared at him, wondering if what he'd said was part of the ritual and

I was supposed to say something in return. My brain was hardly functioning, however, and I finally said the only thing I could think of that encompassed all my feelings for him. "I love you."

I sensed a presence behind me only moments before two arms slid around me. Startled, I turned into his embrace. I didn't actually register that it was Jared until his lips covered mine. The difference between the two was subtle but distinct all the same. My waning desire, suffering from my separation from the stimulus of touch, flamed before my mind caught up with the situation and my reaction was slow because of it, and because I was so caught off guard.

I pushed him away, glancing toward Jerico, almost fearful of his reaction.

"I did something wrong?"

Jerico looked at me questioning before his gaze moved to his brother. As stunned as I was, it was only the beginning. When Jerico opened his mouth, the words that emerged were like no language I'd ever heard in my life. Discarding the last of his clothes, he pulled me close, sliding his hands over me in a way that seemed intended to soothe more than arouse.

Pulling me with him, he settled on the disappearing, re-appearing bed that I finally realized was some sort of hide-a-bed, though I couldn't figure out how it managed to appear and disappear without a sound.

I found I didn't care either. I was still confused about the fact that I'd found myself with both Jared and Jerico and not only were both naked, but it seemed neither of them were surprised by the situation.

Unresisting, I allowed Jerico to pull me between his legs so that I was facing Jared, my back resting against Jerico's chest. Wrapping his arms around me, he kissed the side of my neck. My body reacted instantly to his touch, nerve endings sparking tiny jolts of electricity through me. My nipples came erect, pulsing with blood to make them more sensitive still.

Moisture gathered in my sex as he caught each of my legs in turn and lifted it, hooking my legs over his and spreading my thighs wide. He coasted his palms along my inner thighs as Jared settled to watch.

Vaguely uneasy with the situation, I still couldn't deny that I was also aroused in a way I never had been before-- and curious. Jerico murmured low, against my skin as he nipped the sensitive flesh of my neck, but as before, the words were incomprehensible to me.

I lost interest in trying to figure it out when he cupped my breasts, massaging them, tweaking my engorged nipples gently with his thumbs and forefingers, closing my eyes to hold the acute sensations to me. After a moment, he skated his hands down my belly, caressed my thighs and then very gently parted my nether lips, exposing the keenly sensitive inner flesh.

With an effort, I lifted my eyelids. My heart clenched as I looked down at his fingers and then at Jared as Jerico held me, almost in offering. Mesmerized, I watched as Jared leaned close, watched his tongue as he extended it and licked a hot trail along my cleft.

A jolt went through at the delightful sensation. A harder jolt followed when he covered my clit and sucked the nub gently into his mouth, teasing it with his tongue. I gasped, struggling to catch my breath, to ignore the heat moving through me. When I looked up at Jerico, I saw that his eyes were glazed with desire as he watched Jared pluck at my clit. His gaze met mine. Splaying one palm along my cheek, he dipped his head to kiss me, massaging one breast with his free hand as he had before. I became completely lost in sensation then, too torn by the barrage of stimuli from both keenly tender areas to wrap my mind around anything else.

Despite the confusion of mind and body to so much at once, my body clenched with coiling, rising passion, racing toward culmination. I struggled against it. It felt too deliciously wonderful to end so soon.

After a moment, Jerico lifted his head. Shifting, he settled me back against the mattress and began to kiss my breasts. A sound of protest escaped me as he suckled one pulsing tip and then the other while Jared countered by teasing my clit until I was mindless. Almost before I realized I'd reached the peak, I fell over it, gasping out sharp cries as my body convulsed in hard spasms of climactic bliss.

Jared seemed reluctant to stop, or too caught up in his own pleasure. He sucked my clit until I thought I would pass out from the jolts going through me. I was barely conscious when they finally stopped, allowing the spasms to begin to abate, scarcely aware of the hands that stroked me soothingly.

Before I'd entirely touched down, the caresses became more pointed, stirring the fires once more. I murmured a protest, but I wasn't reluctant.

It felt so good to have them both stroking me that I simply basked in it for some moments. The urge grew in me, though, to caress in return, to give pleasure. Opening my eyes with an effort, I sought Jerico and found him sitting beside me. Shifting, I caught his erection in my hand and ran my tongue along the sensitive ridge of the head of his cock. He shuddered, his hand clenching on my shoulder. Encouraged, I covered the head with my mouth, sucking. He moved restlessly, arching up in offering and I took as much of his cock into my mouth as I could. Encompassing him tightly with the muscles of my mouth, I began to move over him in an escalating rhythm, feeling my own body responding as surely to my labors as if his cock was thrusting into my channel.

The thought had scarcely entered my mind when Jared shifted my hips and placed his mouth over my clit once more, teasing me as he had before. The rhythm of my heart stammered then began to race. I sucked harder, moved faster as my own body began to build toward release again. I was skating the edge when Jared ceased to tease my clit and withdrew. A moment later, he lifted my hips, settling my knees on the mattress and then I felt the head of his cock probing me, gliding through the juices that lubricated my cleft and lodging in the mouth of my passage. I braced myself as he probed deeper, thrusting and retreating until he sank to my depths.

We moved awkwardly for several moments and then I allowed him to set the rhythm. I could feel Jerico fighting against release as my own body struggled toward it. The realization sent me soaring higher. I sucked him hungrily, greedily, feeding my own desire off of his excitement. Abruptly, his cock jerked in my mouth. It touched off my own climax and I groaned, milking him with my mouth as my body began convulsing around Jared's cock. He went still for a handful of heartbeats and then began pumping into me harder and faster as his own release caught him.

I didn't let go of Jerico's cock until it ceased to spasm and my own convulsions began to dissipate. Finally, weak with the expenditure of what felt like every ounce of strength in me, I released him and dropped weakly to the mattress, gasping for breath.

We lay in a tangled heap for some time. Finally, Jerico roused himself and shifted down to align his body with mine and tug at me until I was draped limply across him. Jared shifted, as well, settling snugly against my back and dropping an arm across my waist.

I supposed it should have felt strange. It didn't. It felt so right it was downright scary. Dimly, I wondered at Jerico and Jared's complete comfort in sharing me between them, but I finally decided it must be a twin thing and something I would never completely understand. If it didn't bother them, I sure as hell wasn't about to object. The only thing I could think of that could possibly be better than sharing my body with Jerico was being with Jerico *and* Jared at the same time.

Just about the time my heart and lungs ceased to labor and regained their normal rhythm, Jerico stirred again. "We should take you home."

I grunted. I was in no hurry. It dawned on me that I hadn't had any of my questions answered, but I found I lacked the energy to care.

Several moments passed before I realized that both Jerico and Jared were stroking me caressingly. Jared leaned down and placed a nibbling kiss on my shoulder. "We'd be more comfortable there," he murmured.

I grunted again. I couldn't imagine how we could be. It was a little crowded on the bed with three of us, but I didn't think my bed was any bigger.

"I arranged it," Jerico responded lazily, "just in case-- although I'd begun to think you wouldn't come back. We need time to learn each other. In any case, the job here is done. We have a new one coming up, but we'll have time to ourselves before that."

He didn't wait for a response. Disentangling himself from me, he slid off the bed. Jared came up on his knees behind me, scooped me up and passed me to Jerico. Half asleep, I curled around Jerico, not particularly pleased to be disturbed at the moment since all I really wanted to do was sleep for a little while and then start over.

Curiosity gained the upper hand as Jerico carried me across the room, however, and the thought occurred to me that the three of us were buck naked. Puzzlement widened my eyes a little when I saw that Jerico had moved to the wall opposite the door we'd come in. I lifted my head and stared at the wall, then glanced up at Jerico. When I looked around for Jared, I saw that he'd come to stand beside us. He leaned forward and placed his palm on the wall.

Instantly, an area of the wall began to glow and ripple, like water that had been disturbed. Tensing, I tightened my arms around Jerico's neck and sat straighter. When I glanced at Jerico again, I saw that he was smiling at me. "Welcome," he murmured, dipping his head to kiss me lightly even as he took a step forward.

Blackness engulfed me, as if someone had flipped a switch and turned me off like a light.

Chapter Five

Awareness came to me slowly, like the mists of deep sleep parting. Warmth surrounded me, though, and I found I was reluctant to relinquish the sense of well being for the cold light of day. As usual, it couldn't be denied. Thoughts began to gather and tease at me, bringing me more and more alert and taking me further from the comfort of sleep. Finally, reluctantly, I opened one eye a fraction. Jerico was propped on one arm beside me, watching me, a half smile on his lips. I stared at him for several moments, then glanced behind me when I felt a hand skate along my back.

Jared smiled faintly at my expression.

I think relief was uppermost, that for once I hadn't woken alone to wonder if anything I thought had happened had actually happened. He leaned toward me and kissed me briefly. Jerico snatched me away from his brother and kissed just as briefly, then smacked me on the ass. "Are you going to lie in bed all day, or are you ready to explore?"

I chuckled. "I'm not against laying in bed all day, but I wasn't thinking about sleeping."

His eyes gleamed. "Don't tempt me. I'm weak and need food."

I laughed at that. "Who's cooking?" I teased.

The brothers exchanged a look. "We'll go out," they said almost in unison.

I looked down at myself. "Like this?"

"I think we can find something for you to wear," Jared responded coolly, rolling away from me and climbing out of the bed.

I looked around the strange room I'd found myself in when Jerico followed suit. Cool colors were perfectly harmonized in the room, which was huge and wreaked of wealth. None of the furniture designs looked the least familiar, but from the gauzy draping that surrounded the bed, to the huge bed, and the chests, chairs and tables scattered about the room, it was tasteful and pleasing to the eye.

Jared, I saw, reached a panel in one wall that was roughly the size and shape of a door. It opened, so silently I wouldn't have known it had opened at all if I hadn't been staring at it at the time.

Automatic doors?

"Go on. I'll join the two of you once I've found clothing," Jerico suggested.

Shrugging, I crawled across the bed and got out, following Jared, already feeling anticipation at the prospect of showering with the two of them.

A jolt of surprise went through me when I reached the 'bathroom'. This was only partly because, like the bedroom, it was enormous. Mostly it was because the furnishings were so ultra modern as to be almost unrecognizable. Relief flooded me when Jared exited a small compartment on the other side.

I tried not to look desperate as I hurried toward it and went in.

Need almost abandoned me when the lights came on with the closing of the door and I stared at the potty. There was a hole and seat, however, and my need was too immediate for me to spend much time studying the strange looking thing. There was no paper. Before I could get desperate, warm water bathed my bottom. I jumped, spreading my legs for a look just as a blast of air replaced the fluids. The blast blew my hair back, but it also dried my bottom almost instantly.

The thing closed like a trap when I got up.

I didn't hear a flush, but I heard something.

When the 'throne' opened again it was as pristine as an operating table.

Bemused, I left the facilities.

Jared was standing in an enormous, circular depression. Water pelted him from almost every direction.

There wasn't a sign of a curtain nor any walls for that matter.

I walked smack into 'something' though, hitting it so hard I fell back several steps. Jerico, who'd entered the bathroom as I crossed toward the shower, grabbed me from behind, steadying me. Holding my shoulders, he guided me to a different position and inside. Still bemused, I lifted my hand and waved it in front of me until it connected with something that felt vaguely solid--but oddly yielding at the same time.

I began to feel as if the weirdness had caught me up anyway--it was just a different kind of weirdness.

"You'll grow accustomed. It isn't that different," Jerico said quietly, skating his palms over me in a soothing way.

Diverted, I allowed myself to enjoy the moment, washing them, basking in their attention as they bathed me. By the time we'd finished, I was ripe for another roll on the bed.

They had other ideas apparently.

There were no towels for drying. Instead, Jerico pushed me toward a spot on the floor and warm air rushed over me. Unlike the blow dryers I was familiar with, this actually dried me fairly effectively.

I would still have preferred a towel, but it seemed pointless to complain. He presented me with a robe like gown when I got out. I looked at it a little doubtfully, but discovered when I'd pulled it on that it fit me reasonably well. I couldn't picture going out in public in it, especially when they donned very similar robes, but I kept my reservations to myself.

Jerico slipped an arm around my waist, leading me through the bedroom and out through yet another automatic door. I glanced around the corridor outside, discovering it was more of a landing, or interior balcony, than a hallway and formed almost in a circle which ended in a wide set of spiraling stairs.

The place was a palace!

Unnerved, I refrained from gawking the best I could and allowed Jerico to guide me down the stairs and out the front door. I stopped abruptly when we left the 'house', feeling suddenly as if I was Alice and I'd just fallen down the rabbit hole.

The sun had just crested the far horizon, bathing everything in a multicolored glow and very little of what I saw was even vaguely familiar. The sun looked abnormally small. The trees and plants like no vegetation I'd ever seen, with strangely twisting limbs and trunks, bluish green leaves instead of the bright Kelly green I was used to, and as strangely shaped as the trees and shrubs themselves. Things moved in the sky that weren't planes but looked manmade, beside other things that moved in the sky that weren't birds.

I licked my lips, blinking. The strange scene didn't vanish. "What is this place?"

"Ren Jtanie," Jared murmured. "Our home."

I glanced at him and then at Jerico. "Your home?"

"Our home," Jerico corrected. "It seems strange, I know, but you'll grow accustomed."

"You keep saying that," I retorted tartly. "I'm just not sure why I need to."

Jerico studied me for a long moment. "We are mated. We will live together," he said a little uneasily.

"I expected that," I said at once, unwilling to break the magic and cause him any doubts. "But--what is this place? I have never seen anything like this--the plants are weird--everything is weird and different."

The two brothers exchanged a look. "We felt the same, but one grows accustomed to new places. We travel in our work, so we are only here occasionally. Some of the places you will like, others maybe not so much, but we will not have to stay long if you don't like it--and if you are not happy, you could stay here, or on Earth. But we would far rather have you with us. Even with the gateway, I like to keep traveling to a minimum."

Shock traveled through me in a wave that made me dizzy. Gateway? Earth? Ren Jtanie? The strange language. The strange plants. The weirdness of it all. And still I had a hard time accepting the explanation that explained so many of the questions that had been plaguing me for weeks.

"This is … are you saying this is another … planet?"

Jerico studied me a moment and gathered me close. I didn't resist. I really needed comforting at the moment. "Poor *tshieda*," he murmured gently. "I told you the service was galactic dates and mates. What did you think I meant?"

"I didn't know you really meant galactic!" I complained, trying to fight the urge to give way to hysterics as the full impact settled around me like the collapse of a high rise building. "My boss is going to fire me!"

He rubbed my back soothingly. "No, he won't. He won't remember anything you don't want him to."

I pushed away from him far enough to meet his gaze. "How am I going to stay with you two and keep my job?"

Jared touched my arm, drawing my attention. "These things must be worked out to merge lives. We will find a way so that the three of us can live in harmony."

I eyed him skeptically. Job compromise usually meant the woman gave up hers to support her husband's career. It occurred to me after a moment, however, that I was being a little unreasonable about the situation. True, I'd been to college--twice, for training in two different careers, the last law enforcement, but it wasn't like education was ever wasted. I hadn't been with the force long enough to consider it a career that had actually been launched. Furthermore, solving puzzles was my passion and there would be mysteries to be solved anywhere I happened to be. I wouldn't be 'giving up' anything. I would be gaining worlds more to explore.

I relaxed fractionally.

It was my second passion, actually. My first was the two aliens standing next to me, as hard as it was to grasp that they actually *were* aliens. Life was full of comprises. The important thing to remember was that some were more important and more critical to one's happiness than others.

I smiled faintly. No wonder I hadn't found my soul mate before. They were half way across the galaxy from me--or maybe all the way. I supposed that was why Mrs. Hutchins daughter, Julia, had disappeared and wondered if mama knew just how far away her daughter had moved off. Not that it mattered that I could see. Distance only mattered when it was hard to close and these people had travel down to practically instantaneous.

The important thing for me to remember was that there was always the gateway if I needed to go back for something or just wanted to for any reason at all.

Lifting up on my tiptoes, I kissed Jerico, and then Jared. "I love you--both of you. Let's go. If you don't feed me I'm going to expire."

Chuckling, Jerico draped an arm across my shoulders. Jared settled a hand on my ass and the three of us made out way down the steps toward the strange bullet looking thing I figured must pass as cars on Ren Jtanie. "What does *tshieda* mean?" I asked curiously.

Jerico smiled down at me. "Beloved."

MATING DANCE

Shizuko Lee

The building was exceptional only in how utterly normal it appeared. Whoever it was that had designed it must have intended it to be the most forgettable building in the world. "Are you sure this is it?"

"I don't know...." Val turned in the car seat to look at her a moment. "I guess it must be. I mean, this *is* the address Laura gave me." She turned back to the building, seeming to have as much difficulty as Caitlin did believing this was it.

Caitlin looked again at the building. No Holes Barred. That was what the club's name was, supposedly. This hardly looked like the place you'd find an exclusive adult club. *I guess that's why they chose it. Or built it, or whatever.* That was, of course, provided Laura hadn't decided to play a nasty trick on Val, in which case it would be extremely embarrassing when they went in and asked where all the action was. Caitlin didn't know Laura very well personally. She did know the woman was fond of jokes and had played countless pranks on Val, whose trusting nature insured she would fall for them every time.

"Are you positive you want to go through with this?"

Val nodded slowly to herself. "I haven't been laid in a year, Caitlin. A year. Do you have any idea what that's like?" she ground out. "A whole year of *nothing*. Not just horrible sex, *nothing!* It'll atrophy if I don't get some soon!"

Caitlin tried hard to banish the sudden vision of a withered vagina from her mind. "Damn it Val!"

She knew exactly what Val meant, though, had in fact been without longer than she, but preferred not to point it out. She might be horny, but she was fairly scared. What if she wasn't any good any more? What if she never had been? If she were just *destined* to be alone? She tried hard to shake the thoughts running through her head. Her mother had lived her whole life alone. What if it ran in the family, like some dread, unnamed disease?

It's now or never. It'll be years before I get up the gumption to try again. If I ever do. It occurred to her that she really wasn't starting off on the right foot. *What is it Val was always saying about giving people a fair chance?* Val seemed to have even worse luck with men than her own, yet still tried to find a good one. Caitlin never had figured out if it was blind determination or pure desperation that drove her.

"Well … let's get this over with."

As they stepped from the car, Caitlin wondered yet again how she had even allowed Val to talk her into this. She had decided several years ago to stop looking for love after a string of nightmarish blind dates, set up by so-called great friends. She'd lost most of her friends over the years because she wouldn't go out with their freaky, monstrous, or just plain stupid relatives more than once. *Shit, you would think, being my friends they'd know my taste a little better than that! Or at least know their own family well enough to know they wouldn't be interested in me!*

She had finally come to her senses and just stopped going out on blind dates all together, swearing off relationships while she was at it.

Val was the only friend that she had kept, mostly on account of the fact that Val didn't have any male relatives around her own age. Aside from that, it was almost exclusively her married friends who tried to set her up. *It's almost as if they just can't stand any of their friends not being married after they've tied themselves down. Are they jealous of my being single, or scared that I might get an interest in their husband? As if I'd be like that!*

She had added to her vow just over a year ago, deciding never to have another one night stand either. She tried to block the many horrible experiences from her mind, but one in particular came, unbidden.

She had met the guy at work and had found him wildly attractive. He seemed very interested, too. They had flirted a lot for several weeks until, one day, they had somehow wound up in her bed together. Things seemed to be going great at first, lots of kissing and heavy petting. She hadn't been at all disappointed in his body, which turned out to be nicely tanned and toned. The problem occurred after the clothes were off and she was well past the point that she felt she could say no. When they were actually in the bed together, it turned out he didn't really care if she enjoyed herself or not. Apparently, he thought the kissing and petting from before was all that she needed and that, with that out of the way at last, it was time for him to get his own jollies. He was a dead fish. There was no passion, no touching, just a quick in and out that left her feeling befouled and used. He had grabbed up his clothes and tore out of there like he'd been thrown, without even saying another word. She had not minded that part at all, had actually feared he might make things worse and linger. *Thank God for small favors.* Needless to say, work had been *extremely* awkward after that, at least for her, so she wound up having to find herself a position elsewhere.

"Earth to Caitlin. Come in. Over."

Startled into a sudden awareness of her surroundings, Caitlin shook off the memory and glared at Val. "Yes?"

"You're supposed to say 'over.'" Val giggled at her scowl and pointed across the street at the door. "Are you ready?"

Caitlin nodded once, and, trailing well behind Val, crossed the pavement to the door of the club. She paused momentarily and braced herself as Val opened the door and they entered. She hardly dared to open her eyes. When she finally did, it was only because she'd bumped into Val. She steadied herself, muttering an apology and looking over her friend's shoulder. She let go of a breath she hadn't known she held as relief flooded her. Somehow, she'd gotten it in her head that the club would be nothing but an orgy, a mass of naked, humping bodies her friend would doubtless insist she join. Instead, the crowd on the dance floor gyrating to the music looked and behaved just like they would have in any other club.

"Um. Val? Are you sure this is it?"

Val gave her a stern look over her shoulder. "Come on." She pointed toward one of two sets of circular, wrought iron stairs. "Laura said to go up."

As she followed her friend up the stairs, Caitlin found herself tensing up again. They were met at the top by a veritable wall of a man with beady eyes, who looked them over head to foot before stepping out of their way. His voice, though deep, seemed oddly normal for a man of his build. She'd actually expected something booming.

"You may enter."

Caitlin edged to Val's side as they looked around the mezzanine. There were four doors, each leading, supposedly, to four fantasy worlds. Before she'd even gotten the chance to read any of them, Val pointed to one on the right and said, "I'm going in there."

Caitlin looked at the sign above the world. "Historic dates and mates?" She looked quizzically at Val. *Dates and mates from the past? Ours, or someone else's?* She couldn't think of a single man she'd ever been with that she cared to ever date again, let alone mate with. *I guess maybe its people dressed up in silly costumes? Where's the appeal in that?* There obviously had to be some for the club to stay in business with offerings like that, but it certainly held no interest for her.

"Yeah. Why not? You're allowed to try a different one if you don't like the one you start out with, ya know. Besides, it's the one Laura recommended. You coming in?"

Caitlin shrugged. "Nah. I think I'll go in that one over there," she said, pointing at the one across from Val's room of choice.

"Galactic dates and mates?" Val said and laughed. "Why go to that one? Or are you just saying you want to go there and planning to skip out like a little chicken?"

Caitlin gave her a look, though the thought had crossed her mind, and sighed. *No real reason, it just happens to be closest without being your choice.* "It sounds interesting enough. Anyway, I'm not really into that whole history thing."

"So you'll really go?"

She swatted at Val. "Yes, I'll go. I'll see you in a little bit."

"Shit, you'll see me in a few hours! You can go for a quickie if you want, but I'm here to stay a while! Hey, remember what I said earlier? Take the first empty room you come to."

"Why did Laura say that anyway?"

Val shrugged, "No idea. See ya!" She turned and practically ran through the door. Caitlin, however, walked slowly toward her own, a knot of anxiety already formed in her stomach. She knew now she was going to go through with it. She honestly enjoyed being with a man when it was at least half decent, even if she hadn't had anything like that in a long time. She was already here, everyone already knew what she'd come for, which in itself made her uncomfortable. There was little point in turning back now. She wasn't even sure she wanted to. She looked nervously around the gallery one more time before stepping through the door. Inside was a long corridor filled with people, mostly men, who had their noses stuck to the plate-glass windows which lined both walls. *How do they keep them clean? There's a job I'll never take! What the hell is so interesting, anyway?*

Curiosity piqued, Caitlin stood on her tip toes and tried to look into the first window, to see what all the fuss was about. Inside, a man and woman floated, entwined, in what appeared to be thick water. *How on God's green Earth can they breathe in there! Is it some kind of super water, like that movie I saw that time? Heavy enough in oxygen for people to breath?*

As she stood there, staring, puzzling it over, she was jostled suddenly by several new-comers. It broke the spell and she gave up her spot to them. *Have at it. I'm not much on watching anyway.* She felt confidant she'd solved that little puzzle. *I'll just google it when I get home tonight.*

Moving down the hall, she sidled up to another window when she heard the loud gasps of the onlookers, intrigued in spite of herself. Inside, a naked woman was chained spread eagle between two metal pillars. Some *thing,* some strange and terrible, ugly *thing* had hold of her. It looked like it had a hundred mouths and it had every one of them plastered to that poor woman's body. Caitlin looked at the backs of the men around her, the few profiles she could see, in shock, wondering what that thing was and why no one was stopping it. *Surely it's just animatronics or something.* A loud moan from the woman inside drew Caitlin's attention back to her, belying her last thought. *It can't be fake. I've never heard of anything this good, even in a movie.* She squinted at the glass, certain it wasn't really a screen. The woman was writhing under the mouths, moaning loud enough for the onlookers to hear through the glass. Caitlin felt her own pussy tingle when two of those mouths closed over the woman's mound and the woman moaned again.

Caitlin pulled herself away forcibly, and continued down the hall in shocked silence, a little faster than before. *I hate to say it, but ... I want one! It isn't much to look at but ... my god!* She felt goose bumps run up her spine. *It looked like fun. What the hell am I saying? It's an alien! A real, honest to goodness alien! I knew the government had been keeping it a secret all these years, the liars. I knew it! There really are aliens. So this really is about galactic dates and mates. Would I really want one?* It was obvious they had some that looked nothing like humans, but the first one she saw had. Maybe she could get one that looked mostly human without being like a typical man? She stilled herself, deciding to go ahead and try. *I'm already here. As bad as I've had in the past, an alien couldn't possibly be much worse, right?*

The crowds thinned the farther she walked, and she walked swiftly past the last group, continuing on several minutes. Val had told her to take the first empty room, but she wanted to get as far away from the crowd as possible, too self conscious of her body, and shocked at herself for what she planned to do, to live and stand having all of those men watching, judging her. *It's too much like having your parents come in on you!* She finally stopped at a door, looking quickly back at the peepers in the distance to see if they'd noticed her. They didn't seem to have, at least none of them were looking in her direction, so she went inside and closed the door, leaning her back against it heavily. Unmoving except for her heart palpitations she remained where she was, staring at the room around her and wondering at the implications.

The room was spacious, completely devoid of true furnishings, having only a huge touch screen against the opposite wall. There was a distinct lack of anything male, alien or otherwise, in the room. She found herself worrying that she may have chosen the wrong room. *Is this why you're supposed to take the first empty room?* She didn't really want to go back out again and chance being noticed.

*I think I'll stay here a while. Maybe they'll eventually work
their way down here some time tonight.*

If they don't? I'm going home in a few hours either way.
She turned around to see if anyone had run up to the
window.

"It's gone!" The window was completely gone! There
was nothing there now but wall! She opened the door,
forgetting for the moment the potential of attracting
unwanted attention, and looked in the window. On the
other side was the hand she was using to brace herself. She
drew back inside the room. *Amazing! I've never heard of
glass like this!* She shut the door, studying the glass,
scratching at it with a fingernail, surprised that paint didn't
come off. She wondered just how many public buildings
had this stuff in them now. *Do they install it in shopping
centers to catch thieves? In the jails to keep an eye on
inmates?* The possibilities seemed endless. Truly horrifying
as far as privacy went, was her chief concern. *I can't have
sex in a room with a window! What if somebody wanders
by? They'll attract everyone else's attention and I'll have a
gaggle of men outside* looking *at me!*

She finally left the window and walked over to the touch
screen. "Damn it Val, what am I supposed to do now?" She
looked the screen over and decided, due to its obvious
complexity and her own inability to comprehend even one
of the symbols on the many buttons, to simply leave it
alone. She sat cross-legged on the floor and waited for
something to happen. Nothing did. No alien came out of
any wall, or in through the door. She started to wonder if
she was supposed to tell someone outside what she wanted
before coming into a room, but thought better of asking,
just in case it wouldn't help. She giggled to herself,
imagining a group of men standing outside the window
right now, watching her sit on the floor.

After twenty minutes of sitting and staring at the walls
she finally decided that perhaps she was supposed to type
something on the key pad. It took several minutes after
standing for the numbness and ensuing pain to subside, but
when it had she stumbled over to the screen. She looked it
over harder this time, but only one button seemed to really
stand out. "Let's see. On my DVD player, the little circle

with a line through it turns it on, so...." She pressed the button, but aside from a click, nothing happened.

Shrugging, she tried again, pressing a few more interesting looking buttons. Suddenly a voice that seemed to come from nowhere startled her. She'd already asked what it had said before she realized the sound originated somewhere inside the touch screen. "What language is that? Greek?" Instead of responding, the voice continued as before and seemed to repeat itself several times. She had pressed a dozen more buttons trying to get the language changed when at last it stopped altogether.

* * * *

Killian stared hard at the plain building before him for several moments before looking again in consternation at the card he held cradled in his hand. *This is it. I think.* Nori had told him to expect a normal building, but it just didn't seem natural for it to contain such wonders, yet look so ordinary. *Nori wouldn't lie. Not about this.* He pushed the doubt from his mind and strode across the plaza, pausing only a moment at the door before entering.

It took many moments for his eyes to adjust to the gloom of the interior, but when they had, he felt deflated. Typically, an orgy was in progress. Bodies were everywhere, entwined, lying in clumps all around him on the padded floor. For many, the mating dance was still visible. *I don't know why I expected differently.* He felt the stirring of his own mating dance, which he was quick to squelch.

He'd always been unsettled at the way most people behaved during mating, willing to perform at any time and place, mating so rarely in the comfort and privacy of one's own home, as it was said to have been done in years long past. He longed for monogamy in a world where most women never settled for just one male. Not that there had ever been enough women to go around, even in the grand old days. His brothers always called him greedy to want one all to himself to mate with, alone, at his house of all places. It was such an unnatural desire.

Nori, of course, changed his tune after he had discovered Lexi. The beautiful Lexi.

Killian thought she had the loveliest fur he'd ever seen. He understood Nori's immediate attraction to her, one shared by every man who laid eyes on her. He was the only one who had not performed the mating dance for her, no easy feat, but it had done none of the others any good. She only had eyes for Nori.

The irony that Nori had found first what he himself was so notorious for pursuing was not lost on Killian. Nori had done his best to make it up to him the only way possible, sharing with him the location of No Holes Barred. 'You can get a mate there. A true life mate! You can even pick and choose. It's paradise Killian. Truly paradise.'

It had taken Killian one whole, excruciating cycle to prepare himself for his mate. In that time, he had expanded the small house in which he lived to include numerous other rooms, had amassed a small fortune to ensure her comfort and his own ability to give her just about anything she could ever want. He had even worked to improve his body. He wanted everything to be perfect. In all that time, he had avoided this side of the city, afraid that if he so much as laid eyes on the club, he wouldn't be able to resist going in. Now at last, here he was.

Nori said it would appear like any other bordello, he repeated to himself several times, reassuring himself with that thought. *Why would any male settle for this? Don't they know what's up stairs right now?*

He scanned the room for a flight of stairs. He spotted two sets against opposing walls and opted for the path of least resistance. Killian had to step over many thrashing bodies, nearly tripping over out-splayed limbs twice, but finally managed to gain the stairs. He took the steps three at a time. At the top, a guard scanned him, glaring down at him. After several moments, Killian began to wonder if he would even let him pass, prepared himself to fight his way through, but at last the man nodded and stepped aside. Once inside, a quick scan of his own revealed the obvious choice of doors. *Galactic dates and mates.* His member awakened again and started it's mating dance, too insistent now to discourage. *So close. I'm already so close.*

Pushing through the door, he shouldered his way through a crowd that had gathered to look in through the windows that lined both walls of the hall at the mating couples within. *So there are some who've found their way up.* How many were here, searching as he was? *How many are here just to watch? They'd better have some way to shutter that glass inside. I have no interest in sharing our first mating with anyone.* Anxious now, he dismissed them after a moment, moving well past the crowd before entering a room.

Once inside, it took infinite patience to remove his loincloth slowly, instead of tearing it off. By the time it was off, his member's dance was in full swing. He was filled with pride to see how intricate his dance had become and knew that surely any woman would be impressed with it. From his pouch, he removed the two ear cuffs Lexi had loaned him for the occasion, placing one on each ear. 'You'll need these,' she'd said. 'They'll help you understand what she's saying, just in case she isn't from Earth's future, like me.'

Folding his things, he placed them beside the door before looking around the room. It contained a touch-screen and more than enough empty space to satisfy any man's needs. Walking over to the console, he pressed the power button, responding to the voice prompts that followed.

Yes, he knew the rule of three, yes he was certain he wanted a human woman. No, he didn't care what year she was from. *Definitely one with lots of hair. Oh, and short like Lexi.* He envisioned himself bending down to kiss his mate instead of craning his neck to look up, and smiled. When he'd finished, he entered his own information.

When the woman of his dreams did not immediately appear, he pressed the key for a chair and settled down to wait. *Maybe it takes a while for the system to process that much information? I'm not familiar with the technology. What if I was too specific about the woman? What if there isn't a human like that? What if Lexi is an exception and not the rule?* As he sat for the next six hours, his desperation grew. His member had long since exhausted itself and lay flaccid in his lap. He was bombarded with thoughts he didn't want to acknowledge. He tried once to reenter all of the information, afraid he might have hit a wrong key, but the system would not allow him access. Killian was on the verge of moving into another room and starting over when a sliver of light to one side of the console riveted his attention.

He gasped, *I'm chosen!*

His member, which he had doubted would be able to perform after its previous dance, surprised him by starting anew.

Leeping to his feet, he rushed to the door, and waited in front of it several seconds for his new mate to appear. When she did not, he walked through to find her.

The passage through time and space was disorienting, but he recovered quickly. Killian turned and found himself looking down at the back of what was undeniably an alien woman. *So small. She's almost the size of a child.*

She was standing in front of her own console, still pressing buttons. Long , blue black fur flowed down her head, ending in wisps at firm, round buttocks. He straighten to his full height, proud that among the many men he knew she could have chosen, she had chosen him. Hardly daring to breathe, lest she be nothing more than a dream, he moved quietly up to her. She spoke a strange word and put her hands--lovely soft-looking hands, on her waist. Feeling a sense of wonder, he reached out to touch her, to caress her fragile shoulder.

* * * *

"Now what?"

A hand on her shoulder almost startled her out of her skin and she yelped. "What the--!"

Whirling around, she found herself staring at a very muscular, very naked chest. It was attached to a mountain, but it was definitely human. "How the hell ... did you...."

Even as she stammered the question, of its own accord, her gaze dropped, skimming across a flat stomach and coming to rest on the spot that was definitely alien. Instead of a patch of hair, a cock, and balls, there was a--serpent!

She felt a sudden, searing blush rise from her neck to the top of her head. *My God! It's huge!* It was long, erect, and moving sinuously, dancing quite merrily, in fact. Mesmerized, she stared at it some moments, slack jawed, unable to look away and ashamed of herself for it, feeling heat gathering in her nether regions as his throbbing cock, still dancing, reached toward her.

With an effort, she managed to tear her gaze from his member finally and looked up his body to the handsome face that was attached to the talented cock. *He's bald!* Actually, that wasn't quite right, she decided after a moment. It didn't look as though he'd lost all of his hair as much as it seemed he'd never had a hair on his body in his life. *He doesn't even have eyelashes!* Oddly enough, he not only looked perfectly natural without them, he was amazingly good looking.

An alien!

He grinned down at her and said something in a deep voice. She didn't understand of word of it. She shook her head and blinked at him. "What?"

The grin fell slowly from his face and he said something else, shaking his own head.

"I'm sorry, I just don't understand you. Do you speak English*?" Of course not! He's an alien! Why would he?* She kicked herself mentally, trying to think of something to say that he might conceivably understand.

He pursed his lips a moment and then seemed to remember something. Finally, he pulled a small, plain metal ear cuff off his ear and held it out to her on his palm. She stared down at the clip a few moments, making no attempt to take it.

He motioned toward her ear with his free hand. *A gift?* It seemed oddly out of place to her, his giving her a present, especially given his nudity. The puzzled look she gave him must have said volumes to him, because he took hold of her head and gently tilted it to the side, placing the cuff on her right ear. "Now, as I was saying, how did you manage to understand enough common to get me here when you obviously don't speak it?"

Caitlin felt her jaw drop. "What? What did you just say?"

He raised a hairless eyebrow at her. "I said, how did you manage to understand enough common to get me here when you obviously don't speak it? Is the interpreter not working? Do you understand me now?"

"I--yes, I understand now. I thought you spoke a different language a few moments ago, that's all. What are you? Are you really an alien?" She immediately regretted asking, feeling extremely rude for it. *Of course he's an alien! They don't make those here!* She fought the temptation to look down again at that marvelous cock, whose movement she felt sure continued even now. She was dying to know where he was from, how he had gotten here, everything, but she didn't know where to start!

To her surprise, he laughed. "Is that really what you brought me here for? Questions?" He leaned toward her and breathed deeply, drinking in her scent. "Your fragrance says otherwise."

"Fragrance? I'm not wearing...." She blushed again when she realized what he was alluding too and decided to shut up. *What on Earth have I gotten myself into?*

He seemed to take her silence as a cue and gently took her face in his hands. Caitlin gulped against a knot that felt like a goose egg, but she was more than willing to get to the good stuff. Placing her palms on his chest, she came up on her tiptoes, meeting him halfway. When he pressed his mouth against hers it felt heavenly. She closed her eyes, drinking in his musk as he parted her lips with his tongue, thrusting it inside. Like strong drink his taste and touch went right to her head in a rush. Delighted, she sucked his tongue lightly. He moaned, running his hands down her body, pulling her possessively, almost roughly against his length and wrapping his arms tightly around her.

Feeling movement against her pants, confusion surfaced. His arms were around her. *What* was caressing her ass? She gasped when she reached down to discover what it was and something warm and taut wrapped itself around her hand. Pulling away from him, she looked down and discovered she was holding his cock--or, more accurately, it had twined around her arm lovingly. "Oh my--!"

She pulled her arm away. Undeterred, the cock sought a new target and--nuzzled her. She wondered briefly how such a wondrous thing could have developed elsewhere, and more importantly why men on Earth hadn't developed such fantastic cocks.

Chuckling at her obvious confusion--for he knew from his brother that Earth men were not the same and that his brother's Earth woman had been fascinated by the mating dance--he brushed by her, quickly typing something on the console.

"I don't suppose you can do anything about that?" She pointed to where she knew the window to be.

Killian smiled, pleased that they were of like mind. "I just took care of that. I've never been one for being watched." Returning his attention to the console, he pressed a few more buttons. Feeling an odd sort of buoyancy, Caitlin looked at him in askance.

"Less gravity, more pleasure." He took her hands, pulled her to him and tugged her shirt over her head, looking hungrily down at her exposed breasts, caressing her with his gaze. She felt her nipples perk, moaned aloud when he bent down and suckled her breast, sending a quiver of pleasure all the way to her core. She grew wet as he ran the blade of his tongue over her nipple, as he messaged her other breast with his callused hand.

When she felt his cock rub against her legs, she eagerly unfastened her pants, her fingers fumbling. Finally, she managed to get her pants unfastened and pushed them and her panties to the floor. As if it had a mind of its own, his cock danced closer the moment she was undressed. Sucking in a breath that was part anticipation, part nerves, she spread her legs slightly, allowing his cock to run between them. It rubbed against her thighs and she found herself thrusting her hips against him, toward it. Delight filled her when his cock took the hint and started to caress the outer folds of her sex, moving like a lover's finger and sending wonderful sensations through her.

Within moments, Caitlin found she no longer thought of his being an alien, couldn't really think at all past the here and now, the delirious heaven of his touch. She licked the taste of him from her lips, marveling at how wonderfully this man's hard body felt against her own. Running her hands over his muscled back, up to his hard, broad shoulders, she held him close while he kissed and caressed her with his hands, learning her body. She gasped as his cock pressed incessantly against the nub of her clit, rubbing up and down over it, seemingly of its own accord, driving her need higher and higher until she was moaning, unable to contain it.

After a few moments, he pulled her with him to the floor, licking her wrist with his hot, wet tongue. He left a fire trail with his touch, softly licking her inner arm, sucking on her neck. She'd begun to feel real desperation by the time he shifted, pushing her gently to her back. Positioning his body over her own, he trailed kisses down her jaw to her neck, gently sucking her earlobe. Caitlin gasped as he explored her soft body with his hands, teased her nipples, and lowered his head to suckle them. All the while, his throbbing cock caressed the lips of her sex, her clit, as if two lovers caressed her at once, driving her wild with need.

Too mindless by now to verbally demand what she needed, she rocked her hips back and forth, trying to align her body with his cock, but each time she felt the head right where she needed it, it pulled away from the entrance, moving to stroke her clit once more. She was near faint from gasping for air when at last his cock thrust into her. Hungrily, her body clenched around the offering and she cried out. Disappointment filled her when, after doing nothing but tease her, his cock withdrew once more, pulsing against her thigh.

"Please...." Her voice, full of need, trailed off.

He closed his eyes and shuddered, controlling himself with a great effort. "Not yet."

His pleasure glazed eyes met hers momentarily before he bent again, trailing kisses down her abdomen, his breath hot against her quivering skin. He ran his hands down her legs, moving lower and kissing and licking them. She cried out as his lips brushed her inner thighs, moaning and squirming when he changed directions, moving higher with his kisses. She ran her fingers over his smooth head, delighted when he at last moved over her wet sex, parting her inner lips with his tongue, drawing a moan of ecstasy from her lips. She leaned back, her hips rocking involuntarily. *Oh God, I'm gonna cum.*

Almost as if he'd heard her silent cry, he sat up, pulling her roughly toward him, lifting her legs over his shoulders. She gasped, biting her lip as his hands cupped her firm buttocks, as he drew her clit into his hot mouth and sucked on it. She moaned in momentary frustration when he stopped, the moan turning to one of pleasure as his tongue darted inside of her, thrusting in and out rhythmically. Within moment, the first waves of an orgasm wash over her and she cried out at its intensity, felt her sex clench tightly around his tongue. He continued to thrust in and out, pulling her to greater heights than she'd ever dreamed possible.

When he finally stopped, she lay quivering in the aftermath, wiping stray hair back from her face as he lifted his head, as he moved up over her with a purpose.

Positioning himself between her legs, he kissed and sucked on her neck, his cock rubbing back and forth over her sex, slipping inside of her suddenly, filling her completely with its mass. Caitlin shuddered as he began to thrust into her. Along her channel, which had a stranglehold on his huge cock, she felt vibrations as his member struggled to continue its mating dance. The movement, coupled with the stroke of his cock, skyrocketed her body upwards once more. She bucked, meeting his rhythm, increasing the speed, feeling herself climbing toward another release.

Abruptly, he moaned raggedly against her throat, panting from his effort to exert control over his body and withdrew. She knew he was trying to keep from coming, but it didn't help her feelings. She wanted it back. She could feel his cock, slippery and wet, searching her thigh. She knew it was looking for the soft hot hole he'd deprived it of. Taking his cock into her hand, she closed her hand around his heated flesh, massaging it, moving her hand faster when he moaned again.

"I'm trying hard to save that, but you're making it difficult."

"Sorry...." She let go and met his gaze as he sat up. "I was almost there. You could have...."

He shook his head. "There's only one chance for a first impression. Isn't that what you humans say?"

She was torn at once between pleased surprise that he was determined to thoroughly pleasure her and disappointment that he hadn't finished what he'd started.

He grinned at her expression, still panting slightly. "Our time isn't over yet. Turn around."

She rolled over onto her hands and knees, looking back at him expectantly.

He mounted her from behind, his cock once again thrusting inside of her. Lifting her hair over her shoulder, he kissed her nape and slipped one arm around her, cupping a breast in his palm and teasing her nipple to painful erection between two hard fingers. All the while, he thrust slowly in and out of her, their bodies growing slick with the effort. She pushed back hard into him, gasping when he released her breast and started teasing her clit as he had her nipple.

Her body seemed to clench all over.

"Harder. Oh God, faster--"

Straightening, he caught her hips with both hands, slamming his engorged cock inside of her, increasing his tempo with every thrust until at last she felt herself reach the precipice, fall over it again. As her sex tightened around him in convulsions of ecstasy, he moaned, allowing himself to take his own pleasure at last. She felt his hot seed fill her, felt his cock quiver and buck inside of her.

Weak, quivering in the aftermath of her second climax, Caitlin collapsed onto the floor, closing her eyes languidly as the last of her energy left her. Hissing at the acute residual sensation, he withdrew his spent cock and stood.

Feeling vaguely disappointed, she simply rolled onto her side as he withdrew. She didn't look up at him. *Leaving, I guess. The same thing the last guy did.*

Not true. The last one certainly hadn't made her body sing.

The floor seemed to grow soft beneath her. Feeling movement, she opened her eyes as he lay beside her, taking her into his arms.

"I thought you were leaving."

He looked at her in puzzlement. "I guess I could if you want me to."

"No! I mean, I don't really want you to. I just thought you were leaving, that's all."

He seemed to mull that over, stroking, exploring her naked body with one hand. "Is that an Earth custom?"

"In this kind of situation? Yeah. Pretty much."

He frowned, obviously perplexed over it. "This is acceptable?"

"Not to me, no." At least not currently. There'd been plenty of times she was just as anxious for her 'date' to depart as he was to leave.

She found herself growing hot again as he continued his ministrations. She studied the muscles on his chest, admiring how they moved about as he breathed.

"Is that why you're here? Because the men here do not know how to fully appreciate a woman?"

"Actually, I came because my best friend wanted moral support." That wasn't entirely true. Maybe what they say about hope springing eternal was true after all. "She didn't want to come by herself."

"Where is she now?"

"She went into a different hall--" Her eyes widened on a sudden thought. *Oh my God! If I'm here with an alien, does that mean ... did she really get a man from the past?* It occurred to her that Val had definitely chosen the wrong door. *Men were men, what ever time they were from. Aliens on the other hand....* She looked up to see he was gazing intently at her. "What?"

"What's your name?"

"My--" She hadn't actually noticed that she'd never given it to him. *I just had sex with a man without even asking his name.* Forget what her mother would have thought, she felt ashamed that he'd thought to ask first.

"Caitlin. What's yours?"

He smiled faintly. "My name is Killian. What did you mean before? About Earth men behaving badly in this kind of situation?"

Caitlin merely stared at him blankly as if he'd suddenly begun to speak that strange language again. It was a one night stand. *Surely--- My God, doesn't he know?*

Apparently, he hadn't but he seemed to read enough of her thoughts in her paled face.

"You used me," he said accusingly as understanding dawned. His face grew dark and angry.

Caitlin was suddenly mortified. Guilt swamped her. The fact that she realized she was now in the exact opposite position she'd been in with so many guys didn't help. Somehow, 'I thought you knew' didn't seem like the best thing to say. "I thought we both came here for the same reason," she said finally.

"For a mate," he said, his voice tight with hurt and anger.

It occurred to her that the sign outside had said Galactic dates and mates. *I thought it meant mate as in sex, not mate as in for life!* "I'm so sorry. You're a nice--um--guy and all. It's just that I'm not really ready for that level of commitment!"

Slowly, his anger seemed to drain away. He sighed, his face falling. "So that's it. You're rejecting me."

Caitlin looked into his eyes, at the pain she knew she'd caused there, and felt like a total bitch. It didn't really matter that she hadn't hurt him intentionally. She'd still hurt him and she felt like a dog. She hated herself at that moment, but had no idea how to make things better. Still she felt impelled to try. "Can you take it as a maybe?"

He looked into her eyes at that, studying her briefly. He looked hopeful, but doubtful, as well, as if he wasn't certain she was sincere. "It's better than a positive no…."

She placed a palm on his chest. "It's closer to a yes than I've ever come before." *Of course no one's ever asked me to be their mate before,* she added to herself. "Maybe when I get to know you a little better?" *What am I saying? He's an alien! I don't even know anything about his species! What if I want kids? Could I even have them with him?* A part of her responded that for the right man she'd give up that possibility, that she hadn't even thought of having kids before anyway, but she tried to ignore it.

A question had been nagging her since 'it' had first wrapped itself around her hand. She felt strange asking, but she was dying to know if that was typical behavior or if 'it' had responded particularly to her. *I know better than to hope it's just me.* She really did want to know, though, so she stilled herself for a disappointment and asked anyway. "Does it always do that?"

"What?"

"Your cock. Does it always move like that? Trying … you know, to find a warm hole?" *That could've come out better.* She felt herself blush as his rich laughter rolled over her, and regretted asking at all.

"No, it doesn't usually do that. It just happens to like yours." He sobered. "The mating dance is normal, though."

"Mating dance?"

"The … dance it's performing, even now."

She could feel it moving around, felt her own desires growing again, in spite of the fact that she was just too worn out to go it again.

"So that's a mating dance." *Birds dance and sing. Most animals have some kind of ritual.*

"So, what? The guy with the best dancing cock wins?"

He grinned at her, and she felt her blood warm. "You could say that. There's always been heavy competition for mates on my world. That's why I came here in search of one." His grin faded.

They sat in awkward silence for some moments, the warmth she'd felt ebbing quickly. *Mate.* Could she really go through with something like that? Where would they live, his planet or hers? How would she find a way home if things didn't work out? Why hadn't anyone ever warned her that being with an alien was infinitely more complicated than settling for a human?

"Where do we go from here?"

When he didn't acknowledge her question, she wondered if she'd said it out loud. She was on the verge of repeating herself when he answered.

"You didn't understand the voice prompts." He gestured toward the console. "Did anyone here tell you the rule of three? Your friend perhaps?"

"Rule of three?"

"Two times a date, three times a mate. It means that if we see each other more than one last time, we both understand that it is because we want to be mates."

Only two dates? It seemed so ridiculous that she should be expected to decide to marry a man after only two dates. "Why only two? Why not ten? Twenty?"

"According to the computer, in most cultures, to mate once is to mate for life. The rule of three is … a concession."

"So … where do we go from here?" *Do you even want to see me again, or did I offend you too much earlier for that?* Considering what he could do with his cock, there was no telling what the women where he was from could do. What it if he didn't think she was any good at sex? What if he thought she was awful?

To her surprise, he disentangled himself from her arms, stood and walked to the computer. Returning with a pencil and paper, he sat cross-legged on the floor, his member inert for the first time since they'd met. With great care, he scribed strange symbols on the page that looked vaguely familiar to her. When he'd finished, he held it out to her and she took it.

"What is it?"

"Instructions. On how to call me on purpose next time."

"Oh." She studied them, recognizing them as the same symbols she had haphazardly typed earlier.

He stood again, reaching down to pull her up, as well. She tilted her head up to look at him and he leaned down, pressing his lips against hers in a passionate kiss. His cock brushed fondly against her thighs.

Killian backed away with a sigh and typed something on the console, and a sliver of light appeared beside him. He turned to her.

"I look forward to seeing you again." His look said he didn't dare hope it, and Caitlin again felt like a dirty dog.

She nodded, unsure of what to say, what she *should* say to him.

He passed into the light and was gone.

Caitlin stared at the spot where he'd vanished for a time. Finally, feeling strangely unhappy considering how thoroughly sated she was, she turned and gathered up her clothes.

"Shit," she exclaimed on a sudden thought. "I bet Val's left without me by now."

She dressed in a hurry, smoothing her hair as best she could, and stuffed the address he'd given her into her pocket.

She was relieved to find, when she opened the door, that Killian really had kept the men on the outside from being able to see them. The whole group had moved closer down the hall, but there were none standing outside the door to greet her, for which she was thankful. She wove her way through them down the hall, and quickly descended the stairs.

The club was, by all appearances, just as full now as it had been when she'd gone upstairs. She pushed her way through the crowd and out onto the street. Val was laying back in the driver's seat, asleep with the doors locked.

"Val?" She tapped on the window. "Val, wake up!"

Val started and fumbled with the lock. When she'd unlocked Caitlin's door, she slid into the passenger seat.

"Where've you been Caitlin?"

"Sorry it took me so long. Time … kind of got away from me. I thought you were planning to stay most of the night."

"I did. I mean, I thought I did. It's so strange. It felt like I was there all night, but when I got downstairs and actually looked at the time, only an hour had passed."

"So how long have you been waiting for me?"

Val looked at the clock a moment. "About thirty minutes."

Caitlin frowned, thinking it over. "I guess the whole time thing must have something to do with the club itself. Everyone's still in there dancing. Looks like the same people, anyway."

"So how was it? You were in there a long time. Did you really, you know, *do* it?"

"Yeah. You?"

"That's it? Yeah? Caitlin, I got to be with a knight! A real honest to goodness *knight!* And all you can say about your *alien* is yeah?"

"All right, all right! I met the most handsome man I've seen in a very long time and had the best sex of my life. His cock moved around on its own, which is normal where he's from if you can believe it! After all of that, he even turned out to be a genuinely wonderful man."

"You mean alien."

Caitlin glowered at her friend.

"Okay, guy. Hey, it's not like you were planning to ever see him again anyway, right? I really liked Sir Anthony, but it could never work out! We're from different times, different worlds. Of course, you two are from two *completely* different worlds, but my point is the guy could never fit in here. Could you even imagine a knight here? In *this* city?"

"Or you living with him back there in his time?" Caitlin shook her head. "No, I guess it really couldn't work out." She felt the weight of the paper Killian had given her in her pocket, but resisted the urge to touch it. Their goodbye hadn't seemed so final before. *He really wanted to see me again.*

Caitlin sat silently as Val started the car, gushing the whole way home about her knight in shining armor. At Caitlin's stop, they said their goodnights and she went inside her dark, lonely little one room apartment.

* * * *

A month. It had been one, whole, horribly lonely month since she'd seen Killian. She had tried hard to forget about him. *Val was right. There's no way things could have worked out differently.*

She told herself that every day now. *He's an alien. I'm human. We're from different worlds. Surely he knew I wouldn't be coming back.* She felt like such a coward. *I didn't even really say goodbye. He obviously wanted to see me again. What if he's up there right now waiting for me?*

It would be just like a man to do that to make a girl feel guilty. The asses know that works. Lay a guilt trip on a gal, look helpless, and they're putty in your hands.

By the end of the month she couldn't stand it any longer. Her song had changed. 'It wouldn't work' to 'he's playing me' to 'it would be rude not to go one last time, just to tell him I won't be coming back. He'd do the same for me. Wouldn't he?'

Once she'd made up her mind, she was in a fever to go. She put on a slinky red spandex dress she knew she looked great in and then dug around in the top drawer of her dresser for the address he'd given her and the ear cuff he'd left.

"Yet another reason to see him again," she murmured to herself, glad she'd realized she had something of his that she needed to return.

She took the bus up to the club and went inside. It looked for all the world as though the same crowd were still there dancing. She fairly flew up the spiral stairs. The same man met her at the top, with no more interest in her than before, and moved to let her inside.

"Val?"

Val stood like a deer caught in head lights, one hand on the door to historic dates and mates. Caitlin crossed her arms and walked slowly toward her.

"I thought you said it wouldn't work out...."

"I know I did. To you. I didn't tell *him* that. I just came, ya know, to see him one last time, all right?"

So you miss him. I know how you feel.

"Just one last time. Me too. I forgot to give him back his translator too. I'm sure they're not cheap." She held it out as evidence that she had a *real* reason to be there.

"Oh."

"Well, I'll see ya later."

"Yeah. Later." With that, Val turned and went through the door to find her knight. Caitlin, meanwhile, walked through her own door. A crowd was again gathered to gape at the couples behind the glass, but she paid them no heed. *Killian.* Would he be mad that she had not come sooner, or happy that she came at all? *I'll find out soon enough.* She chose what she thought to be the door she had entered her first time to the club, shutting the door firmly behind her. Rushing to the console, she fumbled in her purse for the paper and translator he had given her.

"There you are!"

Her fingers where shaking as she placed the translator on her ear and unfolded the paper, studying the writing several moments before starting. Stilling herself with a deep breath, she began carefully punching buttons. The system's voice spoke.

"Do you accept the rule of three?"

She pressed the next button indicated, ignoring the computer's voice altogether since she had no earthly clue what she was supposed to say to any of the prompts. It went silent when she hit the last button on the list. She turned around with a smile, disappointed when Killian wasn't there to greet her.

"Damn. Did I type everything up right?" She looked over the paper in her hand, unable to see anything she might have done wrong.

"I thought you'd decided to take a different mate."

She started at the sound of his voice at her shoulder, whirling around and throwing her arms around his neck. "Killian! Are you angry? Please say you're not mad at me." She released him and backed up in case he was. *Damn it! Now he'll have the wrong impression. Sorry, I just seem to be happy to see you. I've really just come to reject you to your face.*

"No, no! I'm not angry. I just thought … when you never came back…."

"I'm sorry. I … well I thought about everything … you know, that you said." *What Val had said.* "And everything else. Killian, I just don't see how things could work out between us," she blurted out. *There. I said it.*

His face clouded up and he looked away from her.

"Killian. It isn't that I don't wish like hell that it could! I … care … about you…. It just wasn't meant to be, can't you see that? I'm so sorry." She waited, but when he said nothing, she turned for the door. "I just … wanted to say goodbye--"

Killian's strong arms wrapped around her waist and pulled her to him.

"That's how you planned to say it? Just 'I'm sorry,' and then a hasty retreat?"

She looked up at him guiltily, knowing that wasn't what she'd planned at all. She'd hoped they could have one last night of wild and wonderful sex. "No...."

"Stay with me. Just one last time. We're already here together."

The moment he made the suggestion, doubt flooded her. She nodded anyway, telling herself that it wouldn't hurt so much to say goodbye this way, but in her soul, she knew she was making things worse.

Satisfied with her answer, he stroked his hands over her in a leisurely way, as if relearning her body. After a moment, he released her, studied the dress she was wearing and, finding no way to open it, caught the hem and slowly pulled her it over her head. After tossing the dress toward the corner of the room, he bent over to tug off her panties. When he straightened, he kissed her deeply, running his hands over her now nude body, holding her close.

Feeling his cock stir, she tugged impatiently at his loincloth, which he was quick to remove. When she felt his hard cock caress her skin and start petting her pubic curls, she spread her legs in invitation. To her delighted surprise, his cock instantly went straight for her opening, writhing as it burrowed deeply inside of her. She gasped, closing her eyes as sensation rolled over her like a tidal wave. Catching her tightly to him, Killian carried her to the floor and rolled over, pulling her atop him. His rough hands massaged her breasts, supporting her as she arched back, rocking her hips back and to, delighted in the motion of his cock. Catching her hips, Killian thrust deeply into her, drawing a loud moan from her lips. After a moment, he slid his hands upward and grasped her arms, pulling her down to kiss her deeply as he slid one hand down to cup her butt, and palmed her breast in the other, kneading the soft flesh and sending fresh waves of glorious sensations through her.

Drowning in a sea of bliss, she explored the sensitive inner flesh of his mouth with her tongue, running her hands across his smooth chest and shoulders.

Abruptly, he changed positions. Lifting her from his lap, he stood up, caught her around the waist and thrust his cock into her. She shuddered as her own weight pushed the squirming member deeply inside of her sex, wrapping her legs around his waist and locking her ankles together for support. He trailed fire across her jaw as he carried her to the nearest wall, placing her back against it and ramming his hard cock up into her. Kneading the flesh of her buttocks, he kissed and licked her jaw and neck feverishly as he pumped into her. A growl issued forth from deeply in his chest and began to thrust into her harder and faster. She felt him stiffen, felt his hot seed fill her, felt his cock thrash against the muscles of her sex. The motion brought on her own release and she screamed with the force of it.

Weak in the aftermath, they collapsed to the floor together this time, once again in each other's arms. *It's actually quite nice*, Caitlin thought to herself dreamily. *Definitely not like anything on Earth.*

"Do all women here have such magnificent fur?" Killian asked as he gently stroked her hair, lowering his head to it and breathing deeply. "It has such an unusual smell…."

The question caught her unaware, confused her for several moments. "Fur? Oh, you mean my hair, right?" She covered a yawn before continuing. "Everyone here has it. Not always long like mine. It comes in all different colors too. The smell is just my shampoo."

He silently considered her answer. "No one on my world has hair. There are only a few species of animals that have fur and only a handful of them with enough to speak of."

"That's strange. I wonder why you didn't evolve hair like us? I mean, you seem so … human." She thought of the prehensile cock that was even now stirring inside of her. "For the most part, I mean."

"We came from Arutagia." At her puzzled look, he tried to explain. "It's a place of … water. We came from the water."

"Oh. Well, we did too." *Just didn't get the full benefit.*

"I love your hair." He fingered a lock of it, twirling it between his fingers. His cock, obviously in full agreement, squirmed inside her sex.

"Killian," she said hesitantly.

He stilled. "Don't, Caitlin."

Their eyes met for a moment before she could look away. The pain in his eyes was evident and made her hurt in response, but she knew she had to say something. "It just wouldn't..."

He placed a finger over her lips, replacing it with his own lips for a brief kiss. When he released her, he stood wordlessly, locating his loincloth on top of her panties, and dressed.

Oh god, this is it. He's leaving now. What the hell am I supposed to say?

"Killian--"

"Caitlin." He stopped at the shaft of light and turned to look at her one last time. "Good bye." He stepped through and in a moment, was gone from her life.

Caitlin felt sick. She felt like she might throw-up any moment. *He's gone. I'll never see him again. He left, just like that.* She moved in a daze, hanging her toes in her panties more than once as she dressed. *He's gone forever now.* She'd never been as miserable as she was at that moment.

She could hardly breathe. Pushing and prodding her way through the crowd, she reached the door at the end of the hall. Outside, Val paced the mezzanine.

"Val!"

"Caitlin!" Val rushed over and hugged her. "Caitlin, don't be mad. Anthony asked me to marry him! Can you believe that? I'm getting married!"

"What?" Caitlin was floored by the announcement. "What are you talking about?"

"I'm getting married!"

"To Sir Anthony? But where will you live?"

Val tried to calm down. "I'm going to live with him. In the middle ages. I never really did ask him what year it is where he's from. Oh Caitlin, can you believe it? I'm finally getting married!"

Caitlin didn't know whether to be more shocked or horrified at the revelation.

"Good god Val! You were saying just a while ago that you were only here to say goodbye, that it couldn't work out!"

"I know what I said." Val stilled. "Caitlin. I'm never going to find a guy like Anthony anywhere else. Especially not in this day and age. He could never fit in here. Hell, what would he do for a living? In his own time and place, though, he could actually be a really good provider." Val patted her stomach. "We'll need that."

"You're pregnant? You're pregnant!" She pulled Val into a hug of her own. "Oh my god! I mean congratulations! But Val...." She pulled away from her friend and studied her face. "Val, you'd be giving up so *much*."

"I know. There's a lot of stuff I'll miss--mostly my best friend in the whole world. But, Caitlin, I'm in *love* with him. I was miserable the whole time I was away from him. I know it's a huge risk and I'll be giving up every modern convenience, but love doesn't exactly come around all that often. I've never been so crazy about any man. Especially not one who's crazy about me too."

"I just can't believe it."

"Caitlin ... I know that we always had a thing where neither of us pries in the other's love life, but ... well, you've been miserable too. I can see that."

She's right. I have been. She shook her head. "Val, there's just no way it could work out."

"Why the hell not? This place is here for a reason. If that kind of relationship never worked out, would they offer it as a choice?"

"I guess I never thought about that...."

Val kissed her on the cheek. "Well do. Anyway, Anthony's waiting in the room. I just couldn't leave without saying goodbye."

They squeezed each other tightly for a few minutes. "Why not give the guy a fair chance, Caitlin?"

A fair chance?

"Goodbye, Val." She sniffled and tried to smile for the last time at her very best friend. "I'll miss you."

"Me, too."

Val virtually skipped to the door leading to the hall of historic dates and mates. "Bye Caitlin!"

In moments, Caitlin was left alone with nothing but her thoughts.

Had she really given Killian a fair chance after all? Enough of one to learn about him, to care, but a *real* chance? *Val is giving up everything for a chance at happiness. Would I really be giving up that much to be with Killian?* She turned toward the door she had rushed out of only minutes before.

They have technology there. Hell, this translator is above and beyond anything we have here. She opened the door, walking down the hall to the room she had just vacated.

I could always adopt children if I really want them. Come back for a frozen pop. Hell, as far as I know, I might be able to have some with him. Ya never knew about these things. She pulled out the crumpled paper she had hastily stuffed into her purse when Killian had left her, and started hitting the buttons on the console.

Would he even be interested now? That thought brought her up short, but she pushed it aside with an effort and finished. *He has to be. He just has to.* Caitlin squeezed her eyes shut and wished with all of her soul that he'd come back.

She sighed, almost sobbing in relief when she felt a pair of strong arms wrap around her. She turned into his embrace.

"Killian!"

"I thought you said it wouldn't work out."

"I know what I said." She tilted her head back and he kissed her lips and face. "I want to give it a try ... if you'll have me?"

He gave her an incredulous look, sweeping her into his arms. She wrapped her own around him, nuzzling his neck, closing her eyes against the light as he carried her into another world.

"Welcome home."

The End

THE AWAKENING

Angelia Whiting

Chapter One

Britenia tossed an expressionless glance at her mentor. "Why should I even bother?"

"You have been wronged Brit. All of your people have been wronged."

Britenia scanned the satellite, located at the end of the gateway that Rupshel had brought her through. It was a colorless piece of rock, floating in the galaxy, bearing nothing except boulders and stones and pits of various sizes. It was as dead as she was, as dead as the enormous bolder they stood in front of that burrowed nondescriptly into the satellite's pebbled surface, looking as much a part of the terrain as any other of the enormous rocks. In its stone façade the words, *No Holes Barred* was carved appearing as though a passerby had haplessly scratched into the surface. But Rupshel told her it was the entrance to the spa club and resort that she would reside at for as many dawnings as it took.

"It doesn't look like much of a place to find deliverance."

"Not true child." Rupshel cast his glance to the large boulder. "Many travelers pass through the cosmic gateways to this satellite play land, some stay awhile and some go. Inside you will find creatures from the galaxies far and wide. Emotions abound."

The elderly man tipped his head toward Britenia and scratched his ancient purple-gray beard. His voice lowered an octave though his tone was still firm. "You may find joy here, my dear."

"I doubt I'll ever have that gift again, Rupshel." Brit stared at the rocky wall in front of her. "Nothing holds meaning for me. I remain empty."

"Ah, child," Rupshel glided over to her, his long flowing robes caressing the ground as he moved. He was the epitome of a life time of wisdom and knowledge, four centuries of learning he put to claim under his belt. "Do I detect despair within you?"

Brit's head snapped around so she could look her mentor in the eye. "It is an emotion, yes?"

"It is."

"Well, it is not a very pleasant feeling." Still, feeling a twinge of an emotion stimulated Britenia's hope, another emotion. Perhaps she would stay awhile.

"Be patient, my student. You've just arrived here. You will learn." A wily smile played at Rupshel's lips. "You may even discover passion in this place."

Britenia stared impassively at her mentor for a moment. "Or anger. Maybe I will find anger here, or hate, or some sentiment I can feel strongly."

"Passion is a strong feeling, child, and encompasses an array of pleasures or displeasures as the case may be sometimes."

Ignoring the man who counseled her, the wise teacher who instructed all of her peoples at the University of Emotional Awareness, Britenia turned away, putting her back to her mentor.

"I should feel hate," she said.

"Do you?"

Britenia stood still, not answering him right away. It was as though she was trying to conjure the emotion. She shook her head with numb regard. On an inhale, she looked at her mentor. "No."

Her soul was an empty shell--void of emotion.

Empty.

"It doesn't even feel strange to feel ... nothing. I feel nothing, Rupshel."

Rupshel placed a caring, fatherly hand gently on her shoulder. "You will, Britenia, as time passes and you witness the vibrancy that naturally resides in others. Study them and what they feel, and your emotions will begin to blossom."

"Like this satellite?" Britenia knew she should chuckle at her own humor, but the sentiment evaded her.

Rupshel chuckled for her. "Beneath it all, my lady royal, I think we'll discover you are quite a delight."

"I would wish to say I believe you." Britenia lowered to sit on a small rock near the big boulder. She folded her hands in her lap. "How will I recognize the emotions when they come?"

"You were one of my finest students." Rupshel knelt in front of her and placed a palm on her cheek. "Just keep your scrolls nearby."

Britenia nodded. Four solar annums she spent at the University for Emotional Awareness. She supposed she was ready. "My scrolls, yes. They will tell me all."

"Not all," Rupshel answered. "Much you will discover on you own."

Britenia would've given him a confused look then, if she possessed the emotion. Instead she merely said. "I have no choice but to try."

"For your sake and for the sake of your people."

"So that I may return to my planet and enlighten them, yes?"

"Yes. And to take your rightful place on the throne." Rupshel stood and stepped back from her. "For now I leave you. There is the welfare of the other apprentices I must see to."

"Just one more question, Rupshel." Britenia stood, causing Rupshel to halt, just as he was about to step into the tunnel that brought them here. "How might I understand the many languages spoken here?"

"A thoughtful question," Rusphel turned and faced Britenia. "The place is equipped with a universal translator. Just speak your own words and others will understand you, and likewise you will understand them."

"Thank you, my teacher." Britenia closed her eyes and bowed her head respectfully. "I will be fine."

When she opened her eyes again her mentor was gone, leaving her standing alone at the entrance of *No Holes Barred*--Alone, but not lonely.

Britenia wondered what loneliness felt like.

Sighing for no other reason than releasing a breath, she picked up her travel bag and knocked on the rock. A tiny stone piece sank inward revealing a hole about the size of her hand. Flattening her palm over the opening, she presented the tattoo on her flesh. It was the symbol that would gain her entrance. "Invited member."

She felt a small tingle on her skin as the surveillance scanner read the mark. The small hole sealed as she dropped her hand and then a crack appeared in the surface of the rock door.

It spread open, revealing a dark, silent cavern.

Britenia stepped inside.

But she wasn't inside at all.

As the rock doorway behind her scraped closed, there was a low rumble and a flash of light. The place began to illuminate and Britenia discovered that she had entered an outdoor garden, full of colorful flowers and trees and soft music. A white, marble brick path ran the center of it. Off to one side there were several small pools and one larger one. Steam rose from the bubbling waters on the smaller ones and she assumed the water in the larger pool was cool. A few guests were relaxing within the waters' depths. Just beyond the pools, there were several raised, cushioned cots. The first four were vacant, but a male lay face down on the fifth one. He was nude except for the towel draped across his buttocks and thighs. A woman was kneading his shoulders.

Another relaxing activity, Britenia supposed, a way to relieve stress. What was stress like?

Britenia began walking along the path, catching the murmurs of conversations, hearing the animation in their voices and watching the assortment of emotions that played on the faces of the guests there. She could feel the tepid breeze of the air around her as it gently stroked her hair. The walkway was cool beneath her unclad feet. The garden that grew around her was an oasis of botanical scents. But despite all the delights the spa provided, Britenia was unable to *feel* any of it.

She could only observe.

From her studies, Britenia understood the various situations that should elicit certain emotions. Still, they evaded her. But that was why she was in this place. To explore--the life in others, the life that was missing in herself.

Passing a grouping of tables arranged along the garden terrace, Britenia's eyes locked unresponsively onto a man indulging in a meal. She stopped.

Something very slight stirred within her and Britenia blinked several times at the unexpected feeling, but it vanished rather rapidly just as every sensation that threatened to surface regularly did.

The man's head lifted and he smiled at her, and she acknowledged it with a nod. She didn't smile back, but did notice the way nearby women were examining the brawny male, bearing a gleam in their eyes that Britenia could only interpret as desire. It wasn't beyond her to comprehend the physical concept that the man was aesthetically pleasing.

Passion. Will I ever fully feel passion?

Her eyes flicked behind the man to an enormous tree, its trunk completely hollowed out. From the brochure the management sent her, Britenia recognized it as the club. Tipping her head she tuned into the sounds inside, catching a more upbeat style of music emerging from it. And there was movement. It was dancing. People were dancing on the main floor. And there was jovial talk and laughter. Her eyes flickered upward. The second level was of interest to her. Special services were offered there, personal fantasies and those of a more intimate kind. A twinge of anticipation seeped into Britenia's chest, a flicker, just a flicker of excitement before it vanished.

She would sample all the services if she could. One of them was bound to awaken her.

Britenia's gaze dropped downward. The man continued to watch her. Did he find her aesthetically pleasing?

No matter. She had work to do, emotions to discover.

Turning her head back to the path, Britenia saw the grouping of thatched roof cabanas. One of them had been reserved as living space for her during her stay, and at the moment her body felt weary. Deciding on a nap before the supper hour, Britenia continued down the path, thinking about nothing in particular.

Chapter Two

Jicar watched the woman as she passed by.

Stunning was the only word that came to his mind and he smiled at her when she halted and looked over at him. Her hair was silvery and long--down to her waist. Soft peach highlights shimmered through it under the caress of the mid-day sun. The expression on her lovely face intrigued him. It seemed to hold much but at the same time, was void of all. Sitting back in his chair, Jicar let his meal settle in his stomach. His gaze remained fixed on the woman as her line of focus went up to the club's second level for a few moments before she returned her gaze to him.

Was she sending a signal?

But then she turned away and continued on to where ever it was she going. A smile played at one corner of his mouth, as he watched the flow of her silky skirts around her body and he caught an enticing view of the curves in her calves through the discreet slit on the side. She was barefooted and wore a sparkling, blue anklet made of *jura* crystal. An expensive piece if it were real. Jicar suspected that it was by the sharpness of its glint.

A sign of royalty.

Interesting. Jicar mingled with many royals when he was on holiday at the various clubs, but this beauty, he'd never seen before and wondered where she had been hiding.

Jicar's eyes drifted upward to the roundness of her bottom, watching it gently sway as she walked. His mind imagined his hands lain upon it, his lips on the naked flesh. A low, craving groan formed in his throat. It had been awhile since he'd had a woman, eons since he felt more than physical need. Yet, here and now, with just a single glance exchanged between two strangers, a sudden yearning was stirring. With quick inference Jicar recognized the feeling.

When had he become so lonely?

He shook the feeling away in a convincing sway of thought. Jicar wanted no woman except for the pleasure of bedding her--an eve of passion shared between them with only the desire to slake their lust.

Nothing more than that.

Still, he would ask the owner of the establishment, Trina Winsleng, about her.

If the woman was willing, Jicar might be offering.

Just for a single eve, he told himself. Rarely did Jicar indulge in a second eve with the same female, preferring to move on, else he might become attached.

Rising from his chair, he entered the club. A few guests danced on the floor, or dined at tables but at this midday hour, the place was more or less quiet. He found Trina in her usual place, at a table in the back corner.

It was unusual, but she was alone, for many sought her talents.

"Jicar," she said smiling broadly as he approached. "Please, sit."

Jicar took the seat next to her and leaning in, he gave her peck on her cheek. "How do you fare, Trina?"

"Business is good … very good." Trina turned over the clean cup that sat on a saucer at the table. She then grasped the flagon from the table and poured Jicar a cup of herbal drink. "Are you enjoying yourself this visit?"

Lifting the cup to his lips, Jicar took a sip and then replaced it atop the saucer. "Tell me about the new royal who visits."

"New royal?" Trina gave him a quizzical look. "I'm not sure of whom…."

"You know who I'm speaking of, Trina," Jicar interrupted with a smirk. "You're familiar with all of the guests who come here."

Trina pressed a palm to her chest and cast an innocent expression in Jicar's direction. "Do I?"

"Discreet as always, Trina." Jicar took another sip of his herbal drink.

"Of course."

"What can you tell me?"

Dropping her hand, Trina grinned. "I don't think I'm at liberty to say."

"Trina," Jicar urged. "Give."

"All right then. I can tell you this. Britenia is a royal and the reason for her visit is to find her emotions."

A hearty laugh burst from Jicar. "I see. Did she misplace them?"

Surely it was only a jest.

"As a matter of fact, she did."

Jicar sobered immediately. Drawing his brows together he stared at Trina, his expression part inquisitive, part disbelieving.

"It's completely true, Jicar. I've met with her and she is indeed detached."

"But how … why?"

Trina slashed a hand through the air. "All I know is that it was a sorcerer's spell cast some forty annums back. All the inhabitants of her planet and their subsequent offspring are cursed...."

Jicar drew his brows together, a serious of questions forming in his head.

"Mistress Wensling." A voice interrupted, and Trina looked up to see two guests, Lehran and Kmol standing at her table.

"Is it time for our match already?" Trina reached beneath her chair and lifted a small box, placing it on the table top. She opened it and removed a cylindrical cup, five multifaceted, clear *Shatib* gems and four compu-score cards.

Jicar took another sip of his tea as the two guests seated themselves.

"May I present…" Trina began indicating Jicar.

"Jicar Adi LarRhe, yes we've met." Lehran's eyes grazed along his torso, but Jicar pretended he didn't notice. On his last holiday at the *No Holes Barred*, he partnered with her for a night, but the sex was inanimately boring. He never sought a second date.

"Pleasantry and peace to you," the man who accompanied Lehran said. "Kmol Fegjr, Labordian galaxy, planet Graxor."

Jicar returned his introduction with nod. "And peace to you as well."

"Care to join?" Trina asked Jicar.

"Sure, why not?" Jicar shrugged.

"Good, then." Trina dropped the *shatib* gems into the cup and pushed it toward Lehran, who tapped a dot on her score pad to indicate it was her turn. She then picked up the container, shook it and turned it upside down. The gems plinked to the table and started to spin, each glowing with shifting colors. When they came to a stop two gems were blue, two were red and one was yellow.

"Humph," Lehran eyed the pieces.

Since blue was worth more points, she picked up the red and yellow, dropping them into the cup. She shook it and dumped the gems on the table once more and was rewarded with more blue and a green. Her score card automatically recorded the points she earned.

Kmol took his turn next, and after two tries came up with only two red gems and three other single colors.

"Guess I'll take the pair," he said and passed the game pieces to Jicar. "You're up."

It was then that Jicar's eyes drifted toward the club entrance. Patrons were beginning to flow through the door, arriving for the supper hour. Scooping the gems, Jicar dropped them into the container. He shook it back and forth listening to the rattling sound they made as they shifted in the cup, but his eyes never left the entrance, his attention fixed on the beauty that had just come through the door.

She stood in a nondescript manner, the fingers of her two hands laced and hanging in front of her as she scanned the club's main floor. Her hair was pulled tightly back from her face, emphasizing her strikingly beautiful features. At the top of her head, the orange sparkle of the gemmed, hair clip that bundled her mane, caught Jicar's eyes, and when she turned her head to the side he notice that the rest of her hair emerged from the clip and hung down her back in loose, but perfectly symmetrical coils. As he stared at her, Jicar had to wonder if she realized the sensual beauty and elegance she emanated.

In Jicar's eyes, she was a vision of grace and poise, yet her expression was blank, almost mechanical. It was as if she was merely going through the motions of living and it wouldn't make a difference to her if she were dead or alive.

Jicar wasn't overly sentimental, but something about her detached façade touched him in a way he was unable to explain.

He wanted to help her.

Call it chivalry or Jicar's enjoyment with meeting a challenge. Either way, he wanted to know more about this woman.

What did Trina say her name was? *Ah, yes*, Britenia.

"Why in the galaxy would you turn that down?" The sound of Lehran's voice jerked Jicar's attention from Britenia.

"What?" he said, his attention shifting toward the group at the table.

"Shatib … you had a Shatib … five blue gems." Lehran lifted questioning brows at Jicar.

"Did I?"

"You did." Trina tipped her head realizing that Jicar was paying little attention to the game. "But then you snatched them up and dropped them back into the cup."

"I guess I'm a bit distracted." Jicar shrugged nonchalantly and handed the cup to Trina.

"It would seem so," Trina answered, her eyes sweeping the club's main floor seeking what seemed to be so distracting to Jicar, but couldn't identify anything.

"The three of you play." Jicar picked up his cup of herbal drink and drained it. He leaned back in his chair, propping an ankle on the opposite knee. "I guess I'm not so much in the game playing mood."

His attention moved back to the entranceway, but Britenia was no longer standing there. Searching the now growing crowd he located her at the bar. A male *Tivartian* was handing her a foaming drink--*Licris*--light on the spirits, spicy in taste. She sipped it and nodded her head in approval. The *Tivartian* then leaned in and whispered something to her. She answered by bending her mouth to his tentacle ear, whispering in return.

Jicar's curiosity peaked as he wondered what they were saying. But when the male pointed to the second level and Britenia turned her head in that direction, Jicar tensed, suddenly feeling possessive of her, though he knew he had no right. Yet at the same time he wasn't about to let the male have her.

"Good game, Trina," Kmol said. "Nice win."

Lehran and Kmol stood and excused themselves, heading for the floor to enjoy some dancing. Jicar was glad they were gone.

"She's caught your fancy?" In the midst of the game playing, Trina had been studying Jicar and it didn't take her long to determine what occupied his mind.

But Jicar, being in the position he was on his planet was a man of discretion, so Trina waited until her guests had left the table before speaking about it.

Jicar looked briefly at Trina before his gaze drifted back toward the bar, and he clenched his teeth. Another *Tivartian* had joined the other and having a penchant for ménages it was obvious they intended to share Britenia. Both were pressing their bodies to her, one from the front and one from behind.

"Invite the woman to sup with us, Trina." Something savage was stirring within Jicar, though he attempted to ignore it. "I want to meet this woman who has no feelings."

Chapter Three

Trina caught the bartender's eyes and sent him a series of hand gestures. It was a method that she used to communicate with her staff, beyond the understanding of her guests, which was most appreciated when one wished to be tactful.

The bartender nodded his understanding and leaned over the bar in front of Britenia, beckoning her closer. She turned her ear and he murmured the Mistress Wensling's request. His head tipped, his eyes fixing in Trina and Jicar's direction. Pulling back from him Britenia followed the line of his gaze and then said something to her male companions.

Jicar was surprised and pleased when she readily disengaged herself from the *Tivartian* men and started walking toward the table. He became immensely smug at the disappointed expressions that fell to the *Tivartians'* faces as she left them, though Jicar knew it was Trina's request that she was honoring rather than his undisclosed desire to have her there.

Watching her intensely as she approached, Jicar took in her entire presence. And then his breath caught when he snagged a view of what she was wearing, well at least with what she wore on top--a single strip of cloth that swept across her chest. Except for shimmering blue threads that weaved through the material, it was otherwise transparent giving Jicar an exquisite eyeful of her perfect breasts. The dusky areolas nicely showing through, and her nipples...

Jicar imagined drawing those jutting peaks into his mouth and sucking on them.

His cock twitched.

What she wore wasn't more revealing than the scanty garments of some of the other patrons. In fact, many, both male and female often donned clothing that was sheer top to bottom, showing off every one of their assets. But Jicar had grown accustomed to the attire and stopped leering long ago.

Britenia's skirt was opaque, revealing nothing except a view of her beautiful thighs that appeared and disappeared through the multi-paneled garment as she approached. The fact that he was unable to glimpse her pussy when many others were so willing to expose, made it that much more tantalizing to explore that part of her.

"Welcome to No Holes Barred," Trina greeted Britenia. "I hope you're enjoying your stay."

Standing at the table, Britenia gave Trina a pensive look. "Enjoy, yes, a pleasurable emotion. I will try."

Her eyes flicked to Jicar and she recognized his as the man she saw earlier.

He stood to present himself. "Jicar Adi LarRhe. Please join us."

Indicating the empty chair between his and Trina's, Jicar pulled it out for her, and she sat down. After seating himself, Jicar lifted an arm and crooked his index finger to signal a server.

Narla, who caught the gesture, was instantly at the table. "What can I get for you, handsome?"

Tilting her head in a curious angle, Britenia studied the woman's face, catching the twinkling of her eyes and the batting of her eyelashes that followed. "She has lust for you, Jicar Adi LarRhe."

Narla's face tightened and her cheeks heated with a discomfited blush.

At the same time Jicar snorted. "And how do you know this, my lady Brit?"

With the utmost of sincerity and a completely blank facade, Britenia righted her head and looked Jicar directly in the eyes. "It says so on her face and her nipples are hard."

A roar of laughter burst from Jicar's mouth.

Mistress Wensling almost spit out her drink, but saving grace, she swallowed hard.

"Stars!" Narla gasped, her arms crossing over her breasts reflexively.

"Are you always so bold to speak, my dear?" Trina swiped at her mouth trying with all her might to keep from joining Jicar in his amusement.

Britenia turned and handed her a napkin. "I don't understand."

"Bring us a bottle of iced Burgin, a platter of roasted Tishi meats and mixed fruit, Narla," Jicar instructed the server, not bothering to suppress the smirk on his lips.

"Right away," Narla choked out and then gulped, her face still red with embarrassment. She shot Britenia a frosty glare before rushing off in a fluster.

"What the mistress means to say…" Jicar leaned closer to Britenia.

Tipping her head to listen, Britenia wondered at the quality of Jicar's voice, thinking the accentuation of his words and smoothness of the sound could be assessed as appealing.

"…you should be a bit more discreet," Jicar continued.

Turning her head, Britenia met his gaze, realizing belatedly that his face was very close to hers, their lips nearly touching. "Why?"

She felt a reaction between her thighs at his closeness. Merely physical, she'd had many of those before. Despite that, her eyes dipped to his bare chest and she noticed how muscular it was.

"Well … well because people have feelings, my dear," the mistress Wensling said to the back of Britenia's head.

"Feelings," Britenia whispered, her eyes lifted to Jicar's mouth. It was a full mouth and she had to wonder at the kind of passion his mouth could induce. "Feelings, yes."

"Of which you have none." Jicar was probing, finding it hard to believe that any creature, not alone an entire race could be completely stripped of emotion.

How did they survive? What motivated them to rise each dawning?

Studying the lady Britenia's expression as she continued to stare at his mouth, Jicar became keenly aware that the simple action was causing his lips to tingle. Sucking in his bottom lip, he scraped his top teeth along the flesh, attempting to tamp the sensation--the urge to kiss her. "Tell me about this lack of emotion your people suffer."

He was curious--*no*.

It was more than that.

Jicar was intrigued, and most especially with the complacent expression she wore. Woman never looked upon him with such indifference. He was accustomed to seeing lust in their eyes, yet this woman seemed completely unaffected.

At his question, Britenia's eyes snapped up to meet Jicar's, but she remained quiet.

"Yes, yes! Do tell." Trina stared intently at Britenia. "I for one am very interested in this sorcerer's spell that's left you and your entire civilization vacant of feelings. What's it like?"

"Indifference is a word to use, I suppose." Britenia answered without removing her attention from Jicar.

At that moment Narla reappeared with a tray. She set the order at the center of the table in a less than gentle manner, the platters and bottle of drink hitting with a clank. A sneer spread across her mouth at the way the lady Britenia and Jicar continued to stare at one another. Turning in a huff, she disappeared back to the kitchens.

Breaking the gaze Britenia held on him, Jicar reached for the Burgin and pried open the cork. Grabbing a mug he filled it and then placed it in front of Britenia.

"What more do you wish to know, Mistress Wensling?" Britenia looked down at the full mug of Burgin that Jicar Adi LarRhe slid in front of her and followed the path of a second that he passed in front of her and offered to the Mistress.

"Is it true you only feel physical lust and physical pain? And please, call me Trina."

"Yes, this is true."

Interesting, Jicar thought. Pain gave them reason to avoid that which might kill them and lust allowed them to reproduce.

"Have you ever tasted Burgin, Brit?" Jicar sipped his drink and then set the mug on the table.

Britenia picked up the mug containing the iced drink, the coldness of the liquid seeping through the container and cooling the palm of her hand. "It's a spirit, yes?"

"Yes, it's a spirit. A strong one."

"An interesting choice, Jicar." Trina shot him a knowing look. "Do you have something in mind?"

Jicar's smile widened. He slipped his arm behind Britenia and rested it on the back of her chair. "I intend to get her drunk."

He took another sip of the drink and Trina lifted her mug in like, nodding to him before also taking a sip of the Burgin.

"I've never experienced drunk, or tasted this spirit." Britenia blinked at him. "But from what I know it loosens the body for the sexing."

Jicar's brows lifted. She was so forward, so outspoken. "What a delightful you are, my lady"

Britenia reached and took Jicar's hand, curling her fingers around it. "Do you wish to sex me, Jicar Adi LarRhe?"

"Damn!" Jicar sucked in his breath as she placed his hand on her breast. His cock immediately hardened.

"Goodness me, not on the main floor, my dear," Trina interrupted. "That's reserved for the next floor up."

At the same time Jicar pulled back his hand, not that he wanted to. He had to. The urge to shed her clothing and tumble her on the table swept through him like a cosmic storm, taking him completely unaware.

Britenia merely looked at him, but she felt something at his withdrawal.

What was it?

Disappointment, yes, it was disappointment, an emotion. But immediately the unpleasant sensation was gone and she was numb again. Her attention drifted to the two circular wrought iron stair cases that twisted their way up to a balcony gallery that circled the first floor. Several guests looked downward, watching the activity below.

"Is it up there that passion is found?"

"Sometimes," Jicar answered, demanding his cock to settle down.

It wasn't listening.

Attempting to ignore his arousal, Jicar attended to the food platters, putting bits of Tishi meat and fruit on the plates and then passed one each to Trina and Britenia.

"I should explore that floor." Britenia looked at her plate. Picking up a red chunk of fruit, she sucked it into her mouth causing a trickle of juice to trail down her chin.

Before he was aware of his own actions, Jicar leaned forward, grasped Britenia by the shoulders and licked the liquid from her flesh. He then cranked his head back, shocked by his own actions, most certainly unapologetic, but also amazed at how natural if felt to put his mouth on her.

"Perhaps the two of you should move to the second level," Trina suggested with a chortle before biting into a piece of meat.

Ignoring Trina's snort, Jicar kept his attention on Britenia, thankful that he did so when he saw the barely noticeable smile that graced her lips for a split of a light second before it vanished, but he saw it nonetheless. Proof of its happening was confirmed when the lady touched her lips with her own fingers.

"Pleasure," she said.

"You felt pleasure?" Jicar grinned. He was most definitely intrigued by this blossoming flower.

"I think, but it's now gone."

"You did feel it however, my lady."

"Yes," was all she said before her eyes fell to the cup of Burgin. "Why do you wish for me to experience drunk?"

"Let's just say the drink has a side effect." The Trina answered for him.

With a nod, Jicar agreed. "Those who indulge in it become, how should I say…."

"Emotional?" Tina finished for him.

Britenia's head snapped around to look at the club's Mistress. She lifted a pensive brow.

"Well if that is the case." Britenia snatched her mug of Burgin from the table and put the rim to her lips. She gulped and gulped and gulped.

"Easy, Brit!" Jicar reached for the mug, but she tossed her head back and drained the drink before he could pull it from her mouth. "The drink has a punch to it."

Staring at her, Jicar waited for a reaction, and then he had it.

Her eyes crossed.

"Oh." A gasp left Britenia's mouth. "I think I'm dizzy."

She hiccupped and then held the mug toward him for refilling.

Jicar obliged, pouring another mug. "Are you always so trusting, Brit?"

"Trust is emotion that could easily be taken advantage of." Britenia took a large swallow of the Burgin and then hiccupped again. She looked at Trina, and a twinge of a feeling emerged. "I believe it is trust that appears for you."

And then she turned to Jicar. "As for you Jicar Adi LarRhe, I'm not so sure."

"A wise woman!" Trina laughed heartily and Jicar joined her.

"I do make my decisions based on intellectual thought." Britenia looked down at her mug and then put it to her mouth, draining yet a second serving of Burgin.

Trina and Jicar exchanged glances. "And does this intellectual thought tell you that if I were to get you drunk just to lure you into bed, it might be wise to abstain from the drink?"

"I wouldn't have to fall into my cups to be sexed, Jicar Adi LarRhe."

"But you know nothing about what I might do to you, what erotic things we might engage in. We've just met."

"I am receptive to explore." Britenia hiccupped yet again. Her head dropped and her bottom slid forward, off of her chair and onto the floor. Trina covered her mouth in dismay and Jicar grimaced as he watched her slither from her seat.

"I believe I am under the table," Britenia said. She raised her mug holding it up toward Jicar. "I believe I shall have another, yes."

"I believe you've had enough."

"Quite," Trina agreed.

Taking the mug from her, Jicar placed it on the table and then reached down to help Britenia rise, setting her back onto the chair. His hands remained fixed on her shoulders until he was sure she was steady.

"Drunk is interesting." Showing not the least bit of embarrassment by her graceless topple Britenia scanned the lounge. Briefly she studied the movements of the dancers on the floor, pondering the enjoyment on their faces and how their bodies seemed to move pleasurably to the rhythm of the music that flooded the atmosphere. "In answer to your question, Jicar Adi LarRhe, sexing is a natural physical act. There would be no reason for me to refuse any male who wished to join."

With that Britenia stood, her focus remaining on the dancing guests.

"You don't mean to say you'll bed any male here who shows desire in you?" Trina frowned with worry.

Jicar on the other hand shook his head in disbelief. First of all, he could hardly believe she wasn't slurring her words or swaying on her feet with all the Burgin she drank. Secondly, her attitude about sex could be a dangerous thing. Especially when indulging at any No Holes Barred club. Many creatures from many galaxies came through the cosmic gateways to enjoy the carnal offerings. But some had sexual tastes that were quite odd or could be threatening to one's health if the body wasn't accommodating. A guest would be wise to select their partner carefully when dating.

"I'll try this dancing, yes," Britenia said.

And before either Jicar or Trina could say another word, Britenia was heading for the dance floor.

"I think we need to attend to her closely, Jicar," Trina said as she watched Britenia mesh into the fold of dancers.

"We?" Jicar returned. Leaning back in his chair he folded his arms across his chest. "I have no intention of becoming a bulwark for a woman so vulnerable she wouldn't know a threat if it stood upright and boomed its presence directly to her face."

Jicar's attention swept the dance floor, seeking the object of their conversation and he found her. "You forget, mistress, I'm here for relax...."

His voice halted before he could finish the sentence, his eyes riveted to Britenia's body. The sway of her hips moved to the beat of the music, the panels on her shimmering, purple skirt drifting aside revealing shapely legs and even more shapely thighs. On closer inspection, Jicar was sure she wore nothing beneath, hints of a dark thatch and bare buttocks teasing him with their brief but tempting appearance each time she twirled. His eyes shifted higher, stopping to admire her bare belly, and her bare naval and the way her waist curved inward, visualizing himself grasping her smooth form, licking her tender flesh as he knelt in front of her, imagining her moans of ecstasy as he sucked on her pussy.

His cock twitched and then thickened.

Higher his gaze went higher, and since she was now at a further distance, Jicar once again allowed himself the pleasure of staring at her breasts. He choked back a groan as he stared at her nipples pushing through her top.

By the hell spirits she was making him insane with lust!

Inhaling deeply as if to bridle his arousal, Jicar tore his gaze from her breasts, his attention shifting to her face.

It didn't help.

She stared back at him and *damn holy starblasters* if he didn't see seduction in those lovely peach-colored eyes of hers, and invitation in her continued erotic moves. Yet she couldn't be aware of the effect.

Could she?

After all she had no emotions, right?

It didn't matter, his cock went fully rigid pressing painfully against the seam of his trousers.

And what was that fragrance permeating the air? It was sensual and arousing. Trina must be trying a new incense.

"Perhaps a single date would prove interesting," Jicar said aloud.

"I suspected as much," Trina chortled. "I think you would find her an ultimate challenge."

Turning his head, Jicar smirked at Trina. "Failing to arouse a female's wild passion would be a first for me."

"If the rumors about you are true, I'm sure it would."

"I do recall you've tasted this rumor … twice."

Returning his attention to the dance floor, Jicar discovered that Britenia had left the spot she was dancing in. His eyes threaded through the aggregate of dancers searching for her, but she was no where to be seen.

Finally he located her standing at the bottom of one of the staircases, staring up to the second floor. She began to climb the steps.

"Shit." Standing quickly Jicar pushed through the crowd chasing after Britenia, but before he could even reach the flight, she was gone, having already gained entrance to the second floor mezzanine.

Chapter Four

Galactic Virtual Fantasies.

Briefly Jicar wondered if Britenia might have gone through that door, but almost immediately realized she likely would seek one of the other services that the club offered, specifically *Galactic Dates and Mates.*

She talked too much about sex and passion.

He was correct, spying her at once after the larger-than-life-itself attendant, upon recognizing Jicar, allowed him entrance.

For the love of the cosmos! The *Largalion* she was allowing to fondle her would tear her up. They were violent during the act of sex, finding climax by chewing and digging with their razor-sharp teeth into their partner's flesh. Britenia's skin was definitely not rigid enough to endure it. When it was over she would be a bloody mess, if she was even still alive.

Jicar stalked toward them. Towering over Britenia and the *Largalion* he narrowed angry, threatening eyes.

The creature looked up at him and sneered. "I saw her first."

"No, you didn't." Jicar returned, his voice low and menacing.

Removing his hands from Britenia, the *Largalion* raised them into the air in obvious surrender. He backed up and then moved away.

Britenia didn't react to the exchange between Jicar and the male, but instead continued to stare through the peeking window. Jicar stepped behind her, intent on making her comprehend the dangers in sexing indiscriminately. "Do you understand what that creature would do to you?"

He looked through the window she stood in front of to see what sex play she was observing.

It was two females, their bodies writhing against each other.

Britenia tipped her head with unconcern. "No. What would he do to me?"

"Had you consented to have sex with him, you would've been ripped to shreds during his climax"

"Oh," she returned casually. "Then I should be grateful you've saved me from my doom."

They both fell silent as they watched the females on the other side of the window. One was a *Mossitian* woman and the other appeared to be an Earth woman, who was arching and thrusting her pelvis, her legs spread wide. The *Mossitian* grinned and then lowered pussy downward, her tongue-shaped clit wagging back and forth, her labia opening and closing, smacking like the lips of a mouth, moving toward the Earthling's mound. Both women began to float as the gravity in the atmosphere was eliminated. Their legs intertwined and their pussies met, the *Mossitian's* clit thrusting inside of her partner's vagina, the labia making suction noises as their pussies rubbed together.

Both females groaned.

Jicar dated a *Mossitian* female some time back. It was quite an interesting evening, but not interesting enough for him to ask for a second date.

Stepping closer to Britenia, Jicar pressed his body along the length of her backside. He propped his hands on the wall, one on each side of viewing window and around Britenia's shoulder, as they both continued to watch the two women through the glass. "Have you had sex before?"

"Many times," Britenia answered. "With six males of my species."

Jicar's brows lifted. "All men at once?"

"No, separately. We mated and parted after awhile, to seek another."

"It seems like a rather detached way of sharing a relationship."

"Not much different from the way many live."

"How so?" Jicar asked.

"The joining is out of biological urges and nothing more," Britenia answered. "No love is shared, no mutual caring. Satiate the need and move on. That is true, yes, especially with the males in many species?"

Jicar grinned at her wisdom. "I suppose."

"It's like that with you, Jicar Adi LarRhe, yes?"

Oh she is truly a sly one, Jicar thought, realizing that her use of his full name impersonalized their acquaintance, friendship or whatever it was that seemed to be passing between them.

It made Jicar desired her all the more.

He inhaled, and caught Britenia's scent, the smell of her arousal taking him by surprise. It was sweet, intense. Jicar had never scented a woman so strongly before. Unable to resist, Jicar tipped her head back and nuzzled his mouth against the flesh of her throat.

"There is a difference between you and the males I am familiar with, however," Britenia added.

"Is there?" Jicar lifted his mouth from the flesh of her neck and gazed into her beautiful eyes.

"Where the males of my world would merely flip up our skirts and mount us when the need to mate struck them, your seduction is much slower ... teasing." Britenia sidestepped, slipping from his grasp. "Arousing."

"You find me arousing?" At first, Jicar wasn't sure if her delectable perfume that continued to tease his nostrils was a result of his presence or what she was watching through the window. He was immensely pleased she admitted that it was him. "And what makes you think I'm trying to seduce you?"

Britenia turned and faced him then.

By the sacred spirits! She smiled broadly. It was a striking smile and Jicar knew there was emotion in it.

"You are here with me on the second level, are you not?"

Cripe. She was right. As much as Jicar tried to tell himself he came up to the second level, following her into the corridor of *Galactic Dates and Mates* for the purpose of protecting her, he had to fully admit to himself that he wanted to have sex with her.

That Jicar wouldn't deny, nor could he deny that the bouquet that scented the air downstairs was not the result of incense. It had been Britenia all along.

Turning her back to Jicar, Britenia once again stepped in front of the peeking window. Jicar's eyes flicked to females on the other side.

In what felt like a natural action, Jicar's arms slipped around Britenia's body, his palms sliding across her belly. With his cock growing fuller and more demanding, he thrust his hips forward, pushing his throbbing erection into the crease of Britenia's bottom.

"Does that interest you?" he asked her, referring to the scene beyond the window.

"That does not," Britenia answered. She pulled from Jicar's arms once more and turned. Her eyes dropped to the bulge in his crotch. "That might however."

"Good." Jicar swept his arms around her, pulling her close.

"Your male part seems to be in wanting," Britenia said, now feeling the hardness against her belly. Her own pussy had begun tingling from the moment he entered the corridor, and now her vagina was growing moist, flooding with need. "Do you wish to mate with me, Jicar?"

"Mate?" he whispered as he bent to kiss her neck. "No."

Britenia tipped her head back as Jicar's lips found the underside of her chin before they skimmed along her jaw line. "Then why do you continue to fondle me?"

"I request a date."

"Explain, please."

"Establishment rules, twice a date, thrice a mate. I wish for an evening of sex with you, no more. I have no interest in finding a wife."

"Yes, I was informed of these rules." Britenia shifted her head, leaning back and putting space between his face and hers. She looked steadfastly, unblinking into his eyes. "On one condition."

"And what might that be?"

"I wish for myself, more than just the feeling of climax between my legs. Help my mind feel passion. Help me cry out in pleasure."

Jicar's chest heaved.

The thought of it lit his cock on fire. But caution seeped in. There was much he could do to inflame her desire, things that his culture reserved only for their lifemates. Affections he'd never given to a woman.

He had to tread carefully or else he would lose himself in this challenge she presented.

He had to get control of his throbbing cock or else he might find himself slamming and thrusting into her, here in the very corridor they stood in, giving the peepers around them an up close and personal view of his raw lust.

Which at the moment seemed to raging.

On a guttural growl, Jicar's hand circled one of Britenia's wrists and, he pulled her further down the hall. He felt no resistance as she paced behind him willingly. Stopping in front of the door of his private dating chamber, he turned her so she faced him. His body met hers, forcing her backside against the door. Cupping her face, Jicar lowered his mouth, pleased when her lips parted for him.

His tongue swept between her lips and he groaned when she sucked on it and then slid her own tongue along the surface of his. Abruptly she pulled back, breaking the contact. "I have never experienced a kiss, Jicar."

"This was your first?" Jicar was astounded. She admitted to having sex numerous times yet none of her males had ever kissed her?

"Kissing is an act of affection, yes?"

"I suppose it is."

"It's called foreplay, yes? What the male uses to bend the female's mind into engaging in sex."

Jicar snorted as he thought about that. "I'm sure there are many females who use foreplay as part of the seduction as well."

"Show me more of this seduction, Jicar." Britenia tipped her face to him, her lips puckering with invitation.

And Jicar obliged, surrounding her lips with his own. His left hand smoothed along the curves of her waist and hip as his right hand hit a small plate on the wall.

Behind Britenia, the solid door that supported her back slid open. She and Jicar fell through.

Chapter Five

Slipping his hands to the back of her head, Jicar deepened the kiss, seizing her mouth, his tongue thrusting inside, tasting her. She responded in like, mirroring his movements in a perfunctory manner. Her body remained stiff and unyielding except for her pelvis, which pushed against his erection in an almost instinctive manner. Jicar knew her body was willing, but her mind did not respond.

It was confirmed when he pulled his head back and saw the blankness in her eyes.

His body however shuddered with urgency and through the haze of his carnal, physical desires Jicar realized the need for Britenia was also flooding his mind.

He was quickly losing control.

Slow down.

On a sigh he broke contact with her, grasped her hand and led her to the bed on the other side of the room. Reaching over the headboard he hit a switch that dimmed the lights to a soothing, softer illumination.

He then reached behind Britenia with both hands, loosening the knot that held her top in place. It floated to the floor. Kneeling in front of her, Jicar grasped her waist and took liberty, kissing and licking her stomach, swirling his tongue around her naval, nuzzling his cheek against her warm flesh. His hands slid lower until the found the top edge of her skirt and he pushed the stretchy material downward until the garment fell, pooling around her feet. Jicar admired the thatch of hair at her juncture, his nostrils flaring at the dizzying scent of her arousal.

And his mouth watered. His cock surged in demand as he brushed his fingers back and forth over the hair there, enjoying the silky feel of her soft curls. On a shaky breath, Jicar stood.

"Sit," he said, his tone gentle and bidding.

Britenia lowered to the bed and watched as Jicar began stripping off his trousers. She studied the ripple of muscles in his stomach as he pushed the waist band over his hips, stared when his shaft jutted free, pointed horizontally and straight in her direction as if it was choosing her. The appendage was of a stature that others would say should inspire awe. A strange sensation swirled inside of

Britenia's chest and seemed to find a path directly to her throat. But as if the feeling hit a barricade, there it stopped, the physical attack leaving her mind untouched. Reaching out, she traced the swollen head with a single finger and Jicar released a gasping breath. But other than that, Britenia didn't know what else to do.

We will have sex, the logic in her head spoke to her. It's what they were in the chamber for.

Abruptly Britenia pushed further on the bed and turned to all fours. Lifting her ass in the air, she offered her body for mounting.

Under normal circumstances Jicar would've grasp her hips and plunge his cock into her wetness, a little slamming, a bit of fondling, a simultaneous orgasm and she'd be gone. Instead, he frowned as he watched her hips wriggle. Though Jicar found her movements quite erotic, the position was simply what she was used to.

But it wasn't what she wanted.

"No," he said and took her hips between his palms, urging her to turn over. "Like this."

"Oh," was her only response.

"Lie down on your back."

Once she was fully reclined, Jicar slipped his hands behind her knees. He drew her legs up and parted her thighs and then settled his hips between her legs.

"This is like hugging, yes?" Britenia asked.

"It is." Jicar had never thought about how intimate the position actually was. He was also keenly aware that he never mounted a woman like this before. It was the traditional marriage position--the *Coveting* position of his culture, reserved for the first mating.

But this was only a date, and what harm could it do? Besides it felt rather nice to Jicar--gentle and warm, almost protective of her body, possessive--the way he covered her. He sank further, pressing his weight down. "How do you feel?"

"Like I'm being crushed," Britenia choked out a gasp.

"Sorry." Jicar eased some of his weight and Britenia sucked a thankful breath into her freed lungs.

This wasn't going very well.

With most women, Jicar had little problem sexing them, pure animalistic lust driving them to climax. Typically he and his sex partner would be entangled by now, humping wildly like two untamed creatures in heat. But Britenia wasn't just any woman. It was pure animalistic lust she wanted to avoid.

"What do we do next?" she asked him.

Jicar thought about how mechanical she sounded, as if she were asking him to read the procedure to her step by step. He pondered that a moment and then said. "We stop talking and start feeling."

When she opened her mouth to speak, he hushed her words by placing a finger on her mouth. Removing his finger, he bent to kiss her, lick her, explore her flesh. His hand found a breast and he fondled it gently.

Her hips began to move and Jicar lifted ready to slide into her, but he stopped when he saw the vacant expression on her face.

Her eyes were wide open, no sign of passion in them. Not even a twinkle.

Frustrated and incredibly horny, Jicar rolled off of her and settled himself to her side. Britenia watched him intensely, but as he bid, she said nothing. Propping his head on his hand, Jicar traced circles around one of Britenia's nipples. It hardened, she jolted and gasped in surprise. He smiled.

A reaction, and a nice one at that. "Did you like that, my lady?"

"Yes," Britenia whispered hoarsely. Her breasts tingled, ached, yearned for more touching. She never felt that sensation before.

"Are you aroused?" Bending, Jicar drew her breast into his mouth, wondering if this was the first time she'd been suckled there.

Britenia's body jolted again. "Yes,"

"Here?" Jicar released her breast and his hand cupped her pussy feeling her wetness, her heat. He flicked his finger across her clit. Her hips tilted upward, gyrating to his touch.

"Or here?" Jicar's hand left her mound and skimmed the length of her body until it reached her head and he lightly skimmed his fingers across her forehead. He lowered his head again, his mouth continuing its assault on her breast, and Britenia, feeling the warm wetness of his lips, the gentle caress of his hand, began to quake all over.

"Touch me," she said. "My body aches, Jicar."

"What about your mind?" he whispered against her breast and then dragged his tongue across her hardened nipple. "Does it scream for my touch?"

Britenia just stared at him. Her body was certainly screaming. But in her head only reason dwelled. Even in this aroused state she could probably read an entire manual and cum at the same time. "It's as if my head is completely detached from my body, Jicar. Like separate entities."

Inhaling deeply, Jicar closed his eyes. Her scent flooded the air so thickly it nearly drove his head into a whirl. How could he make her feel the same?

Slowly. The woman had never been made love to properly.

Jicar grimaced mentally at his choice of works, yet it was true. If he wanted to awaken her, he would have to take her like a lover, not like some rutting beast in the throes of sexual need. He would concentrate on her pleasure, fulfill her needs, and for the moment disregard his own.

"Close your eyes, Brit." And Jicar watched as she obeyed. "Don't think, feel what I do to you."

Tenderly, he ran his fingers along her body, touching her skin in feathery glances, down between her breasts, along her belly, through the hair of her mound. Briefly he grazed his fingers over the area, feeling the swelling of her clit as he did so. Bending he kissed her mouth as his hand moved upward taking one of her breasts, skimming his thumb over the top.

She didn't move, but instead lay quietly as he touched her. His mouth left her lips and trailed lower, taking her other breast into his mouth and he sucked gently at her nipple. Her body twitched and then settled, but her breathing began to deepen.

Ah, Jicar was enjoying this foreplay. It was sweet torture.

Slowly his hand left her breast and skimmed downward again. This time when he reached her mound, he let his fingers delve between her nether lips until he found her clit. He rolled it between his finger and thumb, over and over until a slight gasp left her mouth. Her hips moved subtly, but rhythmically. Without giving second thought to what he was doing, Jicar released her breast and began trailing kisses down her torso, her rising scent driving him, drawing him closer to her core. He slipped his finger inside of her and stroked, groaning at the building wetness and heat as her inner muscles clenched and unclenched.

He inserted a second finger.

She moaned.

And then his mouth was on her, his tongue lapping at her folds, his lips surrounding her clit and drawing on it, sucking, his tongue flicking as his fingers continued to thrust inside.

"Oh, oh." Britenia began to writhe. When Jicar started to touch her she pushed every thought from her mind, concentrating only on the areas he stroked, how he started gently and increased the tempo and pressure of everything he was doing to her. It pushed at her mind and Britenia grabbed onto the sensation, refusing to let go.

Like a key turning in a door, her pleasure center unlocked. An incredible surging force swept through her brain. It was dizzying, exhilarating. It was passion, powerful and steadfast it took control, ripped through her flesh, through every cleft of not only her body but her mind and soul.

Grasping his hair, Britenia thrust up at Jicar, begging his mouth to sex her. He suckled and lapped and thrust his tongue, his hands moving to clench her hips, her moans growing louder, encouraging him. She pumped faster, tensing and relaxing, panting and crying out and then panting harder.

"I can't take it anymore," he rasped against her pussy. His cock was about to bust.

"Please, Jicar, don't stop!"

It was a pleading cry full of incredible emotion.

"I need you now, Britenia!"

And with such quickness that Britenia barely felt him move, Jicar plunged his cock inside of her, the inward stroke so hard, so powerful, a jolt shot straight up her body and exploded in her mind.

She screamed, her hand grabbing his ass, in desperation.

Jicar's passion soared and she took it. Pumping wildly into her, pounding, crying out her name, listening to the sounds of her frantic gasps as she struggled toward the edge of climatic passion, his lips suckling her neck, her mouth, her breasts and she clung to him for dear life and he clung back as her cries of ecstasy escalated and he knew she was cumming hard.

And he was there with her.

In one ferocious rush the power of his orgasm blasted straight through his erection and he thrust into her one more time, before slamming his pelvis tightly against her pussy, groaning loudly as her muscles convulsed around his spilling cock.

They both lay there for some time, their hearts pounding, their breathing erratic, entwined in a lovers embrace. And when Jicar finally lifted his head to look into her eyes, he saw the daze of a woman amidst her settling passion, satiated and content.

"Talk to me, Britenia," he whispered as he planted kisses on her face.

"I ... can't ... speak."

Her eyes drifted shut and Jicar smiled softly. Rolling to his side he took Britenia with him, carefully moving, shifty her leg over his hip, to keep his cock inside of her, allowing it to soften within her folds. His body relaxed fully and his lids closed as he held her, thinking about how good she felt in his arms.

Chapter Six

Jicar's eyes snapped open and the first thing that reached his sleep fogged mind as he yawned and stretched his arms, was how perfectly replete he felt. He smiled and then wrapped his arms around Britenia again, molding against her flesh, feeling the soothing warmth of her, listening to her quiet breathing as she slept.

Planting a tender kiss atop of her head, Jicar grinned widely when he realized his cock was growing hard and that it was still embedded inside of Britenia's body.

He could hardly believe he desired her again.

This woman aroused him more fiercely than any female he'd ever known. The orgasm he had with her was the most intense he'd ever felt.

Slowly, his hips began to move and he pumped, his hand began to roam, skimming her belly, cupping her breast.

He didn't think she'd mind.

"Jicar," she whispered, still half asleep, but her body responded, began moving with his, her leg shifted slightly so he could push deeper inside.

He groaned when he felt her hand come between their legs and she began stroking his balls with her fingers. Moving his hand under her arm, his finger flicked back and forth over her clit and she whimpered at his touch, her slick passage becoming even wetter.

She lifted her eyes to look at him, her detached expression was gone, replaced by a flood of desire that graced her face, her lids heavy, her brows drawing together in sexual anguish--begging, her mouth opening as she drew a passionate breath.

Again he detected her scent, her sweet, arousing scent. It wrapped around him, caressed him, taking hold. "You smell so good, Brit."

His cock stretched, thickened, grew unbelievably hard.

Jicar drew her lips to his, their breathing catching inside of each other's mouths, their tongues brushing in heated arousal, their bodies moving in rhythmic accord.

On heavy panting and increased pumping they found the cadence of mutual desire and their orgasms hit simultaneously, explosively, as one.

Still entwined, they both fell back to a blissful sleep.

A short while later, Jicar awoke. His eyes shifted to the time piece on the wall.

It was dawn.

Shit.

He had shared his bed with her for sleep--for an entire eve. This was something he never allowed another female to do. Worry seized him as he recalled loving her with his mouth, and he thought of her taste, her passionate moans as he licked her intimately.

She almost came in his mouth.

This too was something he'd never shared with a female before. Both were meant only for his mate.

Jicar didn't want a mate.

But last eve he couldn't restrain himself. Her genuine responses to him drove his basic need to awaken her, to claim not only her body's lust but her mind's passion as well. Somehow, knowing he was the first to do this only served to further urge him on. And it didn't help that with her rising climax, her scent increased, imbedded itself in his nostrils, made a home in his mind. Even now, as Britenia slept, her fragrance taunted him.

He slid away from her and rolled to his back, propping his hands behind his head and stared at the ceiling.

"Jicar?"

Jicar glanced over at Britenia. She was sitting up, her beautiful breasts exposed, the bed covering across her hips, her mound only partially covered, hints of curls peeking out from beneath. Strands of her hair fell over her face, swept around her neck, tangled around an arm, a bit mussed but exquisitely sexy.

His cock agreed, twitching.

"Our date is over?" she asked.

Forcing his hands to stay put instead of reaching for her, Jicar clenched all the muscles in his lower abdomen, in his pelvis and groin, attempting to drive away the growing need to pump his hips, to seek her body, her sex, her passion.

"Yes." It was all Jicar could manage to say without fully losing control of himself.

There would be no second date.

No, there wouldn't.

Jicar waited to see if hurt would cross her face, but the expression never came.

With nothing except a removed expression, Britenia pushed the covers aside and crawled from the bed. Jicar tensed further at the sight of her naked body, but willed himself not to move.

Bending, Britenia picked up her skirt and top and put them on. "Thank you, Jicar Adi LarRhe.

Britenia headed for the door, tapped the switch plate on the wall and when the entrance was open, she stepped through. The door slid closed behind her.

Jicar stared at the door for awhile examining his feelings, realizing he had an incredible urge to chase after her and bring her back to his room, cover her with his body, plunge deep inside of her again. Listening to the silence, Jicar waited for a knock, hoping she would return and at the same time hoping she wouldn't.

The knock never came, forcing him to wonder why he was disappointed.

He was horny, that's all.

And confused.

No not confused.

He was just horny.

His attempts to help her find passion had incited him. He found the encounter extraordinarily erotic. Of course it would be arousing.

Grasping his cock, Jicar began to stroke it. Once he had relief all would be well again.

Jicar attempted to form images of the women he sexed before, the carnal positions they'd had intercourse in, their lusty cries as they came, as he came.

What their hair looked like. The way they smelled-- especially the way they smelled. But no matter how he tried, every thought, every sense, every image that crept through his mind brought him right back to one person.

Britenia.

Forget her.

Without satiating himself, Jicar let go of his cock. Sitting up on his bed, he rubbed a palm over his face, and then frowned.

Why had she left so easily?

She looked neither happy nor sad. She looked rather blank.

Maybe he hadn't helped her find passion at all. Maybe she faked it.

No.

Jicar was sure that wasn't true.

Why did he care?

He should've felt relief when she left his chamber without even a backward glance, but instead, her departure left him feeling very much alone.

Chapter Seven

Britenia was suddenly seized with a strange feeling. She found passion last eve, and with it, confusion. She didn't like the latter emotion because it clouded her logical thinking, making it difficult for her to reason why there was a lump in her throat and why her chest felt so heavy.

Maybe she was becoming ill.

Barely having enough time to consider it, she tripped over her own foot as she descended the club's stairs and nearly toppled.

"Easy there, my lady." Two hands caught her before she fell to what was certain to be a skull fracture. "Are you all right?"

"I'm fine," Britenia answered, her stomach swirling at the near mishap. "Thank you."

The two stared at each other for a moment.

"Xander Alik," the man finally said, releasing her and offering a slight bow of his head.

"Britenia," she nodded back slightly.

An awkward silence followed and then Xander spoke again, "I see you're descending the stairs, while I'm going up."

"Yes."

"Pity." Xander stared at her pretty face and then his eyes made a quick scan of body. Finding it delectable, he smiled. "Perhaps I might convince you to turn about?"

Britenia tilted her head up and toward the mezzanine. "I believe I am finished with the second floor."

Studying her, Xander wondered what bad experience she suffered that had her looking so removed, for she certainly didn't look pleased. "Well then, perhaps another time?"

"Perhaps." Britenia offered no other words and once again began moving down the stairs.

Xander's eyes flicked upward and then shifted back to Britenia. "Wait!"

Halting at the bottom step, Britenia turned to look at him.

With quick pace, Xander tramped down the steps until his feet reached the main floor, his body turning to face her as he did so. "Have you eaten?"

"Many times," Britenia answered. "That is odd question, Xander Alik."

Xander chuckled at her matter-of-fact response, her tone lacking both condescension and sarcasm. He knew she wasn't mocking him, but truly misunderstood. "I didn't mean ever, I meant this dawning."

"That I haven't done."

"Then I insist you join me for breakfast." Holding out his arm, Xander waited for Britenia's acceptance. He smiled broadly at her when she slipped her hand around the crook of his elbow.

"Excellent!" Xander said and led her to an empty table.

Jicar watched the byplay between Xander and Britenia from the second floor mezzanine. He resisted the urge to rush down the steps and insinuate himself between them. But now that they were seated at a table, he could merely approach to join them without drawing suspicion from Xander. Having grown up with the royal, Jicar and Xander were not only cousins, but best friends. Xander was pleasant in face and quite sensual in physique. He was like a magnetic force to the ladies. The last thing Jicar wanted his cousin to detect was that Jicar disliked him keeping company with Britenia.

Not because he couldn't shake Britenia from his senses-- that it disturbed him to see her giving attention to another male--*no not that*. It was because Xander much enjoyed competition, and Jicar, never refusing Xander's challenges, didn't want to be forced to compete for the charms of a woman he really didn't want.

Really he didn't.

Aside from that, if Xander got even a whiff of her pheromones, he might be hopelessly lost, finding himself mated with the female. He needed to protect his cousin from her … *yes, he did*.

That logic made the most sense.

Descending the stairs, Jicar approached the table where Xander and Britenia sat. Without hesitation or invitation, he pulled out an empty chair and sat down. They both stared at him, Britenia with a blank look and Xander with a welcoming smile.

"Jicar! Searched for you last night." He smirked figuring that more than likely Jicar was enjoying female company. "So where have you been hiding?"

"Here and there." Jicar's eyes flicked to Britenia. She was studying a menu and paid him no heed. If she was experiencing any emotion, she certainly refrained from showing it.

"My manners," Xander said. "Britenia this is my cousin Jicar, Jicar…

"We've met," they both said simultaneously, both with the same subdued tone.

Silence followed, Xander's eyes shifting between the two of them as their gaze's fixed one on the other. Drawing his brows together he attempted to interpret the looks on their faces. Britenia's expression appeared nonchalant, blasé even. But in Jicar, Xander suspected he was suppressing something.

And then it dawned on him pretty quickly that the two of them had spent last eve together. His lips curled up on one side as he watched them stare at each other. "Then I guess introductions aren't necessary."

Jicar broke eye contact with Britenia and signaled a server. "Have the two of you ordered?"

"Not yet," Xander answered.

Britenia stood. "If you'll both excuse me."

"Where are you off too?" Xander frowned. "You haven't eaten yet."

"I don't believe I'm hungry," Britenia answered.

Before Xander could utter another word, she turned away from the table and headed for the door, exiting the club.

"What in the galaxy did you do to that woman, Jicar?"

"I didn't do anything to her." Jicar glared at his cousin. The man was too perceptive by far.

"Apparently. I met her on the staircase, and she seemed none too pleased." Xander smirked at his cousin. "Did the winky wither last eve?"

In no mood to discuss his sexual encounter with Britenia, Jicar shot him a glaring warning. "Stay clear of her, Xander."

"Why should I?" Xander snorted. "If you had trouble fulfilling her needs, perhaps I might remedy that."

A clear picture was forming in Xander's mind. Jicar fancied the lady, and he'd known Jicar long enough to recognize when he was jealous. What a perfect opportunity to tease his cousin. "We might even share her."

"I'm serious, Xander. Stay clear."

"So you're planning on having her again?"

"No."

"Then what's the problem here?"

"You're weaker in self-control than I am," Jicar stated with the utmost serious tone. "You might not be able to resist dating her, once, twice and then maybe even for a third. Do you really wish to take a wife?"

To that comment Xander laughed loudly. "I do think you project your own sentiments, my cousin. I hardly think a single date with the female will enrapture my mind."

"She's dangerous."

"She's a lovely woman, Jicar, if not a bit sedate. Still, it's the quiet kitten that is often like a wildcat in the bed. I just might be tempted to find out."

Jicar shook his head from side to side. "No, cousin, you won't if you know what's good for you. Her smell, it's overwhelming, must be something from her species."

"I admit it's warm in here," Xander returned, his expression jocular. "But I really didn't detect the woman had an odor."

Jicar rolled his eyes upward. He'd known Xander long enough to recognize when he was teasing. "I'm talking about her pheromones. It's difficult to prevent yourself from being consumed by it."

"I didn't detect her pheromones."

"How could you not, Xander? The scent is everywhere. Even now as I speak to you, it's all around, lingering, though she's left."

"I see, my king. So you're maddened by this female scent that's all around yet no one but you can detect." Xander laughed uproariously. "I think the scent is nowhere except up your nose."

"You're looking to have my boot up your ass, Xander." Jicar really didn't need to ask. He knew what Xander alluded to.

"I'll prepare to depart and make the announcement to your kingdom."

"You'll do no such thing."

"And why not?"

"We haven't even had a second date."

"No? Then I suggest you do so."

Chapter Eight

He wouldn't see her for a second time.

No he wouldn't.

He couldn't.

Well, at least he shouldn't.

Should he?

And why was he stomping through the garden with an aggravated pace? Jicar halted and looked around. It was just a hair past sunrise and most guests were still asleep.

Xander had to be incorrect. Scenting the woman was not an indication that she was his lifemate. He'd caught the fragrance of other females' pheromones before. Of course then so did all the other males in those cases.

He's lying. Xander probably did smell her fragrance but was pretending not to, trying to prove he possessed more self-control than Jicar. *No.* Aside from being acutely honorable, Xander put too much value in their friendship to deceive or persuade him. Xander's comments about Britenia possibly being Jicar's lifemate were spoken with an honest opinion. Rubbing his forehead, Jicar decided he was thinking too hard on it. His head was starting to throb and his muscles ached with tension.

He needed a massage.

Stalking to the cushioned tables, Jicar stepped behind a nearby screen and removed his clothes. He came out wrapped in a towel. After pushing his request on a keypad, he reclined on the table face down. Within moments the masseuse appeared--a female just as he asked for. Her touch would force his thoughts away from Britenia, and if the masseuse was willing, he would date her this evening. It was just what he needed, to erase Britenia and her alluring scent from his mind.

Just what he needed.

Why did that determined concept seem so unconvincing...

And depressing?

Instead of relaxing into the seasoned hands of the woman who massaged him, he became acutely aware of her touch when she skimmed her hand over his ass several times in obvious gesture. It caused Jicar to tense.

The masseuse was willing, but he was rejecting.

Without a word to her, Jicar stood. He stepped behind the changing screen and donned his trousers and vest. He stalked toward the club with every intention of getting drunk, with every intention of drowning Britenia from his thoughts.

Xander sat alone at the table overlooking the spa garden, sipping on a cordial. He saw Jicar enter and waved him over. Smiling he indicated the seat across from him as he took another swallow of his drink. "You look miserable, cousin."

"It's a little early to be drinking, don't you think?" Jicar picked up the bottle that sat in front of the table, turned over the small glass that was sitting next to it and poured himself a jigger.

Lifting it to his lips he jerked back his head, swallowing the spirit down.

Xander lifted a brow. "It's never too early to drink, apparently."

He watched Jicar pour another and down that one as well. "So how many dawnings does this make, cousin?"

"Seven."

"I see. But of course you've found relief with other females."

"No."

"Your faithfulness to her is astounding."

"I'm doing no such thing. I'm just not in the mood."

"Since when?" Shaking his head at Jicar's stubbornness, Xander lifted his glass to take another sip as his eyes drifted to the window. He looked outside and nearly choked on his next swallow.

"Are you all right?" Jicar started to rise from his chair.

Through his sputtering and coughing, Xander started laughing. "Well, isn't that a sight for lust-deprived eyes."

"What?" Jicar looked over his shoulder and through the window to see what had caught Xander's interest. "Holy fucking shit!"

He stormed away from the table and headed outside, stalking directly toward Britenia who stood on the garden path just outside of the club's window. His hand circled her wrist and he dragged her from the path, through a bed of flowers, through a bevy of bushes, to the seclusion of the forest that surrounded the spa.

He stopped and swung her around to face him.

"What in starblazing hellfires do you think you're doing?"

Britenia's brows lifted in questioning. "Walking back to my cabana."

"You know that's not what I mean, Brit." Jicar waved a hand in front of her body. "I'm talking about this."

Britenia looked down to see if something was strange. She was naked and couldn't imagine what was wrong, unless something odd was attached to her somewhere and she couldn't feel its presence. Shrugging, she tipped her head back up to meet Jicar's face. "What?"

"You're naked!"

"Yes?"

"Why?"

"I was cooling off in the large pool."

"You're not cooling off now."

"No, I'm drying off."

"But why are doing it naked?"

"I forgot my towel. It would be uncomfortable to don my clothes while I'm wet. So I didn't bother."

"So you thought it proper to walk back to your room naked?"

"Yes."

"Have you no shame?"

Britenia tilted her eyes upward and askew, as if to ponder that emotion. "I don't think so."

"You should." Jicar snatched the pullover top that she held in one of her hands, righted it and began tugging it over her head.

"Why?" Britenia pushed her arms into the short sleeves and then followed Jicar's movements as he knelt and tugged the hem as far down as it would go.

"Because...." Annoyed that it only reached the middle of her thighs, Jicar pressed his lips together. Standing, he glared at Britenia. "Because all of the men are looking at your naked body."

"And some woman too," Britenia added.

"Don't you give a care?"

"No."

Jicar slapped a hand to his forehead, pressing hard. He shook his head back and forth as he squeezed his eyes shut.

Of course she didn't care, but he surely did! It disturbed him that other males were looking upon her with lust on their minds.

And then he heard laughter.

Britenia was laughing.

Lifting his head he saw the mirth in her expression as she closed her lips, her eyes continuing to twinkle with the humor she found at his expense.

He frowned at her.

Britenia's expression sobered. "I am sorry, Jicar. I should not be finding my amusement at your … your … what is this emotion you suffer … jealousy?"

Jicar wasn't about to admit to that. "It's called frustration, Brit."

Searching her memory for a definition Britenia drew her brows together. Frustration was a disturbing, anxious emotion. "But why do you feel this sensation?"

How much would he admit? Stepping closer to her, Jicar grasped her by the shoulders. "It's you. I'm frustrated by you."

Sweeping his arms around her, Jicar dipped his head. Their lips met, his mouth taking hers in a searing kiss. He pressed his body along the length of her holding her tightly, yearning, craving to be inside of her.

His cock began to riot in his trousers.

Britenia's essence filled the air, wrapped around him, took up residence inside of his head. His chest hammered with an unfamiliar beat, and distraught by the overwhelming feeling, Jicar ripped his mouth away from her.

His mouth fell agape, but no words emerged. All he could think about was how magnificent this woman was, and how beautiful she appeared to his eyes.

With one finger, Britenia pushed his jaw shut. "Does this mean you request a second date?'

"No," Jicar stated firmly and released her, letting his arms drop to his sides.

"Very well." Turning, Britenia began walking away. "I will see you this eve then, Jicar."

"I said, *No!*" Jicar yelled to her back.

"I heard you loud and clear, Jicar Adi LarRhe."

A smile tickled Britenia's mouth as she walked away, and she lifted her fingers to touch it.

Pleasure.

And unlike some emotions, this one showed on her face. Ah yes, it was definitely pleasure.

And something else she was unable to identify.

Chapter Nine

Britenia stood in front of the full length mirror that was near the circular wall of her cabana. Her clothes were made of the finest of materials--sewn by the most talented of craftspeople in the cosmos. She so very much wished to feel the delight of wearing such well made things as the other guests here on the resort seemed to do.

But it was not to be for now.

The choice of clothing was a matter of decision only, what felt comfortable and matched well. Her feet were bare as Britenia preferred, and this dawning she had chosen an emerald gown that rested nicely along her curves. It was made of a light, velvety material and was sleeveless. The neckline plunged to just below her breasts revealing the rounded flesh of her cleavage. A black cinch molded around her waist, and just as with many of the gowns Britenia wore, there were slits on the sides that ran the length of her legs from ankle to thigh. The temperature at the No Holes Bar Club and Spa was very warm, and the openings provided a nice breeze.

If it were not for the dark look Jicar had given her about her nudity earlier, Britenia would've chosen something much more indiscreet, transparent even.

Though she found her pleasure in his frustration, the jealousy he refused to admit did something strange to her heart, it didn't seem a fair thing to upset him. For as much as she enjoyed the obvious emotions that seemed solely for her, equally, Britenia did not enjoy causing Jicar discomfort.

Looking in the mirror, Britenia examined herself, to make sure her clothes fit smoothly and the seams were all straight. She stopped to stare at her lower limbs.

"I've been told I have nice legs," she spoke to her image and then shrugged. "They look like legs to me,"

Her attention went to the time piece that swirled in the orb on the bedside table. It was still early yet and she wasn't hungry, so Britenia curled up in the cushioned, oversized chair in the corner, unrolled the Scrolls of Emotional Awareness and began to read. Her thoughts drifted back to Jicar. She found her passion with him, but the stirrings that were surfacing within her also went much deeper than that. There seemed to be a craving for him that was unbearable ... almost like pain.

Shuffling through her scrolls, Britenia searched for the section on relationship emotions. While reading what the scripts had to say, Britenia suddenly realized she'd been stroking a hand up and down her leg, pretending it was Jicar touching her. She put the scrolls aside.

Britenia's fingers circled higher and then she slipped them inside of the slit at her thigh. As she closed her eyes, Britenia's hand moving directly to her pussy. Flicking her finger back and forth across her bud, the titillating sensation caused Britenia to moan.

She'd never played with herself before, but thoughts of Jicar, his smile, his affectionate touches, his deep, erotic voice kept urging her on. Both her physical and her emotional desire for him spiraled, collided, entwined. Her hips began to move as she thought about how his tongue licked her clit, and she thought about what it would be like to suck on his shaft.

Britenia wanted to do that for him, feel him hard and erect and cumming in her mouth.

Opening her eyes, she caught sight of herself in the full-length mirror and brushed the skirt of her dress aside. She spread her legs and watched her own finger moving over her flesh. Moisture seeped from her vagina, but despite that Britenia sighed and removed her hand.

She needed Jicar.

Standing, Britenia smoothed out her dress and rechecked her appearance in the mirror. She dragged a brush through her hair before heading for the club. As she walked the path, Britenia suddenly realized she had a feeling weaving its way through her veins.

It was called *nervousness* ... and she knew it had something to do with seeing Jicar and possibly being rejected by him.

Taking a deep breath, Britenia moved closer to the club's large opening. The music grew louder, enveloping her as she walked through the open doorway. It mixed with the chatter of an unusually large crowd, that she had difficulty seeing around. Searching for Jicar amidst the wall to wall patrons, Britenia drew a deep breath, wondering if he had arrived or if he was even intending on showing.

Britenia wasn't a fool. She knew that Jicar was making every attempt to avoid her. That is until he reprimanded her for walking naked through the garden.

She found her humor then.

And then he kissed her. She wanted more of his kisses, more of his touch, more of the passion he coaxed from her.

Pushing her way through the crowd as she sought a place to sit, Britenia wondered where the other more pleasurable sensations she was promised were? Though Jicar gave her passion, he abruptly took it away claiming that their encounter was for one time only.

That thought, in and of itself made her empty again. But the emptiness was different this time. It had her heart aching, in both the physical and the emotional sense. The emotion found its place inside of her, and it seemed to be stuck there. It was one sentiment Britenia wished she could rid herself of. That and all of the other unpleasant sensations she seemed to be experiencing of late-- disappointment, anxiety, loneliness and again, the horrible ache in her chest, which she had yet to identify.

Britenia hoped there wasn't something physically ailing her heart.

Perhaps she should seek out a healer, the problem seemed to be growing worse with every dawning.

The song playing had ended and there was a pause before the next set. Dancers left the floor, giving Britenia a better view of the surrounding tables. Scanning the crowd, she looked for friendly faces. Upon spying two females chatting happily at a table, she decided to approach them.

"May I join you?"

They both looked up and one of them nodded. "Why sure!"

Britenia sat down and one of the women pushed a platter of food in front of her. "Help yourself."

"Thank you." Picking up a skewer of roasted meats and vegetables, Britenia started to eat.

"I'm Sheva," one of the woman said.

"And I'm Licress," the other added.

"We're earth cats!" they laughed in unison.

"Earth cats?" Britenia asked.

"Well not exactly earth cats," Licress told her. "We, sort of displaced ourselves to the planet."

"The creatures there are so tasty." Sheva grinned amorously.

"And the food isn't so bad either," Licress added. "So who are you?"

"I'm Britenia."

Sheva leaned in. "Do you shift?"

"Now and then," Britenia answered. "From place to place."

Sheva laughed. "Oh dearling, that's not what I meant."

Xander watched from a distance as Britenia made acquaintance with the two shape-shifting females. He changed the direction of his attention, his eyes moving to the table in a far corner where Jicar sat alone.

Jicar was glaring at him, a warning Xander assumed by the way his cousin narrowed his eyes, that he better keep his distance from Britenia.

Ignoring his cousin's threatening expression, Xander pushed away from the wall he'd been leaning against, and took a leisurely strolled toward the table where Britenia sat. "Excuse me, my lady, but I was hoping for a favor."

Britenia looked up at Xander. "It would depend on the kind of favor you ask."

Xander chuckled softly and held out his hand. "Nothing too dangerous, just an experiment."

"O-o-o-h! An experiment," Licress said as her eyes grazed carnally along the length of Xander's body. "You can experiment with me, good-looking."

Sheva pushed a shoulder against her and chuckled.

Xander grinned at the two felines, and still holding out his hand he said, "I assure you, Britenia, it won't hurt. I'm just curious about something."

"Curiosity killed the cat," Sheva said.

"I'm not a cat," Xander smirked and then nodded when Britenia accepted, flattening her palm against his own.

His fingers curled around her hand, and Xander pulled Britenia to her feet. He stared into her beautiful peach-colored eyes. "You are a lovely woman."

"Thank y...." Britenia hardly had time to respond, when Xander suddenly grasped her by the shoulders and jerked her closer to his body. He buried his face into the side of her neck and sniffed, drawing a long and hard breath through his nostrils.

He pulled back, and Britenia's eyes grew wide in questioning, but before she could say anything else, Xander dropped to his knees and buried his face in her crotch, rubbing his nose back and forth at her juncture and again sniffing.

Britenia's head dropped downward. "What are you doing, Xander?"

"Sniffing you."

"Oh me oh my!" Licress exclaimed. "Will you do that do me?"

"Maybe." Xander said as he stood. He grasped Britenia by the shoulders once more and turned her around. Pressing a hand between her shoulder blades, he forced her to bend. Her hands came up reflexively, propping on the table and she leaned on them.

Xander crouched, and stuffed his nose in the crook of her ass. Again he sniffed.

For the first time, Britenia understood shock. She knew the males of her planet who wished to have sex would act as such, but it wasn't a behavior she expected from a patron here.

Stiffening, she stood and turned around. At the same time Xander rose and faced her. He smiled broadly at her, and then he pivoted, turning to where Jicar sat. Britenia followed the line of his gaze and caught sight of Jicar sitting at a far table.

Her heart skipped a beat and began leaping erratically in her chest. Immediately her pussy clenched with arousal.

Xander looked at her, perceptive of the lust and longing she could barely hide as she gazed at Jicar.

"Are you aroused by him, my lady?"

At first Britenia said nothing because she was attempting to control her breathing, which had become strangely uneven and rapid.

"Yes," she finally said, her voice a hoarse whisper.

Her gaze shifted and she looked at Xander through the corner of her eyes. "You're not going to start sniffing me again, are you?"

"Tell me, Britenia," Xander smirked at her question. "What would you do if I sent one of these sexy women over to sit on Jicar's lap?"

Britenia angled her head, this time facing him directly. "Are you attempting to rile both Jicar's jealousy and mine, Xander?"

"As a matter of fact, I am," he said.

"Jealousy," Britenia decided, "is a ridiculous emotion, and I will not have it."

Xander laughed at her determined expression. *Good for her. The woman would need that stubbornness to be married to Jicar Adi LarRhe.*

But he wasn't finished with his experiment yet, especially now that he knew she was aroused.

His attention darted back to Jicar, and he smiled devilishly before grasping Britenia and pulling her in front of him, so that her back was to Jicar and he was able to keep his eyes fixed on his cousin.

And if looks could kill...

Xander's arms swept around Britenia and he dipped his head, burying his face in her cleavage and taking one last whiff. Moving higher, he planted his mouth upon hers and made every attempt to give Britenia a passionate kiss, but her lips pursed together in resistance.

It was all he needed to know.

Releasing her, Xander straightened and then snorted at Jicar's intense irritation and his flaring nostrils and he knew that Jicar was catching her scent.

Lifting upturned palms, Xander shrugged.

Nothing, he mouthed.

Although Xander was extremely aroused himself, it was more by his own antics than by any pheromone that

Britenia emitted. If Jicar thought Britenia's scent was available to all around, he was sorely mistaken. And since it seemed that only Jicar could smell her, it meant only one thing.

Britenia was his lifemate.

"What a man!" Licress exclaimed as she squirmed in her seat. "Come here tomcat and sniff my ass."

"Licress! How bodacious."

"My experiment is complete, Britenia." Ignoring the she-cats, Xander pulled out Britenia's chair for her and then pushed it in as she seated herself.

He turned and walked away.

"Suck my furry tail," Sheba said. "You're one to talk. If I recall it was your bodacious pussy wriggling as you walked that tree limb, driving Pedris so mad with it that he had to mount you, filling your belly with those kittens."

"Kittens?" Britenia asked.

"Why yes, offspring," Licress answered.

"I had one of those once."

"Once?" Licress asked. "What happened to it?"

"I gave it away."

"Away!" Sheba gave Britenia a stunned look. "But why?"

"I had no need for it."

"Oh my, horrible!" Licress said.

"No more horrible than your luring Pedris from me, Sheba."

"I didn't lure him. He wanted me because he loves me."

"Catshit!" Sheba growled, pushing at Licress' shoulder. "He loves me. You are merely his whore-cat."

"You bitch! Take that back." With that, Licress slapped Sheba across the face.

Chapter Ten

"I'm sure it was necessary to be so thorough," Jicar snapped.

"I assure you, my king." Xander took a seat next to Jicar. "It was for your benefit, and safety I might add. Jicar glanced down at Xander's crotch, noting the bulge in his pants from his swollen member. "I think you enjoyed yourself a bit too much."

"I enjoyed myself immensely." Xander picked up the glass in front of him and took a drink.

Once again, the music began to play, and the guests started moving to the dance floor.

"If I didn't know you better, Xander, I would've been sure you were preparing to hump her at the table."

"Tsk, tsk. I'm more discreet than that. I would've taken her upstairs and humped her in the corridor. I'll bet she has a sweet, little pussy."

"How dare you take liberty talking about my…." Jicar clamped his mouth shut.

"Your … what?"

"Nothing."

"Your paramour?"

"No."

"Your business partner?"

"No."

"Your sister, your friend … your woman?"

"No, no and definitely no!" Jicars voice raised an octave. He inhaled deeply through his nostrils and his lids drifted shut as if he were captured by some exquisite dream.

Xander snorted. He knew that look, had seen it on the faces of many betrothed. "You can smell her."

Jicar's eyes snapped open. He glanced in Britenia's direction but her table was blocked by the dancers crowding the floor. Resisting the urge to stand and search over the tops of their heads, he instead shifted his attention back to Xander. Jicar slumped in his chair. "Even through the smells of the food, and the incense, and the array of perfumes worn by the guests here."

"And I swear on my loyalty to you, that I cannot." Xander tapped the rim of the glass in front of him. "She admitted after seeing you sitting here that you aroused her, Jicar, and still I detected no scent coming from her."

A crash so loud it penetrated through the booming music interrupted their conversation. Several women shrieked. The dancers cleared the area rapidly with guests running for cover. Xander and Jicar both stood and at the same time the music died.

Across the dance floor, on the opposite side of the club, the table that Britenia sat at had been turned over, the food, the drinks spilling to the floor. The two women that Britenia was making acquaintance with were snarling and hissing at each other, feline fangs appearing in their mouths. Long, sharp claws emerged from the tips of their fingers and they were swiping them through the air.

And Britenia stood right in the thick of it, unmoving, her head poised in a tilt, her attention steadfast on the women, as if she were studying them.

That's all Jicar needed was to watch her get the hell scratched out of her or possibly have her throat torn out by being caught in the middle of a couple of infuriated, shape-shifting panthers.

Both he and Xander moved at the same time. Security personal were also closing in. Jicar's heart pounded as one of the woman raised her hand--a hand that had morphed into a big, black paw. She was ready to strike, and spirits help him, Britenia took a step closer, probably to get a better look. He reached her just as the claw slashed, snatching her by the arm and pulling her out of harm's way.

Xander stepped between the women trying to sooth them.

Jicar thought it was an idiotic move.

Security closed in and all hell broke loose. The women completely shifted and two wild panthers leapt over the top of Xander's head and lunged at each other.

Patrons screamed and scattered for the exits. Tables were toppled, chairs were thrown back, and the sound of breaking glass shattered the air.

"This is anger, Jicar." Britenia broke free of his clutches and started to turn back. "I want to experience it."

"You don't want to experience this, Brit." Jicar attempted to tug her away again, but she fought him.

Irritated by her foolishness and lacking the will or the time to argue with her, Jicar bent and wrapped an arm below her bottom. She gasped when he lifted her and tossed her over his left shoulder so that her upper body draped upside down along his back. He didn't care about the indignity of it all.

She probably wouldn't either.

But he had to get her out of there.

Britenia grunted as Jicar readjusted her on his shoulder.
"Put me down Jicar."
"No."
With her firmly in his grip, Jicar headed up one of the
garden paths, the sounds of crashing and growling felines
and distraught guests fading behind them. When he reached
a three-way split in the path, Jicar looked, around, realizing
he didn't know where Britenia was staying.
"Where's your cabana, Brit?"
"I don't know."
"What do you mean you don't know?"
"I'm not sure where we are, Jicar. The only thing I can
see right now is your ass and the ground."
"Which view do you like better?" Jicar smirked and then
jumped slightly when he felt her teeth nip at his backside.
Just that simple gesture sent heat racing through his flesh.
And the fact that her crotch was so temptingly close to his
face, her unique scent taunting him mercilessly, only
served to intensify the sensation which seemed to whirl its
way through his chest and gut merging into a powerful
force that shot straight into his groin.
Jicar blew out a breath, his shaft pulsing, swelling and
throbbing, hardening to a full-blown erection before he
even had time to comprehend what was happening. His
body fell into an instant quaking that had his head spinning
and his knees nearly weakening with need for her.
Despite his resolve to refrain from dating Britenia for a
second time, and holding her thus was pure torment, for
some blazing reckless reason, he couldn't put her down.
Something deep inside of him was erupting, something
obsessive, inherent and completely base. "Just tell me
which path to take, Britenia."
He had to get to Britenia's cabana or he was going to
throw her down and mount her there on the very path.
Pressing her palms against Jicar's butt for leverage,
Britenia lifted her head and twisted to look around the side
of him, but she didn't say anything.
Jicar inhaled and then exhaled, the air leaving his lungs in
lengthy, shuddering breath. "Well?"
"Right."
Jicar took a step.
"No left."

"Which path, Britenia?"

"The world looks different upside down."

"Right, left or middle?"

"Not the middle."

"Then which?"

"Put me down."

"No … which path?"

"Right," Britenia decided. "The cabana at the very end."

Figured it would be the last. Jicar began walking again, his strides growing longer and quicker with each step, and when he finally reached her dwelling, Jicar bent and set Britenia on her feet.

Looking up into his eyes, Britenia glared at him … an actual glare. "Good eve, Jicar."

She turned her back to him, opened the door to her room and walked through.

Chapter Eleven

Jicar stepped into the door opening before Britenia could close it on him. He grasped her upper arm.

Turning, Britenia glanced to where he held her and then shifted to look up at his face. "Did you want something, Jicar?"

Hesitating, Jicar lifted his free hand and smoothed his palm along her cheek. "Let me in."

"You had no right to pull me from the club when I was studying emotions."

"I was afraid you would get hurt." Jicar released her arm and slipped it around her waist, pressing her body to him.

"What I decide to do is none of your concern."

"I'm making it my concern."

"Yet you avoided me for several dawnings."

"I did." Jicar pushed his fingers through her hair. Tipping her face upward he brushed his lips with hers. "I'm sorry."

"What right did you have to order me back into my clothes?" *Especially when I would prefer that you were stripping me out of them.*

"I feared another man would desire you."

"And what if one had?"

"I would've had to kill him."

"I offered you a second date and you clearly said *no*."

"I was being foolish." Jicar pressed his lips to the side of her neck and inhaled her fragrance before suckling her flesh.

"You helped me find passion and then you took it away."

"Let me help you find it again." Smoothing one of his hands lower, Jicar cupped her bottom and pushed at her with his hardness.

"I'm upset with you, Jicar."

"I know." He grinned. "But I want to be by your side for every emotion you experience, Brit, good or bad."

"You do?"

"Let me in."

"No." *I mean yes, I mean yes, yes, yes!*

Jicar backed Britenia into the cabana.

She didn't resist.

Lifting his booted foot he kicked the door closed.

"You're exquisite," Jicar said and pushed the cloth of her dress from her shoulders.

A soft cry left her mouth as he cupped her breasts. Her mind emptied of reasonable thought as desire swept in. Reaching forward, Britenia pushed the vest of him and her hands skimmed his sides, feeling his muscles tense beneath her touch. His mouth came down on hers, their tongues collided, sucking, their mouths sealing hard and demanding.

Britenia's hands found the waist of Jicar's pants, the fastener that held them closed, and she fumbled a bit but finally undid it, and jerked them over his hips pushing until it fell downward. Her hands sought his shaft and she wrapped both her fingers around it, stroking the hardened flesh, running her palms along the length, feeling it pulsate in her grasp.

Her thumb grazed the head capturing the moisture seeping from it, and Jicar groaned with pleasure.

Pulling her mouth from his, Britenia stared into his eyes, noticing for the first time how dark and sensual his gaze was.

She opened her mouth. Her chest heaved and she panted her exhales before dropping to her knees in front of him.

Giving him no time to speak, Britenia sucked his cock into her mouth, her tongue swirling around the swollen head.

Jicar's hips jerked and he gasped out a grunt of approval, his hand thrusting through her hair to steady her head.

He pumped, in and out of her mouth, his lust rising, his chest expanding with his hard breaths of air.

Britenia's tongue swirled around the head and he growled with the pleasure of it. He was close to orgasm, too close, but didn't want their second date to culminate into his satiation from the carnal bliss Britenia offered him right now. Jicar attempted to pull from her mouth and as he did, Britenia sucked harder, refusing to let him go. Stilling his hips, he relinquished to enjoying more of her mouth while struggling to keep from cumming at the same time.

And then she did the most glorious thing. Her mouth slid off of his cock and she licked the underside of his erection straight down to his balls. Britenia's hand came up and she cupped and lifted and squeezed his sack, her tongue lapping at the same time. Swallowing hard, Jicar pulled back and dropped to his knees, his hands still laced through her hair. Tipping back her head their gazes met. Jicar lowered his head and dragged his tongue across the crease of her lips dipping between them slightly as he did.

Britenia explored Jicar's body with her hands. His body was firm beneath her touch, and she felt the physical essence of him, felt the powerful need building inside of her, driving its way to her head. A bevy of emotions ruptured in her brain. She choked back a cry, a mix of her arousal along with sadness, understanding fully that this would be their last time together. When he left her this eve, left her forever, Britenia knew there would be emotional hurt, but she pushed it back, grateful for the comfort of being in Jicar's arms, of the passion that swept her body and mind, even if it was only for this night.

Melting against him, Britenia sighed and pressed her weight heavily against his body, forcing Jicar back onto the floor. One of his arms reached back, the other slipped behind Britenia's back and as he reclined, Jicar brought Britenia down on top of him. Her thighs immediately spread, her knees resting to each side of his hip. Lifting up,

Britenia pressed her palms to his chest and she stroked her pussy up and down his shaft in an urgent restless motion.

"Ah, yes, beauty." She was captivating. Jicar watched the motion of her hips, the head of his cock appearing and disappearing beneath her nest of curls.

And she was hot and wet, her carnal moisture dripping, glistening on his shaft, making it slick as she skimmed along the length.

Britenia arched and threw her head back, her breasts jutted forward gently bouncing with her rhythmic motion. Jicar reached for them, cupped them in his hands, ran his thumbs over her nipples. "Jicar." Britenia's voice emerged in a rough whisper. "Please."

Sliding his hands down her sides, Jicar grasped her bottom and lifted her, poised to slide her onto his throbbing cock, feel her tightness, thrust up inside of her.

But he stopped.

Damn holy hellfires!

He was struck by a compelling thirst.

Jicar wanted to rub his mouth on her flesh, thrust his tongue upward and into her as her juices flowed down. He wanted to know what she felt like, tasted like, smell what it was like to have her cum while he was licking her.

His body quaked, and he dragged her hips forward, slid his body downward until she was seated on his face, and he sucked on her.

On a gasp, Britenia fell forward, her body arching over the top of his head, her pussy on his mouth, shocks of pleasure running through her.

She moved, rotating and rubbing, seeking and feeling, her heart thumping her breath coming in short pants.

And then she was on her back, Jicar still tasting her, his tongue flattening as he licked and licked and then suckled on her. She was cumming. Like tiny little prickles it began, surging when Jicar plunged a finger inside of her. His thumb replaced his tongue, and he pressed it to her clit as he moved over her and sank his cock inside of her.

And the sounds of Britenia's own voice, in the throes of ecstasy, echoed through her mind and her hips moving frantically as Jicar slammed into her. She arched up and grabbed Jicar's ass pulling him hard as the impact of her orgasm hit, burst, rushed through her flesh and seized her.

Jicar was lost in her, swept away by her cries of pleasure, his entire body on a rampage, his hips plummeting, his cock swelling, quaking, rupturing. His orgasm shot through him like a cosmic explosion that culminated into only one thought....

He loved Britenia and she was his lifemate.

Chapter Twelve

"How is it that your entire planet is without emotions, Brit?" Jicar snuggled next to her, pulling the covers of the bed higher, nestling them as their bodies laced.

Britenia nestled her cheek against Jicar's shoulder. "My father, the king, always a man to consume power and control, found that he couldn't suppress the constant civil uprisings against his harsh rule. He feared being overthrown."

"It's something many rulers fear, even the good ones." *She's the daughter of king ... interesting.*

"But a good ruler would never do such a horrible thing as my father did, to his, or her own people." Her father's distorted thinking seeped in and sadness at the insanity of his actions took hold. "To remedy the problem, my father paid an errant sorcerer in priceless gems, items needed to conjure stronger magic. In return he cast a spell that would remove the emotions of my people for the extent of six generations."

"Why six?"

"The sorcerer informed my father the spell would only last that long."

"How is it that you, the king's daughter, were chosen to be the ambassador of emotion seeking?"

"I was born with emotions."

That surprised Jicar and he cranked his head to look down at her. "But how is it you were born with emotions, when all others from your planet were not?"

"Since the king and my mother retained their emotions, when I was born, mine too were intact."

"But why did he strip you, his own child, of feelings?"

"As I grew, I became more aware of what my father had done. I rebelled."

"A rebellious adolescence," Jicar chuckled. "How unique."

"But it angered him, Jicar. Still I was relentless, telling him what he did was wrong. I was angry with him, and that anger intensified when my mother died. I felt so lonely. I made every attempt to teach my people how to feel again."

"I bet that went over well with your father."

"Yes, so well that when he realized he had lost control of me, he summoned his sorcerer and paid him to empty my mind."

"Your father is a sick man."

"It matters not anymore, Jicar. My people need me...."

Jicar was about to ask her more when she revealed the name of her home planet.

"...and since I've experienced emotion it's felt that I'm Reba Lou's only hope."

Jicar went very still. "What did you say?"

Britenia blinked and met his gaze. "I don't know. What did I say?"

Jicar rolled away from her and stood. Anger shuddered through him. "Why didn't you tell me who you were?"

"I did tell you who I was." Britenia sat up and gave him a questioning look.

"No. Not your name, your title, who you were the daughter of." Jicar heard his own voice rising to an irked pitch. "Your planet!"

Hellfires! Was she sent here to spy on him?

"You didn't ask."

That was the truth. He hadn't pried into her background. But he should have.

Jicar reined his anger for the moment and forced himself to calm. He lowered his voice when he spoke, but underlying it he could still hear disdain in its tone. "Your father had a trade pact with my father."

"He did?"

Eyeing her suspiciously, Jicar continued. "He betrayed our trust, invaded our planet, took many of our people into slavery, tortured some, slaughtered others."

Britenia dropped her eyes and shifted them back and forth along the floor. Her father's actions were always questionable. But was he really that evil? "I was unaware of this, Jicar."

Studying her, Jicar wondered if she lying. "Thankfully, we fought back soundly, forcing a retreat. But it was at great loss. My two sisters and my father were killed."

"This is a terrible thing, Jicar." Britenia felt sorrow, it was meager at first, but as it trickled in, the emotion grew stronger.

It hurt to know her father had done such a thing, though she knew her expression didn't show it. What appeared on her face in response to sensed emotions was something that seemed to be inconsistent.

"My people and yours have been enemies ever since," Jicar told her.

The silence thickened between them then, but finally Jicar spoke again, his voice firm, controlled....

Cold. Britenia shuddered from the chill of it.

"There will be no third time for us." Jicar's heart wrenched at the thought. He could swear he felt it shatter.

He couldn't trust her.

"I didn't think there would be," Britenia returned. "You told me yourself, twice a date, thrice a...."

"I know what I said!" Jicar bellowed angrily. He stalked across the room, stopping in front of a dresser. Propping his hands on the surface, he leaned heavily on it. Her lack of reaction only fed his scorn and fury.

By the god spirits, was he really thinking about taking her for a mate!

Jicar lifted his head catching her reflection in the dresser's mirror. "Don't look at me with innocent eyes, Brit. You used me."

"I did?" Britenia lifted her fingers to touch her face, her eyelids. What did innocent eyes feel like?

"You did!" Jicar turned on her. "To gain access to my planet. How clever of you, pretending you had no emotions!"

"It was my understanding that we were enjoying the date, Jicar. I don't know of this deceit you talk about."

Jicar narrowed his eyes. Her calm voice was infuriating. What a fool he'd been. How could he have been so careless as to put his planet at risk? How could he have let her steal a piece of his heart! "You've betrayed me."

When she didn't answer his charge, Jicar took it as an admittance of guilt. He stalked toward her, grabbing her roughly by the shoulders and she yelped at the pain. "You're hurting me, Jicar."

He was hurting her in mores ways than just physical.

"I'll hurt so much more than… " Jicar closed his eyes. If he didn't tamp his rage, his hurt, his breaking heart, he was going to kill her. Opening his eyes, he glared at her. "How could you do this to another person? Don't you care about a damn thing!"

Britenia blinked. Her mouth opened and her body shook. She would examine the reaction to his anger later. But for now….

"I care about you, Jicar." The sentiment was genuine, falling from her lips without regard. Britenia felt it and said it aloud before she could even reason the words in mind.

"Like hell you do!" Jicar pushed her so hard she fell backwards onto the bed, the force of it causing her to bounce. Grabbing his trousers from the floor, Jicar quickly donned them and then stomped from Britenia's cabana, slamming the door behind him.

Britenia pushed out a hard breath, relieved he was gone, fearing he would never return. She felt moisture in her eyes.

It was tears.

Crying is a strange thing, Britenia thought as she touched the drop of moisture at the corner of her eye. From her studies she knew that one might cry for many reasons, sadness, pain and even joy.

This assuredly was not joy.

Britenia was tempted to fight the tears back, but now that Jicar had departed, she knocked down what she assumed was a protective barrier she held up attempting to keep her feelings in check.

Emotions flooded in--distraught, anguish, even a twinge of anger, but most of all devastation--devastation of Jicar's misinterpreted accusation.

Chapter Thirteen

Britenia awoke with a beastly headache that felt as though it were charging through her skull, goring her brain. She had cried herself to sleep, begging the spirits to shed the horrible emotions stomping through her, give her reprieve.

At least now, some of it had subsided.

Her thoughts moved to Jicar and immeasurable hurt set in again.

He blamed her for his planet's woes, his loved ones' deaths.

The throb in Britenia's head pounded harder.

Her stomach didn't feel much better.

"I'll go vomit and then take a bath," she said to the empty room as she rolled from her bed. Just as she reached the bathing chamber a sensation struck her. It was painful, tortuously painful.

Dark and horrifying intense emotions began flooding in-- hopelessness, depression, anxiety, grief, anger … hate … terror….

They seized her in one tremendous sweep.

Britenia started to scream.

* * * *

"I tripped over your sheets this dawning," Xander commented. "Why were they thrown in the hall?"

"I don't know what you're talking about." Jicar feigned ignorance. Unable to look Xander in the eye less his cousin see the pain there, he instead looked around the club's outdoor patio where the three of them sat.

Trina gave Xander a woeful look. "I believe he was growling something about her scent being in the sheets."

"Hmm," Xander's brows rose. "Did tossing them out help?"

"I don't think so," Trina answered. "He still looks miserable."

Jicar gritted his teeth and glared with ire, first at Trina and then Xander. "Will the two of you please let it be?"

Pinching a chunk of fruit on the platter in front of him, Jicar stuffed it in his mouth. He sought to turn the subject. "So what were you doing on the second floor, Xander, like I need to ask."

"Mmm," Xander examined his nails. "Nothing much, just making a couple of kittens purr."

"Good for you," Jicar said dryly. "And where are our rampant kittens now?"

"Inside, cleaning the mess they made of my place last eve," Trina answered. "With their remorseful tales stuffed between their thighs."

An agonizing screech suddenly rent the surrounding air causing the three of them to startle.

"Why that sounds like...," Xander began, but Jicar was already on his feet and running.

Trina signaled security, then she and Xander shot from their chairs and they too ran toward where the sounds were coming from.

The anguished cries grew louder as they neared Britenia's cabana. Rushing toward the door, Jicar burst through it, finding Britenia wrapped in the bed sheets and curled up into a tight ball on the floor.

She screamed between heavy weeps, her hands clutching the top of her head, and her face buried in her arms.

Jicar went on the defense, quickly scanning the room for an attacker, but nothing seemed amiss, nothing was out of place.

"Britenia," Jicar rushed to her and knelt at her side. He reached out to touch her but decided against it. "Are you hurt?"

"Leave me alone, Jicar."

"But you need help."

"You hate me!"

Wincing at her words, Jicar again reached for her. "I don't hate you, Brit."

"My father's dead!"

With a bewildered expression, Jicar looked over at Trina and Xander who were standing by the open door. Trina turned, dismissed her security personnel, and then closed the door, leaning against it. She looked on worriedly.

"She seems to be having a melt-down," Xander stated.

"I am a horrible person! I feel horror ... terrible, terrible horror." Raising to all fours and screeching as though she were in pain, Britenia attempted to scamper away.

Jicar reached out and grasped her by the waist, pulling her backward and into his arms, cradling her between his thighs. "What brought this on?"

"Let me go! I hate you!"

"Brit, talk to me." Jicar knew in part that she was reacting to his anger from last night, but there seemed to be more to it than that.

"Leave me alone. I want to die."

Sagging, Britenia leaned heavily on him and wept. Again, Jicar looked helplessly at Trina and Xander.

They both shook their heads, shrugging at the same time.

Stroking Britenia's hair, Jicar attempted to sooth her. "Did you have a nightmare?"

Did I cause this? He's been so cruel to her last eve and his heart filled with guilt and regret.

"No, no!"

"Please, Brit. Tell me what's going on."

"I am a horrible mother!" Britenia pulled back from him, her hand flying to her mouth, her eyes widening, her head shaking from side to side.

Jicar looked at her in shock. "You have a child?"

"What have I done?"

She tensed and tried to break free of Jicar, but his arms around her tightened. "Please, Brit, talk to me."

"I … I traded my baby to an acquaintance because I had no use for him." Britenia shuddered, her eyes squeezed shut. Anguish riddled her features. "I received a pet to eat the rodents in my garden."

Wrenching, Britenia released yet another hair-raising scream and Jicar couldn't help but to look her over, the painful cry leading him to believe she must be wounded, but subconsciously he knew that the wound was to her emotion heart.

"Oh Jicar!" Britenia screamed. "And you … you… just go away. Stop torturing me."

The sensations simultaneously attacking Britenia were too much for her to bear. Slumping in Jicar's arms, her head fell back over his arm and her body went frighteningly still.

"I'll get a healer," Trina said as she turned and rushed out the door.

Chapter Fourteen

"She's catatonic."

"What?" Jicar glared at Trina with complete confusion.

"I sent word to Rupshel, her mentor and explained what happened before she passed out. He said it's a reaction to the sensory overload."

"You mean every time she feels a strong emotion this … this…." Jicar waved a hand toward the bed where Britenia lay comatose. "Will happen?"

"Maybe a couple of times, if she's too overwhelmed, but as she adjusts to the discovery of her emotions, the catatonia should subside." Trina frowned at the unconscious Britenia. "There's just one problem."

Taking notice of Trina's expression, Jicar's worry escalated. "And what might that be?"

Trina's eyes lifted to meet Jicar's. His anxiety was apparent and it suddenly occurred to her why his mood was less than pleasant the last few eves. "You're in love with her."

Jicar pressed his lips tightly together and gritted his teeth. His body stiffened but then he closed his eyes. He dropped his head and his shoulders sagged because Jicar was unable to deny the overpowering sentiments consuming him.

"Yes," he whispered. "I love her."

His head snapped up, his demeanor becoming rigid once more. "Now tell me what the problem is with her present state!"

Trina bit her lip, but she had to let him know of the consequences. "If she remains catatonic for too long a period of time, her heart will stop beating and she'll die."

Anguish filled Jicar as he stalked toward bed. As he sat down beside Britenia and stroked her hair, a tear fell from the corner of his eye. He swiped it back and gathered Britenia to him, kissing the top of her head, begging. "Come back to me, love. I'm so sorry I hurt you. I'm so sorry I wasn't here to help you through this."

"There's something else, Jicar."

Jicar stiffened, he didn't want to hear anymore disturbing news, but at the same time had to know.

"Her mentor believes that if the emotions she suffered were devastating enough to put her in this condition, she might be detached again if she rouses."

For a moment Jicar was silent as he thought about the consequences.

"When she rouses." He had to believe Britenia would come through this. And didn't care what her emotional condition would be. He just wanted the catatonic state to lift.

And wouldn't leave her until it did.

Three dawnings later, Jicar still sat with Britenia, but there was little he could do. She rested in the bed unmoving and it amazed him how her body was in complete shut down. He thought she would at least wet the bed, but she didn't. The only sign of life coming from her was the continued beating of her heart.

For which he was tremendously grateful.

By the fourth dawning she began murmuring in her sleep. Emotions emerged, laughing, crying, anger, moans that sounded sensual. She spoke his name a few times, though she seemed unaware of his presence. Despite that, Jicar spoke softly to her, words of promise to her, hoping she could hear him, stroked her body gently, hoping she could feel him.

She quieted again and said nothing more for the length of another dawning.

By eve she began to stir.

Britenia opened her eyes and for a moment felt disoriented. Pushing to a sit she searched the area around her and slowly recognized her own cabana.

She felt numb.

Jicar was looking out the window, his back to her and she tilted her head to the side thinking how larger-than-life-itself he appeared to her.

His shoulder length, black hair was tied back in a queue, wet from what appeared to be a recent washing.

Britenia felt a tingle in her fingers, a craving to touch it.

Her attention turned to his clothing. He wore a deep green velvet vest that was tight around his trunk, the hem meeting the waist of the black leather pants that molded nicely around his firm butt and muscular legs.

His feet were bare.

She thought about how well the garments were made for his body and that they were of high quality too. He looked strong in them--powerful.

"Your clothes fit you well, Jicar."

At the sound of her voice, he spun around and stood shocked for a moment, wondering if he was imagining what he was seeing. Britenia sat up in the bed, clutching the sheet, her mass of peach-silver hair tangled around her body, her face pale, dark circles under her eyes, her demeanor appearing fatigued and weak.

She was the most beautiful sight he'd ever seen.

Inhaling an immensely relieved breath, Jicar went to the bedside, and unable to restrain himself he sat on the edge and dragged her into his arms.

A strange feeling swirled through Britenia's stomach, her chest, her mind, as Jicar embraced her. She interpreted it as hunger, for she was feeling a bit lightheaded too.

Britenia took a deep breath. "You smell very clean, Jicar."

Jicar closed his eyes, his heart grieving. She was void again. The comment was simply an automatic response to her olfactory senses.

"I'm thirsty."

"Of course." Jicar released her and reached for the pitcher of water and the cup that sat on the bedside stand. He poured her a drink.

Taking it from him, Britenia guzzled it down, her eyes riveted to his. When she emptied the cup, he took it from her and set it aside. Britenia's eyes drifted shut and she inhaled again.

Realization trickled in.

Jicar didn't just smell clean, he smelled wonderful.

It was then that awareness struck her.

The numbness faded. Every emotion she'd experienced thrived, but as much as they existed, they also seemed to be settled quietly inside of her, finding their place, waiting for the appropriate time to emerge.

"We should talk." Britenia took Jicar's hand.

He looked down wondering about the gesture. If felt like affection.

Not wanting to cause her any more upset, if she could even be driven to that state anymore after what he'd done to her, Jicar shifted his gaze back to her face. Her stoic expression seemed to soften, but he thought he was imagining it--wishful thinking. "You've been catatonic for several dawnings. Wouldn't you like to eat first?"

"No." Britenia slowly shook her head in the negative. Her lids lifted, her eyes meeting his. "I have a child."

"You told me."

"This is an issue for you."

Jicar released a soft laugh. "Not at all. But I am concerned about your sorrow for your...."

"...son," Britenia finished his sentence. "My anguish over trading him away was an overreaction. I see him every dawning. He lives in the castle with a royal guard and the guard's mate. He's perfectly fine."

"I would like to meet him."

"You would?" Britenia blinked at Jicar and a twinge of joy filled her, but it was overtaken by a feeling of shame. She lowered her gaze away from Jicar. "I'm sorry for what my father did."

She's sorry? Jicar furled his brows.

His hope rose. She appeared sincere.

Pouring her another cup of water, he handed to her. "How did your father die?"

Britenia took a small sip and then rested the cup on her thighs.

She sighed as she stared at the liquid in the container. "What goes around has a tendency to come around, hence when the king became critically ill one year later after cursing his own child ... me...." She looked up at Jicar. "No one came to his aid. No one cared. He died alone and no one felt guilty or ashamed."

Britenia took another sip of her water. "And no one grieved, not even me, until...."

Her words broke off and the silence grew thick between them.

"I should've never accused you of the things I did, Brit." Jicar grimaced as he thought about how vicious he'd been to her. "It wasn't a very diplomatic way for a king to behave."

Britenia pressed her fingers to lips. "Your position is understandable. You were thinking about the safety of your planet."

Curling his fingers around her hand, Jicar kissed her the tips and then lifted them from his lips.

He lowered her hand and pressed his palm to the center of his chest. "My thinking was selfish in part. I didn't give you a chance to explain."

"There isn't much more to it than I've already said." Britenia felt the beat of Jicar's heart beneath her flesh. It caught cadence with her own thumping chest. "Other than I'm now leader to an entire planet of numb-minded people."

"Why didn't you just have the sorcerer reverse the spell?"

"That would've been an easy solution if he was anywhere to be found. Unfortunately, he was a deviant. After my father died he had stolen half the stock of gems in our coffers and vanished.

I sent a plea to the reclusive sorcerers who lived high in the Crystal Mountains, asking them to take pity on our plight of her people, and they did, but were unable to remove the curse."

"Rupshel is one of those sorcerers?"

"He is, yes."

Jicar's expression went sullen. "I'm so sorry I hurt you, Brit."

"Why did you?"

"Since the first time I saw you, I've been trying to determine why the savage urges to possess you have been seizing me."

She didn't respond and Jicar was thankful for her silence, giving him time to think about how her scent, how his ferocious need for Britenia kept growing stronger and stronger with each new dawning despite his futile attempts to resist.

Finally Britenia spoke, "Have you determined what it is that taunts you?"

The tension within Jicar drained as he slowly accepted and embraced the flood of emotions conquering him.

"I have." No longer could he deny what his heart was telling him. "You're my lifemate."

"I see," Britenia watched as Jicar stood.

He unfastened his vest and shrugged out of it. The garment dropped to the floor. Britenia swallowed hard. Her body shuddered with instant arousal. "This is a good thing."

"How so?" Jicar pushed his trousers down along his hips and then stepped out of them. He stood naked before her.

The rhythm of Britenia's heartbeat increasing and her chest heaved with longing as she watched his erection grow. Her mind soared with happiness as she tipped her head to look up at his face. "Because I love you."

Jicar expelled an ecstatic groan as he reached forward and yanked the sheet from Britenia's body, exposing her naked form. His nostrils flare at her scent and the sight of desire on her beautiful face.

She opened her legs in invitation and Jicar settled between them, on top of her, stroking his cock along her folds, kissing her mouth, her face. "I want you Britenia. Accept me as your lifemate."

"But I'm your enemy, Jicar." Britenia was acting much like his foe at the moment. She arched and pressed her pussy against his cock, her clit swelling with arousal her mind bending, her heart committing to giving herself only to Jicar.

"I'm calling a truce," he responded hoarsely.

And Jicar sealed the treaty by plunging deep inside of her, stroking into his wife with every ounce of emotion and longing he possessed, whispering to her, the mating words of promise and devotion.

The End

STRANDED

Shelley Munro

Chapter One

The bastard had left!

Cimmaron Zhaan stared around the empty transport bay, shock kicking her in the gut. She strode a tight circle to survey her surrounds--just to make sure. Her footsteps resounded in the cavernous spaceport. A worker droid scooted in front of her, and she snarled under her breath, sidestepping to dodge it. Empty. The echo of her boots mocked, underlining her stupidity in trusting anything the captain had said. The phrullin' male had taken off early, leaving her stranded with minimum possessions and even fewer credits to her name.

Stranded.

Anger burned her gut, and her hands fisted then squeezed as she imagined wringing the captain's beefy neck. The weight of the stares from the maintenance crew jerked her from pissed to controlled and inscrutable. Yeah, she'd known the arrogant bastard had expected her to act grateful when he'd suggested they while away the long voyage from Risches to Stavek by sharing a cabin. Cimmaron had turned him down flat, and he'd transferred his attentions to one of the lesser crew. But Campbell hadn't forgotten her slight. In fact, he'd gone out of his way to make life difficult for Cimmaron. Leaving her stranded on isolated Marchant was the latest in a long line of Campbell-created annoyances.

Cimmaron stalked past the maintenance men and their droid workers with her nose in the air. Inside she seethed. What the hell was she gonna do now? Campbell had told her to wear mufti while on leave, so she didn't even have a uniform to prove she was a pilot. All her papers were on the *Intrepid*. She stormed down a long corridor to the communication center. One hour later, the telecommunications tech put her through to the command of the *Intrepid*.

"Ah, Officer Zhaan," Campbell said gravely. He sat at ease in the pilot's chair, his tunic blindingly white while his dark eyes bore a trace of smugness.

Bastard. "Captain Campbell." Cimmaron jammed the tip of her tongue behind her teeth instead of blurting the obscenities she wanted to level at him.

"You were late. We had our allocated time slot to depart."

Cimmaron's eyes narrowed, but she refused to react any further, giving him the leverage to get her in even deeper crap.

"This will go on your record, Officer Zhaan."

Too late. Seemed the situation was already beyond mere apologies and groveling. "You told me we were leaving at second moonrise."

"First moonrise," he countered. "Officer Zhaan, I have noted on your record you are AWOL."

"You lied. You told me second moonrise."

The tinge of red on his prominent brow told her she should have held her tongue. His pointy ears twitched--a sure sign of impending displeasure. "None of the other crew was late back from leave."

Cimmaron's hands fisted, and she felt the heat of temper crawl across her cheekbones. Phrull, she was probably flashing gold with her emotions, sparkling like the backside of a glow-bug--an unfortunate side effect of being a Dlog. "Are you going to come back for me?"

"Return for one female. I don't think so. Officer Zhaan, I'd say you're officially screwed." A smirk formed on his lips, echoing in his sly eyes. "Over and out."

The phrullin' bastard. The need to scream swelled inside Cimmaron. She wanted to punch and kick and exert bodily harm on the slimy male. He might have screwed her chances of flying with the Coalition again, but she would get revenge. One day, when he was least expecting it. Cimmaron stood slowly and exited the communications room with precise steps, her back stiff with pride. The five staff manning communications had heard. It was obvious by the silence that even now spilled out of the room after her, taunting and full of ridicule.

Desperate to outrun her fears, the panic that threatened, Cimmaron stormed from the spaceport and pushed into the crowd of beings thronging the narrow alleys outside. Market day. Crowds of beings shopped for supplies to fill dwindling reserves on their short stopovers between destinations. Traders and hawkers shouted at the tops of their voices, trying to attract customers and extract credits. No doubt thieves trolled the alleyways looking for the green and the unwary with purses full of gold and currency to lift. She had no idea where she was going or what to do. Blindly, Cimmaron attempted to control the blooming panic, the knowledge that the captain's petty revenge had left her vulnerable. And in trouble. Her record would reflect the transgression unless she could prove her innocence. She'd have to travel to Coalition headquarters on Bezant. Somehow. It wasn't going to be easy with no currency to pay for her passage. The rumors of space pirates and abductions in this galaxy meant people were wary of giving strangers rides.

Deep in thought, she bumped into a short, blue female, almost knocking her to the ground.

"Sorry," Cimmaron said.

"Hoy, watch it," the female said, struggling to maintain her footing on the slick cobblestones.

Cimmaron grabbed the female, holding her upright when the crush of humanity behind threatened to push her over. "My apologies," she murmured in a formal tone when the danger was past.

The female righted the white cowl that covered her shiny, pale-blue head and glanced at the splotches of mud decorating the hem of her robe. "I look like a low-caste." A trace of alarm flickered over her face. "Phrull, I need this job."

"Job?"

"They're hiring at the club. I must go. They'll close the doors when they have enough applicants." The female darted through a gap in the crowds before Cimmaron could question her further.

The female's words kept reverberating through Cimmaron's mind. A job. A job. *A job*. A rumbling sound punctuated her thoughts, and she bolted after the female, elbowing her way through the alley crowded with market-goers as she tried to follow. No currency. She was starving. She had to eat. A job was the solution--the only alternative she had, if she wanted to get off this Goddess forsaken planet and exact revenge from that phrullin' bastard, Campbell.

In desperation, Cimmaron increased her pace, managing to keep the female in sight despite the crowds in the marketplace. The woman turned a corner, disappearing from sight. Cimmaron sprinted around the bend in the street. Where was she? Ah! Cimmaron caught a flash of white as the female entered a nondescript stone building. She ran, fear dogging her heels, when she noticed the door closing. In desperation, Cimmaron shoved through the door, muscling her way inside even though the bulky Maxiom security guard attempted to close it in her face.

"Just a phrullin' second. Let me in." Cimmaron kicked his shins, gaining precious inches when he stepped back out of range. "I want to come in."

The door opened a fraction more, and the Maxiom sneered at her. Cimmaron stiffened, knowing what he saw--mud-speckled trews and a unisex tunic that hid every single hint of a feminine curve. If she'd had her uniform on he would have treated her with respect, but his doubt was clear as his gaze traveled down her body and back up again. "You? Behind a bar." His single brow rose halfway up his bald head to emphasize his doubt.

Phrull, this job was bar work? Crummy bar work. Having her ass pinched and her tits grabbed was not Cimmaron's idea of a good time. But it was better than the alternative.

Cimmaron inhaled deeply, trying to force oxygen into her brain after her sprint through the market place. Her chest heaved under her brown tunic, each breath coming with a wheeze.

"Take a number," the security guard said, his tone off-putting as though he thought she was wasting her time. Cimmaron scanned the room, her breath squeezing halfway up her throat in sudden consternation. Maybe she was wasting her time. The rest of the applicants were clean, for a start. Well-groomed. Cimmaron eyed the nearest one. And they were little--compared to her at any rate. Feeling conspicuous, even more than she had earlier, Cimmaron accepted a white card bearing a number from the security guard and slunk away to find a wall to lean against in the hope of appearing smaller. In her work as a pilot she downplayed the natural good looks of the Dlog. It made things easier on the job, although it hadn't stopped Campbell from propositioning her and taking enough offence at her refusal to leave her stranded.

Cimmaron scowled, guessing the captain's next move would be to pronounce her AWOL officially. Everything she'd worked and strove for ripped from her grasp because one bloody male couldn't keep his gonads under control. She had to get to headquarters first before the *Intrepid* finished its voyage and returned to base.

The rest of the females and the couple of males in the group took a collective breath and straightened. Cimmaron slouched lower against the wall hoping she wouldn't stick out like pustules on an underling's face.

All for naught.

The man was tall. He prowled into the reception room like a sleek tigoth beast from the planet Dalcon. His piercing blue eyes studied the faces in the room slowly, taking his time, before they came to rest on her. And lingered. A frisson of awareness shot through her body and gathered on her lips. They tingled insistently until finally she broke down and moistened them with her tongue. The expression in the male's eyes intensified, making them darker, more compelling. Finally, his gaze moved on, leaving Cimmaron weak and panting. What the phrull had that been about? In confusion, she stared, trying to analyze the sheer need that coursed through her body, tugging at places that hadn't seen light, let alone reacted to a male in this way before.

He was tall, maybe a fraction taller than her. Unusual. Cimmaron towered above all of her shipmates and only felt at home on her home planet. His hair was the color of deep space. Black. But it didn't hold the nothingness of the uncharted territories. It glowed under the lights, the black-blue sheen making her want to touch to see if it felt as soft as it looked.

He turned to speak to the male at his side. Cimmaron hadn't noticed him at first but she saw he was much the same height. His look was more familiar, that of a local Marchant, which was why he hadn't stood out. The deep rumble of the male's voice tugged at her. Cimmaron shook, wondering what the phrull was wrong with her. She was in the worst situation, stranded with no hope of rescue, yet all she could think about was the male. The need to touch was a siren song in her blood. Her fingers prickled, her lips still tingled and the rest of her body was ... aware.

The male spoke. "I will see you in number order. Please form a line. Rico will show you in when your number is called."

Cimmaron scowled down at her number. Last in, she had the last one. Knowing her luck, the jobs would be gone by the time she was called.

The line moved rapidly. Some of the applicants were taken behind the bar and asked to mix drinks. Cimmaron knew if she managed to get that far, she'd gain a job. Years of saving to purchase her way into the pilot program had made her more than competent behind the bar. Not that this looked like a classy joint. The outside had appeared uninspiring--a building she would have walked past if she hadn't been following the female. The inside didn't look much better, although it was clean. She'd worked in better. And worse. Bottles of alcohol from the far reaches of the galaxy lined the wall behind the bar. A gleaming bar, but it had none of the ornate carving of some of the clubs and high-class joints. A dance floor. Tables. Maybe the place would look better when it was full of people and music. Two spiral staircases led to a mezzanine floor above. Cimmaron wondered what was up there, craning her neck to see. It seemed as though a being standing up there would have a good view of the bar and dance floor below. Probably another bar. Maybe private rooms for the rich or those who could afford to pay for privacy.

Time trickled past. Cimmaron fidgeted, trying to ignore the flitting looks she received. Her stomach contracted, and it wasn't just hunger pains. Nerves danced inside as she came closer to her number being called. Desperation. Maybe. No, it wasn't. She hadn't felt really rattled until she'd seen the male conducting the interviews. The casual line that had formed shuffled forward.

"Next!" Cimmaron jerked to attention when the security guard behind nudged her in the middle of her back. "You. Move it. Don't have all moon-cycle for you to dawdle!"

Cimmaron glared at the large male. She'd met his like before--all roar but no guts to back it up when things got tough. Her gaze crawled across his beefy face. She could take him with no problem, if she wanted. A soft chuckle had her whirling around.

"Come on in and take a seat. I'll be back in a couple of microts."

He held the door open for her, then disappeared, leaving Cimmaron staring after him. His scent--fresh, crisp. Green. It reminded Cimmaron of the wide-open savannah country and towering forests on her home planet of Risches. The alluring scent brought a shaft of homesickness. Despair. She would never see home again unless she managed to get this job. Not that she liked to stay on Risches for too long, not with her stepfather harping on about a female's proper place. Mating and procreating. Not if she had her way. Cimmaron generally only stayed two or three moon-cycles at most. Despite their differences regarding the way a female should act, she did love her mother.

Cimmaron sank onto an upright alloy chair, desperately pushing aside the rising panic and anxiety that tangled in her gut and writhed through her heart. Campbell had not only left her stranded--he'd left her vulnerable. Vulnerable was bad. Vulnerable was a stepfather who hated her and made no secret of the fact while he drove a wedge between her and her mother. Cimmaron scowled. She shouldn't have wanted to go home, but she did since she hadn't seen her mother for over one hundred moon-cycles. Before, she'd had the freedom and luxury of being able to return home when she wanted. On her terms. Now a dark cloud hovered above her head. AWOL. Phrull the captain for leaving her stranded.

A soft click behind made her backbone hit the back of the chair.

"So you want to work here." His voice was deep. Husky. It sent a shiver of pure longing pulsing through Cimmaron. Her gut sucked in while blood seemed to pool low. What was wrong with her today? This male--he wasn't her type. If she wanted a male she'd look to her own race, not an otherlander. And that was about as likely as Campbell returning and telling her it was all a joke. There was more to life than mating. And so much more than spending life as a slave to a mate.

"Yes, I am good at my job." True. She was a good pilot. Also a reasonable bar tender.

He nodded, his expression not giving anything away. He glanced through the open door. "Sorry, I'll be back in a few microts."

Tamaki made an excuse to leave the office. He had to. It was a matter of gathering his wits before he did something stupid. Like grabbing the golden woman, forcing her sexy mouth open and shoving his tongue half way down her throat. Hell, he wanted to do more than that. Confusion lay beneath the desperate need coursing through his body. In his job as manager of the club, he'd seen lots of beautiful women. He'd spent time with some of them on the upper level, fucking their brains out for mutual pleasure. He'd only dated, never felt the need to have the woman three times. Twice a date, thrice a mate. Now there was the kicker. He'd never wanted that before. He ambled out to the bar deep in thought.

"Problem?" Rico asked.

"Yeah." Tamaki jerked his head toward his office. "You could say that."

"You want me to get rid of her?"

"No!" Tamaki's reply was instant. No, he didn't want that. He had rather more sensual plans in mind. First he'd strip the ugly tunic from her body. It made her appear sexless. Instinct told him that beneath the brown cloth she bore a pleasing shape. It was the way she held herself, the proud bearing, the flash of vulnerability in her eyes that disappeared the instant she noticed she was being watched, replaced by a tough, no-nonsense attitude. Tamaki imagined sliding his hands under the brown tunic, fanning his fingers out to measure the width of her waist. And slowly moving them up to cup her breasts. He wondered about size. Shape. His palms tingled, and his cock woke abruptly, pushing against the placket of his trews with enough vigor to make Tamaki uncomfortable.

"Earth to Tamaki."

"Huh?"

Rico grinned at him. "I said, Earth to Tamaki."

Tamaki moved so the glossy hi-tech bar was between him and his friend. "We're on Marchant. Remember? Light years away from the blue planet."

"What's up?" Rico stared at Tamaki before his gaze moved down his body. "Ah. I get it. Wee Willie Winkie is exerting his say in the interview process."

"Get fucked," Tamaki muttered.

"Oh, yeah. And I'd sure like that. The microt I can talk my way into Marianna's pants I'll be sure to let you know. Hell, I might even take out an ad in the Marchant Communicator. Hire a market crier or something. Marianna's surrender will be worth celebrating."

Slightly diverted, Tamaki studied his friend and co-worker. Rico had taken one look at Marianna, a local female, and declared this was the woman for him. Yet he hadn't been able to talk the female into a date. Not within the club or a casual meeting in the city. Tamaki hadn't been able to understand why Rico wouldn't go with any other female. He glanced toward his office. Suddenly, it all seemed to make sense.

"I want her, but I can't fuck the hired help. It's against the rules since the company was sued for the Martian scandal."

"Don't hire her, then the rules won't apply," Rico said. "Go and interview the female and tell her she isn't what you're looking for."

"Lie, you mean."

Rico snorted. "Come on, Tamaki. You've done it before."

"Yeah, when I was young and stupid. Lies have a way of coming back to bite you in the arse."

"Hire her then, and keep your hands off. You're the boss."

Tamaki gave a clipped nod and strode back into his office. "Sorry about that. I needed to have a word with my assistant manager. I am Tamaki Grierson, the club manager."

"Where are you from?"

Tamaki found himself grinning. "Who's conducting this interview here?"

"Sorry. I was curious. I don't recognize your accent. The other male, too. He looks like he's from Marchant but his voice gives him away as an otherlander."

"We're from Earth," Tamaki said. "We grew up together in a land mass called New Zealand. We've both worked in several of the nightclubs in the chain."

The woman nodded. "I have visited the blue planet."

Curiosity crept through Tamaki. He wanted to know more about her, but bearing Rico's words in mind, he changed the subject. "Tell me what experience you have. Why should I hire you?"

She looked him straight in the eye, her golden irises surrounded by dark lashes that curled upward in a delicate arch. Her eyes were more elongated than his, reminding him of a cat. Man, he'd sure like to stroke her fur and make her purr. Tamaki strode behind his desk and sat, not wanting her to see his growing erection. Damn, he couldn't get his mind off having sex with this female. And despite knowing he was making a big mistake, he was going to hire her. Even if she didn't know a fiery beer from a guardian's kiss cocktail. Letting her walk out of his life would be an even bigger mistake. Aware he was skirting the rules but unwilling to let her leave, he continued the interview.

"I worked as a bar tender at the Lingam Towers on the planet Dalcon. I worked there for forty cycles. Once I began my training, I worked evenings and week breaks only at the Gallant Dragon on Bezant.

Tamaki was impressed. She'd worked at some high-class joints. She had experience so at least Rico couldn't call him on that. "Why did you go to part-time? What training did you do?"

"I am a pilot. I work for Coalition Shipping."

Tamaki straightened abruptly. "You're seriously over-qualified for working in my club."

Her golden eyes narrowed, emphasizing their shape. Her tongue darted out to dampen her bottom lip. Tamaki followed the move with fascination, lust jolting his cock to even greater prominence. His gut hollowed. She looked defeated yet anger pumped off her in waves. There was a story here.

"I had a personality conflict with my superior officer. The ship left while I was in the city. The schedule does not permit them to return for me."

The bastard had left her stranded. Her calm demeanor impressed Tamaki. Only the tightness of her body gave her away and the way she appeared to glow when her emotions were heightened. Not a shred of emotion showed in her voice.

"The job is yours if you want it. Can you work tonight?"

Cimmaron let out a slow breath. He'd given her a job. Relief made her giddy. "Yes. I can work as many hours as you need me."

"Good. See Rico about a uniform on the way out. The position is worth two hundred credits per week plus a meal while you're on the job."

Cimmaron nodded. At least if she worked tonight, she'd get a meal. Now all she needed to worry about was finding somewhere to live. "Do you know if there are any rooms to hire around here?"

Tamaki frowned, and Cimmaron watched closely, seeing his scowl disappear magically. He was a beautiful male. He tugged at hungry emotions she hadn't realized she had. The thought brought a soft, choked sound. Her pills. They were in her cell on the ship along with the rest of her possessions. Phrull, this day just kept getting worse. She didn't want to mate with any male, but without the pills to deaden the urge..... Maybe she could find an apothecary here on Marchant. The goddesses must be laughing. Her mother had told her she was silly trying to outrun her destiny, all because she wished to travel and command her own starship. Prestige and power before mating and offspring. Cimmaron thought it was a good trade off. She refused to live the way her mother did, slave to that male-- her stepfather.

No, there had to be a way.

"I have a friend who might be able to help."

Tamaki Grierson scrawled a name on a piece of parchment and handed it to her.

"I will see you later this eventide. Don't forget to see Rico about your uniform."

Cimmaron stood, heeding the dismissal. She'd get through her problems one by one, the way she always did. She had a job and maybe accommodation. She'd find an apothecary next and take things from there. Even if she had to steal to do it, she'd fight the Dlog female instinct to mate and procreate.

She'd fight for freedom and personal choice.

And she'd win.

Chapter Two

"I'm not wearing this." Cimmaron gestured at the skimpy costume she held up in her left hand. It consisted of strips of royal blue fabric. Small strips.

"Don't worry, there's more," Rico said with a chuckle in his voice. He reached into a storage cupboard and drew out a pair of thigh-high boots in the same blue as the strips. "Here you go."

Thigh-high slut boots. Cimmaron gaped for an instant before her mouth firmed into a scowl. "The boots cover more than the rest." She shook the blue strips and held them up doubtfully. "I'm sure they won't fit."

"The uniform is made from shrinkton fabric. When you put it on, the material will conform to your size to fit perfectly."

Cimmaron glared at the offending boots. No doubt they were the same. "I'll wear my own clothes." Even though the only clothes she owned were the ones she stood in. She'd get by somehow, and it would be better than having her body showcased for all to see. Loss of her pills was going to prove difficult enough as it was without men and women who frequented the bar staring at her, touching her. Unfortunately, the Dlog people drew attention wherever they went. Cimmaron shivered as stealthy thoughts of sex and coupling slid into her mind. Tamaki Grierson with his piercing blue eyes, his sexy form.... No! She would *not* allow her Dlog hormones to push her into sex with a stranger. Cimmaron thrust the uniform at his chest. "I can't wear this."

"All the female staff wear this uniform," Rico said. "No uniform, no job." Matter of fact, but the threat was there. He meant it. If she didn't consent to wear the uniform, she wouldn't have a job.

Well. Cimmaron's nose and chin lowered as pride took his announcement on board. "If one customer gropes my backside, I'll hit first and ask questions later."

"We have security men to take care of that," Rico said smoothly. "All you need to do is serve drinks."

He was laughing at her. Cimmaron's chin lifted a fraction. "All right," she said in a grudging tone. "What time do I need to be back to start work?"

"At moon wane."

"First or second?" Cimmaron accepted the jute bag he handed her and stuffed the offending uniform inside. She learned by her mistakes.

"First."

With a curt nod, Cimmaron turned to stride to the door and the Maxion security guard who stood beside it. His sneer remained intact when she approached, but Cimmaron noticed he edged away, out of kicking distance.

"See ya later, Hulk." And with a jaunty wave she opened the door and slipped outside.

The crowds had thinned during the time she'd been inside the bar and the narrow lane was almost empty. The closeness of the buildings made it appear later in the day than it really was. An elderly Marchant woman limped home with her shopping, her head lowered against the stiff wind. Cimmaron pulled the slip of parchment Tamaki had given her out of her trews pocket and scanned it with a frown. She should have asked someone at the club before she left. The crease between her brows deepened as a vision of Tamaki Grierson flitted through her mind along with the inevitable sexual tension in the pit of her stomach. No way was she going back in there until it was time to start work.

A rusty chuckle made the hair at the back of her neck prickle. Cimmaron's head jerked up, and she froze, aware of the danger she'd blundered into because she hadn't been paying proper attention.

"Hoya, looki at the Dlog chica," a voice said. "Whatcha doin' so far from home?"

Damn her distinctive coloring, and damn Tamaki Grierson. He had her so wound up she was probably glowing gold again.

The speaker was one of a group of Marchant youths who loitered on the stoop of the neighboring stone building, smoking curve pipes and drinking from frosted flasks. Jostling and nudging each other with their elbows they appeared harmless enough. She'd keep walking as if she knew where she was heading and ask someone else for directions to the lodging place.

"Where's ya man, Dlog?" The male at the front appeared to be the leader. Cimmaron watched his eyes. His cloudy white eyes told her he was high on vroom, the local liquor. Phrull. Her day just kept going down hill. She glanced at the others. Their edgy gazes darted up and down the street to check for witnesses.

Cimmaron cursed under her breath, and prepared to run if they attempted to jump her. Running was probably the only course of action available. One or two youths alone would have been manageable, but five.... She sighed, angry for getting into this position. If only she hadn't been so preoccupied.

"What's the chica doin' alone without her man?" the youth repeated, his smirk revealing a topaz jewel in one of his front teeth. It glinted in the light of the one of the flare-torches that illuminated the narrow lane.

A rich kid slumming it. Great. Cimmaron backed away, even though she'd prefer to box the male's ears.

"If ya don't have a man, maybe I'll take the position." The youth's smirk widened as his gaze strolled up and down her body. He made Cimmaron feel dirty, and the longing to box his ears grew stronger.

"Heard Dlog women are hot," another youth said. "Wouldn't mind some."

Cimmaron caught a whiff of his breath from where she stood. She backed away a fraction more, continuing to watch the leader's eyes for a hint of his next move.

"Sorry, boys." An arm snaked around her waist. "This one is mine."

Cimmaron tensed until she recognized the voice. Tamaki Grierson. She cast a quick glance at his impassive face. Oh, just excellent. Her new boss, the one male who actually tempted her, who made Cimmaron long to give her body, to indulge her Dlog senses. Why did it have to be him? S he inhaled deeply and instantly regretted it when his clean, green scent threatened to undermine the rigid control she kept over her Dlog sensuality. Cimmaron found herself leaning into his muscular body without even knowing how it had happened. And Tamaki, damn his hide, took advantage of her slip. Before she knew it, her back was pressed tightly to his chest and she felt the reassuring beat of his heart.

"Maybe not your woman for long. Ya shouldn't let the Dlog wander," the boy said. "Might find someone betta." His friends sniggered, egging him on.

"And you think you're the one to take her from me?"

Cimmaron heard the leashed danger in Tamaki's voice, but the youths were too befuddled on vroom to take heed.

"Move behind me, out of the way," Tamaki murmured for her hearing only. "It's about time these bullies were taken down. I'm tired of them harassing my female staff." Anger laced his words, and Cimmaron felt the tension rise in him.

Slowly, she edged away, but instead of stepping behind as instructed, she stood by his side. Poised lightly, she watched the youths, waiting for the moment they decided to make their move.

Seconds later, the leader launched himself at Tamaki. His buddies moved in a collective unit, backing up the leader. A mistake, Cimmaron thought, before giving a feral snarl and stepping into the melee. Lashing out with her right fist, she took pleasure in the crunch of a flat nose. The roar of pain and vicious cursing brought a grin. Hand-to-hand combat wasn't something that came naturally to a Dlog female preprogrammed for serving her mate, but she was a pilot, and they were a different breed all together. Cimmaron blocked a punch and kicked the youth's feet from under him. He toppled over, falling into an open drain with a mighty splash.

Tamaki knocked the leader to the ground with a bone-crunching punch, and the remaining two youths melted into the shadows.

"Can't you follow orders?" he demanded.

"No." Her chin lifted in challenge as she silently disputed his thoughts about the reasons the captain of the *Intrepid* had left her stranded. "Not when I'm perfectly capable of helping. I'm not a helpless Dlog flower." Her fingernails dug into her palms while her heart beat faster.

Tamaki smiled without warning, his teeth a flash of white in his tanned face. His dark hair was ruffled from the fight and Cimmaron had the absurd desire to fix it for him. She curled her hands to fists and resisted the urge with all her might.

The leader of the youths stirred with a muffled groan. He spat and his jeweled tooth fell out onto the cobblestones. He grabbed it and rolled to his feet with another groan. "You're gonna be sorry," he growled before limping away and disappearing into the shadows between two of the stone buildings.

"It occurred to me that you wouldn't know your way around the city. I'm going that way." Tamaki took her arm and arched a brow in silent enquiry.

A shiver sped through her body converging in her feminine heart. The slow, seductive flush of arousal seeped back to her mind. Cimmaron swallowed. She was not attracted to this man. "Tell me where to go," she blurted, trying to shake off his touch. It didn't work. Instead, his lips curled upward into a smile of incredible charm that made her heart beat even faster.

"It's no trouble," he said.

Sighing, Cimmaron gave in even as she silently disputed his words. The man was trouble wrapped up with charm and sex appeal. She was in trouble, and she knew it.

* * * *

Cimmaron dressed in the blue strips of uniform with misgiving. The cracked looking glass in her rented room didn't foster much confidence. The fabric lifted her breasts until they were prominent. The smallest strip covered her breasts but left nothing to the imagination, creating a cleavage big enough for hands to get lost inside. If they dared to try! The bottom half of the uniform covered her from just below the belly button to mid-thigh, leaving her belly bare. Then, there were the boots. The soft fabric of the boots matched the rest of her uniform. A modern fabric made with shrinkton, it adjusted to the outside temperature so the wearer never became too hot or cold. Cimmaron sighed and unzipped them. They were too big when she put her foot inside but she zipped them up anyway. They shrunk to her feet immediately. Cimmaron peered into the looking glass, studying the reflection with misgiving. With her golden blonde hair tumbling loose around her shoulders and the uniform, she looked like a showgirl from the planet Veyga.

She rolled her eyes at the sexy image that stared back at her. Cimmaron much preferred her pilot's uniform. The thought reminded her of all she had lost by being stranded on Marchant. Somehow, she would make the Captain regret his hasty decision. But first she needed currency. This job was the only option she had if she wanted to get to Coalition headquarters to clear her name.

Cimmaron grabbed her room key, exited, and locked up before she navigated the wide stairs leading to the ground floor of the boarding house.

"Ah, Cimmaron. Tamaki asked me to lend you a coat." Lissa, her landlady swept from her ground floor receiving room, her pale-green robes fluttering about her lithe body.

Irritation flared in Cimmaron. There he went again, trying to organize her. "Thanks, but I don't need--"

"Lordy, luv! You can't go out on the streets looking like that. You'll cause a riot before you make it past the tavern at the end of the road."

The woman--and Tamaki--had a point. "Thank you," Cimmaron conceded, accepting the long black coat her landlady handed her. She slid her arms into the sleeves and wondered if Tamaki and Lissa had a personal relationship. Likely, she decided, recalling the greeting kiss they'd shared. "Thanks again. I'd better go or I won't have a job."

"Take care, luv. Make sure you stick to the main roads where there are plenty of security droids. Don't be tempted to take a shortcut. Lots of thugs on the lookout for easy pickings."

"Thanks. No, I won't." Cimmaron wanted to screech but managed to keep a friendly smile intact. She wasn't an underling, barely grown with not a shred of commonsense. A being didn't get past basic pilot training without learning street smarts.

Cimmaron lifted one hand in farewell and left the boardinghouse, walking briskly down the well-lit lanes. She crossed the road before she reached the tavern, taking the landlady's words to heart. The streets were quiet. A cool wind blew, chasing everyone indoors. It was mainly a residential area, a fairly wealthy area judging by the number of security droids patrolling the streets. Cimmaron passed a vendor with a smoked capon trolley. The delicious scents of the capon as they roasted over hot coals made her mouth water. She had to force herself to keep moving when hunger pangs started.

A flash of movement in her peripheral vision made her whirl in that direction. A being slunk into the shadows, the cowl and robe it wore hiding its identity. Cimmaron stared at the shadows until a droid urged her on. Aware she'd be late if she didn't hurry, Cimmaron increased her speed. On arrival at the club, she rapped on the front door. The door cracked open. She wondered how customers managed to enter the club if the door was shut.

"It's you," Hulk said, moving aside to let her in.

"In the flesh."

Hulk jerked his head in the direction of the bar. "Rico is waiting at the corner of the bar for the new staff."

Cimmaron strode past him and headed in the direction he'd indicated. The club looked very different when it was full. Loud music pulsed through the large room. Strobe lights flickered, flashing across the faces of the dancers. Customers were three deep at the bar. Cimmaron couldn't see an empty seat anywhere. Two bartenders served behind the bar, both females, and they wore uniforms identical to hers. They didn't seem to worry about the brevity of the outfit, but Cimmaron felt her naked belly and shoulders rubbing against the fabric of the coat her landlady had lent her. One of the bartenders stacked dirty goblets inside a cleanser unit while the other served a group of giggly females. Their pale coloring pegged them as Marchant, but their outfits, made of shiny black leather, were pure high galaxy fashion instead of traditional full-length robes. They'd changed their hair color from black and looked like a bunch of vibrant flowers. Cimmaron pushed her way through the crowds, finally spotting Rico seated at the very far end of the bar.

Rico slid off his chrome barstool the moment he saw her. "Good, you're here. I wasn't sure you'd show."

"I said I would," Cimmaron said, her tone sharp. Talk about character assassination.

Rico ignored her flash of irritation. "There's a small room out the back where the staff keep their belongings. You can leave the coat there. I need you to come through to my office to sort out the formalities."

Cimmaron frowned. "What formalities?"

"We program all the employee fingerprints into our computerized system. That gives you access to the stock plus entrance through the main door into the club without waiting for security to answer."

Cimmaron followed Rico through to a small office that was only big enough for the desk and two chairs. The desk was covered with parchments and ledgers. Rico shoved them aside and pulled a glass disc out of the desk drawer.

"Place your right finger on the middle of the disc," he instructed. Once Cimmaron complied, Rico flipped over a lid so her whole finger was enclosed. He tapped a sequence onto a keyboard then pressed a button. The glass glowed bright red. Cimmaron felt a flash of heat, and a microt later the color faded along with the heat. Rico opened the glass lid, and Cimmaron slid her finger free. "You'll see wall scanners next to the stockroom and the bar entrance. Hold your finger up to the scanner, and the door will open."

Cimmaron nodded.

"I'll take you behind the bar, give you a quick tour."

Rico showed her where the various drinks were kept, where the chillers, the ice and goblets were stored, how to account for each sale, and introduced her to the other bartenders--Zara, a busty Pinkton with a head full of pink braids and Melad, a tiny bald Marse with tribal patterns covering half her face--before leaving her to it.

Cimmaron slotted into her job behind the bar as if she'd always been there. One bar was much like another. She served up steaming blue mercury cocktails along with flasks of vroom and the hours flashed past. Chances to chat with the other bartenders were few since customers lined up at the bar and drinks waitresses kept Cimmaron busy with orders.

"Hey, babe. Three vrooms over here." The speaker was young and well dressed in a slick silver suit. Another local.

Cimmaron leaned over to pull three vrooms from the chiller.

"Nice ass, babe." He reached over the bar to grab her breast when she turned back with the drinks. Cimmaron was too quick for him and his hand brushed against her bare belly instead. His two friends sniggered.

"Hands off," she said maintaining a pleasant tone despite her irritation. Typical chat-up lines. They had to flex their muscles, especially in front of their friends. "I'm here to serve drinks, not offer entertainment."

His friends sniggered again.

His dark brows bristled above his slanted eyes. "But you're a Dlog."

"So?" Cimmaron knew what he was implying but waited for the usual crude comments about Dlog women and how easy they were.

"Do you have a male?" His pale eyes regarded her calmly, but the pinkish tips of his ears betrayed his discomfiture at his friend's teasing reactions.

"Yes, I have a mate," Cimmaron stated bluntly. A lie, but if word spread about her being unmated she'd never get rid of the lines of males wanting an easy lay. The rumors weren't strictly true about them being free with their favors since their genetic makeup propelled them to mate. Usually, they mated within their own race but they could mate with otherlanders just as effortlessly. Cimmaron snorted. There was nothing easy about having a mate! Especially a Dlog mate since they tended to dominate. Hell, she thought with a silent snarl. Why dress it up with niceties? Dlog males were bullies. Cimmaron added shaved icicles to a silver container, secured the lid, and pressed the mix button. That was why she'd decided to train as a pilot-- Shit, her pills! She hadn't found a medicine man to replace her pills. Phrull. Appalled at her lapse, she cursed under her breath. She'd have to take care of the problem tomorrow. Already she was starting to feel the effects whenever she stepped to close to Tamaki Grierson. The mixer finished, but Cimmaron paused a microt longer. Why wasn't she reacting to her male customers in the same way? The Marchant youths hadn't raised a blimp on her sexual radar, not like her new boss did. She tried to think back to her visit to the blue planet. She couldn't remember having this reaction to Earthmen during the layover there. Cimmaron handed the smoking cocktail over the bar to her customer.

"Keep the change," he said, extending his hand toward her.

"Thanks." As a test Cimmaron let their hands brush when she accepted the credits. Nothing. She dropped the tokens into her allocated currency box. Something in her genetic makeup made her susceptible to Tamaki Grierson. There was an obvious solution to the problem. She'd keep right away from Tamaki Grierson--it shouldn't be too difficult.

Cimmaron worked for another two hours, mixing drinks and chatting with customers. The club became increasingly busy, and Cimmaron noticed most clubbers didn't need to knock for entrance. They appeared to have passes that allowed them access. Surely, they wouldn't all have their fingerprints added to the club's database. That didn't make sense. There must be some other means of entry for new clubbers. Cynically, she wondered how much they paid for the privilege since the club seemed so exclusive.

"Cimmaron, you can take a meal break now," Rico called from his seat at the corner of the bar.

Cimmaron nodded. "Thanks. Where do I go?"

Rico pointed her in the direction of the staff room. "Order whatever you want from the kitchen. Be back at twenty bells."

Cimmaron was ready for a break. Her feet ached from working in the high-heeled boots and hunger made her stomach protest. She wove through the clubbers, dodging the flailing arms of the dancers, and headed toward one of the spiral staircases that wound up to the first floor. As she reached the base of the stairs, a woman in a tight red gown brushed past her and sashayed up the stairs. Shortly afterwards a Nolan male sauntered up the stairs, eye catching in his tight leather trews and billowy white shirt. He disappeared into the shadows at the top of the stairs.

An arm curved around her waist, making her start. "You on a dinner break?"

"I wish you wouldn't creep up on me like that," Cimmaron snapped, her heart thudding erratically against her ribs. The warmth from his arm seared the bare flesh at her waist. It was a seductive heat, and she made herself pull away even though what she really wanted to do was lean into him. Perhaps even rub against him. A purr rattled deep in her throat as she stared up at his sexy blue eyes. A shaft of longing pierced her before his cocky grin registered. Cimmaron drew herself up sharply. Phrull, this man kept pushing past her defenses. She *had* to purchase some pills first thing in the morning.

He chuckled, unperturbed by her irritation. "I'm about to get something to eat. I prefer to eat in company."

Cimmaron found herself being propelled through an unobtrusive door near the base of the stairs, his arm around her waist yet again. For a male, he was awfully touchy feely, and she wished he'd stop. To counteract the feeling he generated in her, Cimmaron concentrated on the staff room. The room was smallish and connected to the club kitchen via a hatch in the far wall. A rough wooden table sat in the middle of the room, its top littered with a news tablet, a galaxy gossip zine, and several dirty platters and goblets.

"What would you like to eat? I'm having the special. Buff steak stew, I believe."

"The special is fine." Cimmaron's stomach let out an embarrassing rumble. Just about anything would do right now. She was that hungry. When he turned away to pass on their order, Cimmaron couldn't help but notice his body. So much for shoving him out of her mind. Her stomach hollowed out and it wasn't hunger for food this time. Every time she saw this man, she wanted him more.

Tamaki placed the order and turned around before Cimmaron had a chance to rip her gaze from his butt. The male smirked, his dark brows rising. "Like what you see?"

Hell, yes, but Cimmaron wasn't about to tell him that. Admitting it was the path to ruin. "Why you don't wear a uniform?"

His brows rose a fraction higher. "You'd like to see more skin?"

"That's not what I meant at all," Cimmaron said, her tone testy. Any of the flight crew on board the *Intrepid* would have heeded the warning in her voice. Instead, Tamaki Grierson stoked the flames.

"I'm happy to take off my shirt so you can touch me." He closed the distance between them and stopped an arm's length away. She could practically feel her hormones snapping to attention and that frustrated her. It wasn't fair that she should be slave to her Dlog hormones. Not fair at all.

"I don't do that sort of thing," Cimmaron stated, crossing her arms across her aching breasts. The rest of her body was communicating readiness to mate as well. Cimmaron knew she wouldn't get much rest tonight. "I'm not interested in sex."

Tamaki felt the need to prod despite being her boss and despite the non-fraternization rules weighing heavy on his conscience. "Oh, shame," he said, positive she didn't mean it. With her curves and golden eyes, she was made for loving. His body tightened at the thought of loving Cimmaron. "You must get very bored. What do you do for pleasure?" Her golden eyes widened momentarily and her luscious lips pulled to a tight line. Yeah, that had prodded her all right. Her gorgeous eyes flashed amber warning lights while her skin took on a beautiful golden glow. Tamaki wondered what she'd look like during the sexual act. Would she glow a more intense gold and would the color spread across her entire body? The need to know was starting to consume him and yet he'd only met her.

"I have my job."

But she didn't anymore because her captain had ripped her security blanket from under her feet. "Why do you want to be a pilot? It's not usual for a Dlog female."

Cimmaron's laugh was bitter. "I don't want to be trapped with a mate for the rest of my life. I don't want to be like my mother."

There was a story here, but he wanted her to relax before she returned to work behind the bar. If she stalked out there with her golden glow, every male in the club would want to try their luck. The thought didn't please Tamaki at all. Despite his reassurances to Rico, Tamaki admitted he wanted her. He wanted her so badly he was tempted to drag her up the circular stairs to the level above where mates were chosen and loved three times until the bond was cemented. But even more, he wanted to touch.

The need to kiss her pouty lips registered at the same moment he reached for her. His hands closed around her upper arms and he pulled her to him. His lips covered hers before she had a chance to react. She froze but didn't fight. Encouraged, Tamaki took advantage of her complacency. He nibbled on her lower lip and slipped his tongue inside her mouth the second she opened for him. The female leaned into him with a soft sigh, her breasts flattening against his chest. Funny, he hadn't figured she'd give in to him so easily, but he'd take what she was willing to give. He sank into the kiss, sweeping his tongue inside her mouth to explore. She tasted just as sweet as he'd imagined.

Addictive. His hands slid down her arms and behind her back. Firm, resilient flesh met his touch. His hands lowered to cup her butt and he drew her closer, fitting their lower bodies together. Her hips rocked, forcing a pained groan from Tamaki.

Without warning, Cimmaron jerked from his grasp. Tamaki let her go, his gaze intent as he waited for a verbal reaction.

"Why did you do that?" She glowed a beautiful golden color but her face remained impassive.

"Haven't you ever done anything because you wanted to?"

Cimmaron frowned, and he wanted to smooth away the wrinkles between her golden eyes. She opened her mouth, shut it again, then blurted, "I went to flight school." She thrust back her shoulders in a show of pride, and Tamaki manfully averted his eyes from her bountiful cleavage. Time for that later. "I learned to fly a spaceship," she said. "That's all I've ever wanted to do. I did that because I wanted to."

A bell tinkled, signaling their meals were ready. Tamaki crossed over to the hatch and carried them over to the table. A timely reminder, he decided, even though the need to kiss her again thrummed through his veins. He sat and waited for her to join him at the table. He shouldn't have kissed her, crossing the line between employer and employee, yet he couldn't find it in himself to be sorry.

Chapter Three

"What's up the stairs?" Cimmaron asked. Anything to avoid thinking of Tamaki and the kiss.

Zara shoved flasks of vroom into the chiller, filling the top shelf before she turned to answer. "Private rooms, I guess."

"What sort of private rooms?" Cimmaron frowned in the direction of the stairs. All night between serving customers, she'd seen male and female of different races going up the stairs. Not as many came down, but she guessed it was early if they were attending private parties.

"Two blooming venuses and a blue mercury." Cimmaron turned to serve the customer while she puzzled out the mystery of what was upstairs. She didn't like mysteries. Straight up with no bullshit. That was her preference. She liked to know what was happening in her territory. The club constituted her territory until she saved enough currency to leave Marchant. She continued to serve customers and dodge wandering hands while she calculated how long it would take her to save sufficient currency. Her stomach turned a nervous flip when she came up with several solar cycles. Phrull. Cimmaron glared at the spiral staircases. Looked as though she'd have plenty of time to solve the mystery.

A Luxor squared his shoulders, the bristly tentacles around his face stirring to attract her attention. "Two vrooms. On the ice."

Cimmaron grabbed two flasks from the chiller and poured them into silver goblets. She added several lumps of violet crackle ice. Immediately, the drinks turned crimson red and simmered with lots of tiny bubbles. She shoved them across the bar at the Luxor male.

"Do you know what's on the next floor?" she asked Melad, the other bartender.

"No idea. I haven't been here much longer than you," the tiny female said. She tossed her bald head. It should have looked ridiculous but Melad made the action seem surprisingly sensual. Cimmaron shook herself at the thought and bit back a purr. She was starting to see sex everywhere. Phrull, she had to find some preventor pills tomorrow.

Cimmaron cleared her throat. "Aren't you curious?"

Melad paused and shook her head. "No."

A hand reached over the bar and cupped a breast before she had a chance to move. "Hoy, six flasks of vroom."

"Take your hands off me."

When he merely laughed and squeezed harder, Cimmaron slapped at his hands. Once free of him, she backhanded him hard enough to snap his head back. His arm swept across the bar when he moved, catching the drinks belonging to the group beside him. A blue venetian cocktail splattered

across the ritzy white outfit of a plump Trateck female. Her
shriek of outrage was high pitched and droned endlessly. It
hurt Cimmaron's ears. The next microt, all hell broke
loose. Cimmaron stood back and watched with
bemusement. The Trateck female sprang at him, her face
turning a bright yellow. Her ears stiffened, transforming
from soft and floppy to sharp weapons. Before she could
strike, the Trateck tripped over a stool, knocking over more
drinks and upsetting other customers. Fists flew. Chairs
crashed to the floor and tables overturned. The security
guards came running as more customers joined in the
melee.

"What happened?" Hulk demanded over his shoulder as
he separated two brawling Luxors using brute force.

"He groped me," Cimmaron said, pointing at the culprit.

"So you hit back," Hulk said in disgust. "Why didn't you
call security? That's what we're here for." When the
Luxors resisted, he knocked their heads together. They
crumpled in a heap without making another move.

Two worker droids made soft whirring sounds as they
restored order, picking up chairs and broken goblets and
flasks and righting tables.

Hulk stood back, his arms folded across his chest as he
watched. Once order was reinstated, he turned to
Cimmaron. "If you do that again, you're out."

Cimmaron lifted her hand to her forehead in a snappy
salute. "Yes, sir." She scowled at his back when he strode
away to do more security guard type things. She served a
waiting Marchant female and her tipsy companions.

"Cimmaron, two reebs for my friends here," Rico said
indicating the dark-skinned male and female standing at his
side. They bore tattoos on their faces, the scarring white
against the darkness of their skin. Cimmaron wasn't sure
what planet they hailed from, but they were attractive
specimens. She grabbed the bottles of amber-colored reeb
from the back of the chiller, popped the lids and handed
them over. "Would you like goblets?"

"There are goblets in the room," Rico inserted smoothly.
"If you require anything else use the bar upstairs."

The male nodded abruptly.

Cimmaron frowned. They were going upstairs? She
scrutinized them carefully. They were obviously a couple.

She sensed the current of awareness that zapped between them, and her acute senses picked up the musky scent of arousal.

The male carried the two bottles of reeb and ushered the female through the crowds of clubbers. Cimmaron watched as they climbed the spiral stairs. At the top she caught a flash of a security guard, then everyone disappeared from sight.

"What's upstairs?" she asked Rico.

"Customer is waiting," Rico said, indicating the Luxor at the bar and ignoring her question.

Frustration curled in her stomach, mixing with the slow burn of arousal. Phrull! Cimmaron took the customer's order and served several other customers. Male and female from many different planets. She was the only Dlog, but then that was to be expected. A sliver of loneliness mixed in with the lump in her stomach. Her hand trembled slightly when she reached for a flash of vroom. Cimmaron curled her hand into a fist then slowly uncurled her fingers, exhaling with relief when the shaking didn't reoccur. Phrull, she had to buy pills somehow, or steal them as a last resort. Her sense of smell was becoming more acute. The sexual musk in the air was playing hell with her libido, and her hand had started trembling. Add Tamaki Grierson into the mix and she was in big trouble.

* * * *

"The new barmaid was asking questions about upstairs." Clear disapproval shaded Rico's words, and he underlined it with a scowl.

"She's good behind the bar," Tamaki said. "The customers seem to like her."

"When they're not trying to grab her tits. The security guards had to step in when she hit a Luxor male and created an all-out brawl."

Tamaki chuckled. "She's feisty."

Rico sighed. "Remember the rules against involvement with the staff."

"I'm not involved with her," Tamaki said, but honesty made him admit he'd like to have an up close and personal relationship with the golden woman. "Besides, she doesn't have security clearance to the rooms upstairs. She won't get up there without being turned back by security."

"Perhaps I should remind her that she's here to serve drinks. That's what she's paid for," Rico said.

"Give her a break. You're pissed because Marianna is ignoring you. You need--"

"Don't say it," Rico snapped.

"Sorry." Tamaki patted his friend's shoulder in a conciliatory manner. He'd never seen Rico tied up in knots like this by a woman before. "Why don't you ask her out?"

Rico's shoulders slumped. "She said no."

"Did she give a reason?"

"She didn't want to harm her good reputation by being seen with me."

Tamaki couldn't prevent a snort. The administrative council of Marchant didn't mind taking their rental or the increased currency the club brought to the planet. Previously Marchant had been a trading planet where travelers stayed overnight at most before moving on. The club gates brought new travelers to the planet. Tourists. "Maybe you should give up on her? There are plenty of other females."

"I don't want another female." Rico nailed him with a stormy glare. "Just like you aren't going to phrullin' listen to me about that Dlog female. You know you're going to have her despite the club rules."

"No." Tamaki shook his head enforcing his words, but phrull, he was tempted.

It was late morn by the time Cimmaron wandered downstairs to break her fast. Low voices pierced the stillness of the boarding house. Sounded as though Larissa had a visitor since she seemed to be the only boarder at present.

A sharp pain pierced her gut, and she pressed a hand to her stomach, pausing at the base of the stairs while she rode it out. Inhaling deeply, she made her way into the refreshment area where Larissa had indicated she kept basic supplies for her lodgers.

"Ah, Cimmaron. You have risen from your rest. You have a visitor."

A visitor? Cimmaron entered Larissa's receiving room, stopping just inside the door. Phrull. What was he doing here?

"Good morn, Cimmaron," Tamaki said.

Tamaki wanted to laugh at the dismay on her face. If anyone should worry about his visit, it should be him. He was breaking every single one of his personal rules along with the club rules by being here, yet he couldn't seem to help it. He'd woken this morning with Cimmaron the first thought that popped into his mind. He'd even come up with a decent excuse for visiting. Yep, no doubt about it. He had a bad thing for the Dlog female.

"What are you doing here?" she asked, not moving from her spot just inside the doorway.

They both ignored Larissa's gasp of shock at Cimmaron's bluntness.

"It occurred to me that you might need an advance on your wages," he said, trotting out his excuse without pause. He could lie with the best of them.

She swallowed, appearing distinctly nervous, even though she had no reason. "Okay. Thanks." Cimmaron glanced at Larissa before casting another uneasy look at him. "Can you tell me where the nearest apothecary is located?"

"Are you ill?" Concern filled him. She didn't seem weak or display any symptoms he could construe as illness.

"I ... No, I am not ill," she said.

So why did she need an apothecary?

"There's one quite near the spaceport in one of the lanes. It's not a particularly good area." Larissa's brows drew together in doubt.

"I know where it is. I will escort her."

"That would set my mind at rest," Larissa said. "Would you like some Marchant ale, luv? The servant is making a batch for us now."

"I--"

"I promise not to bite," Tamaki said. "Larissa will vouch for me." He didn't bite this early in the morn. His gaze drifted across her face and then lower to skirt her breasts. Damn, but he could change his normal practices. The uniform she'd worn at work had given him a fair idea of the areas he'd like to bite first.

"Tamaki, really," Larissa said.

Tamaki's grin widened. "I forgot you read minds for an instant."

Larissa gave a haughty sniff. "Believe me, I'm trying to block *your* thoughts."

"Can you read mine?" That was clear horror on Cimmaron's beautiful face, making Tamaki wonder at the secrets she harbored. There was something ... big. Had she told the truth about being stranded? Tamaki dredged up her explanation and shook his head. No, she'd been so indignant and visibly upset during the job interview. There must be something else.

"I haven't tried to read your mind, luv," Larissa said with quiet dignity. "For one, it would be very rude, and secondly, I never read a being's mind without permission. Tamaki's thoughts were so strong they battered down my guards. It *won't* happen again."

The servant arrived with a tray of ale. The spicy scent was rich and intoxicating, reminding him of the mulled wine his mother used to make during the middle of an Earth winter. The servant set the tray on a low metal table and silently padded from the receiving room. Larissa poured the steaming ale into three jeweled goblets.

Tamaki leaned back on the padded divan and idly scanned the hangings on the walls. The colors were muted because they were old but told an interesting story of Marchant's history and the battles fought to gain freedom from the Orkane.

"Luv, take a seat beside Tamaki," Larissa said.

Tamaki purposely kept his gaze on his surroundings, the images of mountains and lakes etched into the doors of a tall chest that was pushed against the wall.

He heard the squeak of her boots on the hardboard floor, the confident footsteps as she crossed the room to sit beside him. She claimed the far corner of the divan, sitting as far from him as possible. That wouldn't last for long. Like many of the items in Larissa's reception room it was old. Roll-together factor would have them sitting closely and probably touching in no time. Tamaki stretched, raising his hands above his head in a lazy move. When he resettled, they were much closer. He could smell her, an attractive scent not unlike the sea on a fresh day. His cock drew up, tightening beneath his trews. Last night's kiss hadn't been nearly enough. To hell with Rico's objections and to hell with the rules. Something propelled him onward.

Cimmaron hadn't objected to his kiss last night, and if she continued to be of the same mind he was going to make his move.

Cimmaron inched back toward the end of the divan, but Tamaki wasn't having that. He stood to accept a goblet from Larissa and handed it to Cimmaron. With both hands holding the goblet, she'd end up toward the middle of the divan. Grinning inwardly, Tamaki took a second goblet and sat beside Cimmaron. Their shoulders brushed as did their hips and thighs. A gust of air whooshed from between her lips. She shivered, a full-body shiver that jiggled her breasts and made him want to groan. He didn't know what it was about this female, but he had never been with anyone who turned him on so quickly with a look, a soft touch and scent.

Tamaki cleared his throat. "Do you like the ale?"

"It's very good." Cimmaron's voice came out low and sexy.

He glanced up, intercepting Larissa's look of worry. It made him wonder if she'd told the truth about reading Cimmaron's mind. The older woman had an insatiable curiosity when it came to her lodgers. He and Rico had stayed with Larissa when they'd been setting up the club.

Cimmaron rubbed against him, letting out a soft purr. "I've never tasted hot ale before."

Tamaki frowned when she rubbed against him again. He didn't want her drunk! He wanted a lover who was fully conscious and taking part because that was where they wanted to be.

"Perhaps you should take Cimmaron to the apothecary now." Larissa stood. "She doesn't appear well."

Tamaki wouldn't go as far as to say that. Her skin shone in the golden hues he found extremely attractive, and she was touching him willingly. She actually seemed to be enjoying it, too.

Cimmaron heard herself panting and knew she had to get to an apothecary *now*. "Which way do I go?" She stood and forced the words out with difficulty. Her body swayed. It was hard to concentrate when all she wanted to do was rub against Tamaki's body and purr like a feline.

"I'll take you." Tamaki touch her arm and it felt as though she'd received a shot from a ray gun. The current simmered inside her body, jolting nerve endings that were already wired and ready for action. Her nipples rubbed against her bindings, intensifying the reaction in her sensitized body. Cimmaron forced her legs to move and almost groaned out loud at the exquisite sensation of fabric rubbing against her moist feminine flesh.

"Hurry," she pleaded, desperate to get to an apothecary before she attempted to jump Tamaki. Why him? Why now after all she'd been through to escape her heritage. Cimmaron wanted to cry yet knew that wouldn't help one bit.

"Don't let any other male near her. Stay with her. Don't even leave her alone with the apothecary. Promise me," Larissa demanded of Tamaki.

Cimmaron fought the hormone surge inside her body, silently cursing out the captain of the *Intrepid* and every other male of her acquaintance. It wasn't phrullin' fair she should crave a male's touch so badly.

Tamaki supported her weight the whole trip to the apothecary, helping her negotiate the pedestrians that thronged the marketplace while she fought the demons inside her mind. Her breasts ached and each step was pure torture. Tamaki wrapped his arm around her waist, pressing her to his side. Her lips grazed the warm skin in the V of his black shirt, his green, spicy scent sending a series of shockwaves skipping through her body. He never hesitated, propelling her along, guiding her down one narrow lane after another.

Heat engulfed her body, and beads of sweat formed on her forehead. Images of two naked bodies writhing together formed in her mind. Tamaki. Her. A loud purr erupted, and the heat in her body intensified. Her whole body tingled on the cusp of orgasm. Suddenly, she didn't care as much about pills, about captaining a ship of her own or maintaining her independence. All she cared about was ripping off her clothes and forcing Tamaki to thrust his cock deep inside her womb.

Chapter Four

Tamaki had no idea what ailed her, but he was seriously worried. She kept rubbing against him and purring like a cat. Normally, he would have enjoyed the closeness and worked on taking it further, but it was obvious there was something wrong with Cimmaron. He was hoping the apothecary would know the cause and have a cure available. Tamaki half-carried her down the lane and shouldered his way into the shop.

It was so crowded with stock there wasn't enough room for more than two beings inside. Jars of mystery items lined the walls. Layers of dust covered every surface, giving the whole shop a musty, unloved scent. It didn't smell much better, reminding him of the stench of tomcat's piss.

"Hello?" Tamaki hoped Larissa knew what she was doing sending them here.

Scuffling came from a room out the back. The sound drew nearer until a stooped male dressed in a khaki green robe shuffled behind the battered counter. "Canna help ya?" He slurred his words together, sounding rusty, as if he didn't speak very often.

Here, Tamaki was at a loss. He didn't know what was wrong with Cimmaron. A quick glance confirmed she wasn't in any condition to answer a series of questions. Perhaps if he described her symptoms. "She seems hot and keeps rubbing against me. She's purring like a cat."

The male shuffled from behind the counter and peered closely at Cimmaron. "Dlog."

"Yes, she's a Dlog."

The male limped over to a pile of jars and unerringly picked up one. He shook it before tugging off the lid. A grunt emerged. "Six left." The male shook them into his gnarled hand before limping back to Tamaki. "Pay first."

"How much?"

"One thousand credits."

"One--"

"Take or leave," the male said.

Cimmaron shuddered before rubbing her full breasts across his chest. A soft flush highlighted her cheeks, and when she opened her eyes, they were pure gold. "Kiss me," she purred.

Oh, he wanted to, but there was something wrong with this picture. "What's wrong with her?"

"Dlog female must mate. Go on heat. Pills stop."

Tamaki studied Cimmaron in new light. She lay weak and compliant in his arms. Quite unlike the female who strutted with real attitude and took no nonsense from anyone. The golden glow was the flush of sexual arousal, not a fever or illness. "Are the rumors true? If a Dlog female has sex with a male they're mated for life?"

"True."

"How long will the pills last?"

"One pill last for a full cycle."

About a week, Tamaki translated. And the male had six pills. "Can you get more?"

"Expensive."

Anger exploded in Tamaki and it must have shown. The male took two hasty steps backward, putting distance between them.

"Hard to get," he said, panic on his wizened face. "No Dlog live on Marchant. Must wait for traders to come."

Tamaki took a deep breath, finally understanding the truth behind the male's words. "I'll take all six. Can she take one now?"

"Take a while to work."

Tamaki gazed at the female in his arms. She rubbed her cheek against his chest, a lusty purr vibrating through her. If she kept rubbing against him in that manner, he wouldn't be responsible for his reactions. She repeated the move, sliding against his groin. His cock reacted to her sinuous stroking, pulling tight and starting to weep. Tamaki gritted his teeth and attempted to hold her away from his body. She fought him, stronger than normal in her determination to mate.

"Hot. So hot," she muttered, tearing at her tunic.

Tamaki struggled to prevent her removing her clothes. "Does she need to swallow the pill whole?"

The male nodded. "With liquid. I get." He disappeared through the concealed doorway he'd entered via earlier.

Cimmaron stopped trying to take her clothes off, and Tamaki relaxed. Mistake. She attacked his self-restraint, brushing her lips across his throat and rubbing against his groin. Tamaki groaned at the sensation that washed through him, the tightening of his balls and cock. He found himself clutching her to him and rubbing back. She groaned, lifting her head and offering her mouth for him to take. Tamaki took what she offered before his brain had a chance to kick in. Their lips slid together. Tamaki's mouth opened in shock and Cimmaron's tongue slipped inside, stroking the softness of his inner cheek and contrasting hardness of his teeth. He shivered, knowing he needed to stop her before they did something they'd both regret yet contrarily wanting to hold her for a bit longer.

The elderly man appeared without warning and slammed a goblet on the scarred wooden counter. "Liquid." The water splashed over the edge of the goblet and several droplets ran over the metal to pool on the counter surface. The man fumbled with the glass jar and finally pulled out a single black pill. He extended his hand with the pill sitting in his palm.

Tamaki wrenched himself free of Cimmaron and grabbed the pill. He pressed it to her lips and handed her the goblet of liquid. "Swallow," he ordered in a stern voice.

Cimmaron turned her head. "Don't wanna."

"Do it!" Tamaki wanted to shake her. He was trying to help. She didn't want to mate with him, and although he wanted her, he didn't want to win her like this. He wanted her fully conscious of her actions and making love to him because she wanted him. *Him*. Not just a handy cock to scratch an itch.

"Kiss me," she pleaded in a throaty voice, turning her shimmering gaze on him.

"After you take the pill." They stared at each other, neither willing to budge first.

"Kiss me," Cimmaron pleaded, and she trailed her fingers across his face, caressing his cheek and tracing the outline of his lips.

His heart thumped so loudly, Tamaki was sure she'd hear and realize how close he was to losing it and giving in to the urgent desire thrumming through his body. God, he wanted her so badly his hands were trembling. Inhaling deeply, he offered her the pill again. "Swallow the pill, and I'll kiss you." Yeah, blackmail, but he couldn't take much more. She had to take the pill. She just had to before he cracked and crossed boundaries.

Cimmaron lifted her tunic to expose the tapes that bound her breasts. "I swallow and you'll kiss me here." She pointed to a rigid nipple beneath her tunic.

Tamaki swallowed. "Okay." The word came out with a hint of croak. He swallowed again and hoped like hell she didn't have any additional stipulations. He didn't think he could take much more.

"Deal," Cimmaron said. "Give me the pill."

He handed it over, still not convinced she wasn't going to chuck it out and jump him instead. In fact half of him willed her to do just that. Hell of a way to go.

She popped the black disc into her mouth and took the goblet he gave her with a trembling hand. She raised it to her mouth and tipped back her head. As he watched, she swallowed. His breath eased out in relief. Now all he had to do was wait until the pill took effect.

Cimmaron drank every drop of liquid before she slapped the goblet on the counter. "You have to kiss me now," she said.

"We'll need privacy." Okay, that was a good excuse.

"You owe me a kiss. You have to pay. You. Have. To." She punctuated each word by poking a forefinger in his chest. Her cat's eyes flashed a light amber color, but he didn't think it was amber for "prepare to stop".

"Please order more pills." Tamaki pulled a calling card from his pocket and handed it to the elder male along with several currency discs. "Call me when they come in."

"Kiss. Kiss." Cimmaron leaned close and puckered up.

"Pills make sleepy," the apothecary said. His gaze skimmed over them both before he shuffled out and disappeared.

Lord, he hoped the pills would make her sleepy soon. "Come on. I'll take you back to the boarding house." He wrapped an arm around her waist and breathed in shallow, careful breaths as he directed her out of the apothecary's shop. She wobbled dangerously when he withdrew his support and almost fell into an open drain. Tamaki grabbed her by the back of her tunic and hauled her upright.

"No further." Cimmaron planted her feet and refused to move.

"Give me strength," he muttered, finally giving up and scooping her off her feet. He walked rapidly toward the club, taking the back streets so they avoided the worst of the market crowds. Just before he reached the club, he turned into a narrow alley. Halfway along, he stopped and let Cimmaron slide down his body and stand on her feet.

She blinked like a sleepy owl. "What's up?"

"You need to sleep."

"Oh. Okay." She continued to stare at him in the same owlish manner before closing one eye in a saucy wink. "After our kiss."

Tamaki cursed silently. Talk about a one-track mind. He scanned his finger and the door slid open. He ushered Cimmaron inside and up a short flight of stairs. At the top of the stairs, he turned right to his private apartment. Rico lived in the apartment to the left.

Tamaki opened his door and Cimmaron sashayed, albeit with a wobble, inside.

"Bed, I think," he said, steering her into his bedroom.

"Good idea. We'll go to bed right now." Her smile was wolfish, and if they'd come face to face in his club he would have worried. Hell, he would have hidden behind the bar. It didn't take much more than a gentle push to get her on his bed. He tugged off her black combat boots so she'd feel more comfortable. "Ooh, good idea," she cooed. "Let's get naked." That said, she ripped her tunic over her head and loosened her bindings, baring her upper body to his sight before he could protest.

Tamaki backed up. "Ah, glad you're comfortable. You should go to sleep now."

"You promised me a kiss."

"All right." Tamaki stalked over to the bed and bent over to kiss her. He aimed for her cheek but at the last moment, she shifted her head. Their lips collided. Tamaki stilled. Her lips moved beneath his, tempting, threatening his wavering resolve to keep things strictly business. Her hands wound around his neck, massaging behind his neck, drawing him in. Her breasts rubbed against his shirt, and she moaned.

"Feels good. I need more." Her hand burrowed beneath the V of his shirt, her nails digging into his flesh. Cimmaron's scent tantalized, rich and redolent, reminding him of the outdoors and the sea. Tamaki breathed in deeply, savoring her scent and the warm female in his arms. Her busy hands scraped across his flat nipple, bringing a shudder of awareness.

"God, Cimmaron. You have to stop."

"But I'm wet for you. I need you inside me. I feel so empty. Please," she whispered. "Please make love to me."

A beautiful woman in his arms pleading for him to make love to her. It should have been a story with a happy conclusion, but he knew he couldn't give in to her. Once the pill kicked in and she realized what they'd done, she'd hate him. Tamaki pulled away, disengaging her arms from around his neck and pushing her flat on the bed.

She trembled, wrapping her arms around her naked breasts. "Please, Tamaki. I need you." She spoilt the plea with a wide yawn.

"Sleep, sweetheart. We have plenty of time to make love once you're rested. Okay?"

"I am tired," she conceded. Her eyes fluttered shut.

Tamaki stared, hoping she really had fallen asleep. He waited to make sure and was relieved to hear a tiny snort, a snuffle and then snoring. He gave a tired sigh. Crisis averted.

For the moment.

* * * *

Cimmaron yawned as she cleared off the tables in the club. Most of the customers had left, apart from a few Luxor stragglers. Normally, she wouldn't still be working but two of their cleaners had run off, declaring themselves in love. Cimmaron made a scoffing sound deep in her throat. She didn't believe in the faithless emotion. There was no such thing as love. Sex, yes. That happened between male and female, but love.... Bah! Males liked to dominate, and she wasn't having that. Tamaki and Rico crossed the dance floor deep in conversation, and Cimmaron scowled. Tamaki had helped her purchase pills and hadn't made a move despite her vulnerability. Most men would have taken what she'd offered, but he hadn't. She didn't understand why, and it worried her. She didn't like owing him.

"Hurry up and clean the stairs," Melad said. "Otherwise it will be time to come back to work before we're finished."

"Sorry." Cimmaron picked up a broom and dragged her weary body up the spiral staircase.

"What are you doing here?" Hulk, the security guard, demanded.

Cimmaron waved the broom in his face. "Cleaning."

"Hurry up," he snarled back.

Cimmaron shrugged. They'd never been on the best of terms since she'd kicked him in the shins. The male held a mean grudge. Half-heartedly, she started to sweep. Quite a comedown from flying a spaceship.

A workman trudged up the stairs, tracking dirt everywhere. His tools clanked against his hip with each step.

"They told me to ask for the security guard," he growled.

"I'll get him." Cimmaron grabbed the opportunity to see a little of the forbidden area upstairs. She strutted over to Hulk, her gaze darting left and right. To her total frustration, she couldn't see a thing. There were privacy guards over all the windows, but she noticed there were lots of rooms with glass windows and in the very center of the room, there was a seating area. Luxurious leather seats sat in cozy groups for beings to sit and chat in private. Over to the side, a small bar provided drinks and snacks, judging by the stack of dirty platters.

"What do you want?" Hulk snarled, interrupting her gawking.

"There's a workman here to see you."

"For the alterations. Tell him to come up, and you, get back to work."

Cimmaron cast a curious glance at the cloaked windows before returning to direct the tradesman to Hulk. The curiosity was going to burn her alive until she learned what went on behind the closed windows and doors. Cimmaron picked up the broom and commenced half-hearted sweeping again, working her way down the stairs.

"Good job," a husky voice said from behind her.

Cimmaron jumped, then whirled about raising the broom as a weapon.

"Steady." Tamaki chuckled and raised his hands in surrender. "It's me. I wanted to know how you were doing. We haven't had a chance to talk."

Because she was embarrassed and kept dodging him. She shrugged, giving into her irritation. "I'm fine." Yes, it was abrupt and rude, but she didn't want to throw herself at him.

And that was exactly what she longed to do. Cimmaron pictured a spaceship. She dredged up every hurtful comment she'd received about a Dlog female being a pilot. It strengthened her resolve to stay the phrull away from Tamaki Grierson. But because she wasn't a total bitch, she forced a smile. "Thank you for the other day. I appreciated your help."

Tamaki nodded, his grin strangely absent. "No problem. You almost done here?"

"Yes, just need to finish the stairs."

Tamaki nodded. "See you on the morrow."

Cimmaron applied her frustration to stair sweeping and finished in no time, her curiosity about the upstairs rooms as strong as ever.

* * * *

The next moon wane was busy. Galaxy rips had created severe storms that kept spaceships on Marchant for longer than normal and gave the crews some unexpected rest and recreation. Security was busy at the door turning away uninvited customers while others walked in without a problem since they possessed the special codes necessary for entrance. Cimmaron didn't have time to ask questions, but that didn't mean she didn't have them. Traffic up the stairs during the night was heavy, but even more puzzling were the huge number of beings who came down the stairs.

A rush of customers prompted Tamaki to jump behind the bar to help serve.

"What is up the stairs?" Cimmaron asked when the rush died down.

"Private rooms," Tamaki said, pinching her on the nose in a teasing manner. She glanced up to see Rico's scowl. The male made it clear he didn't like her, but she was at a loss to understand why. Shoving aside the thought, she returned to a more burning issue. "What sort of private rooms?"

Tamaki tweaked her nose again, and she felt his touch clear to her toes. She was taking the pills but they didn't seem to work very well in blocking Tamaki's charismatic appeal.

Tamaki smiled at her burning curiosity. "Nothing you need to know about." She was wary around him. Part of him was glad--the sensible part--but try telling that to his body. He seemed to walk around with a permanent hard-on these days. Rico had already expressed his disapproval. Clearly. Tamaki figured Rico was frustrated because his chosen was playing hard to get. And Tamaki kept reminding himself about the fraternization rules--for all the good it did.

* * * *

After several moon waxes and wanes, Cimmaron wanted to scream. The need to learn the mysteries of upstairs was killing her. Deep down, she knew it was her frustration at being stuck on Marchant, but that didn't make her need to know any less burning.

She stocked the chiller behind the bar before stomping off to the staff room to have a kafe before the club opened for business. The staff room was deserted because the other bar staff had grabbed the opportunity to hit the market for bargains. Since Cimmaron couldn't afford frivolous expenditure, she'd stayed. Restless, she swallowed the last mouthful of kafe from her goblet and jumped to her feet. She strode back out to the bar, pausing at the base of the spiral stairs. Hulk wasn't at his normal post. Before she gave the matter much thought, Cimmaron was sneaking up the stairs, using careful foot placement so they didn't creak. At the top, she paused again. No Hulk. She checked left and right, then darted to her left, keeping close to the wall. To her frustration, all the privacy screens were in place. She kept moving until she came to the last room. The privacy screen was fully open. Cimmaron peered through the glass window. A very large bed filled a good portion of the room. It was low to the ground and covered with a deep green cover so dark it was almost black. On the far wall she noticed a computer, but she was too far away to see the keyboard. Her fingers itched with the need to explore at closer quarters. After checking in both directions to see if anyone was watching, Cimmaron crept along the wall and tried the door. The handle turned at her touch, so after another quick glance up and down the passage, she slipped inside. Immediately, her heart thumped, her stomach prickled, and worst of all, her nipples pulled to hard nubs.

Tamaki.

She whirled around expecting to see him standing behind her but the room was blessedly empty. Slowly, her breath eased out. She inhaled deeply and the light-headed sensation eased. She laughed, a low, tinkling sound. Guilty conscience. She knew she wasn't meant to be up here. Cimmaron walked a slow circuit of the room. It was beautifully decorated, the walls a shimmering green, a lighter color than the bed covering. Beside the glass window, a dark green button shone like a jewel. After a slight hesitation, Cimmaron pushed it. The privacy screen whirred across the glass windows, hiding her presence from anyone outside.

Cimmaron prowled the perimeter of the room, feeling suddenly edgy and hot. Her uniform clung to her skin, almost as if the shrinkton fabric had decided she'd lost weight. It chafed at her sensitive nipples, and each step she took brought a new wave of heat. Cimmaron paused in dismay. It felt as though she was coming into heat again. The pills must have been faulty. Tamaki had mentioned that the male who ran the apothecary didn't have any more in stock at present. Phrull, what the hell was she going to do? For every step forward it seemed as though she took six backward. At this rate it wouldn't matter if she managed to save enough money for passage from Marchant because she'd be mated.

The sensual tingle in her nether region intensified, making her long for sex. One male's face sprang to mind, and she muttered a curse under her breath. Tamaki Grierson haunted her dreams as it was, and now he was stalking her waking hours as well.

Cimmaron checked out the computer. There were several buttons, but she had no idea what each was for since they weren't labeled. Probably for music and to control the lighting. Cimmaron turned a slow circle to survey the room. Pretty disappointing really. She had no idea what the big secret was and why this floor was off limits to staff. Since there was a bed, it was obvious the room was used for sexual liaisons. She spied a drawer built into the wall, and pushed the green jeweled button to open it. Yup. The array of sexual aids, ties and restraints confirmed her theory.

The click of a door behind her made her leap in fright. She whirled about, clapping her hand to her chest. Caught in the act. Damn.

"What are you doing here?" Rico demanded, his brown eyes narrowing in dislike.

Cimmaron had no idea what she'd done to him, but he made no secret of the fact he didn't like her.

"I'm ... ah ... cleaning." Pity she'd left the broom in the cleaning cupboard downstairs.

"Right," Rico snapped. "On the bed." He stomped toward her. "Put your hands in front of you." He pushed a button on the computer keyboard and chains appeared from a concealed alcove above the bed. Rico grabbed them and before she had a chance to protest, slapped them around her wrists.

Cimmaron leapt off the bed, but the chains jerked her up short. "Let me go. Now," she demanded.

"I think not. Don't want our secrets blabbed to the competition before opening night. I told Tamaki you were trouble. Who are you working for?"

"No one," Cimmaron said. "I'm not a spy."

"Yeah, and I bet you can't fly a spaceship either," he said.

No mistaking that tone for anything but sarcastic. Cimmaron drew back her fist and let rip with a good solid punch aimed at his nose. The chains clanked and halted a full range of movement. She missed him, jarring her arm instead. It hurt like hell.

"You can't free yourself so you might as well sit there." Rico wandered over to the drawer she'd opened earlier and drew out a jade green scarf. He turned and smirked at her. "Nice jade green to go with the rest of the room. What do you think?"

"Bugger off."

"Hmmm, that's not very nice."

Phrullin' man was playing with her. Frustrated by her inability to move and her stupidity in allowing him to restrain her in the first place, she glared at him. If he came within kicking range, she was gonna get him. Right in the gonads, she thought with relish. And she'd enjoy his pain.

He strutted closer, the confident smirk still in play. Bastard.

Cimmaron tensed, ready to lash out, then the strangest thing happened. A shaft of pure sexual need slammed into her, punching every conscious thought from her mind apart from the need to mate. There had to be something wrong with the pills Tamaki had procured for her. They didn't work too well. She was starting to feel like a wind-up toy. Instead of dispersing, the desire thrumming her body grew stronger. She could smell him--or was it because he'd moved even closer. Rico reached out and smoothed a lock of hair from her face, his touch gentle. Soothing. Lover-like. Phrull! Cimmaron realized she was purring and bit down on her bottom lip. Hard. When she glanced down, she noticed her skin was starting to glow. Funny how gold looked so good with green.

Rico cursed without warning, and Cimmaron jerked her head back, startled. For a long pregnant moment, they stared at each other. There was a flush high on his cheeks and his brown eyes were full of heat. Cimmaron sucked in a hasty breath. Please let him touch her again. Her breasts lifted as she fought to free her hands and touch him. To her relief, Rico cupped her cheek and trailed his fingers across her face again. Smiling, he tied the scarf around her eyes, shrouding her sight. She felt the press of lips against her lips. It wasn't enough. She needed more. A whimper escaped.

"Please."

Rico let his hand drift lower. Calloused fingers brushed across her collarbone, then lower, tracing the blue strip of fabric that covered her breasts. Her senses heightened by the dark, waited for his next move. Her nipples hardened to tight points, pressing against the fabric painfully. Cimmaron murmured her acceptance and wished he'd take a more aggressive approach. As if he could read her mind, he bent his head and took one fabric-covered nipple deep into his mouth. The jolt of pleasure was almost too much. Her knees buckled and she sank back onto the bed. Rico followed and slipped one hand beneath the blue fabric to cup her naked breast. Cimmaron moaned.

Suddenly, Rico's hand jerked from her body.

"Phrull." He bounded away from her as if she were one of the deformed from the planet Lepro. After taking a deep shuddering breath, he stood, his footsteps sounding hasty as he strode across the artificial wooden floor. A lock turned and connected with a definitive click. The phrullin' bastard had left her. Stranded. Again.

* * * *

Tamaki looked up at the sharp knock on his office door. Rico looked downright distraught. His mouth worked but no sound came out. Rico started to pace backward and forward in front of Tamaki's desk. He dragged a hand through his hair leaving it sticking up in tufts.

"What's wrong, man? You took terrible."

"I found Cimmaron upstairs in the new room." Rico ran his hand through his hair again, this time in a different direction.

Tamaki smothered a grin. Rico looked like a hedgehog. "It was only a matter of time before she discovered what we do upstairs. She's been like a dog with a bone. I think it keeps her mind off her problems."

"She's a witch," Rico burst out. His gaze slid across Tamaki's face before shooting to his feet.

Alarm surfaced in Tamaki. "Sit. You'd better tell me what's happened."

Rico dropped into one of the seats opposite Tamaki. "I found her in the room. She was behaving strangely, checking everything out. I think she's a spy for Gynorm Enterprises."

Tamaki picked up a quill and tapped it on a piece of parchment. "Go on." From Rico's agitated manner he guessed there was more.

"I chained her up." Rico shrugged irritably. "I thought you'd want to talk to her."

"And?"

"I don't know what came over me," Rico confessed, "but all of a sudden I wanted her."

"Wanted her?"

"Stop repeating me, dammit. Sexually! I wanted her sexually." He shook his head, a picture of misery. "I love Marianna. I've no idea why I kissed her. I touched her, dammit. What am I going to do?"

Jealousy seared Tamaki's gut, and he had to force himself to sit still and not react. Rico had kissed Cimmaron. A growl rumbled deep in his throat. His woman. He hadn't been patient all this time to let another man claim her, and especially his best friend. He studied Rico's downcast head. Not that Rico seemed thrilled with the prospect of stealing Cimmaron from under his nose. He needed a plan. Tamaki frowned and tossed ideas around before a plan formed. "Can we do without Cimmaron behind the bar for tonight?"

"Yes, I think so. If it gets busy one of us can help out."

Tamaki nodded. "I think we should let Cimmaron stew for a while upstairs. We won't open the new room to clubbers until tomorrow and keep it out of bounds for the moment. Are the privacy screens up?"

"Yeah. I locked the door, too."

Tamaki nodded. "She won't come to any harm?"

"No. I mean, she's restrained but she can move easily enough and lie on the bed."

"Good. Once the club closes we'll go and have a chat with Cimmaron Zhaan."

Chapter Five

Tamaki knew he should have felt guilty--hell he did feel a little remorse, but Cimmaron deserved it. She was gonna be spitting mad when they released her. He looked forward to seeing her, and part of him wanted to experience her anger alone. But he also wanted to see how Cimmaron reacted to Rico. He hoped it was merely time for her to take another pill, her hormones working overtime to get her to mate, but it was possible she really was attracted to Rico.

Rico stalked into the office. "Everyone's gone. I just locked the door behind the security man. The travel tubes are locked down until tomorrow.

Tamaki added his signature to a supplier contract and rolled the parchment ready for dispatch. "I'm done." He stood and made for the door. Outside his office, Rico fell into step beside him. They ascended the spiral staircase together and turned left to the newly decked out room.

"I still think green was a good choice for the color scheme," Tamaki said when they passed the privacy screen.

"I like it." Rico halted outside the door and scanned his finger. The lock disengaged, and he pushed the door open. They stepped into the room.

Cimmaron lay on the bed, her uniform in disarray, and her body glowing a brilliant gold. She must have heard them enter because she turned toward the door. Cimmaron writhed, the motion setting the chains binding her clanking.

"Holy shit," Rico breathed. He pushed past Tamaki and hurried over to the bed to unlock the chains. They fell to the floor with a metallic rattle. Rico leaned over Cimmaron and touched his hand to her forehead. He glanced over his shoulder at Tamaki. "What's wrong with her? What have I done?"

"You know she's from Dlog?"

"Yeah. Oh, you mean she's in heat?"

"I think so. She's desperate for a mate."

"Not in heat," Cimmaron panted. "Not."

"But you're burning up. You're glowing golden." Tamaki touched her forehead, too. Pleasure bloomed inside him. He glanced at Rico to see if he had noticed the reaction. Rico was breathing hard, almost panting. Tamaki grimaced. He knew exactly how Rico felt. It was as if every trace of blood had pooled in his groin. His cock jammed up against the placket of his trews. Painfully hard, all he wanted to do was get rid of the constricting clothing.

Cimmaron ripped off the strips of fabric around her chest, letting swollen breasts spring free. Then, she knelt on the bed and cupped a breast in each hand. Almost sobbing, she offered herself to the men.

Tamaki leaned forward and twirled his tongue across her golden nipple. Rico did the same, and Cimmaron stroke their heads, encouraging them with her soft whimpers.

Tamaki suckled her breast, but it wasn't enough. His clothes weighed him down, sexual heat prickling through his body until he thought he might burst. Tamaki suspected both Cimmaron and Rico felt the same way. He pulled away to strip off his clothes, pinching Cimmaron's glistening nipple when she started to protest. Rico ripped off his clothes, too, then as one they turned back to Cimmaron. They unzipped one thigh high boot each casting them aside. The boots thumped when they hit the ground. Rico pulled away the strips of uniform that tangled around her chest while Tamaki dealt with the skirt and the brief black panties she wore beneath. Finally, they were all naked.

A huge relief.

They toppled onto the mattress in a tangle of limbs. At the back of his mind he wondered at the strength of their reactions, but tossed the thoughts aside as unimportant.

Cimmaron pressed close to both of them, undulating her body and purring loudly. The golden glow of her body bathed them, patterning their skin with glints of rich color. Hands stroked breasts, massaged cocks and stroked dappled skin. A harsh breath escaped, blending with Cimmaron's lazy purring. A hand stroked across his flanks. Urgency ripped through Tamaki and his hand trembled when he smoothed a hand over her shapely ass and upper thigh. He followed touch with kissing, moving his lips down her body, licking and nipping at her flesh. Tamaki tugged her legs apart, pushing her flat on her back at the same time. The bed creaked and sheets rustled as Rico and Cimmaron rearranged their bodies. Tamaki leaned over Cimmaron's lower body, nuzzling at her pelvic bone and nipping lightly at the hair-free flesh. The scent of her aroused sex was like a drug that reacted on all of them.

Tamaki kissed the delicate flesh of her inner thighs and glanced up at the same time. Rico winked at him before bending his head to take the swollen tip of her breast deep into his mouth. The sight of her golden flesh and Rico's darker skin made him hot. Raw need pulsed through him. He had to touch her intimately. Tamaki licked a path the length of her cleft, tasting and lapping up her juices. Cimmaron mewed, her body writhing under the twin assault. Tamaki's heart thundered. His cock continued to ache, his balls painfully tight and drawn up high and close to his body. He parted her folds, baring her swollen nub to his gaze. Unable to resist, he lowered his head to taste her, massaging her clit with a light sweep of his tongue. Her flavor was wild and tied in with her scent, reminding him of wide, open country. Tamaki settled in, tasting and teasing and driving himself crazy in the process. He slid one finger inside her pussy. Cimmaron was so wet she took him easily. So he added two more fingers to the mix. A guttural groan sounded, and Tamaki looked up her body.

She'd taken Rico's cock deep into her mouth, her cheeks hollowing as she sucked. Rico's head was thrown back, an expression of intense pleasure on his face.

Tamaki's cock bobbed, a tear of pre-cum forming on the tip. He fisted his hand around his cock and pumped once. The friction was exquisite, but he knew it could be even better. Tamaki moved between Cimmaron's legs and guided his cock to the mouth of her pussy. He thrust slowly, gritting his teeth as her womb tightened around him, gripping him firmly, so sweetly while she stretched to accommodate him. Tamaki kept pushing until he was deeply imbedded inside her body. He shuddered, feeling a ripple clamp down on his cock. Tamaki withdrew and plunged deep again, setting up a rhythm designed to drive them both to climax. Not that it would take long. Tamaki gritted his teeth, the surge of pleasure shimmering through his balls just out of reach.

"Deeper," Rico growled, his voice thick with passion.

Cimmaron took him deeper into her mouth, automatically following instructions. Pleasure shimmered through her body, her breasts, her pussy. She swirled her tongue across the crown of Rico's cock, enjoying the taste of him as much as she loved the full sensation of Tamaki filling her womb. A purr rumbled deep in her throat. Rico pulled back, then thrust back deep into her mouth. Cimmaron squeezed her eyes closed and concentrated on every sensation. The taste, the feel and the sounds as the three of them moved together striving for the magical moment of fulfillment.

The two men moved in counterpoint and increasingly faster. Flesh slapped against flesh. A hand squeezed her breast, and Cimmaron bucked at the exquisite shaft of pleasure that speared her body. Her eyes flickered open just as Rico grasped and massaged her other breast, branding her flesh and causing a corresponding heat in her sex. Desire, liquid and molten washed over her. Her womb clenched tightly around Tamaki's cock. He thrust deep, stoking the fire burning inside, pistoning his hips. The fingers grasping her breasts became rougher, Rico's cock harder and his tempo more urgent. It was a delicious assault, building sensation inside her higher and higher. The light surrounding her intensified until she glowed a brilliant gold. Tamaki thrust yet again, his cock brushing her engorged clit. Cimmaron groaned around Rico's cock. Hot spurts of cum shot into her mouth just as her body convulsed with the force of her release. She swallowed rapidly, waves of pleasure roaring through her. She was dimly aware of Tamaki spilling his seed, his guttural moan.

Rico pulled from her mouth and settled down at her side. Tamaki withdrew and stroked his hand down her body. He kissed her slowly and lingeringly, slipping his tongue into her mouth and lazily stroking before pulling away. Rico took his turn, kissing her deeply, exploring her mouth. Tasting her. He pulled away and smiled at her before stretching out and flopping back on the bed. Tenderness welled in her and she cuddled up to his side, plastering her damp body next to him.

She glanced over at Tamaki. "Come here," she whispered. "I need to touch you, too."

Tamaki trailed a lazy hand over her face as he drew close. He placed tiny kisses, tantalizingly brief across her face and then settled so she was sandwiched between the two men. Warm and cozy, she felt suddenly tired. Her eyes flickered closed and she fell asleep with a smile on her face.

A lot later, she woke to hands stroking her body. Masculine voices hummed as fingers lightly circled her breasts and probed her moist folds. A finger teased across her nub and lower, gathering cream. Languid and lazy hands and fingers woke her body, teasing her puckered rosette, sliding across her clit. She trembled with sensual awareness, her heart thundering as frissons of excitement poured through her body. A finger probed her anus. Another thrust into her pussy, and the sensation of two fingers thrusting into her at the same time sent her soaring high. Cimmaron kissed a shoulder, caressed a hip. Smooth skin. Masculine skin. Her hands glided across hard muscles, and she followed this up with tasting. Cimmaron squeezed her eyes closed and concentrated on her body. The fingers that filled her body with delicious fullness. The brush of a thumb across her swollen bud. Another finger pushed deep into her dark hole, stretching her to the point of pain. She inhaled deeply, savoring the salty tang of sweat, the faint scent of soap and the musky aroma of sex.

Even the intense fullness. Cimmaron arched her body, sensations piling on top of one another. Her hands wandered lower to grasp the steely hardness of an arousal. Cimmaron hummed her approval when she felt the pearl of cum beaded on the crown. She pumped with slow even strokes and was rewarded by a masculine groan.

The fingers probing her anus pulled out, and she could have howled her disappointment. "Please don't stop," she begged.

A husky chuckle met her demand. Cimmaron licked her lips, about to complain again. But to her relief, seconds later, competent hands spread cool lubricant over her rosette. Her stomach muscles quivered while fingers continued to pump lazily deep into her womb.

"You're very wet," a husky voice murmured near her ear.

Tamaki. Her body softened and a gush of cream moistened her body even further. His thumb glided around the rim of her clitoris. Teasing without giving her enough pressure.

"More," she whispered hoarsely. Her plea did nothing to ease the teasing. Just when she thought she couldn't bear it for a moment longer, the blunt head of a cock pushed against her rosette. Cimmaron froze.

"Steady, sweetheart." Tamaki stroked her breasts, teasing her nipples to aching prominence. He bent down to take her into his mouth, his lips closing gently around her nipple. At the same time the pressure increased as a cock pushed into her anus. Cimmaron tensed.

"Easy," Tamaki soothed. "This will make you feel really good."

"But it hurts," Cimmaron snapped.

"Does this hurt?" Tamaki's fingers smoothed down her body to part her folds and this time, he massaged her clit. A shiver racked her body at the same time as the pain intensified. Rico kept the pressure up while Tamaki pushed her higher, stroking in an instinctive rhythm that made the pain bearable. He stroked her clit with clever fingers. Cimmaron gasped, sucking in a wildly excited breath. Rico pushed past the ring of muscle just as she spasmed, filling her completely, impossibly full.

Before she had a chance to take a breath, Tamaki slipped inside her with a powerful thrust of his body. He moaned low at the back of his throat. Cimmaron gasped as tiny tremors continued deep in her womb.

The men moved together. She could feel both of them deep in her womb as they thrust. Desire kicked in her belly. Her heart thundered. Tamaki pressed close when he thrust. He took her lips in an urgent kiss. Cimmaron gave a small start when his teeth bit down on her bottom lip. The small pain ricocheted through her body until the sensations fizzled and bubbled like heady cacjuice. They overwhelmed her. She felt so full. So on fire. A throaty groan escaped as she shuddered with helpless pleasure.

* * * *

The six-bells alarms jerked Tamaki from a deep sleep. Groggily, he opened his eyes, his head feeling fluffy as if he'd drunk too much reeb or vroom the evening before. Warmth surrounded him instead of the normal morning chills common to Marchant. He yawned and stretched lazily, snapping to full alertness when his hand landed on a warm flesh. A breast. A masculine groan had him jackknifing upward. He stared in consternation at Rico and Cimmaron, his brain pounding in alarm. Phrull, exactly what had happened the previous evening? He looked at Rico, his best friend and shuddered. He hadn't? They hadn't? He shook her head, negating the idea even as it formed.

Slowly, images seeped into his brain and his breath hissed out in relief. A little three on three action. Yeah. But he and Rico hadn't done anything more than touch. As he stared in consternation at his friend, Rico's eyes opened.

Rico sat up, his olive complexion a distinct green. "Shit, it wasn't a dream."

"No," Tamaki conceded, trying to stem the jealousy that rippled through him at the idea of anyone but him being intimate with Cimmaron. Last night it hadn't seemed to matter, but now...

"What is Marianna going to say? She'll never have me now." Horror laced Rico's words. "And what about the fraternization rule? We'll lose our jobs."

Between them Cimmaron stirred. Tamaki knew to the microt when she realized where she was and remembered. She sprang from the bed and tensed, her face freezing in an impassive expression. For another microt they all stared at each other.

"What the phrull happened to us last night?" she demanded breaking the taut silence. "I didn't want to mate with either of you, with any male," she said in frustration. "I don't want to spend my life waiting on a male." She raised her arms above her head and flexed her body. The move lifted her breasts, snaring Tamaki's gaze. To his consternation, his cock stirred. He wanted her. Again.

"I don't feel mated," she murmured. "Maybe it will be all right. Dlog never...." She shrugged, dark red appearing on her exotic cheekbones. "We don't have multi partners. I don't think it's possible to bond with two males."

Well, shit. He didn't do multi partners either, and he knew Rico was of the same persuasion.

"How can it be all right?" Rico demanded tersely. He grabbed up his clothes and shoved his feet into his trews in angry, jerky moves. "I love Marianna."

"You don't have to tell her," Tamaki said. He sure as hell wasn't about to tell anyone about their hot session.

"I believe in honesty in a relationship," Rico snarled. He refused to meet Tamaki's gaze, and Tamaki couldn't exactly blame him. Waking up in bed with your best friend wasn't exactly a great start to the day.

"There's such a thing as too much honesty," Tamaki said, aware his friend was hurting. Truth to tell, he wasn't exactly happy with the situation. He didn't understand how it had happened. He'd had sex with an employee. Two, if he added Rico to the equation. Tamaki puffed out a frustrated breath. Too late now. They couldn't undo what was done.

He turned to study Cimmaron.

"Oh-oh. Don't look at me like that." Cimmaron bounded off the bed, scrambling for her clothes. "I refuse to have sex with you again." She eyed his erection with suspicion and backed up a little more as if he might jump her.

Despite the gravity of the situation Tamaki wanted to laugh because the idea was at the back of his mind. Cimmaron eyed his body, and the tension in the room ratcheted sharply upward. His cock jerked. Oh, yeah, his whole body liked the idea.

"I'm going to see Marianna." Rico stomped out of the room, slamming the door shut after him.

Privacy.

He prowled toward her.

Cimmaron scooped up her uniform and held it in front of her. "Keep away from me." Her eyes narrowed, but he saw the golden glow in her almond-shaped eyes. She wanted him too, and it scared her.

"I'm getting my clothes." Tamaki made sure his face appeared the picture of innocence while he grabbed up his clothes. Reluctantly, he stepped into his trews, maneuvering the fabric carefully over his erection, then shrugged into a shirt. He watched Cimmaron all the while, his pulse rate thudding in an erratic manner. Twice a date, thrice a mate...

He was her boss. He needed to keep reiterating the fact because it tempered the need simmering through him to grab. To touch. To sink into her warmth again. Then there was the mating thing. He only ever dated. He never saw a woman a second time let alone the third time needed to cement a relationship. What most customers didn't realize was that the primary purpose of the club was getting couples together. Helping male and female find mates. Life mates. If a couple met once or twice it counted as a date. If they came together a third time and made love they were officially mated and bound together for life. Tamaki had never wanted a mate before because of his transient life style. The club managers moved often. It was a way of keeping them fresh and helping the clubs grow in popularity. Then there was the strict no-fraternization rule.

As far as he knew none of the managers were mated. He didn't think it was a prerequisite. It just happened that way. Cimmaron moved, interrupting his musing.

"Where are you going?"

"Back to the boarding house. I need to wash and take a pill. Not that they seem to be doing much good."

"I'll check with the apothecary to see if further supplies have arrived, but he seemed to think it would take some time."

"I can't afford them," Cimmaron said, her frustration evident from the fisted hands and taut stance. "What are these rooms for?"

"They're for customers who wish for privacy."

"Huh. That's obvious. What else? How do customers get up here? I've seen some walk up the stairs but not enough to keep business flowing."

"Hmm." Tamaki smiled inwardly. He could tell her, but generally they kept the staff from the downstairs part of the enterprise in the dark. Customers traveled from other planets to Marchant specifically for the purpose of having a night of pleasure or some to find a mate. Customers came via word of mouth. They didn't need to advertise since Tamaki had the rooms filled every night.

Cimmaron pulled the door open, turning to leave.

"See you later," Tamaki said.

Cimmaron nodded but fear kicked her in the gut. Whatever had possessed her to have sex? With two men? According to what they were taught by the matriarchs in the family it only took one time. A male offered. They accepted and did the deed, then they were mated until death parted them. The elders had described the mating bonds like invisible chains that clicked into place as soon as bodily fluids were exchanged during the sexual act. Cimmaron didn't feel different. She frowned, purposely striding out to put distance between them. There were no invisible chains pulling her back to Tamaki. She continued her loose-limbed stride down the passageway, past the other rooms that were still privacy screened and down the spiral staircase. Then another thought occurred. She froze mid-step, almost toppling down the last three stairs in her stunned stupor. Perhaps she was mated to Rico?

Cimmaron's heart stalled for a beat. Phrull, no! They couldn't be mated. Rico didn't like her, and he made no secret of his dislike. It was mutual. Or so she'd thought. Cimmaron scowled, acknowledging the truth as she walked to the door leading to the street outside. She'd enjoyed the sex last night.

"A threesome." Cimmaron curled her top lip in a show of disgust and grabbed her coat. "A phrullin' threesome." What had she been thinking? After ripping the door open, she stalked through and slammed it shut, taking great satisfaction from the loud echo. An elderly beggar, stooped and malformed, limped up to her holding out a battered vroom flask that had been cut in half. Cimmaron indicated the lack of pockets in her uniform, drawing a reluctant grin from the beggar. His front teeth were missing, probably sold to procure currency.

She thought about Rico. She thought about Tamaki. A shiver rippled through her. She'd wanted to walk back to Tamaki and run her hands over his naked chest. And the idea of following the path of her hands with her mouth had occurred soon afterward.

Cimmaron stewed until it was time to return to the club for work. She lectured and told herself it was okay to make mistakes. Mistakes were fine as long as you learned from them. Mistakes were fine as long as you didn't repeat them. She wasn't stupid. Any time she had sex with a male was a risk.

"I will not have sex with that male. I will not," Cimmaron muttered as she held her finger up to the scanner outside the club.

"Shouldn't you wait for him to ask first?" a bright spark called from the front of the line that had formed to enter the club.

"Mind your business," Cimmaron snarled, mortified that someone had caught her talking to herself. She usually exerted more control.

The door opened and Hulk peered out.

He grunted. "You."

"Yeah," Cimmaron snarled. "Deal with it." She didn't wait for an answer but stormed into the club.

After dumping the jacket her landlady had lent her inside the staff room, she headed behind the bar to help set up.

The first person she saw was Tamaki. Her footsteps faltered, then she halted completely. It felt as though someone had punched her hard in the chest. Every particle of air eased from her lungs and she panted, trying desperately to replace it. His scent seemed to swallow her whole and a spark ignited in her pussy. Panic roared through her. Stupid Dlog hormones. She'd taken a pill before returning to work. Maybe her stepfather was right, she thought still in panic mode. Maybe there was no way to control the Dlog genes, no way to outrun her heritage. Maybe Tamaki was her fate.

There were worse ways to go, a voice whispered through her head.

Cimmaron drew a sharp breath and reached for a stack of drink mats ready to set out on the bar. Her hand trembled violently, and she snatched it away, hiding it at her side.

"Cimmaron." His husky voice pushed her traitorous body even harder. Her breasts pulled tight, and her stomach seemed to hollow out. She wanted to turn around and step right into his arms. Another tremor shook her body.

"Cimmaron?" He touched her shoulder, and she felt it right to the tips of her toes. They curled upward inside her boots. She was not going to succumb to him again. No matter how much she craved his touch. She was strong. She was a pilot, dammit.

"Are you okay?"

Cimmaron couldn't look at him without giving away how much she wanted him. Like a fire, the need burned inside. "Fine," she muttered, trying to control the shaking of her hands as she started to set up the bar.

"That's good," he said. "Melad has called in sick with Mercury space flu. I'm going to work the bar tonight in her place."

Cimmaron managed a nod of assent. Oh, joy. An evening of torture by close association. She only hoped she didn't break down and start drooling or even worse lick. No! Worse than that would be if she crash-tackled him and licked. Cimmaron shuddered, wanting to carry out the self-prohibited actions. Desperately. Hell, maybe she would even kiss.

Aware that he expected her to speak, she said, "It's good we won't be short staffed. There was a big line of customers waiting outside. Should be busy."

"Yeah, the space storms are keeping most of the ships grounded."

It seemed as though he might linger and chat.

"I'll go to the cellar to get some crates of vroom." Yes, she was a coward. Running away. But it was either that or she'd act on the urgent need to grab him. Phrull, what a mess. Cimmaron forced herself to stomp down to the cellar. If she ever came face to face with the captain of the *Intrepid* again, she was gonna thump him through to the next galaxy. This was his fault.

The club opened not long after she finished stocking the shelves. Cimmaron made sure she worked the opposite end of the bar to Tamaki, dispensing drinks efficiently. Grumbles about the space storms were few since it wasn't often that crews had leave in Marchant. The bar did a roaring trade. The customers were three and four deep at the bar, the dance-floor music loud, and the crowd jovial.

"Hey, beautiful. How about a drink down here?"

A pang of envy struck Cimmaron hard when she saw their uniforms. Space jockeys out for a little recreation. "Sure. Won't be long." Cimmaron finished the carousal cocktails she was mixing for the blue skinned Darians before moving toward the pilots.

"Hi, boys. What will it be?"

"I'd like hot sex laced with you," a golden-haired stud murmured.

Cimmaron shook her head and grinned at the same time. "Not in this lifetime, but I can get you a drink."

"Can't blame a guy for trying." Blondie leaned close, and Cimmaron sensed rather than saw Tamaki's interest in the conversation. An idea formed. Her smile brightened.

"Drink?"

"Don't mind him. He's a terrible flirt," another of the pilots said.

"Takes all kinds." C immaron shrugged allowing her grin to remain in place. She'd show Tamaki how much the previous night meant to her.

"We'll have two vroom, a reeb and three blue venetians," Blondie said.

"Coming right up." Cimmaron walked away with an extra sway in her step. The prickling of her skin told her they watched every move with interest. She bent over to grab two bottles of vroom and the reeb from the chiller. A whistle pierced the air, carrying above the pounding beat of the music. Cimmaron glanced over her shoulder and winked at the pilots before turning back to the task at hand. After placing the flasks on the bar, she made the cocktails and accepted payment with a smile. She moved on to serve the next customer. Another vroom. Didn't people realize the stuff rotted their brains?

"What are you doing?" Tamaki asked in an undertone. His warm breath skimmed across her cheek when he leaned close.

Cimmaron tossed her head, putting precious distance between them, and fought the weakness in her knees. "Merely being friendly."

"Didn't look like that to me."

"What? I'm not meant to act pleasantly toward the customers?"

Tamaki cast a quick look toward the group of raucous pilots. "Not that friendly."

"I work here. As long as I do my job you have no cause for complaint," Cimmaron snapped. She stalked away, her back straight and the hairs at the back of her neck prickling with danger the whole time. Throughout the evening he kept looking at her. Not that she caught him out, but she sensed it. Her body simmered in a state of arousal for the whole session, an annoying prickle rippling across her skin.

"Stop looking at me," she muttered. Edgy and off-balance, she wanted to lash out with more than words.

"Merely observing your technique," he said smoothly. "I need someone to train some new staff."

"Not me," Cimmaron fired back. Luckily a customer stepped up to the bar wanting a refill of his reeb, so she had a good reason to turn her back on him.

"A Dlog," the customer said. His three eyes looked up and down her body. "Are you mated?"

Tamaki stepped up close. She smelled his clean, green scent before he touched her. His arm slid around her waist as if he had every right.

"Yes, she's mated." He stared at the middle eye of the Usplop until all three of the creature's eyes glanced away.

"Pity. I need company on my ship. Gets lonely traveling from trading post to trading post."

"Maybe you'll find someone upstairs?" Tamaki murmured.

Upstairs? Cimmaron scowled. In between customers she'd watched the stairs. She hadn't noticed one person going upstairs. It must be awfully quiet up there. The Usplop wouldn't find a mate up there.

The creature brightened, tiny tentacles stirring at the side of his oblong head. Cimmaron suppressed a shudder. No telling what happened to the creature's body when he was in a state of sexual excitement.

"Take this," Tamaki said, handing the creature a disc. "That will get you past the security guard. If you decide to partake of entertainment upstairs, currency will be deducted from your account. The hostess will answer any of your questions."

The creature hesitated, then gave a decisive nod that sent a ripple through the tiny tentacles. "I will partake. It is no good traveling alone." He took the drink Cimmaron handed him and ambled off toward the stairs. Cimmaron watched him until he disappeared out of sight at the top. Questions trembled on the tip of her tongue, the curiosity almost killing her. Turning to Tamaki, she opened her mouth to ask and shut it again when she noticed his arched brows. Silent laughter lurked in his eyes. Cimmaron whirled away and stalked to the opposite end of the bar, muttering under her breath. "Jerk."

She attempted to keep away from Tamaki, but the infernal man kept brushing past her, the narrow bar not giving much leeway when it came to passing.

"Quit it," she snapped.

"Just doing my job," he countered.

Yeah, right. "It's not busy. Why don't you go and do some paperwork or something equally boss-like?"

Tamaki chuckled. "I'm watching the staff. That's in my job description. What can I get you to drink?" he asked a pilot.

Cimmaron growled under her breath and hurried off to serve another group of space jockeys before Tamaki beat her to it and received the credit tips instead of her.

Tamaki hadn't had so much fun for ages. A buzz of sexual awareness fizzed through him like the bubbles of a newly opened flask of vroom. He pulled a goblet of frothy veeno, glancing down the bar at the golden female who seemed to fill his mind increasingly with each passing cycle. A subtle golden glow emanated from her skin, giving away her turbulent state of mind. The female was just as aware of him as he was of her. In that instant he made up his mind to follow a new stratagem. Trying to remind himself he was her boss wasn't working. They could have one more date without invoking the mate thing. Just one more taste and then he'd back off and leave her alone. He could always lend her the passage to leave Marchant. Even if she didn't pay him back and he never saw her again, it would stop the temptation. Tamaki considered his idea from all angles before nodding. Yeah. That's what he'd do. One more time. If that was what she wanted, too....

The rest of the session trickled past so slowly Tamaki wanted to scream his frustration out loud. It was just pure luck he'd chosen to wear a long tunic instead of his normal form-fitting shirt. At least the tunic covered his bulging groin from curious eyes. His frustration levels, however, remained high.

At last security saw the last customers from the club, and they finished the cleanup ready for the next session.

"Cimmaron, can I have a quick word before you leave?" Tamaki held his breath, wondering how to handle things should she argue about staying.

She cast him a doubtful look, clearly hesitating before finally turning back.

Tamaki waited until the last employee left.

"I wondered if you'd like to see upstairs." He waited, wanting to grin at the expressions that danced across her face. Eagerness. Suspicion. Doubt.

"There's no one up there."

"That's where you're wrong. The rooms are still in use."

Cimmaron straightened abruptly, her golden brows almost meeting when she scowled. "You lie."

Tamaki offered his hand. "Come and see."

Instead of accepting his touch, she brushed past him and stomped up the spiral staircase. The sound of her boots echoed in the empty club.

A victory of sorts. Shaking his head, Tamaki followed. Maybe he should have cajoled her into a wager. He took a moment to admire the curvy butt that swayed beneath the short blue uniform skirt. His lips pursed in a silent whistle. Oh, yeah, baby.

Chapter Six

He lied but she had no idea why. Cimmaron headed for the nearest room. Unlike last time, the privacy screen was open. A sapphire glow emanated from a room, lighting up the passage with the shimmering light and shading everything in its way a delicate blue. Cimmaron stepped toward the window, close enough to peer into the room and see the occupants. She gasped. The Usplop she'd served downstairs was floating in the air, his limbs secured by stout bindings so he couldn't move. The glow came from his body, and his tentacles undulated, sticking out from his body at right angles. A female--well, Cimmaron thought it was a female--licked delicately at the tentacles that stuck out from his groin. An audible moan of pleasure sounded through speakers either side of the window.

Tamaki stepped up beside her, not touching but close enough for her to feel the warmth coming off his body. "Our friend has found a suitable partner."

"Yes," Cimmaron answered, her voice faint. Heat suffused her body, yet she couldn't tear her gaze off the intimate scene in front of her.

"Do you like to watch?"

"No!"

"Some people do. I like to watch sometimes but mainly I'm an action man."

"The male doing the fucking?" Cimmaron asked tartly, her gaze finally snapping off the couple to glare at him.

"I wouldn't have put it quite like that, but yeah. I'd rather run my hands across your body than watch another couple making love."

"What is this place?" Cimmaron's gaze slid from his face, unable to maintain eye contact without giving away the desire that simmered inside. She refused to succumb to his ... his ... charm again.

"It's a mating club. Beings from all over the universe and beyond come to meet others. Some date while others like the Usplop are looking for a mate." Tamaki placed his hands on her shoulders and turned her so he could see her face clearly. "If a couple meet in the rooms once or twice, it's considered a date. Should the couple meet a third time, they are mated."

Cimmaron gasped, searching his face desperately for truth, her gut hollowing with fear. "We ... we've dated?"

She was a Dlog, pre-programmed to mate. If that wasn't bad enough she'd managed to land in the one place that could make her life miserable--a dating and mating club.

"Yes." Tamaki took her arm. "Would you like to see the other rooms?"

No. Not really. It was difficult enough resisting Tamaki without being tempted by spending time with him. Cimmaron attempted to shake her head, but his sexy grin distracted her. Cimmaron's mind took a sharp turn into Temptation City. Tamaki. Her heart pounded a little faster, a fraction louder and her body moistened. All over. Tamaki took her arm and drew her deeper into temptation and trouble. Cimmaron shuddered, trying not to breathe in his scent.

"There are twelve rooms in total. We started with five and have gradually added to the number to increase the club's capacity."

"I don't need to see any more," Cimmaron said, digging in her heels so he stopped his casual saunter down a white passage.

"But you were curious."

Sure, and now Cimmaron knew what had befallen the cat. Trouble.

Tamaki kept walking and she unwillingly followed.

"Okay, I get it. This is punishment."

"No, that is punishment," he said, pointing to another glass window.

There was no glow from this window, but the room inside was very different. Sumptuous in rich red velveteen, a huge bed with a gold and crimson cover and lots of plump cushions. Two beings were inside this room. As Cimmaron watched, the female swished a flogger through the air. It struck the male's back and he fell forward on the bed. She could see his face, but instead of the pain she'd expected to see, his face was screwed up in an expression of ecstasy. Her gaze flicked down his body in the microts it took him to sprawl face down on the bed. His cock was fully erect. Cimmaron glanced at Tamaki and found he watched her.

"Seen enough?"

Heck, she'd seen enough after the first couple. She gulped. The shrinkton fabric of her uniform was faulty. The material had drawn so tight she could scarcely breathe.

Cimmaron nodded because she didn't trust herself to speak without begging him to touch her.

"I need to check the new room. The final electrical work was done tonight, and I want to see if they left it clean and tidy." Without waiting for an answer Tamaki took her arm again and propelled her in the direction of the new room. Cimmaron wished he'd quit with the touching. She was finding it very unsettling.

After directing her down the passage, Tamaki opened the door to the room and tugged her inside. Dropping her arm, he turned in a slow circle.

"What do you think of the room?"

Cimmaron gave the green color scheme a cursory glance, keeping her eyes well away from the bed in the center of the floor. "It's very nice." The desire to shove Tamaki onto the bed struck her unexpectedly. She had to curl her hands into fists to stop from reaching for his broad shoulders. Her Dlog genes. Again.

"I'm pleased with it. You didn't see all the technological advances the last time you were here." He wrapped his arm around her waist, squeezing her lightly.

"Stop touching me," Cimmaron snarled, jumping away from him. "I ... just don't touch me."

"Why? What are you frightened of? I'd never hurt you."

The male might look innocent but she didn't believe it for a moment. "You might not hurt me, but you're ready to have sex," Cimmaron snapped back. "I don't want a mate. I'm a pilot. It's what I do."

"I don't know why you're so bent out of shape." His brows rose in a teasing manner. "I was going to show you the room's features. I don't recall mentioning sex." Tamaki tugged on a handle. A drawer slid silently from the wall--a different one than last time.

Despite herself, Cimmaron craned her neck so she had a better view. An array of sex toys, at least she presumed they were sex toys since some of them were mystery items. The desire to run her hands over his body was a siren song in her mind. Cimmaron closed the distance between them before she was aware of moving. She touched his face, swallowing when she saw the blaze of passion in his eyes.

Tamaki jerked her into his arms and plundered her mouth. When she gasped, he took advantage and slid his tongue between her parted lips. He tasted hot and heady and very masculine. Cimmaron stroked his tongue with hers, reveling in his heady taste, the play of teeth and the dark sound he made deep in his throat. His scent mesmerized her. It was as seductive as his taste: rich, green, redolent of the outdoors.

Their clothes melted away, and they fell onto the large bed. With increasingly urgent hunger they tasted each other, limbs tangling, desire exploding between them. Cimmaron guided his cock to her slit and he thrust inside one tiny increment at the time until she was fully impaled. They rocked together, the sensation building rapidly. Cimmaron exploded with the force of her release. The ripples in her womb continued for long moments, clasping at his cock. He groaned, thrust several times in deep, fast strokes before freezing fully impaled in her womb. Cimmaron felt the spurt of his seed, gloried in his moan of release. She clutched him to her, squashed by his weight but enjoying the intimacy of being in his arms.

Tamaki slipped from her moist sex and turned on the bed, pulling her into his arms. He kissed her, a slow and lingering mating of their lips. Her hands dropped to cup his buttocks, her fingers delving between his cheeks to massage his puckered rosette.

"Again?" he asked in a husky voice.

Cimmaron nipped at the delicate skin of his neck and waggled an impudent finger, dipping it into his rosette. She felt his erection spring to life with renewed vigor and smiled against his neck as she moved her hips against him. The hunger remained and only he could appease it. "Yes, again," she whispered. "I ache. I need you to fix it."

His clever hands danced across her body creating magic with each touch. Cimmaron groaned softly, undulating her body, silently encouraging him to dance a seductive tango with her.

* * * *

"Had to call backup," the security guard said. "I've never seen the like. Not even in vroom addicts, and you know how violent they can get."

Tamaki listened to him, frowning through his explanations of the brawl in the new room on the second floor. The male was his best security guard, but this morn he bore battle scars. His bulbous eyes were streaked with red and an angry scratch marred the scales on one cheek. The male's tunic was in complete disarray, which was highly unusual in the warrior species.

Tamaki tapped a quill against a piece of parchment and ignored the splotches of black ink that splattered across the pristine white. "I understand the couple who hired the room had a violent disagreement and came to blows."

The security guard nodded then winced. "Yeah. It was a Clart and a Martian, both peaceful races. The Clart female battered the Martian until he lost consciousness. She left via the travel tubes before my team had a chance to intervene."

"Probably the influence of the full moons."

His security guard nodded, and Tamaki hoped he was right. They needed that room for financial viability. He'd had to fight to grab custom from the other entertainment businesses on Marchant, and he wasn't about to take backward steps when the club was doing so well. "Rico and I will double-check the equipment in case there's a malfunction causing the problem." The threesome between Rico, Cimmaron and him hadn't exactly been normal. Hell, Rico still refused to look him directly in the eye whenever they were together.

An abrupt tap sounded on his door before it opened. Rico peered in and seemed to relax when he saw the security guard.

"Everything seems fine out in the bar. I thought I'd take a ten minute break," Rico said.

Tamaki nodded. "What about upstairs? Is the new room in use?"

Rico tensed and wouldn't meet his gaze. "Yeah. No problems."

The communicator on the security guard's belt beeped without warning, breaking the uncomfortable silence. The male glanced down and silenced the piercing beep. "Problem, boss. Second floor."

They glanced at each other before erupting into action. Tamaki and Rico followed the security guard up the spiral staircase and turned left to head for the new room. It was empty when they arrived. Two ashen faced security guards waited at the door.

"What happened?" Tamaki demanded.

"Two females hired the room. They left before we could grab them," one said.

The other shuddered. "There was oozing green blood everywhere. They had sex but it was brutal."

Something worse than full moons was afoot here. Cursing under his breath, Tamaki issued orders. "Tell the females on reception that we're not hiring out this room again tonight. Rico, schedule the cleaning droid to do the new room first." He waited for the security guard to leave and shut the door behind him before waving a hand at Rico. "Take a seat." He started speaking again before Rico had taken possession of a seat. Thankfully, his matter-of-fact behavior seemed to put his friend at ease. "What do you think the problem is? Any ideas?"

"Most beings who enter the room seem to want to have sex." Rico looked him straight in the eye for the first time since the torrid threesome in the new room. "Even though it's not what they would have done normally."

Tamaki sighed, his rapid tapping with the quill sending another shower of ink over the once clean parchment. "It seems that way." He thought of his second bout of sex with Cimmaron and coughed to clear his throat. The sensation jolted the length of his body making him all too aware of the way he reacted to the Dlog female. Two dates. One more time, and they'd be mated. Tamaki wasn't sure how he felt about that. A club manager moved around often, which was why most of them only dated when they took advantage of the club's amenities. And never with staff.

"Tamaki!"

Tamaki jerked to attention. "What?"

"Are you all right?" Rico appeared ready to bolt.

Tamaki chuckled. "Relax. I'm not about to jump you."

"Yeah, my head knows that, but I can't help it. I've never done anything like that before." He glanced at Tamaki and grinned suddenly. "Not before I met Marianna either."

"Yeah. Me neither. Come on. We'd better check out the room."

"Ah-ah. Not in my job description," Rico said. "I don't get paid danger money."

"We'll wear masks and full suits. It has to be something in the atmosphere that's making everyone act that way."

The room appeared warm and welcoming, which was exactly what they had intended when they drew up the plans and decided on fitting it out.

Tamaki smirked at his friend through the transparent mask he wore over his face. He pushed open the door and stepped inside, his suit rustling loudly. The room looked normal. Tamaki turned to speak to Rico. His friend stood just outside the door, his pale and sweaty face obvious even though the mask.

"Coward," Tamaki taunted.

Rico nodded, and flapped his arms like a chicken. "Bwawk, bwawk, bwawk, bwawk."

"I don't feel anything weird." Tamaki strode over to the controls and examined them. His fingers flew over the keyboard as he typed in commands. "Nothing wrong that I can see. You're the expert with the electronics. Come and take a look."

Rico brushed past him and ran the electronics through a series of self-tests. "Looks fine."

"Do you feel anything?" Tamaki ventured.

"Nothing. Do you think it's the suits? That would mean the problem is airborne."

Rico studied the unit that pumped suitable breathing air for each species through the room before glancing at Tamaki. The expression on Tamaki's face brought a scowl. "Aw, shit. We're going test it."

"There's already talk about the room. It's best if we keep as much in-house as possible before we lose customers. We'll prop the door open. If you feel anything weird get out."

"Fuck," Rico said, but he propped the door open then strode to the middle of the room. "You go first."

Tamaki took a deep breath. His gut crawled with apprehension despite his casual ease. He wasn't too happy about the situation himself. He counted silently to three then ripped his mask off. Seconds later Rico did the same. They stared at each other in total silence. Tamaki took another cautious breath. The air seemed okay. No weird scents.

Without warning it hit. A wave of lust that made his knees buckle because of its intensity. "Out," he gasped.

"But I want…." Rico backed up, his eyes glowing with need. "Don't wanna seem over familiar," he ground out, his face screwed up in torment. "But you have the sexiest butt."

"Marianna," Tamaki gasped. He jerked his gaze off Rico and struggled with the multitude of feelings crashing through his body. His blood thundered through his veins. His heart pumped, and his hands shook with the need to stroke Rico's face, his skin. Wasn't gonna happen. Was. Not. Going. To. Happen. "Out," he ordered. "You first."

Rico edged toward the door, but Tamaki could see it was a huge struggle. Rico swallowed loudly and licked his lips. Tamaki followed the movement avidly before he realized what he was doing. He ripped his gaze away, his body in a hot sweat. His cock thrust against the coveralls he wore, reminding him of the urgency to mate. The thought pierced his confused brain. If he weren't damned careful, he'd end up mated to his best friend. "Out!" he hollered.

The blast of sound prodded Rico to action. He attempted to walk but fell. With an anguished groan, he crawled across the synwood floor. Tamaki watched his slow progress and fought the urge to race across to his friend and drag him into his arms. Aghast at the direction of his thoughts, he attempted to dredge up Cimmaron's face. Her almond shaped eyes and the flash of gold that captivated him. He fought his need to go to Rico, concentrating on Cimmaron and how she felt in his arms, the smooth flow of skin across skin, the glide of lips. Her taste. Tamaki shuddered. Oh, yeah.

Suddenly, the blinding need for sex died. He inhaled deeply and turned toward the door. Rico stood just outside the room, gulping in huge drafts of air.

"You okay?" Tamaki called.

"I am now. You?"

"As soon as you were outside the urge to mate stopped."

Rico scowled. "Houston, we have a problem."

* * * *

Rico plonked onto a chair in front of Tamaki's desk and stretched his legs out in front of him. "Custom is down on the second level."

"Yeah. The receptionist said it had been quiet. The rumors are flying faster than a Naxmus fighter ship."

Tamaki leapt to his feet and paced back and forth behind his desk. "If only I could find the cause. It's ticking me off. I know the problem is something to do with the conditioning unit but I've changed the machine, the filters and every other conceivable part. If I'm on my own I'm fine, but the moment someone else enters the room, all I can think of is sex." Tamaki paused. "You don't want to know what I nearly did to the droid," he added wryly.

"What are you going to do?" Rico asked.

Tamaki sat on the corner of the desk and was pleased his friend didn't jump out of his skin each time they were in the same room. Things were almost back to normal now they knew their behavior was somehow chemically induced. "I'll be upstairs in the room. I've been leaving the door open while there are no customers around, so if you need me holler from the door. I thought I'd go through everything once more before I go to the experts. You don't need me down here."

"No, we're fine. I didn't approve of hiring Cimmaron initially, but she's a damned fine bartender. Custom has increased since she arrived."

A pang of jealousy shot through Tamaki. While Rico had finally returned to normal behavior, Cimmaron was avoiding him. Normally Tamaki would have taken it on the chin, mentally shrugged, and moved on. After all, what did he want with a mate? Or problems with his bosses and probably termination of his contract. Yet a part of his mind hungered for her touch, her laugh and smile. God, he missed her sassy tongue and no-nonsense plain speaking. Cimmaron didn't play games, which was why he was trying to do the right thing and keep away. It wasn't easy when she continually dwelled in his mind.

Chapter Seven

Cimmaron let herself out the front door of the boarding house and pulled the door closed, testing it to make sure it was firmly shut. The local youths were in their normal place on the steps of an old warehouse. They had taken to calling Cimmaron names whenever she passed but the harassment didn't go any further than that. She marched past, her nose proudly tilted upward but not far enough that she wasn't aware of what was going on around her. The leader sneered at her, and Cimmaron allowed her upper lip to curl with disdain. Childish but necessary if she was to win the silent battle that waged between them.

"Hear there trouble at club," he called. His friends cackled like a group of broody Martian hens, nudging each other with their elbows. The leader smirked proudly, puffing up like a Martian rooster keeping his hens in line.

"Don't know what you're talking about," Cimmaron snapped, barely breaking stride. Score one for the enemy.

"I hear sex good in new room."

It was the smug satisfaction in his voice, the knowing tone that made her halt and turn around to scan his face.

"Good trickie, chica, huh? Don't get mad, get even."

Without thought Cimmaron prowled toward him ready to choke the truth from his scrawny neck. If he knew anything, she'd get it from him. Damn, she'd had sex twice with Tamaki. Twice. Not sex, a small voice hummed at the back of her mind. Made love. Cimmaron cursed, her eyes narrowing as a wave of rage swept her. She didn't want a mate. She would not mate. Cimmaron intended to fly ships.

The youth's friends backed up in alarm, leaving the leader isolated. Alone. The target of her wrath.

Cimmaron advanced again, stopping close enough to the youths that she smelled vroom fumes with each uneasy breath the leader took. She inhaled and gagged at the stench of their sweaty bodies. They obviously subscribed to the latest fad idea regarding cleanliness as being unhealthy. Cimmaron inhaled through her mouth, closing out the worst of the stench of unwashed bodies and fear.

"Tell me," she gritted out, impatient for answers. She glanced at her timepiece and scowled. Time was wasting. "Tell me now."

"Bitch," the leader growled, and before she could grab him, he whirled away. He melted into the shadowed alley that ran between the buildings, followed closely by his friends.

"Phrull." Cimmaron stared after them for a moment, before deciding she had better head for the club. She'd worm the truth out of them the next time she saw them.

Cimmaron stomped past beings laden with produce who were leaving the late night market. Did the youths know something or had they heard the rumors and decided to capitalize on them? Cimmaron replayed the words as she dodged a pair of droids pulling a cart laden with Marchant dried vegetables and dehydrated fruits. The leader had talked about revenge. He looked the type who didn't forgive easily, especially when his pride was involved. Cimmaron gave her timepiece another glance and broke into a run. She scanned her finger and the door opened to let her inside.

"Late," Hulk said.

Cimmaron sneered at him, and Hulk glowered right back. She bit back the urge to grin. The male carried photos of his offspring in his currency belt. She'd caught him showing them to the other security guards. Cimmaron shook her head, bemusement making her frown. The offspring had looked ugly. Cimmaron didn't get why he was so proud, even though it was kinda cute.

"You coming in or ya gonna stay there?"

"I work here," Cimmaron snapped, instantly more comfortable with their usual repartee. "Course I'm coming in." She stomped past Hulk and headed for the changing rooms where she'd left her thigh-high boots. In the dressing room, she slipped off her coat, pulled off her pilot boots, and thrust her feet into the hated boots.

Cimmaron sighed before heading back out to the bar. Her currency didn't seem to grow much. The pills to suppress her Dlog hormones had arrived at the apothecary. They were expensive, but she had to have them since without them all her plans would turn to solar dust. At this rate she was going to remain stranded for many more moon cycles. "Bloody male."

"Talking about me?"

Cimmaron came to an abrupt halt but not quite quick enough. Her breasts brushed the hard wall of Tamaki's chest before she jerked away. Frissons of heat ricocheted through her body, traveling through her breasts and lower to her sex. Cimmaron inhaled sharply, trying to control her wayward body. A soft chuckle snapped up her head, and she glared at him.

"Don't touch me."

"I didn't mean to. I thought you saw me coming."

Cimmaron bit the inside of her lip in consternation. She should have noticed him standing there. She was growing soft working in this bar, losing all her pilot instincts.

"I'm late," she snapped.

Tamaki merely grinned. "I don't think the boss will dock your currency earnings. Do you want to have dinner with me?"

Cimmaron gaped. "No."

Tamaki reached out and brushed his hand over her cheek before she had an inkling of what he intended. Another series of lightning bolts shot through her body before she reacted and stepped away.

"You have to eat. I don't want to mate with you," Tamaki said. "I thought we were friends and you might like to eat together."

"I don't have friends," Cimmaron snapped. What was wrong with the male? Why wouldn't he leave her alone? Every other male she came into contact backed off once she'd made it clear she wasn't interested.

"I'm your friend, Cimmaron. I'm going to work in the Green room. Page me when you're on a dinner break, and I'll come down." Raising a hand, he walked away, leaving Cimmaron staring after him.

The loud buzz of a Marchant midge made her realize her mouth hung open. She snapped it shut so the insect didn't fly inside and hurried off to the bar, trying to outrun her jumbled thoughts. "You're late," Rico said.

"Blame Tamaki. He wanted to talk," Cimmaron snapped. Phrull, he wanted to be friends. "What do ya want?" she snarled at a waiting pilot.

His teasing gaze slid across her bared skin and the tight uniform before settling on her scowling face. He sighed. "I guess I'm gonna have to settle for a drink. An Earth whiskey. No ice."

Cimmaron nodded and turned to fix the pilot's drink. After sliding the drink across the bar, she accepted the handful of credits he gave her. Cimmaron moved on to the next customer, her mind still on the male she'd just served.

He was much prettier than Tamaki, and he had music in his drawl. He hadn't caused a single blip on her hormone radar while Tamaki--Cimmaron slammed a flash of vroom on the bar, splashing a few drops over the shiny surface. It sizzled on contact before turning a milky white color then pink when the flash of lights caught it. "Sorry," she murmured to the customer as she ran a cloth over the spill.

Cimmaron moved on to the next customer, ignored their flirting while she hummed along with the live band. Not bad for a change. The laughter became louder, more raucous as the night passed. Cimmaron took her break and didn't page Tamaki as he'd requested. Guilt assailed her briefly, but she shoved it away, telling herself she didn't have time for a long break. They needed her back behind the bar because it was so busy. Time passed and eventually the punters started to leave in twos or threes, wobbling unsteadily through the door into the frigid Marchant morn.

Cimmaron swiped an errant lock of hair from her face and wearily started to restock the drinks behind the bar. On the other side, droids collected empty flasks and goblets, stacking them on the bar for washing.

"Have you seen Tamaki?" Rico asked.

"No." Cimmaron pushed aside the tiny bit of hurt that flashed through her. He hadn't meant the friend thing. Friendship wasn't possible, not since she was a Dlog. Dlog females didn't have friends. They had mates.

"He's not answering his page, and we need him to sign off on the stock and send the transmission to head office."

"Send security to get him." Cimmaron scanned the remaining customers who were finishing off drinks. A curse echoed through the club. "Phrull, those idiots are gonna fight."

Rico ran a hand through his hair, making it stand up. "I'd better help security. Go and get Tamaki. Remind him he needs to do the sign off."

"Yeah. Okay."

Rico grabbed her forearm as she passed. "Don't go inside the room. Talk to Tamaki from the door."

"Why can't someone else go?" Cimmaron muttered, frantically searching for a way out. Avoidance was best. Every time she came within touching distance of the male she wanted more. She wanted taste as well as sight. She wanted...

Phrull!

"Go, Cimmaron," Rico ordered, and before she could rally another argument he leapt across the bar and waded into the skirmish.

A chair crashed over on its side. Hulk grabbed two beings by the scruffs of their necks and threw them toward the door.

Cimmaron dodged a groaning Vercops. His eyes bulged from their sockets--all six of them--while distress calls from his mate filled the air. She ran up the stairs, her boots clunking noisily. At the top of the spiral staircase, she turned to the left and hurried to the green room. The microt she spied the privacy screen for the green room her heart started to pump faster. Something close to alarm prickled the hairs at the back of her neck. She halted outside the dense metal door. It was closed too. Cimmaron reached for the door handle then hesitated. She wiped her moist palm on her shrinkton skirt and then tried again.

"Phrull," she whispered, when her hand trembled violently. Each time she saw Tamaki, it was harder to resist his good-natured charm. And the longing.... The longing grew stronger and stronger. She was a pilot, dammit. Cimmaron threw her shoulders back and thrust open the door.

"Tamaki." Cimmaron cleared her throat and repeated his name in a firmer voice. "Tamaki. Are you there?"

The fight downstairs was escalating. A loud crash echoed up the stairs. A male roared in his native tongue, sounding fierce and furious.

Damn. Cimmaron peered around the corner. Someone was sprawled on the floor. All she could see was legs, but she thought it was Tamaki. "Tamaki?" No answer. Cimmaron inhaled sharply. She was going to have to go inside. Gingerly, she walked into the room, breathing in slow pants and holding her breath in between.

Tamaki was out cold. She skimmed her hands over his body but could see nothing that indicated a wound. "Tamaki." Cimmaron shook him and was rewarded by a groan.

The scuff of feet overhead made her jerk her head upward. A ceiling tile wasn't on straight. She caught a flash of color. Someone was up there.

"Come down here, coward."

A laugh resounded. Cimmaron froze. She knew that laugh.

"Not so smarti nowa, chica," a voice sneered.

"Cimmaron, you shouldn't be here," Tamaki murmured. He pushed to a sitting position. "Man, my head hurts. I heard a noise but before I could turn around, someone zapped me with a stun gun."

"You have no wounds," Cimmaron said.

"I have a headache."

They stared at each other for a long moment, and suddenly her uniform felt heavy and burdensome.

"God, you're beautiful."

"All Dlog are beautiful," she countered. Phrull, was that flirtatious tone her? Cimmaron shook her head in an attempt to clear it, but all she could think of was Tamaki and how he felt when his cock was buried deep inside her body.

Tamaki smiled and placed his hand on her thigh, the naked skin between her thigh-high boots and her skirt. His hand was warm and sent a shower of tingles surfing through her body.

Their gazes met and it seemed as though a gossamer cord drew them closer. Cimmaron swallowed, the sound loud inside the quiet room. Tamaki's fingers continued to stroke her thigh until a purr erupted from deep in her throat. They shouldn't do this. She should leave. His fingers stroked across and up, edging toward the plain pilot regulation panties she wore beneath the skirt. Her skin color deepened to a brilliant gold.

"We need to leave the room. Now. Before something happens." Cimmaron thought about standing and leaving. She tensed for a scant microt, then Tamaki's finger slipped beneath the leg binding of her panties. It moved with unerring accuracy, stroking moist feminine flesh and grazing across her clitoris. Cimmaron sucked in a hasty breath, the ribbons of sensation making her body arch.

"Do you want more?" Tamaki whispered. "I do."

A sneering laugh rang out, jolting them both from the sensual web binding them together. They jumped to their feet, staring up at the ceiling. A fine mist showered down on their heads, then the scurry of feet made it clear their watcher had retreated.

Cimmaron gulped trying to retain the return to sanity, but Tamaki touched her. He trailed his hand across her bare belly. She shivered and leaned into him so her breasts brushed his chest, losing the fight for reason. Her nipples tightened to hard points, and she stroked her hand down his cheek and chin.

"I want more." A tiny voice at the back of her mind protested for an instant until Tamaki leaned in and kissed her, stealing her breath as he traced the curve of her lips with his tongue. Cimmaron gasped, and his tongue slipped inside her mouth. Slowly, he explored her mouth until pleasure coursed through her body. He tasted of spearmint, of spicy heat and male. His muscles flexed beneath her questing hands, and the bulge of his groin pressed into her lower body.

Tamaki pulled away from Cimmaron glancing down at her with a grin. "I believe we can give you more." He tugged at the strip of cloth that covered her breasts, expertly removing it before she had time to blink. He let the blue cloth drop the floor before he traced the delicate veins visible beneath the surface of her skin. "You're so beautiful." His fingers drifted across her collarbone and dropped to cup her breasts. Tamaki pinched one nipple until it turned a deeper gold. A sharp tug brought a corresponding pain. A good pain that made her cry out for more and arch her body into his touch. Between her legs, her moist folds grew wetter. Needier. Her heart lurched painfully as the hard ridge of his cock pressed into her belly. Without warning he scooped her off her feet and carried her over to the large bed. Cimmaron bounced lightly before Tamaki covered her, his bulk preventing her from moving again.

"Kiss me, Tamaki. Touch me. Please."

"Oh, I intend to," he promised and trailed his hands and mouth across her hipbone.

Cimmaron felt the tingle of teeth and the roughened pads of his fingertips when he explored her body. She smelled his hot male scent and reveled in the way he made her nerve endings vibrate. She parted her legs for him as he silently requested, her folds engorged and wet. So wet. Cimmaron shifted restlessly as he tested her readiness, his thumb teasing the sensitive nub nestled at her core. A jolt of pleasurable excitement made her breath catch. His sweetly invasive fingers drove her higher as they pumped deep inside her, brushing and teasing her clit. Fire whipped her sensitized body, then he slipped her hands beneath her buttocks, lifting her to his mouth. His tongue teased her swollen flesh, flailing it and driving her impossibly higher. Cimmaron sucked in a breath, releasing it on a moan. By the Goddess his touch felt good. He delved between her legs, stoking her need higher, but not giving her enough pressure for release.

"Tamaki, please." Phrull, she never begged, but she wanted to right now.

"You're so wet and swollen for me. Your skin glows gold and gleams for my possession." He pressed a kiss to her inner thigh, the stubble on his lean cheeks rasping against her soft skin. His tongue journeyed the length of her cleft, making her shudder with helpless need.

"Yes," she whispered, a purr rumbling deep in her throat.

With one final lap at her moist folds, Tamaki moved up her body. He kissed her lips and she could taste her essence on his tongue. Tamaki pulled her over his body and desperate to have her pussy filled, she impaled herself on his cock, increment by increment until he was fully seated. Then, with her need to be filled appeased she rode him, driving them both closer to fulfillment. His cock seemed to grow larger with each lazy swivel of her hips until he filled her impossibly full. He reached out to capture her breast with his hands before taking her in his mouth, drawing sweet agonizing circles around her nipple with his tongue. His eyes were a deep, dark blue and they caressed each part of her as she swayed above him. He made her feel beautiful. He made her feel powerful. Tamaki made her feel like a woman--a woman worthy of him.

As desire flared between them, Cimmaron's pace quickened. Tamaki rose to meet each downward stroke. Sensation grew, tingles spreading outward until she convulsed with the force of her release. Deep in her womb she felt the spurt of his seed. She heard his groan of completion. Cimmaron fell forward until she lay against his chest, panting to regain her breath. Tamaki's arms came around her, holding her so closely she was aware of the thunder of his heart.

Cimmaron soaked up the novelty of being close to a male and the sense of rightness at being with this male. She didn't want to move.

* * * *

"Oh, my God. You two have been at it again." Rico hovered in the doorway, strain on his dark face.

Cimmaron let out a squeak that had no business coming from her throat. She scowled at the un-pilot-like sound and attempted to hide her naked body behind Tamaki's greater bulk. The male chuckled and drew her close so her breasts squished against his chest.

Then he stretched, looking like a lazy cat, supremely at ease with his nakedness. "Yeah. Life is good."

Rico raked his hand through his dark hair. "That's three times."

"Four actually."

No mistaking the smug tone in that voice.

The sensual fog was starting to clear from her mind. Cimmaron stiffened and her eyes narrowed.

"Thrice a mate," Rico said.

Cimmaron let out a screech that made Rico wince. Mated? They were phrullin' mated? She thumped Tamaki over the shoulder, but the lazy lug merely grinned.

"Great, isn't it?" He pressed a kiss to her bare shoulder and eyed her heaving breasts with interest.

"But I've been taking pills." The words came out as a wail of horror. All that currency spent to keep her free of a male. She was mated. Mated to Tamaki. Despite all her careful steps to remain unmated. She wanted to qualify as a pilot, not act the slave for some male. Phrull, the idea of popping out offspring every solar cycle made her want to upchuck.

"No!" She yanked from Tamaki's grip. The instant they were no longer touching, she felt a physical wrench in her gut. Cimmaron took several steps away from the bed, aware of the pull toward Tamaki intensifying. The desperate need to touch him and reassure herself brought a scowl. They couldn't be mated. They couldn't.

"I'm so sorry, Cimmaron," Rico said, his voice edged with painful sympathy. "There's nothing you can do. You and Tamaki are mated for life."

It was the quiet pain in his voice that made her accept the truth. Cimmaron turned to the male she'd mated with, part of her hating him even as the mating bonds writhed through her blood, tempting her to touch him.

"Phrull," she croaked as she took a step toward the bed. "I'm stranded." Her voice held pain, bitterness, frustration and deep disappointment. "Stranded for life."

Chapter Eight

"No!" Tamaki watched his mate pull on her clothes with quick, abrupt moves. He had feelings for her. He'd never wanted another female like this. He ... hell, he loved her. She belonged to him, with him. And somehow, he'd prove it to her.

Tamaki watched the flash of bare butt as she hurriedly dressed and her long, luscious legs as she thrust her feet into her boots. He watched the angry swish of her hips when she strode across the room and winced at the strident tap-tap of her heels. Despite it all, he couldn't restrain a grin. His mate was a babe.

"Take that damn smirk off your face," Rico snapped.

Tamaki sat up on the bed and stretched lazily before scratching his belly. His muscles felt well used but he couldn't wait for another go round with his mate.

"Did you hear me? You've broken the no-fraternization rule. You'll lose your job, man!"

Tamaki smiled lazily and stood. "I don't think so. Don't dither at the door like a chaperone, Rico. I believe it's safe to enter the room now."

"No thanks," Rico muttered with heartfelt sentiment. "I'm not stepping foot in that room until I know it's safe."

"There was someone in the roof. I believe they've been misting a version of Earth's Spanish Fly drug into the air.

Just enough to make the occupants of the room desperate for sex."

"But Spanish Fly makes you keep going and going like that advertisement on Earth television claims about its batteries. You know, the one with the bunny rabbit." Rico stopped when he saw Tamaki's rising brows. "Or so I've heard."

"I believe this is the version discovered on the planet Talon. You know, the newly discovered planet?"

Rico glanced at his timepiece. "Shit, I came up here to remind you about the reports for head office. They're late. The window for transmission communication is almost closed."

"Hell." Tamaki bounded off the bed and hurriedly scrambled into his clothes. "Why didn't you say so?" He sprinted from the room, down the corridor, and bounded down the spiral staircase. At the base of the stairs, he came to an abrupt halt, and Rico barreled into him from behind. The main bar and seating area was a mess with chairs lying drunkenly on the floor, upturned tables and broken goblets strewn across the room. A security guard lay flat out on the floor with one of the barmaids squatting beside him. She dabbed at splotches of purple blood on his face with a worried expression.

"What happened?"

"There was a fight," Rico said. "Never mind that. We handled it. Get the figures through to HO before the transmission window closes. We don't want an auditor droid landing here. They have no sense of humor."

Tamaki gave a terse nod before striding through to his office. Luckily the figures were completed and ready to go. He plugged his code into a keypad to hook up with the satellite and after checking the files were in the send box, he hit the transmit button. The transfer process started smoothly, and Tamaki leaned back in his chair while he considered his problems. Or blessings, he thought with a sudden chuckle. Being mated to Cimmaron was worth the aggravation. He sobered. How the hell was he going to get past the company strictures about fraternization? There were very clear guidelines as Rico had reminded him. After the scandal and lawsuit on Mars all managers and senior staff had to sign the no-fraternization clause. He loved his job and didn't want to give it up, but he was mated now. They were a team for life. A done deal. Tamaki tilted his chair back on two legs, closed his eyes and concentrated. There must be a way.

His keyboard beeped and he punched in another code, an added security feature. This shunted the information through the final stage. While the figures were finishing transmitting, Tamaki continued to puzzle about Cimmaron. He liked her very much. He liked being with her and was happy with being mated. *Okay*. He loved her, dammit. A grin broke out. Hell, yeah.

He loved her.

The mating process had merely hurried the relationship to a conclusion. Tamaki snorted. Not that Cimmaron would accept defeat. He needed to find a way to make her happy otherwise neither of them would find happiness. But what?

An abrupt tap sounded on the door and Rico walked in. "Did you get the info to head office?"

"Yeah. It's still sending." Tamaki let his chair settle on all four legs. "How are things going with Marianna?"

Rico brightened. "Better. She's accepted my offer to take her to the Marchant picnic on Founder's Day."

Tamaki did an internal eye roll. Man, he hated the pretentious Marchant upper-class sector, and he didn't like Marianna's superior manner. But since Rico was happy to move in those circles and was steadfastly hooked on Mariana.... He studied his friend closely, his mind working at speed. Was it possible? "I have an idea." Tamaki glanced at the transmitter and tapped his forefinger on the hard surface of the desktop. "Can you stay for a bit longer or are you seeing Marianna?"

"Yeah, I can stay." He didn't add any further explanation so Tamaki figured Mariana was busy. None of his business, but he thought his friend could do better.

"Okay, listen up," he said. "Here's what I was thinking."

Cimmaron went through the motions of cleaning behind the bar, immersed deep in her thoughts. Phrullin' male!

"Where did you disappear to?" Melad asked, breaking into Cimmaron's mental cursing.

Cimmaron concentrated on a dirty spot on the shiny bar, scrubbing her damp cloth across it with brisk moves. It did nothing to settle her ruffled mood. "Rico asked me to find Tamaki urgently." Her voice was sharp. Defensive. And it gave away almost as much as the color of her skin. Phrull! She refrained from looking at Melad, not because she was worried about lying convincingly but because her skin was giving off a golden glow. She knew her eyes would be flashing a brilliant gold, bright enough to dazzle. A sure signal. Anyone with half a brain would guess the glow was sexually induced.

"Wish he'd sent me," Melad said in a dreamy voice. With sure, competent moves, she stacked goblets in the sterilizer. "I'd like to know what Tamaki looks like under all those black clothes he wears."

"He's our boss." Thank goodness Melad hadn't seemed to notice anything strange.

Melad's head jerked up. A flash of surprise shot across her face, and Cimmaron forced her lips to a stiff smile to counteract the sharp tone.

"Sorry." Cimmaron sucked in a deep breath, attempting to stuff the surge of jealousy in the far reaches of her mind. Melad shrugged and turned back to stacking the bronze goblets. She pulled out another rack and stacked the silver goblets separately. Cimmaron resumed her cleaning. Tamaki didn't belong to her despite his assertions they were mated. After another inhalation, Cimmaron felt marginally calmer. The answer was simple.

She'd leave.

That's what she'd do. Paying for the suppression pills had cut into her funds, but the tips plus the part of her wages she'd been able to save had added to a decent amount of currency. Maybe she could hire on as a deckhand?

When a Dlog mated they were planet-bound. This mating was different. It was against her will. Cimmaron suppressed a blip of excitement as she thought of Tamaki and the way he made her feel when he touched her, when his cock was deeply imbedded in her womb. The mating *was* against her will, dammit. She couldn't afford to stay here on Marchant, not if she wished to clear her name and graduate to full pilot status. Tamaki kept creeping into her mind, and she whirled with a huff of impatience to stock the chillers.

As usual, the vroom compartment was totally empty.
Cimmaron worked quickly, efficiently stocking the white
flasks of vroom and other drinks as she made plans. Her
mind kept drifting. Tamaki. Tamaki. *Tamaki*. She picked
up the empty crate, stomped from the bar, and slammed the
crate onto the pile awaiting pickup by the local brewer.

A snarl built low in her throat, easing out in a feral growl.
That was it. No matter who she had to sign on with or what
demeaning job she had to take, she was going to leave
Marchant. She'd depart tonight.

Cimmaron made haste to the boarding house but still took
care to keep to the brightly lit streets and alleys that were
patrolled by security droids. At the boarding house, she let
herself inside and went directly to her room. Packing the
meager belongings she'd accumulated since being on
Marchant, she left out enough currency to cover her
lodging and scribbled a brief note to Larissa. Cimmaron
dressed in her plain brown tunic, trews and boots and left
the blue shrinkton skirt and top on her sleeping mat along
with the thigh-high boots.

As she let herself out and walked off without looking
back, Cimmaron pushed aside the loneliness that suddenly
assailed her. Her steps faltered momentarily, then she threw
her shoulders back and increased her pace. She was used to
being alone. Ever since she'd decided on training as a pilot,
she'd traveled a lone road. Once she cleared her name and
was reinstated the hole wouldn't seem quite as large.

Cimmaron strode down the brightly lit streets but instead
of heading for the club, she turned toward the spaceport.
Vagrants loitered in the shadowed recesses of buildings.
Cimmaron kept moving in a confident manner, knowing
that the slightest trace of fear would lead to disaster.

A sudden sharp pang of pain in her chest took her by
surprise. She gasped and staggered at the intensity of it.
Clutching at her chest, she attempted to breath through the
pain. The shuffle of feet behind her made her spin with an
instinctive feral growl. No way was she succumbing to
vagrants intent on stealing her possessions and currency.

"Back off," she snarled.

A gnarled and stooped male wrapped in a grubby white
cloak held up his hands in a peaceful sign of surrender.
"Not me to worry bout," he whispered, his voice hoarse

from years of smoking the harsh local tobacco. "Rich young males slummin'. Thems cause worry. Hide!" He slipped into the shadows and disappeared from sight.

Cimmaron glanced over her shoulder. Phrull! The same group that harassed her most days. Had they followed? She'd been so leery of what was in front of her, she hadn't checked behind. Cimmaron slid into the shadows and hastened her pace, moving swiftly through the dimly lit areas of the rutted streets. A wave of pain crashed through her chest again. Phrull. She'd taken a pill before she'd left for work. Determined footsteps behind made Cimmaron suck up the agony and move.

Dilapidated stalls and areas to display traders' wares were in evidence now. Another bolt of cramp hit and with a silent grimace, Cimmaron sank to the ground behind a pile of discarded display tables. Her boot went into an open drain, the splash too loud for her liking. She froze, hoping they hadn't heard.

"Where chica go?" a sing-song voice called.

"No see," someone answered. "No see."

"Tricky chica. Tricky. Tricky. *Tricky.*" Cimmaron recognized the leader's voice. Phrull. Just once she'd like to level the playing field and have a one on one confrontation with the coward. Her top lip curled upward in disdain. It would never happen--not with his rich parents and their currency behind him.

A spaceship roared overhead, taking off from the spaceport. The flare from the propulsion unit lit the whole street for an instant while the rumble from the engines filled the air. Cimmaron crouched even lower glad of her nondescript brown tunic. It would be difficult for them to spot her. All she needed to do was wait them out--if the stench of rotting rat-creatures didn't kill her first.

"Chica must 'ave gone other street," the leader said. "Back track."

He wasn't going to check behind all the piles of rubble in the street? Surprise made her blink. She'd thought him brighter than that. Or.... Perhaps he was. Cimmaron remained where she was for long moments after he'd spoken and she'd heard them retreat. The cold ground cramped her legs, matching the throbbing in her chest. She shifted uneasily but the pain grew worse. When she was about to move she heard a soft curse and then footsteps. Cimmaron's heart thundered with sudden apprehension. She'd been right to wait before moving. The leader had tried to smoke her out with trickery. Pain hit again. She curled up in a tight ball trying not to make any noise in case they came back. A shiver racked her body. Phrull. Cold. So cold. Tamaki would know how to warm her freezing body. As the thought slipped stealthily into her mind, the cramps eased. Cimmaron listened carefully and heard the murmur of voices to her left. The shuffle of feet. The swish of a cloak. She pressed a fist to the nagging ache emanating from her chest and concentrated, trying to discern if it was the gang of youths or others.

"Psst!"

Cimmaron threw her head backward and thumped against the stone wall behind her. For a moment, she saw stars. A groan squeezed past her lips as she tried to figure out which part of her hurt worst--her head or her chest.

"Psst, they've gone." A male in a dirty white robe appeared in front of her. It was the vagrant she'd seen earlier. "Leave now. Peaceful street. Don't want trouble."

Well, that was telling her. Her presence was not required. "I'm going." Cimmaron turned away from the vagrant and his silent friend and walked briskly toward the spaceport. They might be vagrants but they were right about the gang of youths' possible return. The sooner she reached the relative safety of the spaceport the better.

The agony in her chest intensified, robbing Cimmaron of breath. Clutching at her chest, she pushed through the growing throngs of beings exiting and entering the spaceport. The microt she entered the port, Cimmaron made a point of standing straight and pretending her chest didn't hurt like the devil. Once she found paying employment on a ship leaving Marchant she'd have time to recuperate from whatever ailed her. Meantime, she'd suck it in.

Cimmaron decided she'd go to the workers' canteen first. Gossip was usually the best source when it came to searching for employment. And if she had to use her Dlog looks to gain the information, then so be it. The knot on her head continued to ache in harmony with her chest. A film of sweat broke out on her forehead.

"What happened to you?" a male in oil-stained coveralls said.

Cimmaron frowned. "Nothing." She stuck her nose in the air and attempted to sidle past.

"The side of your head is bleeding."

"Where?" Cimmaron prodded the lump on her head. A sharp pain shot through her head. She winced. Her hand came away bloody. "Oh, that. I hit my head. Tripped," she added. "Are any of the ships hiring?"

"You?"

"No, the King of Mars," Cimmaron snapped. "Of course it's me."

"Not many beings willing to hire a Dlog. Too much trouble."

Cimmaron drew herself up tall and stared down at him in distaste. "I am not a Dlog." She maintained eye contact but it was difficult with the persistent throb in her chest. All she wanted to do was curl up in a ball of misery, or even better, lie down with Tamaki at her side. He would make her forget the pain. They'd touch each other, stroke, fondle. Kiss.

A maintenance droid dropped a tray on the floor with a loud clatter, thankfully yanking Cimmaron from her traitorous thoughts. Tamaki. Bah! The male had set her up. Tricked her. Not that she believed anything about them being mated. She didn't feel different. A vision of Tamaki formed inside her head, and her whole body jerked, shock freezing her rigid. The bloody male was naked, his erection thrusting outward. He was flaunting himself.

"Are you all right?" the male asked.

Cimmaron shook the vision from her head. "Yes. Anyone hiring?" she demanded out of patience with the male. She'd asked a simple question. Was it too much to expect an answer?

He waved his hand in the direction of the far wall. "Check out the notice board over there."

"Thanks." Cimmaron walked in the direction he'd indicated. Each step was pure torture. Beads of sweat formed on her brow again even though she'd wiped it earlier, and her meager possessions felt as heavy as two crates of vroom. Her chest continued to ache with sharp flashes of pain striking like punches. Cimmaron transferred her scruffy bag to her left hand and raised her right hand to massage her chest. It didn't help. With each step she took, the stabbing pangs spread through her chest. She gasped, her bag dropping from nerveless fingers. It hit the floor, falling in front of a trader. The trader tripped and fell headfirst onto a table laden with trays of Marchant stew and flasks of vroom and reeb. Crashes and colorful curses filled the air as chairs scraped across the floor and the beings seated at the table leapt to their feet. A pungent stream of Marchant stew dripped over the edge of the table.

"I'm so sorry," Cimmaron croaked. Her hand pressed against the middle of her chest but still the pain intensified. She wobbled then crumpled to the ground, her legs unable to support her any longer.

The nearest being, a pilot from one of the freighters judging by his uniform and boots, knelt beside her. "You okay?"

"Looking for job," Cimmaron gasped out, her mind focused on the one thing that was important to her. A job. Freedom. Independence.

He touched his palm to her forehead. "You're sick."

"Not. Need job."

"We have a job available. For a pilot. Not a ... ah...." The male trailed off while several of the others laughed.

"Not a Dlog concubine," a female pilot said with a disdainful curl of her lip.

"I am a pilot," Cimmaron snarled. With great effort, she stood. When she wobbled precariously, the male who'd helped her grabbed and held her upright. "Second pilot on the *Intrepid*."

"Yeah, right," the female countered, before turning her back on Cimmaron in a pointed snub. The rest of the pilots did the same.

The male pilot pulled a cloth from his tunic and wiped her forehead. "You're not well. Why don't you find lodgings until you're feeling better? Phrull, I hope whatever you have isn't contagious."

"There's nothing wrong with me!" Staying would mean facing Tamaki again. Cimmaron scowled even though the chest pains had eased a fraction. The stupid male thought they were mated. Yeah. Okay. They'd had a little fun together, but they weren't mated. She'd know if they were mated since she'd have trouble leaving his side. She'd turn all obedient. Subservient. She'd want to touch him all the time and be touched in return. She'd ... Phrull. Cimmaron definitely had the touch thing down. Her fingers practically itched with the need to touch, to run her hand and tongue and lips across his naked torso. And lower.

"No one will hire you if you can barely stand."

Cimmaron sighed, aware the male was taking most of her weight. If he let go she'd likely fall flat on her face. "But I need to leave Marchant!"

"Not gonna happen." The male checked his timepiece. "Time for me to head back to my ship."

"Thanks." Cimmaron retrieved her bag and found an empty chair to sink onto before watching the pilot stride away. Envy sat uneasily in her gut. That male was going to fly a ship out of Marchant airspace while once again she would remain stranded.

Chapter Nine

Tamaki strode down the narrow alley, his lips pursed in a silent whistle. The Marchant morn was cool and a puff of steam erupted with his exhalation. He drew his cloak around his body to keep the worst of the cold at bay and increased his pace. Cimmaron. His mate. He couldn't wait to see her again. First he'd kiss her golden lips, then he'd swing her into his arms and carry her off to her room where they could be private, their loving as noisy as they wanted. He'd strip her lean yet curvy body of every scrap of clothing. Next he'd tie her hands and legs with the silken scarves that he carried in his pockets so she couldn't move. He'd tease her breasts and nipples until they stood erect with lots of kissing and nuzzling in between. He'd kiss the vulnerable skin of her neck and behind her ears. He'd draw her taut golden nipples deep into his mouth and suckle. Gradually, he'd work down her body. Yeah. Tamaki grinned. He'd delve into the dip of her belly button with his tongue. She'd be hot for him by this time.

Impatient.

Cimmaron would writhe against the silken scarves that kept her bound. Hell, she might even start to beg. Tamaki chuckled at that thought. Somehow, he didn't think his mate would ever beg. She might demand in that imperious way of hers. Captain mode. Life between them would never be smooth running, but that didn't trouble him. They'd function well as a team.

What would he do to her next?

Ah, yes. Maybe he'd skip a few parts. Stoke her impatience even higher. He'd massage her feet and calves with a delicate scented cream. Maybe a cream scented with moonflowers and a hint of jabo aphrodisiac to make them both even hotter for each other. Desperate. Tamaki paused to open his cloak to the morn chill because suddenly, he burned with heat. A sharp pain tore through his chest, and Tamaki drew in a sharp breath. Damn, he'd had a cramp in his gut all morning. He breathed through the twinge of pain before continuing his brisk pace. He thumped on the door of Lissa's boardinghouse, his feel-good mood returning once the pain in his chest faded.

The door opened. Tamaki grabbed Lissa in a firm hug and squeezed her until the air hissed from her lungs and she started to protest.

"Let a lady breathe," she gasped out.

"But it's such a fine morn. Has Cimmaron risen from her slumber?"

"Cimmaron's gone. You'd better come inside." She led him through to her meeting room and gestured him to take a seat. "She left a note."

"Gone where? I didn't think she had enough currency yet." Tamaki sat but bounded to his feet microts later and started to stride from one end of the sumptuous room to the other. He dodged a green velveteen cozy chair and paused briefly to stare through the privacy slats at the windows. His gut churned. He'd thought.... A heartfelt groan emerged. God, with Cimmaron one should never think or assume. She was so strong and independent. "Gone where?"

"She didn't say. I thought she would have told you since you work together."

"We're mated," Tamaki said bluntly. "I didn't plan for it. The mating happened by mistake, but I can't be sorry. I love the stubborn female. Damn, what the hell am I going to do?"

"If you love her and want to remain mated, go after her."

"I don't understand. The mating bonds are tight. She shouldn't have been able to leave."

Lissa handed him a goblet of ruby red cranfruit wine. Tamaki's hands curled around the warm goblet as he puzzled over Cimmaron's leaving. Hell, she must really hate him. The thought was sobering. A mate who hated him so much she'd left rather than face him again.

"That's what I'd heard, but possibly it's something to do with her Dlog genes?" Lissa sipped from the steaming goblet. "The two of you are a good match. Go after her. Talk to her. Have you told her how you feel about her?"

"No."

Lissa rolled her eyes. "I thought you were more sensible than most males. You know she wants to fly more than anything. Stopping her flying would be like clipping a bird's wings."

"Yeah, I know." Tamaki scowled, a pang of regret lancing through him. He loved Cimmaron, but he'd known all along this wasn't what she'd wanted. Now he'd driven her away. "That's what I wanted to talk to her about." Tamaki prowled about the room, pausing to pick up a delicate blue urn before setting it back down.

A thump on Lissa's door stopped him mid-step.

"Carry on," Lissa said with another eye roll. "Don't let me stop you. I'll get the door." She glided across the room and disappeared into the passage beyond.

The soft murmur of voices reached him as he trod another circuit of Lissa's room. In the distance a door thudded and then footsteps approached.

"You have a visitor," Lissa trilled. She stood aside for someone else to enter the room.

Tamaki froze. "Cimmaron."

"I'll leave the two of you alone," Lissa said, shutting the door before Tamaki had a chance to reply.

He took two steps toward Cimmaron before stopping. Space. She needed time and space to accept him and their new situation. He opened his mouth to speak, then closed it, frightened he'd spook her.

Cimmaron stood poised just inside the doorway as if she might bolt. "I tried to leave, to get a job on one of the ships flying out. I wanted to leave, but I couldn't damn well stop thinking about you." Her golden eyes flashed with temper, and she stepped closer, jabbing him in the middle of his chest with her forefinger. "What have you done to me? Why can't I get you out of my head?" Her breasts heaved with indignation beneath her brown tunic. "Why?"

Tamaki's heart flipped over on seeing her pain, hearing it in her voice. He loved her. Wasn't that worth something? Another realization crept into his mind. The pain in his chest had faded the moment Cimmaron had stepped into the room. A part of him wanted to smile even though so much rode on how he presented his case to her. Right now it was difficult. All he wanted to do was touch. He drew in a sharp breath knowing he needed to wait, that waiting would be worth it. A ripple of nerves closed his throat. Tamaki coughed and then swallowed, trying to dislodge the nerves. "Cimmaron, I didn't mean for this to happen." But he wasn't sorry either. Not the time to tell her that.

"But you didn't stop it." Tears coated her voice and her golden eyes looked suspiciously damp.

"I'm an innocent victim, too. Do you think I planned on this? I could lose my job for breaking the fraternization rule."

A stricken expression crossed her face. She blinked rapidly. "All I ever wanted to do was fly ships. When I was an underling I used to watch the birds glide on the airwaves. I wanted to do the same thing. Fly and explore space."

His mate's misery brought another lump to his throat. Aching to comfort her, Tamaki stepped closer and drew her tense body into his arms. For an instant her body was stiff, then a wispy sigh sounded and she relaxed against his chest. Her body trembled, but it felt so right to have her in his arms. Perfect.

Then his body reacted to her proximity. His cock pulled tight. Wrong time. Wrong place. Tamaki pulled up cold images inside his mind but it was difficult with the warm body of his mate in his arms.

Yet again, he cleared his throat. "You can still fly, Cimmaron." Dammit, his plan had to work. He held his breath waiting for her reaction.

Cimmaron yanked away from Tamaki, aware that once again she'd succumbed to the magical power he seemed to hold over her. And the blasted aches and pains that had assailed her at the spaceport had all disappeared. The only ache she had was a sexual one. Her folds were moist and aching, her body desperate for his possession. She shifted from foot to foot, the brown tunic feeling heavy and burdensome on her sensitive skin. She summoned up a glare. "How? Tell me how I can fly when I'm trapped on this forsaken planet with you? The captain of the *Intrepid* has probably filed his AWOL report by now. I'm doomed to stay, chained to your side." Bitterness coated her voice, even though logically she knew Tamaki wasn't entirely to blame for this situation. As he'd pointed out, he was a victim, too. Cimmaron paused, trying to think. Yet no matter which way she turned the situation, she couldn't see a solution.

Stranded.

Mated.

Trapped.

Cimmaron sniffed, trying to regain control of her frazzled thoughts. "I tried to leave but I couldn't. My body shut down. The pain in my chest was so bad I couldn't stand on my own. Because of *you*."

"I know." Caring laced his words.

Cimmaron snapped her eyes closed on hearing his sympathetic tone. Why couldn't he yell so she could shout back? A suspicious moistness built behind her closed lids. The truth--he really did know. The funny thing was that if she'd been looking for a mate, she would have loved to find Tamaki. He was a good male. Strong. Handsome. Demanding yet fair. The customers liked him, which was why the club was becoming so successful. He was a male worthy of love. Cimmaron's mind repeated the thought then stuttered over the concept. Was that what this new emotion closing up her throat and pulsing through her veins? This burning in her heart? The need to throw herself at him and never leave his side? Was this love? A tinge of fear snapped at her. Phrull.

Stranded.

A tear leaked past her closed lids and she scrubbed it away with the back of her hand.

"I've transmitted a report to my head office." Tamaki closed the gap between them and stroked his fingers across her cheek.

Cimmaron shivered and bit her lip to stop a purr of contentment erupting. Kissing would feel so much better. Tamaki coughed, and she realized she'd drifted into daydreams again. She couldn't seem to concentrate on anything but Tamaki.

"Did you hear me?"

"Yeah, a report. But what about the fraternization rules Rico was spewing about?"

"I decided honesty was best. I told them everything. About the sabotage. About our mating."

Alarm made her heart pump. She cared about Tamaki. He loved his job just as much as she adored flying. "What ... what happened?" They couldn't both lose the things they loved.

"Rico takes over management of the club--"

"They're firing you! But you built this club up from nothing. Rico said your club is the top earner in this part of the universe." Cimmaron grabbed his shoulders and shook him vigorously. "You can't let them do this. You must fight them!"

"--and I take over the management of the club on Vegamont."

"Fight! Vegamont? Did you say Vegamont?"

"Yep." A tiny smile played around his lips.

Cimmaron sighed, a pang of acute envy piercing her heart. "You're so lucky. That's the home base for Vegamont Shipping. And the training school for pilots is there. I'd give anything to move to Vegamont."

The tiny smile bloomed to a full out grin. "You're my mate. I thought you'd come with me."

"With you? You'd really take me with you to Vegamont?" Cimmaron felt her heart thump against her ribs as she searched his face for truth. The male meant it. He really meant it. "You would?"

"Of course I would. You're my mate. You know those pains you had in the chest?"

Cimmaron nodded, unable to squeeze words past the lump of emotion that twisted her gut.

"I had chest pains as well, although they didn't sound as acute as the ones you experienced." Tamaki frowned. "Maybe it's something to do with your Dlog genes."

"The pills aren't working as well as they should either. Ever since I ... we ... had sex."

"Made love, my mate. Made love." Tamaki cupped her face in his hands and kissed her. Their lips clung together, their breath mingling as they tasted each other. His hands slipped beneath the hem of her brown tunic and slid upward until he cupped her breasts. His thumbed rubbed backward and forward over her nipples, and a series of pleasant shockwaves traveled straight to her clit. Cimmaron purred and her skin took on the familiar sparkle of arousal.

Slowly, Tamaki pulled back. He stared down at her, his brown eyes full of emotion. "You're my mate. I love you. Where I go, you go." His fingers played across her breasts until she shuddered helplessly.

"Lo ... love." Phrull, she couldn't seem to string her words together. He grasped her nipple and twisted. "Phrull."

"Yeah, scary, huh?" Tamaki gave her nipple a final tweak before removing his hands from beneath her tunic.

"I ...," Cimmaron trailed off, then looked him straight in the eye. "I never thought I'd say this to any male, but I feel the same way about you."

Tamaki's hands tightened on her shoulders, his fingers digging into her flesh. His face held an air of urgency. "Say it. Give me the words."

"I love you." Cimmaron felt a moment's uncertainty until a brilliant smile lit his face.

"I knew it," he murmured, stroking her face again.

Cimmaron lifted her hand, finally giving into the need to return his touch. "Um, it's good that we're going to Vegamont and you have a new job, but what about me? I'm not cut out to be a full-time bartender. I'm at the stage where if one more male hits on me, I'll run amuck. That won't create a good first impression, and I can't be a stay-at-home mate."

Tamaki laughed, his eyes dancing and twinkling. "We can't have that. Did I happen to mention I have a friend at

Vegamont Shipping? He hires the pilots. I could put a good word in for you. And we can stop off on Bezant to clear your name with Coalition Shipping."

"I could fly again?" Please, don't let him be teasing. Cimmaron stared at her mate, hope in her heart. "You'd let me fly?"

"You're my mate, Cimmaron, not a possession. I love you and I want your happiness. Flying makes you happy. From what I've learned about the mating process, once you stop fighting the bonds, the cramps and chest pains will disappear. We'll be able to spend some time apart as long as we intend to get back together again."

"Tamaki!" Cimmaron shrieked. She threw herself into his arms. She was going to fly again. Captain. She might even manage to gain captain status. Cimmaron rained kisses on his face and pressed her body to her mate.

Tamaki laughed, the sound rich and full of amusement. "I'm glad you approve. What say we adjourn this meeting to the bedroom? We could make love without coercion." He paused to press a lingering kiss on her smiling lips before taking her hand and leading her toward the closed door. He opened it and halted to steal another kiss.

Cimmaron led him up the stairs toward her room. They stepped inside, closing the door after them for privacy. "Were the serviceman able to fix the green room?"

"Yeah. Rico and I have decided to press charges. I don't care how rich the kid's parents are."

"Good." Cimmaron unfastened the toggles on his shirt and pushed the fabric aside to display his muscled chest. Her fingers danced across his skin. Hers. Her mate. The passion bubbled up inside and her eyes moistened again. Phrull. Not a good look for a pilot. Leaning closer, she nibbled and teased a flat masculine nipple to prominence. An unknown emotion flooded her body, her mind. Phrull, she was smiling. Actually smiling. And it was a toothy grin. Tamaki grinned back as he toed off his boots and removed his boot linings.

Cimmaron shoved the shirt down his arms and it fluttered to the floor. She unfastened his trews and pushed them and his undergarments down his legs until he stood in naked splendor in front of her. Unable to resist, she ran a finger the length of his erection, tracing the bulbous head.

Tamaki groaned. "I can't wait any longer." He yanked sharply on her tunic, the sound of the ripping fabric loud in the silence of her room. "I'll buy you a new one."

"I didn't like that tunic anyway."

He dealt swiftly with her boots, trews and undergarments until they were both naked. They fell onto the bed in a tangle of limbs, skin on skin. The start of a delicious assault. One of his hands cupped a breast while he parted her legs with his thigh. A moan fell from her lips when he guided his cock between her legs. A rush of moisture trickled from her pussy, easing his way. With one seamless thrust he filled her aching womb.

"Tamaki," she whispered, raising her hips to meet his next thrust. That this male would change his life to make her happy.... The emotion welled even more, threatening to make her cry. She would fly again, and once she'd completed her journey she had a home and welcoming arms. A mate. Tamaki filled a gap she'd never realized she had. Her hands wrapped around his shoulders and she clung to him. He invaded her mouth, exploring the inner surfaces of her mouth, timing his flickering tongue with each deep thrust of his cock. Cimmaron panted, the heat swirling through her veins. She inhaled deeply, drawing his scent deep into her lungs. Intoxicating. Addictive.

Tamaki lifted his head and brushed a kiss across her pursed lips before withdrawing to the tip of his cock then driving deep. "God, you feel so good." He withdrew again and pushed deeply, hitting her clit at just the right angle. A tiny ripple started slow and then gathered momentum until the sensation filled her, filled her heart, her very soul. And in that moment it felt as though something clicked into place. The Dlog mating! A gasp of surprise escaped Cimmaron along with a sense of wonderment. Now she'd willingly accepted Tamaki, the Dlog mating chains had cemented them together just as her mother and the Dlog elders had told her.

They were doubly mated. Cimmaron smiled. No longer was she alone, drifting without purpose. No longer stranded. She'd come a full circle.

Cimmaron Zhaan was home.

The End

Printed in the United States
49009LVS00002B/121-978

9 781586 087890